Praise for *You Never* [...]

'Breathes new life into the psycho[...]
captivating and gripping storyline[...]
an action thriller. I coul[...]
C.L. Taylor

'A truly pulse-pounding thriller. The relentless tension is
leavened only by its heart-rending emotion'
Christopher Brookmyre

'A barnstorming, rocket-paced thriller about an ordinary man
thrown into an extraordinary situation. Fans of John
Connolly and Linwood Barclay will love it'
Mark Edwards

'You Never Said Goodbye is the complete package: a
breakneck paced, twisted thriller that delivers a real emotional
punch. A stunning book. I loved it!'
Miranda Dickinson

'Both a heartfelt and emotional tale of family love and
betrayal, and a pulse-pounding thriller. I've been a fan of
Luca Veste's books since the beginning and this is his best
yet. Totally gripping!'
C.M. Ewan

'Action packed suspense'
The Sunday Times Crime Club

'Thoroughly recommended and a must for everyone who
enjoys high octane thrills'
Belfast Telegraph

'This is an electrifying edge-of-the-seat thriller, a must-read
for fans of Harlan Coben'
Candis

'There are many gasp-inducing revelations before skilful
writer Veste produces a gripping and surprise climax'
Peterborough Telegraph

Luca Veste is the author of several police procedurals and standalone crime novels including *You Never Said Goodbye, The Bone Keeper* and *The Six*. He is the host of the Two Crime Writers and a Microphone podcast and the co-founder of the Locked In festival. He plays bass guitar in the band The Fun Lovin' Crime Writers. He lives in Liverpool, with his wife and two daughters.

LUCA VESTE

Trust in Me

HODDER &
STOUGHTON

First published in Great Britain in 2023 by Hodder & Stoughton
An Hachette UK company

This paperback edition published in 2024

1

A CIP catalogue record for this title is available from the British
Library

Paperback ISBN 978 1 529 35740 0
ebook ISBN 978 1 529 35739 4

Typeset in Plantin Light by Manipal Technologies Limited

Printed and bound in Great Britain by Clays Ltd, Elcograf S.p.A.

Hodder & Stoughton policy is to use papers that are natural, renewable
and recyclable products and made from wood grown in sustainable
forests. The logging and manufacturing processes are expected to
conform to the environmental regulations of the country of origin.

Hodder & Stoughton Ltd
Carmelite House
50 Victoria Embankment
London EC4Y 0DZ

www.hodder.co.uk

To Mark B, Mark E, Craig, and Susi – my fellow QCs.
Thanks for getting me through the past few years with quizzes,
laughs, and support.
Now, question one . . .

BEFORE

I *had known I would tell Jack from around a month into the rela-*
tionship. I just hadn't been sure when. Whether I would wait for us
to be married, to be parents, or much later. On my deathbed, maybe.

When it finally came, it wasn't as if I'd planned it. It just sort of
happened.

It was ten years since the night Adam died. Since Dan and I
decided to make the biggest mistake of our lives.

Since then, I'd met Jack. Left England. Moved to the east coast
of America.

Left it all behind me.

Only, my parents were still back there.

'The cancer has spread,' I said, and Jack's face fell. He reached
out to me, held me in an embrace I never wanted to end.

I was there, back home, when my father passed away. Sitting at
his bedside, as he breathed his last. My mum on the other side. Each
of us holding onto his pale, aged hands. The next few days were a
blur. Arrangements were finalised. Childcare for our two young chil-
dren organised.

I was in a fog of disbelief. As if real life wasn't happening around
me. Everything tinged with the sense that it might be a dream. As if
the world had twisted on the plane ride over and now I was living
in a nightmare.

At the funeral, there were only a few of us surrounding his grave.
The chapel had been filled with strangers' faces, but now, only me,
my mum, Jack and my father's brother and sister-in-law.

Not much. Not enough.

I held onto Jack's hand. Clasping it tightly in my own, as if I were scared of letting go. Of letting myself be untethered.

Then, I saw him.

Standing next to some trees, a hundred or so yards away. I couldn't see his face clearly, but I knew it was him.

My body went stiff. Nervous energy firing through me. Jack seemed to sense something and placed an arm around me.

I couldn't stop looking at him. Wishing I was imagining him being there.

Then, he was gone.

We filed back to the car. Jack still holding onto me. Before we got into the car, I turned to Jack. He lifted a hand and brushed away tears on my cheek.

'Jack,' I said, my voice barely above a whisper. I turned back to where he'd been standing near the treeline, hoping to see him again. Any proof that he had really been there. I looked away when none came. 'Jack, I need to tell you something.'

AFTER

The children were quiet.

Sitting, heads bowed, at the kitchen table, as if they knew something was wrong. She tried a smile, but they wouldn't even look at her.

They wouldn't be there much longer. The school bus would be picking them up in a few minutes down the street. It didn't stop her trying to ease their worries.

'Why did the cookie go to the nurse?'

She waited for a response that was never going to come. She ploughed on regardless.

'Because he felt crummy.'

Olivia raised her head, but it was only to roll her eyes in the way children do. That look that says, *I'll never be as uncool as you when I'm a parent*.

JJ didn't so much as flinch.

Jack came into the room, the tie hanging around his neck undone. She stepped forwards to fix it for him, but he shook her away. She stepped to the side, trying not to show any hurt at his dismissal.

'Come on, kids, you'll miss the bus.'

She followed them down the hall, waiting for Jack to turn. To maybe give her a kiss goodbye. A moment of love. Something for her to hold onto once he was gone.

Instead, by the time he turned around, all she could see were the dark rings of sleeplessness under his eyes and a desperate air emanating from him. A desperate need to get away.

'I'll call you,' he said, before turning on his heels and pulling the door closed behind him. She caught it in time, opening it back up, trying to find words that would make him stay with her. To keep him by her side. Even after all that time together, she couldn't think of a single thing she could say.

She was alone.

She stepped out on her front porch and waved the kids goodbye, not that they could see her doing so. They were already disappearing into the distance.

She would die for those two children. She would do anything for them.

Yet, there she was, waving them off onto a bus that she wasn't driving. With other people she couldn't control. Sending them off for hours at a time, where she couldn't protect them.

The thoughts came and went quickly, before life slipped back into focus.

On the other side of the street, Pam Caulfield was standing outside her door, arms folded across her chest and the *Westport Newspaper* dangling from one hand. She gave her a blank look before turning and going back inside. No cheery hello, no catch-up about local events. No gossip shared.

She knew it was going to be a tough road ahead. That she couldn't expect them to suddenly forget everything that had happened in the past week. It might be a while before they were invited to neighbourhood barbecues and parties. Before conversations would no longer suddenly fall silent if she was noticed on the periphery.

It might take a while for that suspicion they were feeling to dissipate.

She went back inside, closing the door behind her slowly, carefully. As if she was worried about making too much noise. Looked down at the hardwood floor, the early-morning light streaming through from the back of the house giving it a sheen that couldn't be replicated in photographs. Closed her eyes and sighed softly.

Then, she clasped her hands together and allowed herself to be drawn through the house. She floated through, as if she wasn't in control of her actions. As though someone else was controlling her body, making her move, making her blink, making her breathe.

She passed the living room, perfectly still, perfectly clean. The dining room opposite, the same. Into the kitchen, the source of the light that ran throughout the house. Stole a glance out back to her perfectly manicured garden. The blue of the pool water looked so inviting, even in the cold wash of early spring.

She turned away before she could be tempted, down to the locked door at the back.

She pulled the key from the pocket of her jeans and twisted it open. The door opened and the darkness within escaped into the hallway.

The office was small, but large enough for a desk and a couple of bookcases. A small window that looked out towards the pool and barbecue area. The blind had been pulled down, probably at some point the night before. Possibly Jack, if he had come inside to do a bit of work in the evening, when she wasn't around. The kids never came in there, so she didn't think it was them.

Maybe it had been her. She couldn't remember.

She didn't *want* to remember. It was much easier this way – to pretend she was being guided in all her actions. That she didn't have full control of her body, her mind. That there was some unseen force making her move.

He was still dead.

Nothing had changed since a few hours earlier. No matter the amount of wishing she had done.

She had to do something. He couldn't stay here. It wouldn't be long until someone would notice.

She took a step closer, expecting the body to move. Grasp hold of her wrist and not let go.

That wasn't going to happen.

As she felt the tears she'd been holding onto since he had taken his last breath begin to roll down her cheeks, she got to work.

He wasn't going to ruin her perfect life.

Not any more.

She had made sure of that.

BEFORE

1

In the beginning, there was a girl. She became a woman. A wife. A mother.

We raise our children with one thing in mind. To keep them safe. Fed, watered, aware of the dangers that can lie out in the world.

Then, we pack them up each morning and send them into the unknown. Somewhere we don't control, where things can happen without us knowing.

Such is the life of a parent.

It was that thought that ran through my head for a brief moment every morning. That ache of loss that I wished didn't exist.

Jack emerged from the bathroom and planted a kiss on my forehead, as I lifted myself up on the bed, leaning against the headboard. Rubbing sleep from my eyes, as I heard the kids talking down the hall.

'Morning,' Jack said, his voice like silk. He was already dressed, almost ready for work. His aftershave tickled my nostrils. He stood up straight, all six feet two of him, and checked himself in the mirror.

I couldn't hear him say *I'm still looking good, for a forty-two-year-old*, but I could definitely hear him think it. The idea made me smile. I couldn't disagree with him. He had kept himself in shape over the years we'd been together – a mix of running and good genetics. I had a memory of meeting him for the first time and thinking he looked like John Travolta – in his *Grease* days, rather than the later *Pulp-Fiction*-and-hairpiece period. An intensity in his eyes that still made me melt.

In a perfect world, the smile wouldn't fall away so quickly. There wouldn't be a moment when an intrusive thought would push its way to the surface of my mind. Breaking its way through the base level of happiness and contentedness that I felt at the start of every day.

The idea that I didn't deserve any of this.

That I shouldn't smile. Shouldn't laugh. Shouldn't love.

Shouldn't live.

Once, I had been called Sara Drummond and lived at 42 Broadgreen Terrace, Chittinhill, Somerset. A small village, just outside of Yeovil, in the south-west of England.

I'd had an accent that would put people in mind of the countryside, with two syllables.

Only, I'd escaped from that small town. Moved to the big city, gone to university, ended up in northeastern USA, and got married to a wonderful man. Had two children and lost that country accent.

Ended up in another small town.

That should have been my story.

A nice, normal girl, who grew up to be an accomplished woman, with a great career, a great family and a great life.

And yet, every morning, that same feeling came to me. That gnawing away at my mind, the anxious twisting and turning in the pit of my stomach.

You don't deserve this.

'Morning,' I said, before squinting as he shook open the curtains and the morning light stung my eyes. 'Do you have to? You've been up half an hour longer than me.'

'You'll lie there all day if I don't.'

'Not a chance,' I replied, throwing his pillow from the bed towards him. He caught it with a chuckle. 'The kids wouldn't let me lie in on a weekend, never mind a school day.'

'I have to be in early this morning,' Jack said, slipping a tie around his shirt collar. 'So I won't be here to see the kids off to school.'

'Oh,' I replied, not a question. An acceptance of the inevitable. 'Okay.'

'It can't be helped,' he said, turning towards me as I stood up and pulled the bed covers over. 'We're just crazy busy right now.'

'Will you be home for dinner at least?'

'We'll go to Stephanie's restaurant,' he replied, an act of contrition at least. 'I'll try and get back early, so we can go together.'

He must have suspected I didn't quite believe him as he continued.

'You know I hate being away'

I was already preparing for what I would tell them when he didn't get home until gone eight in the evening. Nine, sometimes. Putting on my best impression of it being no big deal. No problem at all.

It didn't matter that I would have been working all day myself. That I didn't get to pick and choose how late I worked. I *had* to be back for the children.

'If you need to work late, let Stephanie know. She only has a couple of hours in between lunch and dinner shift to come around.'

'Yes, of course,' I replied, rolling my eyes at the sound of Jack's sister's name. 'Although, it would be easier if we could just pay for someone to come and watch them instead.'

'She's family,' Jack said, with a long sigh. A breath of air that barely hid the irritation of a long-standing argument. One that kept coming up. 'And she loves spending time with them. Saves us a fair few dollars as well.'

'Of course,' I replied, losing the argument before it reared its head again.

He worked so hard, I reminded myself. For them. For us. I couldn't ignore that. Still, there were moments when I wanted to ask him what was really important in life – whether working all these hours was really worth it. Yes, it gave us a more comfortable life, but the cost was not being able to enjoy it. Not properly, anyway.

One of those things in married life that every person has – the things we don't say to our significant other. That you would *never* say, because you could guarantee it wouldn't be taken well.

'I'll see you this evening,' Jack said, crossing the room and stopping in front of me. He looked down at me before reaching and softly raising my chin to look into his eyes. They were the same sea blue I'd been lost in all those years before. He smiled, his eyes unchanged. He kissed my forehead. 'Love you, S.'

'Love you too,' I murmured back to him, my eyes closing momentarily. When I opened them, he was gone.

I heard a commotion outside of the room. The soft padding of feet on the hardwood floors. Excited voices, hushed whispering. My shoulders slumped a little, before I shook my head and made my way out of the room.

JJ was waiting for me as soon as I left the bedroom. Still in his Marvel PJs, his light-brown hair sticking up at odd angles. Barefoot and barely constraining his energy.

'Mom, Olivia stole my iPad and won't give it back.'

Before I had chance to answer, I heard a simultaneous screech of '*No, I didn't*' from Olivia down the hall and the front door closing downstairs.

'Olivia,' I said, rubbing my temples and hoping against hope that a headache wouldn't be the way I was going to start the day. 'You know you shouldn't take things from JJ's room.'

'I didn't take it from his room,' Olivia replied, not even bothering to hide the indignation from her tone, as she appeared in the doorway to her bedroom. Her arms were folded across her chest, dark hair framing her scowling face. 'It was on the floor in the bathroom. *I'm* looking after it properly, that's all. Unlike him.'

'You have your own,' I said, rubbing my forehead and briefly remembering a time when I didn't have to deal with arguments at seven in the morning. It felt like a million years ago at that moment. 'Give it back to him and if you find it somewhere it shouldn't be, tell me or your dad, so we can deal with it.'

There was a moment when I didn't think she was going to move. Then she turned on her heels and stomped back into her bedroom. JJ had a smirk on his face, enjoying seeing his sister cut down to size.

'And you,' I said, turning on him now. 'Do you realise how much these things cost? If I find you leaving anything that cost more than ten dollars on the bathroom floor – or on any floor for that matter – then they'll be taken from you and you'll never see them again. Your tablet, your Switch, whatever it is. Now, go get dressed, JJ.'

I watched him slope off, muttering something under his breath. I waited a few seconds, hoping to catch him saying something he shouldn't, and then went downstairs when I didn't. I managed to get ready and also prepare breakfast in under an hour. Some kind of record, which I guessed I shared with millions of other parents across the land that morning. Everything put nicely away when I was done. Couldn't have Stephanie judging me for a bowl missed.

I liked her just enough that I held my tongue as she judged me.

I watched them leave at eight thirty, feeling that familiar pang of loss as they walked the short distance to where the school bus picked them up. Across the street, Pam Caulfield gave me a smile and a wave. I waved back and went inside before she could start talking at me about the latest uninteresting gossip.

Enjoyed a moment of silence – being alone in the house for those brief few moments before having to leave myself. A silence that was welcomed, but somehow also screamed out to be missed too soon.

I was out the door a few minutes later, pulling out of the driveway and trying not to sing tunelessly along to the radio.

It was a thirty-minute commute into Stamford on a good day. All the way down Merritt Parkway until I reached Exit 34 and then a short drive south into the city.

It was ticking past nine a.m. as I turned left onto Long Ridge, which didn't give me enough time to stop for a coffee at the diner there. A luxury I sometimes afforded myself.

Fifteen minutes later, I was pulling into the lot outside the office park. My usual spot was empty, as were many beside it. A combination of more businesses moving out and going online, and increasing rent prices, meant the building had seen its tenants reduce in numbers. Still, the board of directors at Better Lives were hanging on.

I always preferred seeing people face to face anyway. Zoom and Teams meetings could never really replace the feeling, the closeness, of being in the same room as a client.

In the lobby, Steve the security guard nodded his head and waved me through. The building could seem small from the outside, but it was still home to a number of other businesses – a massage therapist, an art studio, an acupuncturist, even an escape room that seemed to be clinging on somehow, despite the impossibility of existing during social distancing. Better Lives took up the entire top floor, the elevator opening up to its very own lobby.

Gina on reception gave me the same bright and impossible smile she did every day and a far too cheery 'good morning'.

'Morning, Gina,' I said, placing my bag down on her desk for a moment. 'Nine thirty is my first, right? Mr Robertson?'

She shook her head and I was already thinking about that diner and what I'd missed out on.

'Cancelled, sorry. But it's okay – new client has taken his place.'

I waited a beat, hoping I wouldn't have to beg for more information.

'I don't know much,' Gina continued, her smile threatening to give me glaucoma. 'Although she asked for you personally. Said she liked your picture on the website. Given you were free . . .'

'I'll take it,' I said with a sigh, taking the thin manila folder from Gina's outstretched hand and picking up my bag. 'Who else is in today?'

'Everyone,' Gina replied, as if I should have known. 'It's Monday.'

'How is he?'

Gina made a face, knowing exactly who she was talking about. 'He's in one of his moods.'

I rolled my eyes, sharing a smile with her for a moment. 'Good old Simon, never letting us down.'

'He's asked if you'll meet him later.'

'Probably wondering why we're not getting as many clients through the doors. I'm just glad to be seeing people face to face again. I couldn't do another year on Zoom.'

'Couldn't agree more,' Gina said, leaning forward. 'You're best going to prepare, right?'

'Of course,' I replied, already moving through the glass doors and past the other offices. Mine was at the end of the hall and I was greeted by the smell of vanilla and pine as I pushed my way inside.

I hung up my jacket and smoothed down my trousers, wishing I'd made the effort to hang them properly in the closet after ironing them a couple of days previously. Jack was always particular enough to get that right, at least. Next to him, I looked like Aunt Sally.

I turned on my computer and made myself a coffee using the machine I kept in my office. Chose a pod at random and carried it back over to the desk when it was finished. Opened up the folder regarding the new client, as I simultaneously opened my email and saw too many new messages to deal with that early in the morning.

The information was sparse. As it tended to be more and more lately, regarding new clients. All I had was a name, an age, and a list of possible issues and complaints.

Anxiety, tired all the time, can't sleep, insomnia, worry, empty feeling inside, low mood . . .

It was as if someone had googled a list of symptoms and relayed them to whoever had taken her call.

Still, at least it was a new client. I wasn't about to begin dismissing that things were a little more difficult than they had been.

A few minutes later, the phone on my desk beeped and I lifted the handset. Gina breathlessly announced my new client's arrival, and I stepped out from behind the desk and walked down the corridor to greet her.

And that was how I met Ella.

2

At first, it was just like every other day. Every other arrival into work. Every other new client.

When you've been counselling people – listening to problems, issues, no matter how big or small – for over a decade, things can get a little samey, I guess. Thankfully, I was professional enough to treat anyone new coming into my office with the same respect and openness as if they were my first.

On the surface, anyway. Inside, I would allow my mind to wander. I would think about what I would have for dinner that evening. What new sport JJ had suddenly taken an interest in and how to juggle Olivia's swimming sessions with Little League or Soccer.

Soccer.

I could almost feel what was left of my family back home in the UK shuddering as I called it that.

The first thought I had when she stood up from the waiting area was that I knew her. That feeling you get sometimes, when you see a face pass you by on the street, or in a crowded room. A sense of familiarity that is stopped in place when you can't instantly recall a name or a memory of meeting before. An evil déjà vu that can't be explained.

I stepped forwards in the corridor and offered a hand. After a beat she took it. 'Nice to meet you. Shall we go straight to my office?'

She nodded back at me, staring at the floor, and then followed me inside.

'Can I get you anything? A water, coffee?'

The young woman shook her head and sat down carefully on the sofa without a word. She couldn't have been more than twenty-five, I guessed from looking at her. I'd already forgotten the personal details in the folder, from the quick glance I'd given it. Not that I would have remembered them if I'd tried harder – I always preferred to learn as much from the client as possible.

I took the chair next to my desk, rather than sitting behind it and creating a barrier between us. A little trick that most people fully understood and expected, I guessed, but important, nonetheless.

'So, Ella, is it? Do you mind me calling you Ella?'

'Yes, of course,' Ella replied, shifting a little on the sofa. Her hands were clasped tightly together on her lap. 'Do I call you doctor, or something?'

'No, I'm Sara. No need for formalities.'

Ella nodded softly to herself. She was pale-skinned, a flush of red on her cheeks appearing and disappearing every time she spoke. Her blonde hair had been tied back into a tight ponytail, a hint of make-up that didn't overwhelm. She was slim, tall as well. I imagined she would be used to a lingering stare from the opposite sex.

'Are you British?' Ella said, still not meeting my eye. 'I mean, if it's not too personal a question.'

'I was once,' I replied with a practised smile. 'I've lived here more than fifteen years now though. Still can't totally lose the accent, I guess.'

'Sorry, I just noticed is all.'

'So, tell me, Ella, what made you come here today.'

Another shift of discomfort. 'I'm not sure really. I probably shouldn't have come.'

'Well, I'm happy you did. Think of this office as somewhere safe, where we can talk about anything or nothing. A confidential place, where all your thoughts can be shared without judgement. We have an hour to chat about anything you'd like, so if you decide that it's not for you, we'll have lost nothing but a little bit of time. Doesn't sound so bad, does it?'

'I guess not.'

'Why don't we start by you telling me a little bit about yourself.'

Ella sighed quietly to herself, letting the silence hang between us for a little while. 'I'm not sure where to start . . . do you want to know about the things I told the woman over the phone? She called me after I sent the email.'

I shook my head. 'Let's start with talking about you. Your background, your life, what brought you here this morning?'

Ella swallowed and looked past me towards the window, as if she was hoping someone was hovering there to answer for her. She shook her head almost imperceptibly and resumed looking at the floor again. 'I don't know how this type of thing works. I've never done this before.'

'Well, why don't you tell me a little bit about yourself.'

'I guess you know my name. I had to give my age and address to the woman on the phone.'

'Okay, but that's not really *you*, is it?'

Her head snapped towards me, looking me in the eye for the first time. I thought at first there was anger in her look, but I quickly realised it was fear.

'What do you mean?'

'Those are just facts, Ella. I'm more interested in you as a *person*,' I said, trying to placate her. Soothe her, before she tried to run out of the office. I'd had that happen to me before. A fair few times, if I was truthful. Sometimes, people found this office to be the worst place in the world, despite my intentions. Despite the nice décor, the plants carefully chosen, the prints on the wall of Monet and Matisse paintings. The muted colours, the soft furnishings. Despite my intentionally soft tone, my welcoming nature.

Sometimes, none of that mattered when you were asking people to confront the things in their lives they most wanted to change. When you didn't have all the answers. When you didn't have an instant fix.

Ella looked away but seemed to accept my reply. 'I'm not sure any of that matters though. Maybe I should just tell you why I'm here?'

'We can get to that,' I said, leaning back a little in my chair and letting the folder drop onto the side table next to me. 'First, I'm more interested in your background. To give me a fuller picture. This is about you, Ella. The time we spend together, you're the most important person in the room.'

There was silence again, which I decided to wait out. I studied her, wondering if that sense of familiarity would make itself known to me. I couldn't think of a single occasion when I'd seen her before, but that feeling wouldn't leave me.

'I live on my own,' Ella said, her voice breaking the silence with a shock. 'I mean, I don't have a roommate or anything. I moved out of my parents' house when I went to college and just never went back.'

'I see,' I said, already making assumptions I wasn't supposed to. Already mentally forming a picture of a young woman, living alone, probably working in a job she hadn't anticipated doing when she went to college. Unable to form relationships that lasted longer than a Tinder match and a one-night stand.

I had to put that all to one side, of course. Pretend everyone who walked into my office was different, with unique and varied reasons for ending up with the need to speak to someone like me.

The dirty little secret that I, and so many others in my profession, knew was that you ended up seeing mostly the same people over and over. Moms who didn't know how to cope with all the pressures of family life, middle-aged men who couldn't deal with the choices they made and needed validation that having an affair wasn't all that bad and was probably because of their childhood anyway. And young people.

Young people. More than ever before.

Teenagers who felt under pressure daily to be someone or something they weren't. In my first ten years of practice, I hadn't seen as many teenagers . . . children, really, as I did now. Social media had changed everything. While Ella was mid-twenties, it seemed to me that teenage strife was extending itself by a few years.

'I'm okay on my own though,' Ella continued, as thoughts flew through my mind. 'I like it for the most part.'

'I enjoy my own company too,' I said, sensing an early opportunity to build rapport. 'Sometimes, I'll take a walk down to the beach near where I live. Just look out to the sea and enjoy the quiet. It gives me a bit of a recharge, you know? It's always good to have that reset, do you think?'

I could see her eyes brighten a little, but she still refused to look up from where her hands lay in her lap. 'I like that too.'

'So, you live near the coast?'

'No, not really. But I'll drive down every now and again. It's not that far away.'

'Same, I guess, for me.'

'Do you live close by?'

I shook my head. *Careful.* 'Not too long a commute here.'

She finally looked towards me. 'Not Greenwich. I think you would have lost the accent quicker if it had been. I'm guessing east of here. Westport or Fairfield.'

I didn't react. I had learned that most of the time, when a patient tried to get into my personal life, it was because they were hoping for some sort of reaction. Some sort of denial or acceptance. I knew it was just a way of giving them the opportunity to not share something difficult themselves. A deflection from something painful they themselves were feeling. A sense of power that they didn't feel over anything else in their life.

This didn't usually happen within a few minutes of them coming into my office though.

'You might be right,' I said, keeping my voice soft and open. 'You might be wrong. But we're here to talk about you, aren't we? You live alone, but what about friends and family? Are you close?'

She held my gaze for a few moments, then looked away. 'I have a couple of friends. Not many. Not any more.'

'Family?'

Ella showed the first hint of exàsperation, her jaw moving as if she were grinding her teeth. 'I still speak to my mom, but not as much as I used to. I see them during the holidays.'

I nodded and leaned forwards. 'This is a safe space for you, Ella. Feel free to speak about anything you like. If you don't want to talk about your family or friends right now, we can come back to it. Why don't we talk about why you got in touch with us here at Better Lives? What prompted you to reach out?'

Ella looked up and fixed me with a cold gaze. I didn't blink, waiting for her to speak.

'I had to come here. I needed to speak to someone.'

'Okay,' I replied, feeling a sense of relief that she was finally beginning to talk. 'Start wherever you'd like then, rather than me trying to lead you somewhere you don't want to go right now.'

'I don't really want to be here,' Ella said, closing her eyes for a few moments and lifting her head towards the ceiling. 'I just feel like I'm going to explode if I don't talk to someone. If I don't talk to *you.*'

'I'm listening,' I replied, hoping she wasn't an avid watcher of a particular TV sitcom. 'Talk freely, Ella.'

She didn't wait. Didn't give any preamble. Just laid it out for me, in a single sentence.

'I killed someone.'

3

I didn't react. Didn't say a word. It wasn't as if this was a regular occurrence – I couldn't think of anything close to it, in fact. This was the first time someone had confessed to murder in my office, and I had to quickly think of the consequences of what she had said.

There would be investigations. There would be questions. I could end up in a courtroom, having to explain every last detail of what I said and did in that room in the next few minutes.

I needed time to think. To absorb. To control what happened next. Time I didn't have.

'I'm sorry,' Ella said, wringing her hands together, anxiety exuding from her in waves, threatening to take me down with her. 'I shouldn't have said that.'

I almost breathed a sigh of relief. I was about to launch into a rehearsed spiel about trauma and how that can have an effect on how people view actions and consequences. How it's okay to be confused, to beat yourself up, to call yourself a murderer when you were the furthest thing from that.

I was going to do all that, until she continued talking.

'I mean, not just like that. Not without warning you first. I should be more careful. But you're the first person I've told that to, and I had no idea how to say it other than to just, you know, come out with it.'

Ella was more open now, as if just saying the words had removed a dam that she had built within herself. Which I imagined to be true – there are truths we all hold that can never be said aloud. Everyone is the same. We would all love to be completely honest with each other every day, but it wouldn't last long. I could never tell Gina on reception that she needed to take it easy on the eyebrow shaping, because they looked stranger every day. I couldn't tell JJ's teacher that I had to hold my breath during parent-teacher conferences because his halitosis made me feel nauseated. Or that I didn't want to hear another of Jack's *oh so interesting* work stories when he came home late, smelling of aged whisky and freshly sprayed aftershave.

Those were things we kept to ourselves.

'I just had to tell someone.'

I blinked and was back in the room with Ella. I swallowed and thought of how to approach this. 'Why don't you tell me what happened?'

Only it was as if I wasn't there any more. Not as a person. I was just an avatar, a presence for Ella to not feel alone any more.

'I was scared of saying that out loud,' she continued, becoming calmer by the second. 'Like, if I actually spoke those words, there would be cops bursting into the room instantly. But there's just us here and no one else.'

I shifted in my seat uncomfortably. I quickly scanned her, looking for any indication that she may become violent. Looking for a weapon she had concealed. A knife, a gun.

'Why don't we take a deep breath, Ella,' I said, trying to keep calm, all the while thinking of the quickest way to get out of the room if she suddenly turned on me. 'I know you might be feeling a little overwhelmed right now. Emotions running about the place, your mind fizzing with wanting to tell me everything all in one go. But this will be easier for you if we can approach this calmly and step by step. Does that sound okay to you?'

I caught a flash in her eyes, before she turned away. Irritation? Anger? I wasn't sure. It made me tense a little.

'Okay, I guess,' Ella said, finally, breaking apart her hands and laying them on the sofa, palms down. 'Where should I start?'

'Let's take it from the beginning,' I replied, feeling the tension slip out of the room a little. 'You came here because you were feeling anxious, not sleeping, feeling worried about something. How long have those feelings been going on for, Ella?'

'Since I killed someone.'

I took a deep breath and thought about the likelihood that this young woman, barely a hundred and ten pounds in weight, around five feet five or six inches in height, who looked like a strong wind would be a battle for her to negotiate, could kill someone.

She was the opposite of the 'type'.

Of course, I wasn't the best judge of that.

'Right, and when did this happen?'

Ella was rocking slightly now. A nervous energy replacing the fear. 'A while ago. Sometimes it feels like a dream, but I know it happened.'

A dream. 'Okay, so since it happened, you've not been sleeping. Feeling worried all the time. And this began after this . . . this event?'

Ella nodded, twice, strongly. 'Definitely.'

'What about before? How were you feeling before that?'

She turned towards me now, a moment of confusion flashing across her face. 'Before? I don't understand . . .'

'How were you feeling before this event occurred? Was everything fine? You were sleeping okay, not feeling anxious or upset? Worried about anything?'

She took a few moments to answer, as if she were contemplating her words carefully. 'Normal worries, I guess. Nothing out the ordinary. I suppose I've always got a little worried about things, back in high school and college, but just like everyone else.'

'And then this occurs and you have trouble sleeping?'

'Yeah, every night,' Ella said, on more solid ground. 'I keep seeing it happen, over and over.'

'Like a nightmare?'

She nodded, strongly. 'Exactly. It plays like a movie, in my head. No . . . no not a movie. More like one of those True Crime documentaries on Netflix, right? Where you're not supposed to know what's going to happen next, but you've already googled the case and know the guy killed his wife or something. I'll sometimes hear 911 calls and re-enactments that didn't really happen, like my brain is trying to change the story. It's so weird.'

You've got that right, I thought, but didn't show any sign outwardly of being shocked by what she was telling me. Of judging her in any way. I was being *professional*, all the while I was becoming increasingly uncomfortable about what she was saying to me.

Of all people.

'So, does it feel real when you're having these nightmares?'

'You know, it's like I'm reliving it over and over. Does that make sense to you?'

Far too well. I smiled thinly, warmly. 'I understand. I don't want to push you on the bigger event here – we have only just begun this journey and I need to hear about you as a person. To get a more rounded picture of the situation, if you can?'

Ella hesitated, as if she wasn't getting the response she wanted. 'I don't know why that's important.'

'Indulge me then,' I said, trying to keep a light tone. A sense of normality in what we were discussing, while every moment that passed led me to think that what I had in front of me wasn't a murderer, but someone troubled. 'How was college? What did you study?'

'I majored in History, but . . .'

I cut off her protestations before they came. 'Oh, that sounds interesting. So is that the field you work in now?'

Ella shook her head. 'No, I work in an office. Administration.'

'What college did you go to?'

'UConn. None of this has anything to do with what I'm here to talk about though.'

I smiled at her again, this time catching her eye, as she continued to steal glances my way. 'You'd be surprised what is useful and important to the big picture, Ella. Please, go on, how was college?'

The truth was, I needed to be the one controlling the conversation.

'It was okay, I guess,' Ella said, almost a reluctance in her tone. There was something else there though, under the surface. 'I went to class, a few parties here and there, but nothing major. I wasn't really interested in all of that side of college. I was there because that's what I guess I was supposed to do.'

I caught the wording and filed it away. I felt I knew what was under the surface of her reluctance now.

This was a woman unused to being the centre of attention. Unused to being listened to. She was finally being *heard*.

'Did you feel pressure to go to college then?'

Ella shook her head. 'No, it was just . . . just, like, a natural progression, you know? Like that's what I was supposed to do next.'

'And History was your choice?'

A slight pause, but not long enough for me to know if she was going to lie.

'Yes, it was. I really enjoyed it in high school.'

'What about relationships during college?'

'Nothing serious. I wasn't there for that really. As I said.'

More than once, I thought. Which made me think that perhaps it wasn't a choice. She may be attractive – but then, she was mid-twenties and to me they all looked like fresh-faced beautiful women. They hadn't had to clean the bathroom at three a.m. because Olivia had woken up in the night with an upset stomach and enough time to redecorate the tiling.

Ella was staring at the back of the photo frame on my desk. The only thing that was personal to me in the room, if truth were told. I hadn't put it away before she'd come in, which I mentally chastised myself for, but kept quiet.

I didn't like leaving anything out that could be used by clients to try and switch the focus.

'So, you left college and went into work straight away?'

'Yeah,' Ella said, tearing her eyes away from the desk and back to me. 'I wanted to stay in state and not go back home. I was already working in a restaurant near campus and had saved some money. I ended up in New Haven first and now close to here.'

'How long have you been working in your current job?'

I could see the annoyance rising to the surface within her now. That I'd ignored why she'd come here – to get something off her chest. To hear someone take her words seriously. I'd pushed away a little too much.

'Can we just talk about what I've done?'

'We can talk about anything you like, Ella.'

She nodded to herself. 'Good, because that's all I want to talk about really. I don't want to waste time on all of these other things that don't matter. I need to tell you what I did. Please.'

'Go on,' I said, leaning back slightly in my chair and waiting for her to continue. 'I'm here for you to tell me anything you need to.'

'Okay,' Ella replied, then she began to tell her story.

Only it wasn't *her* story.

It felt too familiar.

It felt too real.

It felt too much like *my* story.

4

The only sound for a moment was the ticking of the clock on the wall. A grey and white, almost featureless addition I'd made to the office recently. Mainly because it gave clients something to focus on when they became long-winded.

I like my job. I don't always love it.

I was trying to listen to what Ella was saying, but as she continued to talk, I could barely hear her over the sound of my own heartbeat.

'I met someone. Just in a bar, nothing weird. I don't like online dating. It's always awkward and men on there always seem to think it's an easy way of having a one-night stand rather than actually building something properly. An easy hook-up and no strings attached. Not for me. So, I went to a bar with a couple of friends. Anyway, this guy was standing at the bar and he was turning round holding a couple of drinks and bumped into me. He didn't spill all that much down my dress, but he was so apologetic it became funny. I sometimes think, what if I'd gone to the bar a few seconds later. Or, if someone else had gone instead. Maybe I wouldn't be sitting here now.'

Ella's voice had changed now. As if this was a story she'd been waiting to tell all her life. One she'd gone over in her head many times – there was almost a rehearsed quality to it.

I should have been professional, but instead I was sitting there like I was watching TV, waiting for the next beat of the story.

'We started chatting. Nothing serious, just about who we were, what we did, that kind of thing. He was with his own group, on the other side of the bar, but we couldn't seem to stop talking. Eventually, someone came over from both of our groups to get their own drinks. We just got locked into each other somehow. I guess that's what they call love at first sight, maybe?'

'It sounds lovely,' I said, finding my voice. Wanting her to continue. To hear what she had to say next.

'I know it sounds made up. Like some kind of romcom or something. Those types of thing don't really happen in real life, but it *did* happen. It was like the universe had brought us together and then kept us there, talking, listening, learning, laughing. It was . . . it was so unusual for me, but so right.'

I knew the feeling she was talking about. All too well. A fleeting memory came to me then, of a different time. A different life.

Jack was all I needed now. All I wanted. I felt blessed to have found him when I had. Grateful. That didn't mean I didn't sometimes go through the rolodex of my past dating life to enjoy the memories. Just for fun, of course. Nothing other than that.

I was lucky to have him.

Now.

Only, there had been a time in a bar, years earlier, when I'd met a different man. When I'd fallen in love at first sight, just like Ella.

'We talked for hours, until the bar closed. Our friends had left us there. He walked me home. He wouldn't come inside my apartment though, despite me asking him to. Told me it wasn't time for that. He wanted to see me again soon, for a proper date. Do things the right way. We exchanged numbers and I remember walking into my apartment feeling that I had just met "the one".'

Ella shook her head slowly, stealing a glance towards me. 'I know, it sounds ridiculous. A chance meeting and suddenly I was picturing a life with someone. But that's how he made me feel.

Like I was special. Like I was the only person in the room. Like I was who he had been looking for all his life.'

I knew the feeling, of course. Those beginning stages of a relationship, that frisson of excitement, that sense of anticipation of what was to come.

I didn't know at that point that Ella was perfectly describing my own experiences. My own life, only eighteen years in the past.

'Go on, Ella,' I said, crossing one leg over the other. 'You're doing great.'

She smiled quickly to herself, before it disappeared as soon as it had arrived. 'We met the next night. An Italian restaurant, because we'd talked about the fact we both loved the food the night before. We were there for hours, just talking and talking. Only, he was asking me all the questions. If I asked something about him, he would give me a real quick answer and then move back to me. I told him about my family, my friends. My job, my future. Everything. Right down to what shows I'd been watching, my love for old television. My collection of theatre programmes. All of it. It was like no other experience I've ever had.'

I checked the clock on the wall while she wasn't looking and saw we'd covered half of our allotted hour. 'It's always a thrill when someone makes us feel important. You shouldn't feel bad about that.'

'I don't feel bad,' Ella said, snapping her head towards me. I could hear the barely constrained anger in her tone and almost flinched at it. She looked away slowly. 'That's not what I'm feeling.'

'I'm sorry,' I replied, emotionless. Wondering when she was going to get to the part that was most intriguing. 'Maybe I didn't word that quite right.'

Ella shook her head. 'It's fine. I just don't want you to think I was some poor little girl who didn't know what she was getting herself into. That's not what this is about. I knew *exactly* what I was doing.'

I studied her closely, as she brought her hands together again. Watched as she seemed to massage life into them. Her nails were perfect, I noticed. Painted red. Deep, almost crimson. The colour of blood. I had the same shade tucked away somewhere. I couldn't remember the last time I'd worn something similar. The last time I'd tried to make a statement with something as simple as my nail polish colour.

'We slept together for the first time that second night,' Ella said, her voice cold and almost a whisper. Almost guilty. 'It was . . . it was amazing. He seemed to know my body without having ever been near it. Not like anyone I'd been with before. It was like an out-of-body experience when I think back on it now. I'd never been with anyone like him before in my life.'

For the first time, I allowed an element of a frown appear. The way she was talking was less robotic when she described the first time she'd had sex with this man. As if she weren't just saying lines in a movie. I hadn't noticed the difference until now. I tried to shake off the feeling.

'We were inseparable from that moment,' Ella continued, wiping away an invisible tear from her cheek, as her voice became a little more choked up. 'He came back the next night, then didn't seem to ever leave. I noticed one day that he'd brought some stuff over. It didn't matter to me though. I was just so happy. Happy that someone had . . . had *seen* me, if that makes sense? We would stay up late, talking and talking. Watching TV shows, movies. He was funny, he was serious. He could have these long discussions about any subject. It was like he was an expert on everything. He'd catch a little news report and be able to talk about it at length. Like, I'd see something on Twitter, or Insta, or whatever, and mention it to him, and he'd already know all about it. Have opinions about it ready to go, if that makes sense?'

It made complete sense to me. I'd known someone like that. A long time ago. A time before Twitter and social media – MySpace was still in its infancy at that point – but TV made up for that.

Turned out that he wasn't as clever or witty as I'd first thought when we'd met. The façade had dropped little by little – usually when he was challenged by someone who wasn't me. Who wasn't hanging on every word he said.

By then, of course, it had already been too late.

'My friends either liked him instantly, or hated him within minutes. He was a real-life love-him-or-hate-him figure. The ones who loved him, he'd encourage me to see. Would enjoy their company. He knew the ones who didn't like him, though. The ones who wouldn't laugh at his jokes, or listen to his stories. Those friends . . . those friends I don't have any more. They disappeared.'

'We can take a break any time you like, Ella,' I said, as she stopped talking and ran her hands through her hair. She was trying to stay confident as she spoke, but I could see the strain it was having. 'Just take this as slow as you like.'

'I'm okay. I can get through this,' Ella replied, a smile crossing her face, fleetingly. 'I should have known at that point that maybe he wasn't everything I thought he was, but I was already in too deep by then. I loved him within weeks. I'd been in a few relationships before then, but nothing like this. He consumed my life. I thought about him every minute – what he was doing, where he was, who he was with. And not because I was worried that he was doing something behind my back. It was because I was jealous of whoever had him for that time I didn't. That they were spending time with him when I couldn't. I know this sounds stupid . . .'

I shushed her soothingly. 'Not at all, Ella. This is your story.'

'I guess it is,' Ella replied with a sigh. 'Anyway, it was intense from the beginning. That's what I'm trying to say. I was like a silly little girl, because I didn't really *know* him, did I? Not after a few weeks. Even though I was totally in love with him and was already planning out my entire life, I didn't know what he was really like.'

There was a beat of silence and I waited for her to continue. I knew she had more to say.

I knew, because I'd been there myself.

'He was never violent towards me. He never hurt me. I just want you to know that. It wasn't like that. He would have taken a bullet for me, I think. So, I was there, through it all, because I wanted to be. There wasn't a reason for me to leave, I guess, but that doesn't mean I shouldn't have gone. I should have gone as soon as he started talking about bar fights and spending nights in cells. That wasn't anything like what I wanted.'

With every word Ella was saying, a strange sense of déjà vu fell over me.

I could have been saying these exact words.

I *had* said these exact words.

'When it happened, I don't think he meant for it to go the way it did. It was stupid. If we'd just gone home, everything would have been okay. I wouldn't have to live with it. We could have been happy. He would have calmed down by the next day, I know it. Only we'd had a couple of drinks and I guess that was all that was needed.'

I knew what she was going to tell me next.

She was going to tell me about the night a man was murdered because of what happened in a bar, late at night.

She was going to tell me about the biggest mistake I ever made.

She was going to tell me about the night I watched it happen and didn't stop it.

Didn't *want* it to stop.

5

On one level, I knew she couldn't be talking about me.

On another . . . it was impossible for me to ignore the similarities. Mainly because I thought about that night every single day.

'The music was so loud in the bar,' Ella said, her voice low, a monotonous drone that was still somehow utterly entrancing. 'It was giving me a headache. I wanted to leave, but he wouldn't listen. Then, there was this guy suddenly watching me. I could feel his eyes on me. When I went to the bathroom, he followed me there. Cornered me as I was waiting in line. I can still feel his breath on my neck, as he leaned in to speak to me. I don't even remember the words now – just the intent.'

I swallowed, placing a hand absentmindedly against my neck, below my right ear. It felt warm. 'What was his name?' I cut in, trying to sound nonchalant as I asked. She couldn't say the same name I'd known – I was sure of that. Still, there was a part of me expecting her to say *his* name.

Daniel Emerson.

I tried not to think about him. It didn't stop me. If my mind lingered too long, I would think about nothing *but* him.

'Why do you need to know?'

I held my hands out. 'It will just make this easier to follow. If you don't want to give me a name, that's fine.'

I could almost see the machinations of thinking going on within her. I didn't know if she was about to lie, or give me a real name.

'Brandon. That was his name. Brandon came round the corner and saw him, us, and knew instantly that there was something wrong. I started stammering, trying to get away, but this guy put his hand against the wall and wouldn't move. Brandon came up and pushed him away. Started shouting, but I didn't stick around to find out what was being said. I just wanted to get out of there. Brandon came back a minute or so later and I told him I wanted to go. I remember placing a hand on his arm. I could feel how tense it was, the muscles barely beneath the skin, screaming in response. I told him the guy wasn't worth it.'

I blinked and saw myself in a bar. My hand on my boyfriend's arm, trying to pull him away. Trying to get him to leave.

'I should have run as soon as the guy came up to me,' Ella continued, shaking her head to herself. 'If I'd just done that, said nothing about it, I wouldn't be sitting in this room right now. I told Brandon I'd had too much drink and wanted to go home, but it was too late by then. He thought he'd hit me or something and that's why my head hurt. I tried to tell him I just had a headache, but he wasn't really listening to me.'

Ella breathed in. 'Then, he said to me, "We were having such a good night and then that guy goes and ruins it. I can't let that just go on without doing something about it. He can't just go unpunished. It's not right." I knew then it wasn't going to end well.'

Almost word for word. I could hear him saying the words – loud enough for me to hear over the music.

'"Yes, it can," I said, you know, trying to calm him down. He said, "That's how these types of people get away with it. They think they can do what they like and there's no consequences. It's not fair."'

She was going to describe them leaving next, and Ella would say it was because she thought he was listening to her finally.

I couldn't speak.

'I thought he was listening to me. That he was calming down and taking on board what I was saying. That everything was going to be okay. Instead, he was working out what he was going to do next. How the night was going to end. And he couldn't have been more wrong. We left and I remember I was smiling, thinking that everything was going to be okay then. He took my hand and led me out of the bar and onto the street. We didn't share a word, as he pulled me along the side of the road to where he'd parked the car earlier. It wasn't until we were sitting inside his car and he was staring out front, that I realised we weren't going anywhere. He didn't make a single move to drive away. To make a joke about only having had a single beer, so being fine to drive. Knowing he'd had at least three or four.'

It was as if she was in my head. Reliving my memories. I wanted to say something. To stop what she was saying.

'I tried again, to get him to leave, but I remember him turning, slowly, and there was a blankness in his eyes. As if he were staring right through me. He shook his head and said he couldn't. That he was sorry. That I deserved justice. We sat in the car for forty-five minutes waiting. I tried to reason with him, but he wasn't listening, until I realised there was no point in trying. Instead, I laid my head against the window and tried to ignore the increasing pain in my head. Closed my eyes and pretended I was back at home, lying in bed next to the man I loved. Dreaming of a future together. Dreaming of what would be. Dreaming of what would *never* be, it seemed. Not waiting for whatever he was going to do to that man in the bar.'

A silence began to grow, as Ella stared past me. To the window behind me, looking out, blankly, at the blue sky and buildings in the distance. I cleared my throat, knowing if I didn't, the first words that would escape my mouth would be strangled.

'What happened next?'

There was the hint of a grimace, as she swallowed something back and shook her head. 'I must have fallen asleep, because when the car's engine turned over beneath me and it began to pull away from its parking spot, I was frightened. My heart was beating so hard in my chest that I couldn't catch my breath. Brandon just said, "There he is," and I knew there was no way back. There was so much hate and anger in just those three words. I could barely believe that he hadn't been able to calm himself in the time since leaving the bar. Instead, he'd sat behind that wheel and become even worse. Stewing in his own rage. I tried again, but he ignored me. In the headlights in front of us, I could see the guy from the bar and he looked so young. Almost a child. Couldn't have been more than seventeen or eighteen in the cold light of night. But then, we weren't much older. Barely in our early twenties.'

I didn't need Ella to tell me what happened next. I was already seeing it play out. Her words still came, but I barely heard them.

I saw myself being thrown into the dashboard as he slammed on the brakes. The door opening, almost in slow motion. Hearing his voice. Hearing his shouts. Seeing the man take a step backwards, before stopping and throwing his hands out and pushing him back.

'*Think you can touch any woman? Think they're asking for it? Is that it?*'

I liked to believe that what happened next was a blur. That I didn't see it properly, starkly, right in front of me.

As if I couldn't recall every second of what came next.

The man was standing one moment, then not the next. He disappeared from view. A mighty thud echoed in the darkness.

'I got out the car, I think to stop it. Because by then, it had already escalated. Brandon was just raining down on the guy. Everything was muffled, like I was under water. By the time I came round the front of the car, the guy was lying there on the ground, not moving. Brandon stopped when I got to them, shaking his hand out. I remember seeing blood on his knuckles.'

I swallowed slowly, trying not to remember.

'Brandon started talking to the guy. Telling him to get up, nudging him with his foot, pulling on him, but it was too late.'

I'd known by that point. I had seen the blood pooling underneath the guy's head, the way his face looked, the contorted nature of his body.

It was the suffocating silence that made me *know*.

'I got on my knees next to the guy, shoving Brandon out the way. I put my hand on his chest, against his neck, as if I knew what I was doing. I knew enough to know that his chest wasn't rising. His neck wasn't pulsing. Brandon was next to me, kneeling down, his hand on my shoulder, just asking over and over . . .'

Is he . . . is he dead?

A tear escaped Ella's eye and I had to check my own cheek to make sure I wasn't reciprocating.

'I tried to do something, I swear,' Ella said, something catching in her throat, as she glanced across at me. Her eyes filmy wet. Her breath coming in short bursts. 'Something, anything.'

'Except the one thing that might have saved him,' I heard myself say, the words escaping before I had chance to stop them.

'That's right,' Ella replied, looking down at her hands. 'I didn't call for help. Instead, I held onto him. All the way until I felt his last breath.'

I knew what she was feeling.

I knew what she was thinking.

I knew *everything*.

She was talking about me.

6

I was holding my breath, my chest tightening, restricting me.

It was like I was back there. In that moment.

'I didn't know what to do,' Ella said, sniffing back a tear. 'I could only hold onto him, as it all came to a stop. Then Brandon, he . . . he pulled me away. I remember not wanting to let go, because then it would be real, if that makes sense? Like if I was close to the poor guy I could stop it from happening. But that was just me going mad, I guess.'

I swallowed and managed to sneak a breath. 'When did this happen, Ella?'

A ridiculous question. I knew when it had happened. I had been there. I had seen it happen. Felt it.

She was talking about me.

Only she wasn't. She couldn't be. I had to forget that line of thinking. I wasn't the only person in the world who had gone through a traumatic incident in their life. Even something like this, which was less common, of course. Still, it was impossible. She couldn't know. She couldn't *possibly* know what I had done.

I had to focus and help Ella. Not think of myself.

Yet, I couldn't shake the feeling that something more was going on.

I knew this girl. Somehow.

She just looked so . . . familiar.

Maybe it was just that she reminded me of myself.

'A while ago,' Ella said, dismissing the question. Eager to continue. 'It doesn't matter. All that matters is that it happened and I didn't do anything to stop it.'

'What happened next?'

Ella took a deep breath, as if she were about to step onto more uneven ground. Only, it didn't feel that way to me. There was a red warning light blinking constantly in my mind. As if it were me who wasn't on solid ground.

'It was obvious he was . . . he was gone,' Ella said, sunshine appearing from behind me and lighting one side of her face. 'Brandon started panicking . . .'

'Okay,' I said, unsure if she was being truthful about the name. There was a slight pause each time she said it, as if she were remembering what she'd said last time. I logged it away, knowing it wouldn't be enough anyway. I could hardly find out anything about a person from a single name. 'Please, go on.'

'Well, Brandon started panicking. Saying he didn't mean to hurt him. I knew that wasn't true though. We'd waited for him to come out. Until he was on his own. Brandon had been waiting until he was definitely alone before he did anything. The poor guy didn't stand a chance – he was drunk, young, and couldn't even defend himself.'

That was a little different to my own story and I almost exclaimed in relief. I managed to keep my composure.

'I didn't know what to do. Brandon was almost crying and I was holding onto this guy, trying to bring him back to life. I know it sounds stupid, but I didn't know what else to do. I held onto him and just rocked back and forth. Then I felt Brandon's hand on my shoulder and I almost ran away. There and then. I was so scared.'

Ella took a moment to wipe away another tear, only I couldn't see anything on her cheek. I could hear the pain in her voice, but it didn't seem to be having any physical effect on her – despite her attempts to show that it was.

I wasn't sure why that might be the case if she was telling the truth. If this was her story. If this had happened to her.

'He said to me,' Ella continued, taking a quick glance at the clock. Forty minutes had gone by now. 'He said, we need to go. But I couldn't leave just like that. Not with him lying there . . . dead. It would have made things even worse. Because I knew, I knew that someone would find him. That they would be able to know exactly who was involved. They could do DNA testing or whatever. I'd breathed on him. That would be all it would take.

'I remember looking around for surveillance cameras straight away. We were in a dark parking lot though, so I couldn't see any. Brandon saw me looking and suddenly started muttering to himself. Holding onto his own body, like he was trying to stop himself from running away. He was talking to himself. Saying over and over, *he had it coming, he had it coming.* He was trying to convince himself.'

That line wasn't an exact match, but I remember something similar.

Dan had been saying, *it was his fault, it was his fault,* as he held onto himself.

Close, I guessed. Not exactly the same.

Still.

'I didn't know what to do,' Ella said, turning to me now, as if she were trying to make me believe her. Again, the same blankness in her eyes. 'I knew we couldn't leave him there, but even that quickly, I knew that Brandon had killed someone. That I hadn't done anything to stop it, either. All I could think about was that we'd end up in some courtroom, all over social media, that kind of thing. They wouldn't care that this man had tried to assault me in the bar. Sorry . . . that he *had* assaulted me. He touched me without my consent, that's assault, right? Anyway, they'd be more interested in the amount of time we'd waited for him to come out. That we'd waited until he was alone, before attacking him – and that's how it would be. It wouldn't be Brandon. It would be *both* of us. I was involved now.'

I couldn't speak. I was hearing my own thoughts being echoed back at me.

I thought about JJ and Olivia. What they would think of their mom, what she had done. That's why I had spent the past eighteen years trying to forget.

There's only so far you can run from your past before you meet it coming round the corner.

And that was what was happening.

I was spiralling.

'It sounds like a terrible situation, Ella,' I heard myself say, as if from another room. Another planet.

'It wasn't just terrible,' Ella said, spitting the words back at me. 'It was the worst thing I've ever done in my life. Because we didn't just leave him there. We didn't contact the authorities, the police. We didn't call 911 and try and save his life. We did nothing. We stood there, hoping he would suddenly spring back to life, but that wasn't going to happen. He wasn't moving, it was late at night, and Brandon had just killed him.'

'Ella . . .'

'But that's not even the worst part,' Ella continued, not hearing me. Or ignoring the interruption. 'Because all I could think about was that if someone found out what happened, then I'd lose Brandon. I wasn't thinking about anyone else. Not about the dead man on the ground, not about his family, his loved ones . . . only Brandon. And myself, of course. Because I was there too. I would be part of this. Our life – *my life* – would be over. Nothing would ever be the same again. I couldn't have that. I couldn't let this mistake take over our lives.'

'What did you do?'

'I made the decision. Not Brandon. Me. I turned to him and said we needed to do something with the body.'

And there it was. Those were the same words I'd used. All those years earlier. *We need to do something with the body.* Not the lad, not the guy, not the man.

The body.

I had already reframed the situation. The person was no longer there. It was just a body to me.

I could feel the gnawing in my stomach. The swirling feeling of anxiety and guilt.

I was being *seen*.

'I just remember holding onto the body and seeing this gold chain next to where he was lying. I remember picking it up, turning it over in my hand. It was just a simple thing, torn from him as Brandon had . . . anyway. It had an initial hanging from the chain. I don't know what I did with it. I stared at it for a while, but then heard heavy breathing coming from Brandon. He didn't know what to do. He was panicking, so the first thing I did was try and calm him a little. I left the body on the ground and moved towards him. He flinched from my touch, but eventually he let me wrap my arms around him. He was cold, shivering, despite the warmth of the evening. I held onto him, afraid to let go. I needed him to try and think straight. To try and act alongside me.'

Ella took a moment, as I realised my leg was bobbing up and down. Slowly, rhythmically. I wasn't thinking about anything else at that moment. Only that I had finally been found out. I looked towards the door, expecting it to burst open and for a dozen cops to force their way inside. To pin me down to the floor and take me away.

My thoughts ran into each other, colliding and spilling out.

'We weren't thinking about him any more. We were only thinking of ourselves. That's what we had to do. There was no other way, I thought. I had to think about us, not him. And in the end, didn't he deserve it? He had touched something that didn't belong to him. That's how Brandon put it. I belonged to him. My body was his. He had tried to steal something that didn't belong to him and that's enough, isn't it?'

I couldn't answer the question. I stared at Ella, wishing she would look up at me, so I could look into her eyes. See if she was real. A real person sitting there, describing my life to me, and not some manifestation of the guilt I'd been carrying for so long.

'It doesn't matter now,' she said, shaking her head. 'I guess I just have to live with what happened and try and move on. I know it changed me that night, though. I know I've never been the same since. I'm less of a person now. I carry all this guilt, of course, but there's something else as well. It's *hate*. I'm angry all the time. I argue with people I say I love. I snap at people in coffee shops and restaurants, if they do something wrong. I flip people off in traffic. I can't just be happy with what I have. I always want more and more. It doesn't matter if I'm around people who want me to be happy. I just want to hurt everyone, because of what I did.'

I couldn't think straight. I was only thinking about that necklace. 'What was the initial?'

'What?'

'On the necklace,' I said, hearing the slight wobble in my voice. Willing it not to break. 'What letter was it?'

She looked at me. Made no attempt to break eye contact, once it was fixed.

'A.'

I felt the world underneath me shift. I gripped hold of the arms on my chair, as if I were about to be lifted away. Thrown to the ground by some unseen force.

She got to her feet suddenly and I almost flinched back into the chair. 'Wait . . .'

'I can't do this any more,' Ella said, glancing my way for a second and then turning her back to me. 'I have to go.'

I tried to stand up, but my legs betrayed me. They felt as if they weren't part of me any longer. I managed to get up just as Ella reached the door and opened it.

Then, she was a blur, as I crossed the room behind her, my heart crashing against my chest as I could only think of one thing, over and over.

I can't let her leave.

She knows.

She knows.

7

I made it out into the corridor outside my office, but Ella was already gone. I could hear my breathing, heavy, hard. I smoothed down my dress and tried to maintain control. Tried to think straight.

It wasn't easy.

I could only think of Ella. Out there, no longer under my supervision, able to tell my story to anyone she wanted to.

I made it to reception and Gina lifted her head as I entered, looking bored and distracted.

'The woman who was just here . . .'

'She left?'

I sighed. 'Yes, Gina, she left. Did you not see her?'

'Sorry, I was in the bathroom.'

A lie. I sensed that instantly. Most probably, she was looking at her cell phone. Or on her computer. Trying to find a date in the area, I guessed. She was forever going on about her dating apps and the many failed hookups she'd been on. As if I was interested. Idle gossip that I endured rather than enjoyed.

I hated her in that moment and then, because I never wanted to feel that way, hated myself for thinking that.

I took a breath and tried to stay calm. 'She can't have got far.'

I didn't wait for a response, almost jogging towards the elevator and pressing the call button rapidly, until a few too many seconds passed by and I chose to take the stairs instead. I went down two at a time, almost losing my footing as I turned in the stairwell and continued down. The heels on my shoes echoed a click-clack all the way down.

I was out of breath by the time I reached the exit, pushing through the doors and scanning the parking lot outside for any sign of Ella.

It was empty.

I saw a car off in the distance, pulling out of the exit, and I took off in that direction. I wasn't sure what I was going to do – I wasn't likely to catch up to a moving car. It wasn't as if I was thinking clearly in that moment, though, so I kept going until I was out on the street. I wanted to catch up with her and make her explain what she'd told me. Tell me what she knew and, more importantly, who she would tell.

And *how* she could know.

It was in vain. The young woman was gone.

I made my way back to my building and entered, my hands shaking as they reached up for the door and pushed inside. Adrenaline was coursing through me, but it was more than that.

It was fear. Running through my veins, to every part of my body.

I had to try and think straight, but I couldn't stop the way my body was reacting.

I'd had almost twenty years to prepare for this moment, but it was as if I were surprised that it had finally happened.

There was a bathroom before reception and I went inside quickly before Gina spotted me coming back in. Went straight to the wash basin and turned on the tap. *Faucet.* The small delineations within a common language. Water gushed out and I watched it for a few moments. I wanted to reach towards it, cup it in my hands and splash reality onto my face. Only, I knew I couldn't go back into the office with make-up smeared across my features.

I couldn't let Gina know something was wrong.

Instead, I turned the faucet off and went into a stall behind me. Closed the door and then pushed the lid down on the toilet. Sat down and put my head in my hands.

How could she know?

I forced myself to slow my breathing. In for five seconds. Out for five seconds. Closed my eyes and saw black stars. Felt my hands shaking against the back of my head, slowing and slowing.

My insides churned with terror. Dread.

She couldn't know.

I thought about it, as my breathing slowed and I started to get a handle on myself. Only two people were there that night. One was thousands of miles away from here, probably already dead. The other was me and despite the feeling of recognition, I could swear I had never met the woman who had entered my office that morning.

I wouldn't tell anyone about that night.

I couldn't imagine Dan would be telling people either. He had disappeared quite quickly afterwards. Racked with guilt, unable to deal with what happened, as his temper had finally gone too far. I sometimes checked the local press in the UK for news about him, expecting to read that he was dead or in prison.

That wasn't my only way of keeping tabs on him, of course. I had other ways.

I hadn't checked in a while.

If Ella had gone into another room, with a different therapist that morning, would she have told the same story?

Of course not. She had wanted to see me. She would have simply waited until I was available.

Why?

Who was she?

I wasn't going to achieve much sitting in that bathroom stall, but it felt good to be cocooned away from the world. A momentary still of silence, save the pounding thoughts running through my head and the idea that I wouldn't be alone for much longer. For the rest of my life, I would have the company of other people – violent people.

I would be incarcerated for what I'd done.

Only it wouldn't be here. In the US. Home, now. It would be back in the UK. A place I tried not to think about too much.

I would be forced back there to answer for what I'd done.

Or not done, more aptly.

I wasn't a good liar and would crumble under any questioning. I would accept full responsibility for everything that happened.

Wouldn't I?

I'd always believed that, but maybe things were different now. I was a wife and mother.

And I thought about JJ and Olivia. They hadn't been far from my mind since Ella had begun talking. Nothing abnormal in that, I thought about them almost constantly. What they were doing at odd moments throughout the day. If they were okay, if they were happy.

I thought of them then, saying goodbye to their mom, as she was led in handcuffs onto a waiting plane, ready to take her back to the UK.

They wouldn't look at her the same way ever again. They would be forever known as the children of a killer. Or at least someone who had let it happen, but the details wouldn't matter. The association would be enough.

Then there would be social media. There would be documentaries, there would be a relentless focus on me. My family.

I couldn't let that happen.

And something twisted inside me. The fear began to slowly dissipate and anger began to take over.

I needed to find this Ella and ensure she didn't tell anyone else what she'd told me that morning. Not until I could be sure that it wasn't my story she was telling.

And then what?

I shook away the thought. Something to worry about another time. For now, I had to pretend. Pretend everything was okay, pretend that I hadn't had my world shaken to its foundations. Pretend that there was a way out of this.

I had done that enough times over the years.

Gina was sitting at reception as I made my way back to my office, watching me closely as I approached, a wary look on her face.

'Was I supposed to keep her here or something?' she asked, a hint of worry in her tone. 'She paid up front for the session, cash as well, which is weird I guess . . .'

I waved away her words. 'It's okay, it was just a tough session, that's all. I was a little worried that it ended abruptly. I'm sure she'll return. I think it would be good if we could do a little digging anyway, just to be sure. Can you find as much information about her as possible, please? I want to make sure she is who she says she is, for her own safety.'

Gina frowned a little, but seemed to accept my request. 'I'll get right to that. She didn't seem all that well when she arrived. Almost like she'd seen a ghost, the poor thing. So pale.'

'You didn't recognise her, did you?' I asked, trying to sound as nonchalant as it was possible to do. 'Not seen her around here before or anything?'

Gina thought for a moment, then she shook her head. 'I'm usually a good one for faces, but she didn't look familiar at all.'

'Okay,' I said, still unable to shake the idea I'd seen this woman before. It didn't make sense to me, but sometimes the brain senses things it doesn't always make apparent. 'Well, I think my next client is a half-hour away, so I'll be in my office.'

I turned and made my way back to my office in a daze. Closed the door behind me and sat down at my desk with a thump.

There was a moment of calm, and then the feeling of being watched came over me. I snapped my head towards the window, but I was several floors up and no one was out there. Of course.

I shook my head and thought about her.

I might have been able to put it all down to coincidence. I might have been able to think that two people had similar stories, that was all.

Only, there was one detail that she could not have possibly known.

The gold chain around his neck. The initial hanging from it.

A.

That was no coincidence.

I had seen it before. I had held it in my hands, just like Ella had described.

She knew.

Now I had to work out what she wanted.

*

Ella left the office, breathing heavily by the time she reached the car waiting for her. They were already sitting in the front seats, not saying a word as she bundled herself into the back.

'Drive,' Ella said, looking out of the window, then over her shoulder at the building. 'Quickly.'

They still didn't speak to her. She was forced against the seat as the car took off with a squeal of tyres, out onto the street in seconds.

She saw Sara emerge into the parking lot, just as they moved out of sight.

From that distance, she couldn't see her expression, her eyes, but she could almost hear her thoughts.

'Anywhere in particular?' Colby said from behind the wheel, his Bostonian drawl a comfort blanket. The woman sitting beside him looked questioningly at Ella in the rear-view mirror.

'Just . . . just drive,' Ella said, settling back and leaning her head against the headrest. She closed her eyes, trying to think. Trying to work out what to do next.

She had set the bomb now. She just needed to be there when it finally went off.

8

I found the information about Ella that Gina had given me earlier and scoured its contents, as if it would contain answers to the thousands of questions running through my mind.

Who she was, where she came from. What she would want from me.

There was nothing there, of course. The list of complaints I'd read earlier, expecting the usual kind of patient to come into my office into my office. A young woman with a cross to bear and enough money to pay for a session, in the hope it would make her feel better. Only, that wasn't the case, was it? She may have been disturbed, but not in the way I'd expected.

And was she really *disturbed*? Or someone who had information and wanted me to know it?

I ran through the endless possibilities then. Money was the obvious answer, yet Ella had run from my office without even an acknowledgment that she was trying to screw with me.

If only she had been older, I thought. Maybe I could have played it differently. Maybe she could have been really the one to blame and I would have got away scot-free. Just like I had for years.

I wasn't making much sense, even to myself.

I wanted to call Jack. I wanted to hear him tell me everything was going to be okay. Only, I knew that wouldn't be what he'd say. Instead, he'd go into full problem-solving mode. Just like so many other men – there was no story he could hear without having a solution to it. I would want emotional support and he would give me chapter and verse on how to deal with the situation.

That wasn't what I needed to hear right then.

Usually, I didn't mind the way he approached any issue that occurred in our lives. In some ways, it made my life easier. I remember when my father fell ill and I couldn't get in touch with the hospital to find out about his health status. Jack stepped in and took control. He knew exactly what to do, how to do it, and got it done. If he'd simply stroked my back and offered his shoulder for me to cry on, I'd still have been none the wiser as to what was happening with him.

Then, he'd been with me when we'd travelled to the UK for the funeral.

That had been the last time I'd been there. I'd always thought I'd never go back after that. I had no real family there now. A few aunts and uncles, cousins too, but we weren't close. I wouldn't be able to pick them out of a line-up, I bet.

I had a new life. I had built a career, a home, a family.

And now this Ella had walked into my office and threatened that.

Jack would understand. Jack would know what to do. I reached into my bag and pulled out my cell phone, found his number in my recent contacts and pressed the dial button. Waited for him to answer. Hoped he would.

I knew he wouldn't.

I didn't leave a message, instead firing him a quick text to call me back.

Then, I saw it was almost time for my next client and tried to compose myself. I had to try and remain calm. To get through the day, without anyone else suspecting something might have happened.

I was already calculating how today would look if it came up again in the future. How people would talk about me, my reaction.

I would have to do something about Gina, because she would think it strange that I'd run after a client leaving early. I needed to seed something there.

Maybe I was more like Jack than I realised. Problem-solving, ensuring everything I did made me look innocent.

Instead of screaming and rolling into a ball like I wanted to.

It didn't stop the feeling of anxiety sitting inside me like a metal ball all day. It didn't stop me counting down the hours before I could leave work and go and pick up the kids. It didn't stop me thinking about what to do next.

One thing was for sure. I wasn't going to wait.

I needed to find Ella.

*

My first appointment after Ella's that morning was a blur. I mostly pretended to listen, as Dana complained about her husband not doing some menial housework she had decided was so important for the sanctity of her marriage. I knew why it meant so much to her – it was indicative of the way her husband treated her as a whole. Yet I couldn't find it within myself to care.

So I sat there, pretending, while she went on and on. When really I wanted to scream at her that it meant nothing. That she should stop wasting her time with this man, because soon enough, she'd be in her fifties. Her children would be grown and out of the house, and she would be stuck with him then.

I wasn't supposed to say things like that. I was supposed to gently guide them to discover their own path.

It was becoming more difficult.

None of it mattered anyway. In a few days' time, I wouldn't be there. I'd be on a plane back to England, with handcuffs round my wrists. That's the truth.

Unless there was some way of finding Ella and making sure she didn't say another word.

I didn't know what that would mean, but it was becoming clearer to me as the hours slipped by.

There was no way I was going to let my past ruin my future.

My second appointment was with Alex. A thirty-eight year old woman, who had moved to the state in the past year. Originally from out west, she'd told me. She'd left an entire life behind and run as far as she could.

She was in law enforcement, but she wouldn't tell me what her role was exactly. She didn't look like your typical cop – not that I knew what typically they looked like. She could have told me she worked as a yoga instructor and I would have believed her.

Alex had problems.

I was doing my best to help her through them. Only, that morning, I was more concerned that she would be able to see through me and know that I was hiding something. And there was a part of me that wanted to tell her everything. To confess and have it be done with.

I liked her. She seemed to like me too. I knew she'd been forced in some way to come and see me, but after a few months she'd begun to let the walls come down a little.

Forty minutes in and I had almost forgotten about Ella. About the teenager who had been killed in front of me. About a life less well led.

'There's just a different kind of sunset out west,' Alex said, a wistful look on her face. 'Know what I'm saying?'

'I've never had the pleasure.'

'You've been here over fifteen years and you've never been to the west coast?'

I shook my head. 'My husband wouldn't step foot in California, never mind Washington and . . . erm . . .'

'Oregon.'

'Right,' I said, clapping my hands together. 'Portland, right?'

'Yeah. But why wouldn't he want to?'

I shrugged. 'I have no idea. We've been down to Florida. New Orleans, Dallas, one time we even stopped off in Tulsa, Oklahoma, but that's as far west as we've been.'

'You should really go,' Alex said, leaning forwards and fixing a smile on her face. 'I miss it every day. Especially during winter.'

'I've always wanted to do Route 66. Maybe, one day . . .'

Alex was telling me a story from her childhood. That seemed to be her favourite subject and I knew why. It was avoidance. She didn't want to talk about anything that happened in her life post eighteen years old.

Too difficult.

I would get there with her. That was what I did.

I helped people.

I hoped I would still be able to.

'Anyway,' Alex said, getting back to her story. 'There was this moment, when we were all sitting watching the sun go down, that I thought . . . this is what it's like to be part of a family, right? Just the four of us, watching it fade away, not even talking. Just being together.'

'Sounds lovely. Would you say that was a favourite memory of yours?'

Alex continued on, but my mind began to wander elsewhere. Five minutes were left of the appointment, and they were starting to drag.

'I think that's why I ended up in law enforcement,' Alex said, as I tuned back into what she was saying. 'Because my dad might not have been there for every moment, but when he was, it made things even better, because it had to matter, right? If you're spending your life making sure everyone else is okay, then when you're back with the ones you love, you make even more of an effort, does that make sense? I just always assumed I'd have a family at this point to make an effort with, that's all.'

'Do you wish you had your own family?'

Even distracted, I sensed the opening. We'd been meeting for a while now and despite the fact that I enjoyed her company, I knew I had to move her towards actual therapy at some point.

Alex sat still, looking back at me, refusing to break eye contact.

'I don't know what you mean . . .'

'You speak so much about how you had such a happy childhood, surrounded by your family. I'm wondering how you feel about the fact that you've never spoken about your current situation.'

Alex opened her mouth to answer, but then closed it. Thought about it. I checked the clock and saw seconds left.

'I . . . I don't know.'

'We've been avoiding the reason you're really here, Alex,' I said, feeling on steadier ground. This is what I wanted to do. I didn't want to think about possibly being uncovered for what I'd done eighteen years ago. I wanted to do *this*. *This* was what I was good at. 'So far, we've talked about your childhood and how happy it was. And the situation from last year that prompted your current predicament – that was in a very quick session that I didn't push because I could see you weren't ready to talk about it. We haven't spoken about what brought you here. Now, I'm happy to listen to as many stories about your childhood as you like, but I also know you're not here because you really want to be. There's something more.'

'I know,' Alex replied, a long exhale. 'I guess, this is easier to talk about.'

'I understand. But if there's something more I can help you with, I want to be able to do that.'

'Right. I just don't know how to start.'

'Why don't we begin with your initial intake form,' I said, sifting through her folder. 'You were having trouble sleeping. Racing thoughts was your main complaint. It was beginning to affect your work. Do you feel that has got better since you started seeing me?'

Alex shook her head. 'Not really.'

'And you know why that is, don't you?'

'Yes, I know,' Alex said, running her hands through her hair. It was cut short, just above the neck line. I could see dark roots coming through the blonde. 'It's just easier this way.'

'I get that, I do. And I know you need to trust me, in order to open up. So, just so you know, I'm not going anywhere. I'm here for you to talk about anything. I won't judge, I won't make you feel bad. I'm here to listen and help you feel better.'

'It's just hard. I don't want to think about what happened.'

'I understand, but at some point we'll have to talk about it. But in your own time.'

A shooting, was all I knew at that point. On the job, I guessed. I didn't know the full details, but I knew that Alex had been on desk duty for a while and wasn't happy about it.

'Until then, when you start to feel anxious, try and close your eyes. Just for a minute. Clear your mind and think of somewhere you feel comfortable.'

'A happy place?'

I smiled. 'If you like.'

'I'm not sure I have one of them.'

'It can be anywhere,' I said, pressing home the thought. 'Listen, mine is an actual place not far from here. Bluff Point. It's nothing special, just a pile of large rocks that jut out to the sea. A beautiful view out to the ocean, but you can get that anywhere on the coast, I guess. But that's where my husband proposed and I just remember it being an amazing moment in my life. I remember looking out and feeling . . . content. Do you think you can come up with something like that?'

'Well, no one has proposed to me recently. I'll try and think of something,' Alex replied, but without much conviction. 'And now our time is up.'

'I want you to come back tomorrow.'

'Really? I'm not due back until Friday . . .'

'I want to strike while the iron's hot.'

'Okay, I can do that.'

'Think about this, Alex,' I said, leaning forwards and giving her a comforting smile. 'We need to find out why you're here and maybe there might be more to discuss then. We can start slowly, don't worry about it. But I know so much about your childhood now, that I want to hear about you as an adult, okay?'

Alex nodded and then got to her feet. 'I will. Think about it, that is.' She moved towards the door, stopped, and turned back to me. 'Thank you. For listening. I know it's your job, but I feel . . . comfortable. Here, I mean.'

'You're welcome,' I said, feeling pleased for a second, before my mind betrayed me and reminded me what had happened in that same room only hours earlier. I cleared my throat. 'It is my job, but that doesn't mean I don't care about the people I see. And, Alex, I care.'

I showed her out and then collapsed into the chair behind my desk. Threw my head in my hands and tried not to scream.

9

Ileft work and was home by four thirty in the afternoon. I had two more clients, both of whom received a shabbier form of therapy than they were probably used to. Not that they would have noticed. Most of the time, people just want to be heard. Want to be listened to. And that's where I came in. There to lend a supportive ear and sometimes, gently, carefully, suggest things that might make them feel better.

Things they could then ignore later on.

The latest was a 'worry diary'. I used this for my patients with high anxiety, which could probably have included most of the population at that point. The previous few years hadn't exactly been what anyone sane would call 'normal'. Instead of them piling worries onto each other, until they're spiralling out of control, I would tell them to write down a new worry into a notebook and then put it to one side, not to be looked at or considered once it was done. Another was 'worry time', where they were only allowed to worry about things in a certain space of time, say one hour per day, dedicated to simply worrying about all those things that they couldn't control.

Most of the time, these acts alone didn't work. You can't control your mind just like that. Repetition helped, of course, but I wished I had a better way of helping those people who came into my office at the end of their tether. Unable to sleep, unable to function. Desperate for an answer that I couldn't give them.

It was impossible, of course, to help everyone, I knew that.

That day – apart from Alex, maybe – I'd helped no one in any practical sense. Every time I'd looked at that sofa, I'd seen Ella sitting there again, telling me my story.

I had spent the day trying to work out how I would find her.

Yet the moment I walked into my home, and saw my children, the stress and worry began to dissipate. I was safe there, with the solidity of normality.

I imagined their faces if they knew the truth, and tried to shake it from my mind.

'Can we have pizza for dinner, Mom?' Olivia asked, in her sing-song voice she stored for special requests. It was impossible to say no, her eyes wide and pleading. 'Please, Mom, we haven't had it for ages.'

She stretched the last word out and brought her hands up in a prayer motion. I brought her to me and she snuggled into my chest. 'We'll see, darling, I'm not sure what we're doing yet. I'll have to talk to Daddy.'

JJ had already run up the stairs and into his room. I wouldn't be getting a cuddle from him any time soon. He was approaching that age I had been warned about – when he would move away from his parents and become a sullen teenager. It was still a couple of years away, but it felt closer than ever.

Olivia was still not in double digits. Nine years old, going on fifty is what most people said. So precocious, so intelligent.

She was still scared of the dark, though, so still my little girl.

'Homework?'

Olivia pulled away from me and thought for a moment, as if trying to work out a lie. She either decided against it, or couldn't think of one. 'Can I watch some YouTube first?'

I shook my head. 'Do it before dinner, or you'll never do it. Go on, you can use the office.'

Olivia's shoulders slumped down, her dark hair swishing around her face. I'd tied it up that morning, but just like every day, by the time she got home it was loose and flowing all around her.

'Okay, Mom,' Olivia said, slinking away to the back of the house. I followed behind her, but went left as she went right, and into the kitchen.

'JJ was unusually quiet on the way home.'

I glanced at Stephanie, Jack's sister, who wasn't looking at me. She was standing with her back to the room, inspecting the contents of the refrigerator. There must not have been anything to catch her fancy, as she closed the door and slowly moved away. She looked me up and down quickly, then grabbed her keys from the counter.

She was almost as tall as Jack. With a body that could only be achieved through endless exercise and no spare time. I'd always felt like she looked down upon me, but after yet another of her recent relationships failed, I stopped feeling offended and instead was sorry for her. She came round to watch the kids for an hour between them getting home from school and me returning from work. It made little difference to her day and Jack thought it best that family look after the kids rather than a stranger. She was almost forty, but we hadn't seen much of each other for the first decade or so of our relationship. At the start of 2020, she had come back to the state, back home, and now ran a restaurant in a town close by.

Mummy and Daddy's money helping her, of course.

She still had other businesses elsewhere in the country. A couple of restaurants and a few coffee shops. They had barely survived the past few years, and she now wore an air of desperation that she failed to keep under wraps at all times.

We didn't always agree on things.

'Hey, Stephanie,' I said, stopping in my tracks. She paused with her keys in her hand as I blocked her exit, unintentionally. 'How's the restaurant?'

She rolled her eyes. 'Don't get me started on that subject. Anyway, about JJ . . .'

'I'm surprised you've only just noticed,' I said, dropping my bag and keys on the table. 'He barely says a word to us these days.'

'That's boys for you. I remember Jack at that age.'

'I can't imagine him being a sullen pre-teen,' I said, leaning against the counter, wanting so badly to shake off my shoes and let my feet breathe, as my grandma back in England used to say. 'I always think of him as being thirty when he was born.'

Stephanie chuckled softly. 'Oh, I could tell you stories about your husband. If he hadn't told me the moment you met that I wasn't allowed to.'

'That was over fifteen years ago,' I said, wishing I'd had more chance to speak to Stephanie over the years, one on one. Maybe it wouldn't be so difficult now, if I had.

'Still,' Stephanie replied, holding up her hands. 'He'd kill me if I started telling tales of young Jack.'

'Maybe some other time.'

She hummed a response. Perhaps a brick in the wall that had been formed between us fell to the ground. I couldn't be sure.

It wouldn't take long for it to be replaced if she knew what I'd done before meeting her precious brother. And that was nothing compared to what their parents would say. Would think.

'Anyway, I'll talk to JJ,' I said, giving Stephanie a warm smile that was almost entirely real. 'See if everything is okay. I know he's had a few problems with some of the boys in class.'

'I'm sure you know what to do,' Stephanie said, in a tone that seemed to say the exact opposite. She stared at me. 'You look tired.'

'Thanks,' I replied, ready for her to go now. Every time it felt like we were getting somewhere, Stephanie had a way of pushing my buttons. 'That's always good to hear.'

'Sorry, don't mean to cause offence,' Stephanie said, passing by me and pausing at the door that led out into the hallway. 'I know Jack is working so hard that it probably leaves you picking up the slack, but you know . . . a bit more effort might make him less likely to stay in the office that extra hour.'

I bit my lip, knowing an argument wouldn't help matters. Stephanie was one of those people who mistake honesty for cruelty sometimes. I gave her a pass. 'I'll think about that,' I said finally, hoping she could hear the bitterness in my tone. 'I think we're at the restaurant tonight? Jack was telling me that he wanted to stop by.'

Stephanie rolled her eyes theatrically. 'That place. Honestly, I don't know why I try sometimes. The chefs are fantastic, but a nightmare to deal with. The wait staff aren't much better. Everyone seems much younger than they should. I'm almost forty and sometimes I think there was ten-year gap at some point, where no one aged. Physically or emotionally.'

'I know exactly what you mean,' I said, shaking my head. 'The joys of getting older. Previous generations said the same about us, I bet.'

'You're not wrong. Although, we don't have to act our age all the time.'

And with that, she was gone, leaving me alone in the kitchen, staring at the various implements I could have used on her for that last comment. Just because I looked all of my forty-two years, and she seemed to wear hers more easily.

I thought about how quickly I could have removed her body afterwards. How I could swear that she left the house totally alive and well.

That feeling of hating my own thoughts came back to me again. Only this time, it was easier to ignore.

10

Jack managed to call by five thirty, which was earlier than I'd been expecting.

'Hey, sorry I'm late . . .'

'It's okay,' I cut in, before he could give me more platitudinal apologies that I'd have to accept and he didn't want to really give. 'Are you not going to make it?'

'Yeah, I'm just running late is all. I'll meet you there.'

'That's fine,' I said, meaning it. I already had my car keys in hand. I even had JJ and Olivia on standby ready to leave. 'What time are you going to get there?'

'An hour at most,' Jack replied, sounding sincere as he under-estimated. 'I promise.'

'We'll see you there.'

I knew it would be close to seven by the time he arrived, but that didn't mean I'd wait around. I knew the kids would be getting hungrier by the second. I loaded them up and made the short drive to Stephanie's restaurant.

The clink of silverware against plates and the murmur of con-versation assailed us as we pushed our way inside. In the past year, Stephanie had transformed the look of the old place, but it didn't seem to be helping much. There were only a few tables filled and the speed at which one of the servers approached us made me realise how few customers Stephanie must be getting.

The waitress didn't recognise us until I told her our name. Another fresh face. Every time we visited, there seemed to be someone new in the place. It didn't take long until we were seated near the window at the front, a booth that seemed to cut us off from the rest of the restaurant.

'Can I get you drinks while you wait?'

I shook my head. 'I'm going to order for the kids now, if that's okay. I don't know when he'll be getting here.'

She shrugged and took our order. JJ and Olivia got their pizzas, as requested. My stomach churned at the thought of eating. My thoughts turning to what had happened that morning, as I sat watching my children eat and waited for Jack to arrive.

The more time that passed, the more I could almost pretend that nothing had really happened. That Ella didn't really exist. That my secret was safe.

It would be so much easier to embrace delusion.

Only that wasn't the case. No. Ella had been real.

She had told me an incredibly familiar story, but perhaps I had heard some facts wrong. Maybe I hadn't been listening properly.

The mind is a strange beast. This was the first time a young woman had been in my care with a story that felt so similar to my own. And given how I'd never really let those terrible events far from my memory, was it any wonder if I had somehow had a little mental breakdown and filled in some gaps with my own experiences.

I tried not to think about it too much as I watched JJ and Olivia eat like they'd been told there was a time limit. I couldn't help but smile, thinking of myself at the same age.

'You'll give yourself tummy ache,' I said, knowing it wouldn't make a lick of difference. 'Slow down, you pair.'

JJ didn't even look up. Olivia at least made an attempt to pause between mouthfuls, even as she talked. I thought about telling her, once again, not to speak with her mouth full, but I didn't have the energy.

JJ hadn't said a word the entire journey. Even now, as his sister detailed her day in great detail, he still refused to speak. Didn't tell her not to talk so much, didn't roll his eyes and sigh loudly.

It wasn't normal behaviour.

And as much as I wanted to find out what might be the problem, I couldn't in all good conscience do it at that moment. I wouldn't be able to focus on what he said, help him in any way. I was thinking about myself too much to be a good parent.

That realisation hurt me.

Stephanie appeared from the back, seeing us at the front of the restaurant and catching my eye in an instant. She gave me a frown and then made her way over.

'Where's Jack?'

'He'll be here soon,' I said, making a show of checking my watch and seeing he was probably still at least a half-hour from arriving. 'He got stuck in work.'

'The pizza good, kids?' Stephanie said, seeming to ignore my explanation. 'I told them to make it extra special for my two favourite people.'

JJ shrugged, but Olivia made a big show. 'It's delicious, Aunt Stephanie. Best pizza ever. Way better than Outpost.'

'I'm glad to hear it,' Stephanie said, a smile on her face that for once didn't look forced. She turned back to me. 'Are you going to wait for Jack?'

I nodded. 'He'll be here any minute,' I said, hoping repetition would make it more likely.

Stephanie came closer. I could smell her perfume, liberally applied, but not overwhelming. Her skin was somehow even more perfect up close. I could feel the envy burning inside me. Not for the first time, I wondered how it was that she hadn't been married, or even in a long-term relationship. Independent, wealthy, beautiful . . . it was hard to imagine she was short of offers.

'I was thinking,' Stephanie said, leaning next to me, trying to keep out of earshot of JJ and Olivia and probably failing miserably. 'About what we talked about earlier. About Jack.'

'Yes,' I replied, when she didn't continue. 'What about it?'

'Do you think he might be . . . I don't know. He just doesn't seem his usual self these days.'

I couldn't disagree, but I knew why. 'He's working on something. I don't know what it is, but I think it must be big. He's just tired from working long hours, that's all.'

'Yeah, I guess that must be it,' Stephanie said, but didn't sound convinced. I could hear under the surface of her words – she thought it was something to do with me. That it had to be my fault why her brother wasn't his usual jolly self.

Well, it wasn't. Not yet.

She shaped to say something more, but was interrupted by the door opening and Jack appearing in the entrance. He looked across and spotted us. He smiled and I almost forgot completely about what had happened that morning.

I was safe now.

He came over, embracing Stephanie quickly, before slipping into the booth next to me. He pulled a face at JJ and Olivia, earning a laugh from only one of them. JJ was too busy concentrating on his food.

He planted a kiss on my cheek as he reached for the menu.

'You didn't need to wait,' Jack said, scanning the menu in front of him. 'You could have grabbed something with the kids.'

Stephanie had disappeared without me noticing. I looked towards the back of the restaurant and thought I saw someone I recognised. I was still looking as Jack cleared his throat. I turned back to him slowly.

'It's fine, I was okay waiting.'

'I got caught up, I'm sorry,' Jack said, not looking up from the familiar words in front of him. I knew he'd go through every item and then order the same thing he always did. My eyes left his and went back towards where Stephanie had disappeared. Tried to find the face of someone I had only just glimpsed, but came up short.

'Order me the usual,' I said, standing up and sliding past Jack. 'Just going to the bathroom.'

Jack gave me a grunt of acknowledgement, as I walked away towards the back of the restaurant. Passing a few tables, but not checking out our fellow diners – the people who were just about keeping Stephanie's business afloat. I was looking towards where the door that led through to the kitchen and the back offices had just closed shut.

I paused at the bathroom door, then took a step to my left and pushed my way through a door that was supposed to be off-limits. The noise level increased a few feet in, as I heard the raised voices from the kitchen area, orders being shouted, the hiss and squeal of frying and food prep.

At the end of the corridor, Stephanie's office door was closed. I thought about going directly there, but I could hear her voice coming from the kitchen. I couldn't hear the words, but I could sense that she was arguing with someone. I made my way down towards her office, the back door that led outside opposite.

It was just closing.

I quickened my step, thinking about the flash of blonde hair I'd seen at the back of the restaurant. The pale skin. The sleek shoulders.

I pushed my way through the exit and a blast of cold wind swept towards me. I kept one hand on the door, as I looked outside.

I saw a figure in the distance, just rounding the corner. 'Hey,' I cried out, surprising myself a little. Only a little. Because I knew who I thought it was.

Her.

'Sara?'

I turned quickly, my heart skipping a beat or two. 'Sorry, I was just looking . . .'

'Is everything okay?' Stephanie said, coming towards me quickly. 'What are you doing back here?'

'Yeah, it's fine,' I replied, trying to think of a reason for being back there. 'I thought I recognised someone, but I was probably mistaken.'

Stephanie cocked her head at me, a furrowed brow giving away how odd she found me in that instant.

'One of the servers?' Stephanie said, not enjoying the words that came out. The question. It didn't make sense to her. Not sounding convinced. 'Yeah, you probably did.'

'No, it was . . . it was nothing, sorry,' I said, wishing to be anywhere else in that moment. 'It's been a long day, I guess. I was acting on autopilot.'

'Right, okay,' Stephanie replied, sounding like it was anything but that.

I shook my head, finding my feet finally. 'Sorry, I'll get out of the way. I don't know what I was thinking.'

Only I did know. As I slipped past a still-frowning Stephanie, I knew exactly who I thought I'd seen.

Ella.

11

I was standing in the kitchen, braced against the counter and looking out to the back yard. The pool was covered up, but I began thinking about the months to come, when we'd have parties again. When friends would come over and Jack would stand at the barbecue and make jokes. When the kids would jump in and out of the pool and laugh and play.

I would drink a glass of wine and feel light-headed. Share gossip. Then, late into the night, sit on the deck with Jack after everyone had left and talk about old times. About where we might be in ten years. Twenty. When we were too old to even imagine.

It felt further away than usual.

'Where's Dad?' JJ said, his voice quiet behind me.

I turned slowly and smiled at him, pleased to finally hear his voice. 'He's just catching up on a bit of work in the office. You can go see him, if you want? I'm sure he'd be happy to talk with you.'

He shrugged back at me and made to leave. I reached out and touched his shoulder. He moved away quickly and murmured something about going back to his room. Olivia was in the living room, quietly staring at the TV as some Disney show played last I'd checked.

I turned back to the yard outside, thinking of all the things I wanted to say but couldn't.

Jack, this morning someone came into my office and confessed to a murder that she couldn't have done, because it was me.

So, take that and party.

All the things we'd love to say to our loved ones, but never do. Left unspoken. Instead, I cleaned up and tried to make the place tidy at least. My bones were aching, my muscles feeling tight. I'd shower once the kids were in bed.

I pulled out my cell phone and brought up the email Gina had sent me earlier that day. I had saved it until I was alone, able to absorb it as much as possible and work out a plan.

> *Sara,*
>
> *Not much I'm afraid. She paid cash, as I said, so we don't even have a card on file. She told me she was waiting for a new one in the mail. I took the usual information down. I've written it below. She did request you personally, after going on the website, which isn't unusual. Putting all our pictures on the website tends to do that. I didn't think it would be a problem, as it wasn't some guy with a thing for one of you. I thought because she was a woman it would be okay. When I called her after she filled out the form online, it took a few times to organise an appointment. It was only confirmed late yesterday afternoon, after you had a cancellation after leaving for the day.*
>
> *One more thing . . . when I finally got her on the phone, it sounded like she was working. I could barely hear, because she was talking so quietly. Sometimes, they want to talk about their problems on the call to me, but she was trying to get me off the phone. I heard voices in the background, so I guess she was at work or with family. I'm not sure.*
>
> *Anyway, hope this helps a little. Sorry I can't be more help. I'll try calling her again before leaving.*
>
> *G*
>
> *Ella Morley*
> *25 Maple Dr – Apt 8*

Norwalk
CT
06850

There was a phone number listed below Ella's address and I copied it down. I began typing it into my cell phone, but then stopped before getting to the final digit. I wasn't sure what I would say to her. If I was right, then she had a lot to answer for, I guessed, but if I wasn't . . . then I was calling a client with significant issues at home to ask them what? Why had they confessed to a murder and then run out my office? Had they somehow heard about the death of someone over four thousand miles away and known I was there?

I could have just asked her to come back in. Tried speaking to her again to confirm whether she was telling the truth or not. It would still have been more than a little strange.

I tried to think about how I would approach things if this was a normal client. My brain wouldn't let me.

I had an address, so I typed it into Google on my phone and checked it out. It looked like a nice place from the street – tree-lined and clean. Just across from the hospital in Norwalk.

There wasn't anything to suggest that it was a bad place to live. The opposite in fact. I shut down Google Maps and pulled up Facebook. Typed her name into the search bar and then started scrolling.

Hundreds of results. Thousands, I guessed. I tried to narrow the search by placing Norwalk with her name, but that didn't help. I scanned each profile picture to find her face, but no luck. So many were using some generic picture, meaning I had to click into each profile, which made me realise how much better people had become about privacy settings.

I went back to Google and placed her name and town in the search. I got much the same result. Nothing that gave me any information. I wasn't sure what I was hoping to find anyway – it wasn't like I was going to get any answers this way.

I needed to speak to her again.

I turned my phone off and placed it back in my bag. Stood up and turned on the overhead light. Blinked at the brightness and tried to rub some life into my eyes. It didn't help much.

'JJ, Olivia, shower,' I called through the house, hearing the break in my voice. The call of normality sounding more foreign than it ever had before. 'I'm coming up now.'

Every part of me ached with tension. But I forced my tired, guilt-ridden body through the evening routine.

At least I wasn't alone.

At least I had my family.

I just had to make sure I kept them.

Jack had looked tired after dinner. Still, he had dragged himself through the house and towards the office, promising he wouldn't be too long.

I knew he was working hard for a reason, but right then it felt as if he was close to burnout. Right at a time when I could have done with his full attention.

I wanted to tell him what had happened.

Wanted him to bring me close to him, tell me everything was going to be okay. That he had a thousand solutions, ready to go.

Only I couldn't. Not then. I couldn't add to his stress.

Instead, I went upstairs and put the kids to bed, with few complaints thankfully. I showered myself, feeling refreshed afterwards, for a few minutes at least. I had washed away a fine coating of the day, but it managed to crawl over me as I sat on the edge of the bed, a towel wrapped tightly around me. I began to feel cold as the water dried on my skin. I thought about Jack.

Back when he was first promoted, I would pop my head into the office and see how he was getting on. Whether he needed anything, as he continued to work late into the evening. He had always turned slowly in his chair and greeted me with a warm smile. Sometimes, he would arch an eyebrow and pat his thigh for me to sit on his lap. I would pad across the office and fall onto him. Place my hands on his face and feel that rough, days-old stubble on his cheeks and nestle my face into his neck. Be assailed by the scent of him. The warmth of him.

I couldn't remember the last time I'd done that. Months, possibly years earlier. Not since he'd stopped greeting me with a smile but instead with a sigh and a pointed finger in the air telling me to wait.

I'd stopped going in to check on him after the fourth or fifth time of seeing that finger in the air between us.

There was nothing I could do about the situation. He worked long hours to provide everything we had. Not that I didn't bring home my fair share – we would never have been able to afford to buy the house on his income alone. Yet his was the more important job in the marriage, I felt.

I just wasn't sure if sometimes he didn't think it was more important than the marriage itself.

I shook the thought away as I dried my hair, rubbing a towel through it quickly and then brushing it out. I sat at my dressing table and thought about Ella.

I thought about Dan.

It had been so long that it was difficult to remember everything about him. Faces go first, I'd found. I could remember certain things from our short time together – the feeling of his hand in mine, the way he made me laugh. I remembered jumping in his car – a blue-green Ford Focus with an added spoiler on the back that didn't look right – and driving for miles and miles.

I tried to recall the way he looked, but it became more blurred the longer I concentrated. I could remember his voice better than anything.

The man he killed . . . I remembered his face. Only, I knew on some level my mind was adding detail that didn't really exist. It had been dark, the incident in the pub before it had happened so quickly that it would have been impossible for me to describe him in any great detail.

But I had held his head in my hands as he breathed his last. Maybe that had helped lodge his face in my memory.

That wasn't the face I imagined, though. The one that came to mind easily was from the multiple news reports and social media pages, which all contained the same photograph, over and over. From when he would have been around fifteen, I'd always guessed. Looking much younger than he would have that night.

There wasn't any more I could do. This was simply something I had to live with and had been for a long time. I had grown used to those fleeting moments when his face came back to me. When I thought of the past, no matter how hard I tried not to.

Now, this Ella had sat in my office and brought it out into the open.

Well, I wasn't going to let it hurt me. Not let it beat me.

I wasn't fully at fault for what happened. And what was done was done. I had a family now. I helped people every day, more than most did in a lifetime. I actively made people's lives better.

I had paid for what I'd done, maybe not in prison time, but morally. I gave back.

I felt emboldened. My family would come first. Not this stranger. Not her story. Not her plan to make me feel whatever it was she wanted to make me feel.

I finished getting dry, put my PJs on, and made a decision.

My bare feet were silent on the carpet outside my bedroom, down the stairs, before slapping against the wooden floors of the hallway and along the corridor. As I got closer to the office, my heartbeat began to quicken a little and doubt began to creep in.

What if he rejected me again? What if he gave me that look that said he was tired of my presence? What if he ignored me entirely?

All questions that I feared facing every day – what if his job was more important than anything else?

I paused outside the office and listened. Heard the shuffling of paper. Then, I could swear I heard a whispered voice. I frowned for a moment, before knocking on the door softly, entering before he had a chance to say anything.

Jack was sitting behind the desk, only the top of his head visible. He was leaning towards the computer screen and whispering softly to himself – work-related things I would never understand, I guessed.

I stood in the doorway, waiting, knowing he was already aware I was standing there, but unwilling to look up just yet. Not until he was ready. I was getting cold, unable to work out what to do with my hands. I didn't want to place them on my hips, as that wasn't the look I was going for. I could put one up, I thought, as that was slightly more appealing. The other one held onto the door.

I waited.

This time, he didn't even hold up a finger to tell me to wait.

A minute passed by. My legs began to ache, as I stood, tense and ready. My bare feet on the wooden floor would be numb in not too much time at all.

Finally, he looked up. Didn't say a word, just looked at me, waiting. I smiled, but it felt strange. Like I wasn't doing it right. His facial expression didn't change, but I heard an exhale of breath.

'Everything okay?' I said, trying to sound light, inviting. 'Are you still working?'

He stared at me for a second or two and then nodded. 'Sorry, I've just really got to get these final reports done before morning. Probably best you go to bed without me.'

'I was thinking that maybe you could stop for a while . . .'

He was already looking away, but I couldn't stop myself. I needed to be close to him, to feel safe again. I moved away from the door and closed it behind me. The key was in the lock and I turned it.

'Sara . . .'

'Shush,' I said, moving across the office and pausing at the edge of his desk. 'Let's not talk any more.'

I walked around the desk and then behind his chair. Placed my hands on his shoulders and thought I felt him flinch a little at my touch. I couldn't be sure. I began massaging his muscles and heard him sigh. I smiled a little and felt a little less nervous.

Then, I reached down and stroked his chest with both hands. Moved my head towards his and found his lips. He responded, his hands moving away from the desk and around my body.

I closed my eyes, as we kissed and our bodies touched. I began to move my hands further down, but he pulled away.

'Let me just finish this and I'll be upstairs,' he said, placing a hand on my face. 'I won't be long.'

'Why not just do it here?' I replied, trying to push closer to him again, but he pulled away. 'What is it? It wouldn't be the first time . . .'

'Sara, I'm really sorry, I want to do this, but I just wouldn't be able to concentrate. Honestly, give me half an hour and I'll be upstairs. Okay?'

I tensed, standing up and walking back to the door. I unlocked it and tried to hide my face from him. I didn't want him to see my expression, because I knew what it would look like. Hurt, sad.

Angry.

'Okay,' I said, surprised by the light tone of voice coming from me. I felt anything but that. 'Don't take too long though. I'll be waiting for you.'

'I won't,' Jack replied, but as I stole a glance towards the desk, I could see he was already looking at the computer screen.

I backed up out of the room and closed the door behind me. Paused for a moment in the corridor outside and exhaled. There was a moment when I wanted to cry out in frustration.

Only, I knew that would make things worse.

There was no chance Jack would be up any time soon. As I moved back through the house, upstairs and into my bedroom, I felt myself slowly slipping away.

It didn't stop me going to the bedroom window. Looking out onto the street. I could almost feel eyes on me out there. Watching me as I stared into the darkness.

A feeling inside me that I couldn't ignore. That I was being monitored. Somehow, I knew, that woman was out there. Knew where I lived, knew who was in the house.

I closed the drapes and got into bed, where I lay staring at the ceiling.

I was still awake when Jack finally came up two hours later.

I pretended to be asleep. I could feel him standing over the bed, looking down at me. Then, he swore softly under his breath, called himself something he shouldn't have, and then went into the bathroom. Crept under the covers a few minutes later and was asleep in no time at all.

I wanted to turn over, feel his arms around me. Feel his warmth, his love.

Instead, I lay there for hours, hoping against hope that I wouldn't think about what the next day would bring. And the day after that.

Life, going on, waiting for the inevitable to happen. I could never be happy. That wouldn't be right.

I had been lying to myself for years that it would be possible.

12

Jack told me he loved me as he was leaving. He paused in the bedroom doorway and looked back at me. Opened his mouth to say something else, then decided against it.

An apology, I guessed. A *mea culpa* that last night he hadn't come upstairs in half an hour like he'd promised. That he hadn't taken me in his arms and made me feel less lonely.

But I could see the strain in his face. The dark rings under his eyes. The guilt weighing heavy on his shoulders.

He was working too hard and I didn't – *couldn't* – add to that pressure. He did so much for us all, I knew that.

I couldn't tell him what I'd been going through since the day before. It would break him.

I saw JJ and Olivia off to the school bus and then made my way to work. Only that morning, I stopped at the Lakeside diner. Took a seat in a booth near the window and looked out to the busy road outside.

'The usual?'

I looked up and smiled at Mary, the waitress who always served me. It wasn't busy that morning – any morning, really, post nine a.m. – but it wouldn't have mattered. Mary would still have been there, with a pot of coffee and a two-word greeting.

'Thanks,' I said, adding milk to the black coffee she poured. I knew what was coming next.

'You Brits . . . never take it black.'

'You Yanks . . . never miss an opportunity to point out a difference in people.'

Mary rolled her eyes at me and then moved to another table further down from mine. I could hear the muted conversation coming from there and wished I wasn't sitting alone. Wished there was someone sitting across from me, ready to listen to my troubles.

I couldn't speak to anyone about them.

I stared out the window, thinking about what to do next. Finding Ella Morley wasn't going to be easy, but that didn't mean I wasn't going to try. I had a few tricks up my sleeve still.

My thoughts turned to Dan.

There were many times over the years I'd thought about him. What he'd be doing now, how he was. After that night, we hadn't so much drifted apart, as spun out of control. He was petrified about what might happen to him if anyone found out, while I was determined that no one ever would.

There was no love there any more, of course. No lust or desire. That had ended that night.

I'd been disgusted by what had happened. Couldn't bear to be in his presence, never mind console and comfort him.

It had been all his fault.

I became aware of someone standing close by and slowly turned. Blinked a few times, as I tried to make sense of the person standing a foot or so away.

'Hey, sorry,' Alex said, almost statuelike as she tried to decide what to do next. 'I was just getting coffee and wasn't sure . . .'

I should have sent her on her way. She was a client. She was troubled enough. She was law enforcement of some sort. And I was thinking about my ex-boyfriend with whom I had killed a man.

Instead, I smiled thinly and gestured to the opposite side of the booth. 'Please, take a seat, it's okay.'

Alex still didn't move for a few seconds. I thought she might walk away and wasn't sure if I would feel relief at that or not. I wasn't sure why I'd even offered a seat in the first place.

It wasn't exactly a smart move.

Alex finally moved into the seat opposite, before signalling to the waitress. 'I wasn't sure if we should speak outside of the office.'

'Well, I'm not going to start counselling you here,' I said, placing a hand around my coffee cup. 'That would be inappropriate. But there's nothing to say that we can't just run into each other in the outside world and have a conversation.'

'I guess not,' Alex replied, but she didn't sound too sure of that. Neither was I.

I tried to think if I would have done this before yesterday. The answer was pretty obvious – no, I wouldn't have. I would have made an excuse and got out of there. Tried not to be rude about it, but I didn't want to see clients in the real world, while they were still going through sessions with me. It wouldn't have worked. Yet there I was, leaning back as Mary returned with a coffee for Alex.

The answer as to why I was sitting there, I was struggling to work out.

'I've not seen you in here before,' Alex said, checking over her shoulder, before she added some sugar to her coffee. 'I come here most mornings.'

'I stop by occasionally,' I replied, wondering if two or three times a week counted as 'occasionally'. 'Usually when I need a sugar fix.'

My plate of pancakes arrived. I doused them in syrup and tried a mouthful. My stomach welcomed the food finally coming in at first, before my appetite began to slowly disappear again.

'The food is good here,' Alex said, watching as I cut up more pancake and placed it carefully in my mouth. 'I wouldn't be able to stay in shape if I ate here like I wanted to though. What's your secret?'

I shook my head, placing down my knife and fork, and wiping at my mouth with a napkin. 'I'll be on the treadmill at home later, paying for this, believe me.'

'I hear you.'

'So, you live near here?'

Alex took a sip of coffee before answering. 'Close. Kind of half-way between work and home.'

'Same here,' I said, grasping hold of the first similarity between us. 'A nice pitstop, if you like.'

'I'm on day shift, but not for another half hour or so. I was awake early, so went for a run. Still had some time to kill and came here.'

I could sense my pancakes cooling, but I wasn't sure I could eat any more in front of Alex. She couldn't see the churning in my stomach, but I could definitely feel it. There was part of me that wanted to ask her advice. To ask what I should do about Ella. If anyone was going to know, I had a feeling it might have been her. Only I knew that would be a mistake.

'I've wanted to ask something,' Alex said, trying and failing to maintain eye contact across the table. 'I didn't think it was appropriate in our . . . meetings. Would you mind?'

I wasn't sure I was breathing. Maybe she knew about Ella already. About Dan. About Adam. I tried to stay calm, but inside me, my heart began beating hard. 'Of course, go ahead.'

'I know you're not from here originally, right?'

'No.'

'English, right?'

'That's right,' I replied, wondering where she was going with this. 'I moved over here about fifteen years ago. Still haven't managed to lose the accent totally.'

'Yeah, I noticed,' Alex said, a chuckle escaping her lips. 'And sometimes you slip and use the wrong words or pronounce things different.'

'You say the wrong words,' I said, 'we had the language first.'

The chuckle became a laugh. It was a sweet sound from her. One I hadn't experienced in conversations with her before. 'I guess that's right. Technically. My first language is Spanish. I don't know why I care enough to notice.'

The coffee went down quickly for both of us, as we continued to talk, and Mary seemed to appear from nowhere to refill it.

I realised how long it had been since I'd sat somewhere with someone I wasn't related to. A friend, despite Alex being anything but that. Sure, we socialised within the neighbourhood – barbecues, parties, whatever. But I wouldn't have called them friends. Jack had friends, but their wives weren't calling me or keeping in touch. And I wasn't exactly making the effort either.

I hadn't been aware of just how little interaction I had with the outside world. But, of course, I knew the reason for it.

Alex was talking about something she'd seen on the news, keeping her voice low as she shared her own opinion. I listened, but wasn't about to share the fact I had no idea what she was talking about.

'I guess they do things differently down in Florida,' Alex finished, checking her wrist and shaking her head when she saw the time. 'Damn, I'm gonna be late now.'

'Just blame me,' I said, almost standing up with her as she got to her feet. 'I'll write a note if you like?'

I said it with a smile, but wasn't sure if Alex got the joke.

'That's okay,' Alex said, pulling out a couple of bills to pay for her coffee. 'I'm just glad of the company.'

'Same here,' I replied, meaning it more than I realised. 'Listen, this doesn't affect our work, okay? I can separate the social from the private, I promise you that.'

Alex hesitated, then nodded. 'I know.'

Then, she was gone. I sat back in the booth, wondering if it had been a mistake to invite her to sit with me. Whether I'd crossed a line and affected Alex's therapy moving forward, just as we were perhaps about to make some kind of breakthrough.

I had needed it though. Some semblance of normality for just a few minutes at least.

It didn't matter that Alex worked in law enforcement. I knew what I was doing.

I put down my cup of coffee with a shaking hand. Looked up as the door opened and a couple walked in. For a moment, I thought they looked directly at me, but they approached the counter and sat down. Talking and laughing with each other. Suddenly, I felt exposed. As if everyone could hear my thoughts, see me for what I was.

Everything I had built over the years was on sand. I was sinking.

I pushed the plate in front of me aside and opened my purse. Threw a few bills on the table and got up. Nodded towards Mary as I was leaving, grabbed the door and got outside, breathing in the fresh air that hit me.

I hurried across the parking lot to my car and glanced back at the diner. I couldn't see through the glass, but I thought everyone in there was looking at me as I left.

There was something in my mind – a calming voice, which was struggling to be heard – that told me I was being paranoid. That I needed to stay relaxed and in control.

That there was nothing to worry about. All I had to do was find Ella and make sure she wasn't going to tell anyone what she'd told me.

Only, I knew it wouldn't be as easy as that.

Someone else knew what I'd done. And I didn't know what they were going to do with that information.

I got in my car and started it up. Laid my hands on the wheel and closed my eyes. Rested my forehead against the steering wheel and tried to control my breathing.

Tried to control my thoughts.

Tried to control my anger.

*

'That was her?'

Colby gave a nod. Some sort of noise that came from the back of his throat. An 'uh-huh'.

Penny turned around on her stool and watched as Sara hurried across the lot and into her car. 'I was expecting something else. She looks . . . professional.'

'Doesn't really matter,' Colby said, still facing the other way. His hand curled around his coffee. 'We know what we have to do. Should be an easy job.'

'I guess,' Penny replied, but didn't really believe that. They never were. It seemed like every time they were told something was going to be easy, it took months to get paid off. This didn't strike her as anything different. 'What's the plan then?'

'Follow her back to her office. And wait.'

'Do we have time to eat?'

'Always.'

Penny stared out the window and watched as Sara Edwards pulled out and drove away. Made sure she turned right and in the direction of where she worked.

'I never like these jobs,' she said quietly. Colby wasn't listening, staring at the TV above the counter, as images of war flashed across the screen. 'They always turn out bad for us. Waiting forever to be paid. If we ever are.'

'Don't worry about that,' Colby replied, dismissing her with a wave of his hand. 'The money's good and we're not exactly in a position to argue. We're settling a favour, at the end of the day. We just do exactly as we're told and everything will be fine.'

Penny had heard that before. *Everything will be fine.* Yeah, as long as you were able to ignore the nightmares. The screaming in the dead of night, from long-gone victims. Because that's what they were, right? Victims.

Their victims.

She guessed there was nothing else she could do. She had dropped out of high school early. Fell in love even earlier. They had tried to work legit, but nothing ever seemed to work out. Now, they were stuck in this type of place. With this type of job.

They were paid for what they did and moved on. Half upfront, of course. Half on completion.

'We've seen a lot of the country, at least,' Penny said, voicing her last thought. Colby looked towards her with a frown, but it didn't last long.

'You're doing it again.'

'What?'

'That thing, where you start in the middle of a conversation, expecting me to know what was running through your head beforehand.'

'It's been twenty years,' Penny said, a smirk on her face. 'You're not used to it by now, you never will be.'

'I guess not.'

'I'm just saying,' Penny continued, not filling in the blanks for Colby's benefit. 'There are upsides to what we do.'

'Like not having to worry about how we're going to feed ourselves? Keep a roof over our heads?'

'Well, that too.'

Maybe, she sometimes thought – late at night lying in a motelroom bed, in some random town, in some random city, in some random state – if they had both just tried a little harder, life would have been different. But it didn't matter now. They'd made their choices and this is where it had landed them.

In an admittedly nice diner, watching a woman who was wearing an outfit that probably cost more than they'd been paid so far.

'Anyway, as I was saying, there's no more pointless animal than a wasp.'

'They must do something,' Penny said, still looking out of the window. 'Every animal has a purpose.'

'No, I'm telling you, wasps are pointless. They do nothing. Add nothing. If they disappeared tomorrow, no one would notice.'

'I think some people would . . .'

'I mean, the food chain wouldn't notice. It would just carry on as normal.'

'You know there's a more pointless animal, right?'

Colby tilted his head, trying to think of one. Failing.

'Us,' Penny said, shaking her head. 'Humans.'

'We'll eat and then follow her,' Colby said, as Penny slowly turned round back to the counter. Colby beckoned the waitress over and gave her his trademark smile. Penny knew what that smile could do to people. What it could do to her.

'What's good, honey?'

Penny didn't want to be anywhere else. This is what she was good at. This is what *they* were good at.

13

Gina was sitting at reception when I entered the building and made my way up, ready with a warm smile and a pile of paperwork.

'Sorry, we've been asked to update some records,' Gina said, as I reached across and took the files from her. 'Mostly clients who only did one or two appointments. He-who-must-not-be-named wants to know why we couldn't keep them on the books.'

'I'll get to it later,' I replied, hooking them under my arm. 'Any calls come in?'

Gina frowned at me, as I tried to remain calm. If she thought a little about it, she would know what I was really asking. I didn't want to come right out and say it though. I didn't want to bring any more attention to it than necessary.

'Nothing important,' Gina said finally. 'One reschedule, one extra appointment. Ethan Jackson. That's not until Thursday though. He sounded pretty worked up on the phone.'

'Right, good,' I said, already moving away and towards my office. 'Just update my calendar.'

'Wait, one more thing,' Gina called me back. She was standing up at her desk, leaning over. She lowered her voice. 'I tried to get your client from yesterday who left in a hurry back on a call, but her cell kept calling out. I did try running some more of her information – see if she'd visited any hospitals in the area in the past, but they had no record of her. I left her a couple of messages.'

I bit down on my lower lip. 'Okay, thank you. Hopefully she'll call back.'

'Was she . . .' Gina began, then seemed to second-guess herself. I knew why. She knew the importance of being discreet, but I don't think my reaction had helped matters in this instance. I had piqued her interest and now it was going to be difficult to put her off becoming more invested in the outcome.

'Was she dangerous or something we should be worried about?'

I shook my head. 'No, nothing like that. Probably just me being overly cautious, that's all. Nothing to suggest that anything bad was going to happen to her or anyone else.'

'That's good,' Gina said, sitting back down in her chair. 'I don't want to have to deal with cops showing up here, demanding to know why we didn't have more information about her, or following up on something we should have.'

I tried smiling, but it felt alien on my face. 'That's not going to happen, Gina, don't worry.'

There was a moment when I thought she was going to continue probing, but she seemed to accept what I'd said. I moved away and towards my office. I had forty minutes before my first appointment – Marie Ennis. A thirty-seven-year-old mom of three, who was dealing with a cheating husband she couldn't kick out and two kids diagnosed with various behavioural disorders. She would unload for fifty minutes, not listen to anything I had to say, and come back the next week with much the same complaints. An awful case of someone who couldn't imagine a better life for themselves.

Or, as I thought of her, my bread and butter.

Most of my clients were women. At least two thirds. Ranging in age from teenage to fifties. I hadn't had a client older than fifty-five in years. It seemed like if you didn't have it together by then, there was no point in even trying in some people's eyes.

I closed the office door behind me and threw the paperwork in a tray under my desk. Pulled up my chair and sat down at my computer.

There were things I wanted to google, but not on my own cell phone.

I waited for the computer to turn on, considered another coffee and decided against it. I could feel the effects of the three cups I'd already had that morning. Rather than making me feel less tired, they seemed to be exhausting me instead.

I pulled up the browser on my desktop and almost checked over my shoulder before typing. Even writing those words were enough to make my heartbeat quicken.

Adam Halton missing Somerset.

The story went back so far at this point, that I had to dig through a fair few unrelated posts before finding what I was looking for.

His family.

I always remembered his father's face, more than his mom or sister. I wasn't sure why that was. Maybe because he was holding back his pain, his fear, of what happened to his son. While his mom and sister were an open book. His dad, on the other hand . . . he was stone-faced. A slab of concrete on human shoulders. No emotion whatsoever.

But I had seen it in his eyes during a small press conference that was shown on local TV back in 2006. Burned into my memory, watching alone in my bedroom, where no one could see me cry at strangers pleading for news on the screen.

It would have been difficult to explain.

On every anniversary, there would be something new. There was a Facebook page dedicated to his disappearance. I clicked on it and the latest post was from almost a year ago.

Still missing, still missed.
We'll keep looking for you Adam. We all love you so much and just want you to come home.

The screen became blurred, as my eyes watered. There were many likes on the post, heart and care emojis clicked. Comments listed underneath, which seemed to be supportive.

I couldn't read them all.

I scrolled down, seeing post after post, reaching back over a decade. Pleas for information, desperation seeping from every word.

They just wanted to know what had happened to him.

It hurt so much to not be able to tell them. I thought of JJ. In a few years time, he'd be a similar age to Adam Halton. If something happened to him and I didn't know . . .

I couldn't dwell on that for too long.

I had often thought over the years about doing something for the family. Maybe telling them where Adam was. What happened to him. But I knew it wouldn't ever be just as easy as that. I'd be found instantly, that's the way the internet worked.

Twenty-four hours had passed since Ella had entered my office and I could feel the weight of that fact increase. I had felt this way only once before, since moving to the States.

I had barely survived it that time.

I continued to scroll, before it became too much and I pressed the back button. Found the latest news story, which was dated 2015.

Ten years on . . . what happened to Adam Halton?

He was nineteen years old. A trainee electrician, who had only gone out for a few drinks with friends. Ten years later, he is still missing, and his family are left with so many questions unanswered.

His mum, Denise (64), has never given up hope of finding Adam. 'I just keep expecting him to walk through the door,' she says now, sitting on a threadbare sofa in the living room of her home in Yetminster, just outside of Yeovil. She has lived here for the past thirty years, and it has seen better days. She'll never leave this house though. 'If he suddenly reappears, he won't know where to go other than here. This is his home. I can't leave it.'

His sister, Christina, lives nearby with her husband and two children. The oldest is four years old and named after her missing brother. She sits with her mum as they talk about Adam. 'He was a happy-go-lucky lad. Always walked around with a glint in his eye. Always getting up to some kind of mischief. But he wouldn't hurt a fly, you know.'

This is slightly in opposition to what the police have to say about Adam, which the family has always pushed back on. When Adam first went missing, they believe the police didn't investigate as properly as they should have, given his past. 'Yes he sometimes got into trouble, but nothing serious,' Denise says now. 'It was just normal teenage-boy stuff.'

The last time Adam was seen was leaving the One nightclub in the heart of Yeovil – a popular club for younger people, which is still open today. He was caught on CCTV walking away from the club.

The next day, his mum raised the alarm when he wasn't in his bedroom when she checked on him after midday.

He was out with a few friends, but they don't remember him leaving. Police sources have said they weren't very helpful to their enquiries, due to the amount of alcohol they had consumed.

They also believe that he may have tried to walk the six miles home that night, after not being able to secure a taxi ride. With a number of rivers, and a large reservoir on his journey home, the fear is that he may have fallen in and not been able to make his way to safety. However, the police say they searched the rivers and reservoir and didn't find Adam.

'We just want to know what happened to him,' Christina says, holding her mum's hand. 'Until we're told otherwise, we're going to keep trying to find Adam, because we know he would do the same for us. He loved his family first. So, we're not going to give up on him . . .'

I couldn't read any more. I'd read this article before – a few times. There was someone missing from the story, of course.

Adam's father.

He'd died six years after Adam went missing. A massive heart attack in woodland twenty miles from home.

He'd been looking for Adam's body, they said. Some kind of clue to his whereabouts. By the time someone found him, he'd been dead a couple of hours.

Another reason for me to feel guilty. Another death that was my fault.

I didn't want any of this.

I moved back to the Facebook page, pulled up the most recent post and clicked on comments. I wanted to write something that would ease their hurt. That would stop the pain of not knowing. I wanted to reach out and tell them everything I knew. That it was just an accident, none of it was supposed to happen.

Instead, I did nothing. I couldn't. Because self-preservation was more important.

That gnawing feeling inside me grew worse.

I was about to shut down the page when I noticed a comment on the latest post. Written only a few days earlier. Any other time I would have dismissed it, but now I couldn't.

I know you will have answers soon. I promise. They can run, but they can't hide.

*

I couldn't remember anything about my first appointment of the day five seconds after it had ended. I wasn't concentrating. And I think my client noticed.

It wouldn't matter. Not in the end.

It was all minor in the grand scheme of things. A distraction I didn't need. My phone had been lighting up in my purse the entire appointment, which thankfully the client didn't see. Once she left, I grabbed it from my bag.

Five missed calls. All from an unknown number.

My phone began flashing in my hand as I stared at it. I answered instantly and put it to my ear.

'Hello . . .'

'Sara.'

I slumped back onto the chair behind my desk. 'Who is this?' I said, swallowing fear down my throat. 'What do you want?'

'Outside, your car, now. You have thirty seconds, or I drive to your children's school.'

I began to answer, but realised the call had ended. I lifted the phone away from my ear and saw an empty screen staring back at me. I wanted to call back, to make some threats of my own, but I knew I couldn't.

It hadn't been Ella.

It had been a man's voice.

My heart was threatening to burst out of my chest. Someone had opened the box of my past and Pandora was now having some fun.

Thirty seconds.

I started running.

14

I made it outside, sprinting to my car, just as my internal clock went past thirty seconds.

No one was standing next to my car. No one at all in the parking lot. I had my keys in my hand, but I didn't unlock the car, thinking that if someone was in there it would be pointless anyway. Instead, I stared at the thing, waiting for something to happen. Finally, I found my feet and walked around the car, looking for anything that didn't look right. That didn't fit.

I couldn't hear a foreign sound. Not a scrape on the asphalt, not a stone being kicked, not a shout in the silence. Nothing.

I began pacing. Up and down the pavement . . . sidewalk. Did it matter? I could think about these things in my mother tongue, right? I could have my own thoughts.

Fifteen years I'd lived in the US. Jack didn't like it when I used British expressions, so I'd worked hard to shift my speech. I didn't quite have the accent down, but it was more transatlantic than ever.

Diapers instead of nappies. Stroller instead of pushchair. Pacifier instead of dummy. I'd remembered all of those when JJ was a baby.

Now, I barely ever slipped.

What was I doing? Who was I waiting for?

Thirty seconds went past. Then another minute. I was about to give up when I saw a car entering the parking lot.

Maroon red. Old.

My heart quickened a little. Then a little more, the closer it came.

I was backing away, my shoes scraping on the asphalt. I wanted to run, but shuffling backwards was all I could manage, before the car came screeching to a halt in front of me. I could see the front two seats – both occupied. A man and a woman. The driver got out first – a guy in his mid-forties, I guessed. A little grey at the temples of his closely cropped hair, a few inches over six feet tall. He didn't take his eyes off me and I found I couldn't tear mine away either.

I heard the passenger-side door open, but my focus was on the man.

I had stopped moving, shutting down in fear.

'Sara, right?'

I turned towards the woman, who was smiling at me. She was a few years younger than the man – dark hair, tied tightly against her head into a ponytail. She wasn't that much smaller than him. The closer she came, the more she towered over me. Her hands were thrust inside the pockets of a long, dark coat. I could hear the clack of heels on the ground as she walked, before coming to a stop next to the man.

'What do you want?'

My voice sounded wrong. As if it were coming from someone, somewhere else.

'You know why we're here.'

I shook my head. 'There must be some mistake . . .'

He took two steps and I could smell his aftershave. Cologne.

'You know, it must be hard for you.'

I turned as the woman spoke. Her voice was soft, head tilted in sympathy. I envied her. She didn't look like someone with the weight of the world on her shoulders. It didn't look like she couldn't carry it, either – there was a quiet sense of power emanating from her.

'Why did you call me? What do you want from me?'

'This has been coming for a long time, Sara. You must have known that on some level – that you couldn't outrun what you did.'

'I'm going to call the police,' I said, hoping she couldn't hear the lie in my voice. 'You threatened me . . .'

'It has to be so difficult for you,' she continued, her voice cloying the atmosphere between us the more she spoke. 'Living a lie. Your whole life, carrying around the knowledge of what you did. What you are. I can't imagine what that's like. Having to lie to everyone. Pretending that you don't know, every single minute of every single day, that you shouldn't be here. That you shouldn't have this life.'

'I don't know what you mean . . .'

'I think you know exactly what we mean,' the man said, taking a step towards me. 'It's time, don't you think? To start telling people the truth.'

'Your whole life isn't real,' the woman said, coming into line with the man. 'Aren't you tired? Don't you wish you could just be the real you? That you could tell the world who you really are. What you did to someone so innocent. It must be like a little voice inside you, every single day, wanting to be heard. Wanting to confess. Over and over, it must drive you crazy. Don't you want to silence that sound for once?'

'I want you to leave me alone.'

'That's not going to happen,' the man said, his breath on my skin suddenly. I made a move backwards, but he was quicker. He took hold of my wrist and then I was on the ground, without a second passing. I tried to scream, but the woman's hand was across my mouth in an instant. The air sucked out of me on impact, as I looked up to see their two faces staring down at me.

'Listen, Sara, we don't want to hurt you,' the woman said, gripping me by the face, hard. Her hand was like a vice and I couldn't move. 'That's the last thing we like to do in a situation like this. But, it's very important you listen to that little voice inside you.'

'Yeah, the little voice,' the man continued, getting on his haunches and crouching next to us. 'That's right. That's your conscience talking – telling you that you've done wrong and never made it right. Well, we're here to make sure you start listening to it. You know what you did. You know what you have to do.'

I found something within me. I started struggling, snapping my head back and forth, until the woman's grip finally loosened. I didn't think – I curled my hand into a fist and launched it towards her. I felt the impact, as my fist landed against the side of her head, travel up my arm and across my chest. I heard her swear in a whisper, but I was already moving. I almost fell, as I turned and stumbled, then started running.

I didn't get very far.

At first, I wasn't sure what hit me. I just saw the ground coming towards me and then the thud of impact. I felt the air leave my body as my back hit the ground, my right arm twisted underneath me. I felt a weight on me and then I felt my head snap back and hit the concrete.

My vision clouded for a second or two, a grey film flitting across what I could see.

'I told you we didn't want to hurt you,' I heard the man say, as he turned me round and I looked up into his eyes. 'But that doesn't mean we won't if you won't listen to us.'

I tried to struggle again, but he lifted me by my shoulders and slammed me back into the ground again. I heard a moan escape my lips.

'We trust you'll do the right thing . . .'

'Col, we've got to go,' the woman said, no fear in her voice. Flat, decisive. 'Now.'

I tried to move again, but the man's weight was still holding me down.

'Think about it. We hope you make the right decision and relieve yourself of the burden you've been carrying.'

Then, the weight lifted and I was free. I tried to get up, but I felt sick immediately, my head swimming and the world spinning around.

I lifted a hand to the back of my head and when I brought it away, I saw blood. I could feel tears escaping my eyes, my stomach churning, as the adrenaline began to release its hold.

There was a screech of tyres in the distance, and then, a few seconds later, a voice.

Calling my name.

I knew who it was, but I couldn't focus. I don't know if it was the shock, or the fall to the ground . . . all I knew was that I wasn't right.

I lay back and waited.

15

I was conscious the whole time. Thankfully. Anyone who is unconscious for more than a few minutes has a hell of a problem on their hands.

So I heard Gina calling 911. I heard her calling Jack.

All the time, I just wanted to move. To tell her to stop. To tell her I was okay and didn't need her help.

I couldn't stop thinking about what had been started. What was going to happen. Who would be next? My neighbours? My work?

My kids?

I needed to find Ella and put a stop to all of this.

EMT arrived. I was moved inside the building, two paramedics giving me the once over.

'We should take you in,' one said, after shining a light across my eyes. 'Make sure everything is okay. You may have concussion.'

I shook my head. 'I didn't lose consciousness—'

'It may be that you didn't realise,' he said, cutting across me. 'It's better to be safe than sorry, right?'

'No, really, I'm okay. I just need to rest a little.'

I could see the two share a look. I wanted them to leave, but it took another fifteen minutes of refusing before they finally accepted I wasn't going to go anywhere.

Then, it was the cops. Two guys in uniform, who couldn't look less interested.

'And you didn't know them? Hadn't seen them before?'

'It all happened so quick,' I said in reply, not exactly lying. 'I don't even really know what happened.'

'Your friend there, she didn't see anyone. You think she came out too late?'

Gina. Not exactly helpful. Not to know. 'I think they were trying to rob me, but I didn't have my purse with me.'

'Why were you down here? Your office is a few floors up, right? And you're down here without even a jacket.'

Now I would have to lie. 'I sometimes sneak down for a cigarette. But, I forgot to bring my secret pack down with me. I was about to go up and get it when they came up behind me.'

'And you think it was a man and a woman?'

I hesitated. 'Like I said, it all happened so fast.'

'Your friend,' the other guy said, this one older than the first. About twenty years or so. A lot more pounds on this one too. 'She said the building had surveillance cameras, so we'll take a look at them.'

I nodded, knowing that they wouldn't help. They covered the entrance, the parking lot out front, but not the side of the building. I knew all they'd find was the car pulling in and then going out.

I wasn't even sure if they'd used the main entrance to drive in. There was another entrance, which you wouldn't always know existed. If they'd used that, then there would be no evidence at all.

Me leaving the building and walking up the side of the building. That would be it. Gina following me out, because I'd rushed out of the office. Probably coming to check I was okay. Not quickly enough, of course, to be of any use.

They may question how much time I was out there, but that would come later. For now, I just needed them to leave.

They did, just as Jack arrived. Leaving me a number to call and a promise that they'd be looking into it.

I wasn't listening any more. I was looking for Jack. Looking for normal.

'Are you okay?' Jack said, as he reached me, taking me in his arms as I got to my feet. He pulled away from my embrace, looking over his shoulder. 'The cops were here?'

'I'm okay,' I replied, pulling him back around to look at me. I was aware of Gina standing close by. No sign of our boss, of course. He had come downstairs for a few seconds, then excused himself. I knew he'd be sitting in his office now, worried about how all this looked.

'What happened?'

I glanced towards Gina. 'Let's go somewhere. I need to clear my head.'

He frowned at me, then placed an arm around my shoulders. 'Of course, let's go get you a coffee or something.'

I let myself be led out of the building, towards where his car was sitting – parked askew, not in a space. He'd obviously driven here quickly, erratically. And that hadn't let up when he'd arrived.

'I'm sorry, I didn't want them to call you . . .'

'Are you kidding? Of course they should.'

He opened the passenger-side door for me, then jogged around to the other side. Got in, looked over at me, and then faced forwards again.

'I'm fine, Jack,' I said, seeing his hands shake a little as they reached for the steering wheel. 'Just drive somewhere, so I can get away from this place for a while.'

He nodded, shifted into drive and pulled out of the parking lot. His eyes fixed on the road. Only every now and again, they would flit to the rear mirror, as if he was checking behind him. He drove for a few minutes, taking turns seemingly at random, before coming to a stop on an empty street. He looked all around him and was quiet for a minute. Possibly two.

I could see that he was breathing hard – a million questions probably running through his head.

'Tell me what happened.'

I could feel my hands shaking. Betraying me. I knew where this was going and I didn't want it to. I wanted to pretend I had no idea, but that wasn't going to work. I knew this had begun yesterday, with Ella.

In fact, it had begun years earlier, when a young man named Adam was murdered, but that felt less important in that moment.

I took a breath, then took hold of his hand. 'I'm so sorry,' I said, feeling the tears pricking at the corner of my eyes. I couldn't start now. I was scared I'd never stop. 'I didn't mean for any of this to happen. I thought it was all over.'

'Tell me what's going on.'

'Yesterday, I had a new client. A woman called Ella. I didn't think anything was wrong – just a normal client, who told me she had some problems. But when she started telling me why, I knew she was lying.'

I breathed in, trying to slow my heartbeat a little. I was sweating. The car suddenly felt like a coffin – constricting, narrowing by the second. I didn't want to move, yet at the same time, wanted to run away from everything.

'She confessed to something. A terrible thing. If it had been anyone else receiving counselling in that room, I would have had a moral quandary on my hands, because what she said was the worst thing that someone can do.'

'She killed someone . . .'

I didn't answer Jack. 'She told me everything that happened. How she was involved, what she'd done. But when she started explaining it all, I knew what she was going to say next. I knew exactly what happened, how it happened. I knew her whole story.'

'How?'

'Because it was *my* story. I don't know how it's possible, but she was telling me all about what happened to me. Or, what I should say is, what I *did*.'

Jack shook his head and began muttering to himself. It sounded like the word 'no' over and over.

'Before I had chance to ask her anything about it, she bolted out of the office. I tried to catch up with her, but she was already gone.'

'I don't understand, Sara,' Jack said, his voice small, quiet, barely reaching me. 'A stranger, what? Came into your office and accused you of being a murderer? That doesn't make any sense.'

'She didn't accuse me of anything. She didn't acknowledge me at all. She just told her story and then left. There was nothing else to it. I was too shocked to say anything.'

'Sara,' Jack said, reaching out and laying his hand on mine, instantly stilling it. 'How could she know? Who would have told her?'

'I don't know . . .'

'It's okay,' Jack said, stroking the back of my hand with his thumb. 'We're going to get through this. Again.'

And I felt like I was going to be okay. Because Jack was there and he would never let anything happen to me. He wouldn't judge me, or leave me.

Because he already knew the worst thing about me and was still there, in that car, sitting next to me, as I cried and let my fear out in full.

16

Penny was staring into space, zero expression on her face. She got like that sometimes – until someone prodded her and she snapped back into reality.

Colby often wondered what she was thinking about during those times. Whether it was about what they'd done over the years. About the choices they'd made. Or if it was just about the next paycheck and where it was coming from.

Most of the time, he just assumed that if it was important, she'd tell him.

'She wasn't that banged up. She was fine when we left her.'

Colby waited for Penny to answer, but she was still staring into nothingness.

'Look, I know,' Colby said, reaching out for Penny's hand and taking it in his own. 'We just do the job as best we can. These people . . . it's not like we're dealing with normal people, right?

'Uh huh.'

Colby sighed and let go of her hand. Moved away from the car he'd been leaning against. 'We need to keep on top of them, don't you think? I don't want to have chase anyone in the end.'

'They never run all that far.'

That was right. Something about them standing at the end of their beds at three in the morning was usually enough to get people's attention.

'Still, we're only doing this for so little money as a favour,' Colby said, throwing his empty coffee cup towards the trashcan. Almost made it. 'And that means we have to make sure we're not stiffed on the tiny amount we are getting. You know how it is with these types of people.'

'I guess you're right,' Penny replied, peeling away from the car and stretching her arms out.

Not for the first time, he thought about how lucky he was.

'So, we'll call in and see what the lay of the land is like.'

'I wouldn't mind a lay of the land round about now,' Penny said, a knowing grin appearing on her face. 'If you know what I'm saying.'

Colby shook his head, but couldn't help but return the smile. 'If I know what you're saying? That trashcan over there knows what you're saying. And I'd love nothing more, but we don't have time right now. None of this seems on the level and I'm not wasting my time if we're not going to get paid at the end.'

'We will. We always do.'

That was fair, Colby thought. 'Okay, but maybe this time we won't have to remove anyone's fingers to get it. Wouldn't that be nice?'

Penny shrugged and Colby knew that for her, it didn't matter either way. For him too, he guessed. He was just happy being there, anywhere that wasn't locked up behind bars, or dead in the ground. Being upright and breathing was a win for him each day it happened.

'What do you think of all this?' Colby said, walking towards the motel-room door. They had been there a few days now – a choice made because it was the only one in the area with a parking lot where they could have their car waiting right outside at any given moment. One that seemed to charge by the hour for other visitors. Still, it had a comfortable enough bed, its own bathroom, and enough cheap places close by to eat. 'You think there's a good endgame for anyone here?'

'I don't think so,' Penny replied, coming up to his side and slipping an arm through his. 'I've thought that from the beginning. I did say.'

'You did say,' Colby said, feeling around in his jacket pocket and then smiling as he produced a box of Milk Duds. He opened the box and tilted it to his mouth. 'I don't tend to think about that type of thing usually. I just get on and do what we're asked.'

'I guess we should all be a bit more like you – just get on with life and not sweat the small stuff.'

'You got that right,' Colby said, placing the Milk Duds back in his jacket as they reached the door. Once inside, he threw his keys down on a small table near the window. 'And anyway, it's not like we're here for all that long. Should all be done by the end of the week, I think.'

'Maybe we should take a few weeks off. Go somewhere nice for a change.'

'Yeah, that'd be nice.'

Only, he knew that wasn't going to be the case, because if he really thought about it, this job wasn't right.

The way it had come to them, what little they knew . . . it all felt off. And he didn't like that. It was hard enough to keep on track at the best of times.

If his gut was right, he didn't think they would be finishing this one so easily.

17

I don't know how long we sat in Jack's car, but at some point he took his hand away from mine. They went cold instantly. I shivered and wrapped my arms around myself.

'Who do you think they were?'

'I don't know,' I said, feeling the ground beneath me shift and fall away as the weight of what had happened to me began to tell. 'Ella didn't say anything about these two people. She ran away from the office, without accusing me of anything.'

'Well, the two things are connected, I'd say that.'

I couldn't tell what Jack's thoughts were. He was stony-faced, expressionless, turned away from me now and staring out onto the street ahead.

'They're working together, I guess,' he continued, scratching at the stubble on his jawline. 'Maybe they're trying to just confuse you by throwing as much as possible at you at once. Put you in a position where you can't see any way out, other than to do exactly what they want?'

'Maybe,' I said, barely listening. My attention was focused on what I was going to lose. My children, my job, my life. It would all be gone once this came out. 'They haven't asked for anything, but I guess that'll be next.'

'I'm guessing they'll want money,' Jack said, disgust thinly veiled in his tone. The first emotion he'd given in the past few minutes. 'That's what this always comes down to. And we don't have much to give them right now. Soon, but not soon enough for them, I would guess.'

'I'm sorry,' I said, wishing I could say more. Wishing there was something else, something better that I could say. 'I've ruined everything.'

'When you told me about what happened,' Jack said, his voice softer, warmer, 'I promised I wouldn't judge you for it. Didn't I?'

I nodded, unable to speak.

'Not just that, but I took a vow,' Jack continued, turning back to me now. 'I told you that it didn't matter. That I loved you for who you are now, not for what you might have been in the past. What you might have done. Sharing that with me was so hard for you and I never forgot the trust you put in me . . . in us. You didn't hide from me. I'll never forget that. So, I'm with you, every step of the way.'

I wanted to feel less scared. I couldn't. I opened my mouth to speak, but I didn't have any words.

'Sara, these people seem dangerous,' Jack said, sensing my emotions. 'To turn up to your office in broad daylight and attack you? For this woman to come into your office and say these things to your face? It's all so . . . so . . .'

'Brazen,' I finished for him. 'They feel like they're in the right and maybe that's the case. So, they don't care about being seen, because what am I going to do really? If I tell the cops about them, they have more on me than I do on them.'

'We need to do something before anything happens to involve the kids.'

'I'm not going to let anything happen to them,' I said, before Jack could continue. Never more sure of anything in my life. 'I'd die for them. You know that.'

'It's not just about that,' Jack said, shifting in his seat. 'It's not just about them being in danger. They're not going to hurt our kids, if you think about it logically. It's all about *you*. If they want money, they're not going to get that by hurting JJ and Olivia. They don't need to. They can just threaten to tell the police what you did and that's enough. They're just trying to scare us.'

I didn't agree, but didn't want to make the situation worse. If they didn't get what they wanted by just targeting me, it wouldn't be long before they went after the people I cared about.

'Well, they've succeeded in scaring me.'

'Right, but this isn't the end of it. They'll keep coming and coming. So, we have to make a decision. About what exactly we're going to do to get ahead of this, before it gets any worse.'

I got it then. What he was intimating. 'I can't do that, Jack . . .'

'I'm not saying you should—'

'If I confess everything to the police, then it'll be over. For me, for us, for the kids. That's all we'll be known for. We won't be able to go anywhere without people knowing what I did. I'll be sent back to England and locked up for God knows how long. By the time this is over, the kids won't be kids any more – they'll be adults. They'll have lived years without me. They won't know me. And would you wait? Would I even want you to? No. I can't do that. I can't let that happen.'

'Sara . . .'

'No, Jack,' I said, my voice echoing around the car. I thought I saw him recoil slightly, but it might have been my mind playing tricks on me. 'I won't let one mistake define me. I've done nothing since that night but try and make up for it. I didn't even do anything.'

'I know, I know,' Jack replied, reaching for me and then awkwardly bringing me to him across the car. My face fell into his chest and I thought the tears would fall freely then. I thought I'd start crying and never stop.

Only that didn't happen. I was simply breathing hard, trying to stop the anger that I was feeling from overwhelming us both.

'It's going to be all right,' Jack said, then kissed the top of my head. 'We'll get through this somehow.'

I pulled away from him. 'How do we do that? I can't find this Ella. And now there's a man and a woman attacking me in a car park . . .'

'Parking lot.'

'Not the time, Jack,' I said, brushing my hair away from my face and glancing towards him. He looked tired. Older than the last time I'd really looked at him. There was grey in his temples that I couldn't be sure was there the last time I'd seen him. Of course, it had been, but it was a reminder of the age we actually were, rather than the age I sometimes thought we still were. 'Do we just wait until they come back to us? What if next time it's at our house? What if they're waiting for us at home?'

'Then, we deal with it,' Jack replied, his jaw tensing. 'I'll protect us.'

I knew he would want to, but I also knew that Jack wasn't one for confrontation. Not physical.

Not like so many of my ex-boyfriends. That's what had attracted me to Jack in the first place.

'We need some kind of plan.'

Jack nodded, but seemed lost. As if he didn't know what to do next.

'If it's money, maybe that'll be for the best. We can find that, at least. If it's to make me go to the police, then we have a different problem. But, we'll cross that bridge when we come to it. Right?'

'I guess so,' Jack said, and I could almost hear his brain whirring with thoughts. 'We have to find out what these people want.'

I didn't think I'd have to wait long.

I also knew I wasn't going to be doing this alongside Jack. This was my problem. Not his. I knew if I said that out loud, though, he would dig his heels in further.

So I kept quiet.

They weren't going to just go away. Ella would be back. I had no doubt about it.

'We also can't just sit and wait for her to come back around,' I said, putting my seatbelt back on. 'I need to find Ella and see what she knows. Because, right now, all I have is what she told me and those two turning up at my work. That's not enough for them to go to the police. It'd be my word against hers.'

'Right . . .'

'Which isn't enough, understand? I can just say that she doesn't know what she's talking about. That she's making it up, I've got no idea where she got any of it from. It's my own guilt that will bring us down if I let it, so I'm not going to.'

'What if she has more?'

'Then, I don't know,' I said, growing impatient. I thought I was thinking clearly, but Jack seemed determined to pile on the fear. 'But right now, she has nothing.'

'Who do you think they are? Do you think they're related to . . . to the man that was, you know, killed?'

I shook my head. 'I don't know. She had an American accent, but I guess you'd know better than me if she was putting it on.'

'I think you would probably spot it too,' Jack said, slowly putting his own seatbelt on and starting the engine. 'So, the question is . . .'

'How would they know?'

Jack pulled away and began driving back in the direction of my office, while I thought about that last question.

How would they possibly know? There was only me and Dan who knew about what happened that night. And Jack, of course, but I knew he wasn't going to tell anyone. I trusted him. And even without that trust, the fact he'd stayed with me for years after I'd told him meant he was just as implicated now.

That left Dan.

I hadn't spoken to him in years. Had no idea what he did, where he was.

But it wasn't like I'd be difficult to find. I might have moved thousands of miles away, but I wasn't trying to hide.

So it made sense that maybe he wanted me to know he hadn't forgotten.

'Dan,' I said, and glanced over at Jack. Saw the knuckles on his hands whiten as they gripped the steering wheel. 'That was his name, I don't know if I told you before.'

'Yeah, you did. What about him?'

'It could be him.'

'You think so?'

The more I thought about it, the more it fit. I knew I hadn't left him in the best of ways. He was drinking more. Wasn't working. His life had seemed to end that night and he was struggling to move on.

'It's not a stretch to think maybe he found out where I was,' I said, as Jack made his way down increasingly busier roads. We came to a stop at a set of traffic lights. 'He was in a hell of a state in those last few days before I left him. He may have got worse. If his life has got even worse over the years, then he may be capable of anything.'

'Can you get in touch with him?'

I hesitated, and then lied to my husband. 'No, I don't think I can.'

I knew I could.

I just didn't want to.

18

I'm not sure why I lied to Jack. It's not like I made a habit of lying to him. It was difficult to even tell him little white lies over the years we'd been together. That's why he knew everything about my past.

I didn't want to spend my life worrying about him finding out something I hadn't told the truth over. It was as simple as that.

I didn't want to hide anything from him.

Which is why it shocked me that I had lied about Dan.

'Well, then I don't know what we're going to do,' Jack said, not even blinking at my untruth. 'But we have to do something before this gets any worse.'

'I'll find her,' I replied, determined that the answer lay with Ella. 'She is the one who can stop this. I'm sure of it.'

'And how will you find her?'

I knew the answer to that one and I didn't like it.

'Maybe it would be better to just tell the police everything?'

I looked across at Jack, wondering if he had lost his mind. 'Everything?'

'Well, obviously not everything. Just what happened with this Ella and these two people. Like you said, it's only going to be their word against yours, right? And they've already shown themselves to be less than trustworthy.'

I shook my head. 'It'll only make things worse. The best way out of this is to deal with it myself.'

'I want to help you,' Jack said, reaching across and taking my hand again. 'This doesn't just affect you. It affects us all. And it's important that we face this – whatever *this* is – together.'

I smiled, despite feeling worse than I had in a long time. 'I know you're with me.'

I felt it stronger than ever at that moment – that I wasn't going to come back from this. Ella, the two people who had attacked me . . . all connected to what I'd done all those years ago. I had never been punished properly for that and now it was coming back to haunt me.

I knew I had to do this alone. If I brought Jack with me into this, then he would be just as guilty as me.

So, I lied again.

'We can do this.'

*

My hands were shaking. I laid them on my kitchen table and willed them to stop.

I had no one I could call. No one I could ask for help. No one who would understand and help me.

I couldn't lay this on Jack. I had to protect him.

I had to protect us all.

Yet, there was part of me that wanted to give up there and then. To just lie down and never get back up. The feeling was over-whelming, the desire even more so.

It would be so easy to just give up.

Only that wasn't what I'd done all those years ago. I could feel that familiar sense of anger swell inside me.

I had never given up before.

I wasn't like Dan. I wasn't just going to live the rest of my life looking over my shoulder. I had got out of that place and look where I'd ended up – in a million-dollar house, with a husband who I couldn't love any more than I did, and the two best children any mother could dream of – all thousands of miles from where I'd almost lost it all.

I had become *someone*.

That was worth fighting for.

And that was what I was going to do.

I had left work early – cancelling the few appointments I had left that day and going home. I wouldn't have been in any fit state to do any good work with my patients anyway, but I still felt guilty about leaving them in the lurch. I was almost certain they could handle a missed session, but I would never really know if that were true.

I swiped across the touchpad on my laptop and brought it to life. Entered my passcode and opened Google Chrome.

There wasn't just the one lie I'd told Jack, about me being unable to contact Dan.

He also didn't know about the fake Facebook account I'd created seven years earlier to check in on him.

I signed in – remembering the details by heart, having committed them to memory all those years ago. I hadn't signed in for a few years, but they came back to me easily.

Then I was in the account of Michelle Denholm. She only had a few photographs – all copied from someone's else's account that I couldn't recall now. Everything about the page was fake. Michelle had eighty-six friends. She liked a number of pages that showed off her eclectic taste. All British culture. *Bake Off*, *EastEnders*, even bloody *Love Island*.

She shared twenty mutual friends with Dan. That was how the friend request had been accepted in the first place – I had scraped through his entire friend list and tried to add as many as possible. A ten per cent hit rate had been enough.

I hadn't ever used Michelle to speak to him in the past. But I must have known this moment was going to come, otherwise why had I made the page in the first place?

It was time now.

I navigated to Dan's page and clicked on the message box.

Dan . . . it's S. I know it's been a long time . . .

19

Colby saw her coming. It was hard to miss her. She stood out in that neighbourhood. Too young, too blonde, too clean.

Penny side-eyed him, probably to make sure he wasn't eyeing her up.

Ella was walking with confidence. Striding towards them, as if she belonged. As if she owned the place. Which, he guessed, might not have been out of the question. It wasn't like he knew all that much about her.

'Thanks for coming,' she said, when she finally reached them. No looks over her shoulder. No furtive glances. She handed over an envelope that disappeared into Colby's inside pocket in an instant. 'That should be enough for the next few days. Now, tell me what happened?'

Colby brought her up to date, noting the smile that played across her lips when he described how scared the woman had been. Penny earned a look when he told her about the blow she'd taken to the head. Penny shrugged, like it was nothing.

'So, it was a little more physical than we'd discussed,' Colby said, matter of fact. He had to make sure she understood how in control they were. 'Couldn't be helped.'

'What happened afterwards? Tell me you stuck around to find out.'

'Of course,' Colby replied, lifting himself away from the side of the car. 'From a safe distance, of course. EMT turned up. Checked up on her. Cops too, but they looked uninterested even before they reached the parking lot. Then, the husband arrived. They went together a few miles away and parked up. Looked like a serious conversation.'

'Okay, would have been good if we could have heard what they said to each other. What she told him, how much he knows.'

'I can bug the cars, if you want? Shouldn't be too hard.'

She thought for a moment and then nodded. 'That'd be perfect. The house too?'

Colby weighed it up and shrugged. 'Probably the same level of difficulty. You'll have to pay for expenses. Not cheap to get something that'll give you the quality you want. Tech being the way it is now, you'll be able to listen in to them live. And we can make sure they'll never even know it's there. Right, Penny?'

Colby glanced at Penny, who gave a small nod.

She didn't even look at Penny. Not even a glance. She was talking to Colby and Colby alone. 'I'll meet you tomorrow, but there's enough in what I've already given you today to cover it now, if it can wait?'

Colby thought it over. 'You're good for it.'

'Okay. I want it done as soon as possible.'

'Who are these people?' Penny said, breaking her silence.

This time, both she and Colby looked at Penny. Colby wanted to tell her to be quiet. To not provoke this woman into walking away from them. It was easy money – something they lacked right now.

He resisted the urge. Probably because he wanted to know the answer as much as Penny did.

'Why do you need to know?'

'Just curious is all.'

Colby turned away from staring at the side of Penny's head, willing her to stop talking. Shook his head and tried a disarming smile, which he knew didn't quite land right. 'It's okay, we're not interested in details, we'll just get the job done.'

'That's what I want to hear,' Ella said, turning back to Colby now. She was impossible to read – almost dead behind the eyes. Beautiful, but you wouldn't want to look at her too long. Far too much intensity.

He wouldn't say he was scared of her, but he was sure as shit that anyone who was on the wrong side of her should be.

'I trust you'll be discreet and not get caught,' she continued, pulling her jacket tighter around her as the wind picked up. 'I know the favour you're doing for me. My father always talked well of the both of you. I know you both know what you're doing.'

Colby picked up on the subtext. Sometimes, he worried that Penny was going to get him into trouble one of these days, but it wasn't going to be any time soon if he had anything to do with it.

Besides, any trouble that came Penny's way was his too.

He'd kill anyone – no matter how much they were currently paying him – who crossed her.

'You can count on it.'

'Good,' she said, then looked at Penny, seeming to size her up. Penny stared back, unflinchingly.

The woman held Penny's eyes for a few more seconds, then walked away.

He waited until she was down the street some before he took Penny by the arm, and said softly, 'Did you really have to do that? We're the hired help here. We don't need to be asking too many questions.'

'I'm sorry,' Penny said, rolling her eyes. 'You must feel it too though, right?

'Feel what?'

'That it's all an act. That this isn't some simple job of intimidation. Nothing about it makes sense. We're bugging the car and the house now? Why?'

'I don't care,' Colby said, walking around the car. Got inside and waited for Penny to join him. Shifted the car into drive and pulled away from the curb. 'We'll do the house first. See if we can find keys to the cars on the drive, make that easier. We can get what we need over in Stamford.'

'We can get what we need that easy?'

'You'd be surprised what you can buy in a department store these days.'

'Would I really?'

Colby didn't answer her, knowing that she was yanking his chain.

'You didn't answer me,' Penny said, once they'd been on the road a few more minutes. 'What do you really think the end game is here?'

'Does it matter?' Colby replied, with a sigh of annoyance. 'Makes no difference to us.'

'Aren't you curious?'

This time, Colby didn't answer because he was scared of what he might say.

20

I pressed send on the message to Dan and waited a few minutes. I didn't think I'd get an answer instantly, but it didn't stop me waiting to see if he read it at least.

I thought about him reading it. Maybe remembering me, the time we'd had together. Whether it would be an instant positive thought, or if he'd go straight to the negative one.

Probably the latter, I guessed. Dan hadn't exactly been in a good way the last time I'd checked in on him.

I went back to his Facebook page, looking for anything new. He wasn't a prolific poster. The odd meme, inspirational quote. I didn't look at it for very long. His profile picture was at least a decade old.

There was part of me that wondered what would have happened to us if Adam hadn't died that night. Whether we would have lasted any longer. Whether we would still be together now.

It was hard to imagine.

Looking back on it now, it felt like someone else's life. I couldn't always remember the small moments that meant so much all those years ago – as if they never existed. I couldn't remember the feelings I'd had, the thoughts that had run through my head.

They had all been overshadowed by Adam's death. By Dan's part in it.

Dan had known it was over as quickly as I had. After that night, it had been more about keeping out of prison than it had about staying together.

I thought about how long it had been since I'd seen him. Years had passed.

I hadn't known that would be the last time, of course.

Moving to America had been a way of putting some distance between myself and the life that was crumbling in front of me back there.

And escaping the guilt.

That had been the hardest thing to deal with through it all. The overwhelming feeling that we hadn't done the right thing. That we should have tried harder to save his life. That was right, of course, despite what it would have meant for both of us.

But chances were, I'd do the same thing all over again. Self-preservation is innate.

When I remembered that night, I could still recall every moment of it. In a split-second, I was back there, in the darkness, wondering if I was going to survive until the morning.

Hoping I wasn't going to end up in the same place as the dead body.

I remembered Dan's eyes, as they found mine. Somehow glowing in the darkness. And I knew then that I had made a deal with the devil and was never going to get out.

Yet there were also moments I'd forget from when Jack and I had met. When we had dated and fallen in love. Sometimes, I tried to concentrate on all those feelings I'd had and bring them back into the present. I almost always failed.

I didn't sleep well that night. Almost as if I were waiting for someone to break into the house and take things further. Even listening to Jack's light snoring wasn't enough to calm me. As it normally would. Instead, I got maybe a few hours, before light started pushing its way through the darkness outside and I knew I wasn't going to get back to sleep.

Dan still hadn't messaged me when I checked.

I called Gina once Jack and the kids had left.

'I'm sorry, but can you cancel anything I have this morning,' I said, realising I hadn't thought of an excuse yet. 'I have to take one of the kids to the emergency room.'

'Oh, nothing bad I hope?'

Another pang of guilt. Using my kids and the possibility of one them being harmed. I was going to hell, I was sure of it. At least I hadn't named the child, so it could be either of them. 'I'm sure it's nothing. Just a fall as they were getting off the school bus, that's all. Probably the school being over cautious. Really sorry to do this on such short notice – make sure they're rescheduled quickly and at their convenience. And let Simon know I won't be in until later. I don't want him thinking I'm trying to skive off.'

Gina didn't say anything other than a puzzled sound. I realised she was trying to work out what I'd said.

'Sorry, that was a British word,' I said, shaking my head. Two countries, divided by a common language. 'I mean . . . I don't know. Trying to get out of work for no reason.'

'I'm sure he'll be fine about it.'

'Thanks, Gina,' I said, then hung up before she could ask any more questions. I could feel my cheeks becoming redder, the more I lied. The more sure I became that guilt was written across my face and in my voice in big block capitals.

I got outside and put the address in my sat nav. GPS. Whatever. I needed to get it together.

A twenty-minute drive down the 95, according to the directions. Only, I knew it would be at least twice that at that time of day. And it wouldn't inform me until I was actually on the road. Everything takes longer than it should – every commute, every trip.

At least the scenery outside was nice enough. Not that I could concentrate on that. My hands were shaking on the wheel and I couldn't bear to change lanes, as I was sure I'd crash into someone, given my level of distraction.

25 Maple Drive.

It was just before ten a.m. when I turned off the turnpike and into Norwalk. Passed a Lowes and numerous small stores. A place on the corner of the street as I turned onto a side road caught my eye. Naughty Nancy's.

I wasn't in Westport any more.

It was still a world away from the council estates of England. The houses may have cost less, but at least you didn't have to share a wall with your neighbours. That had always been the thing that had struck me the most about the difference between the UK and USA – terraced housing. It didn't really exist over here.

And they were the ones who thought we all lived in castles.

I pulled up outside a row of red-brick homes – white sidings and door – and shut the engine off. There was a pretty white house standing alone, looking almost discarded next to the bigger building. A colonial-style home, with a driveway. Number 23. Number 25 looked in worse shape – an apartment building that seemed to have been an afterthought. Plonked down in the middle of the street and called affordable housing.

I stared at the building from my car for a few minutes, working up some kind of courage to move. It wasn't coming easily.

There was a moment when I decided to simply drive away. But, I knew that I couldn't do that. I couldn't keep running.

I got out of the car and walked towards the building. The number was affixed to the side of it, a white box with red faded lettering.

I hesitated as I reached the door, my heart pounding wildly against my chest. I wasn't sure what I was going to say. What I was going to do.

There wasn't much choice in the matter.

I reached across and pressed the buzzer for apartment eight. A horrible noise greeted me – grating in my ear, distorted. I waited, then buzzed again.

I looked up at the single window above, the side of the building a brick wall staring back at me. An air-conditioning unit hung precariously from the bottom of the window.

Still no answer.

A minute had passed. If there was someone inside, they weren't answering. I moved to the side and tried to spy any other windows. To see if Ella was up there looking down and deciding against speaking to me. Perhaps her heart was beating as madly as mine – about being discovered, at being confronted.

No one was in any of the windows.

I made as if to walk away, before changing my mind. I went back and buzzed apartment seven. Then, nine as well. Just in case.

Number seven answered.

Well, I say they answered me. Instead, the buzz back told me that I was being let in without even a conversation. I thought for a moment and then pushed my way inside.

The smell of fresh paint and despair was the first greeting. I took a breath before moving towards the stairs in front of me, reaching for the banister before deciding against it. I didn't want to touch anything.

There were only three floors, with a corridor leading further into the building. They must have been tiny apartments, as there were three on each floor. I reached the top floor landing area and the doors of apartments seven, eight and nine were staring back at me. Number seven opened, just as I tore my eyes away from number eight.

'Yeah?'

I smiled, feeling it stretch the skin on my face in a painful way. 'Hi, I'm just looking for a friend . . .'

'Won't find many of them here.'

The door opened wider and a woman of around the same age as me stared back. She looked tired, the remains of the night still weighing heavily on her shoulders. She was still wearing what looked like a nurse's uniform, but not quite. Long black hair and a clear complexion.

'Sorry, she gave me this address but doesn't seem to be opening the door.' I pointed towards apartment eight and then reached out and knocked on the door a few times.

'Won't get an answer,' the woman said, yawning through the last two words. She shook it free finally and then looked me up and down again as I turned back to her. 'No one lives there.'

I could feel my shoulders slumping at the news. Of course I didn't expect Ella to actually be there really, if I thought about it logically. Still, I was hopeful it wouldn't be a dead end.

'Right, that's what I was afraid of,' I said, acting as if I already knew that was going to be the answer. 'I wrote the address down, but wasn't sure I'd got it right.'

'No one has been there for a while now,' she said, leaning against the doorframe. 'Been empty since at least last summer. There's a listing online, a few people come round, but the economy being what it is, maybe the rent is too high for a single person. Not exactly big enough for a couple here.'

'Yeah, she did live alone,' I replied, working out how to move the conversation towards Ella. 'Maybe you might know her? Ella Morley?'

A blank look on the woman's face. I didn't think it was the type of place where people were on first name terms with their neighbours.

'Doesn't ring a bell,' she said, shaking her head. 'I work night shifts, so don't really see the neighbours.'

'What about apartment nine?' I asked, turning around to the only other door on the landing. 'Could she live there?'

The woman shook her head. 'Older guy lives there. Think he's in his sixties. Lives alone. I've never seen or heard anyone but him.'

'Maybe downstairs then? She's around twenty-six, twenty-seven. Blonde hair, blue eyes, about so tall.' I settled my hand around my own shoulder height. 'I wish I had a picture, but I thought she'd be right here.'

'I'm sorry, I can't help you,' she said, making as if to close the door. 'I hope you find her.'

'Wait,' I managed to get out, but the door was already closed. I considered knocking again, but I wasn't sure what else I could say.

I was looking for someone I could barely describe, who had more than likely given me a fake name.

I sighed and turned towards the stairs. Tried to think of what I could do next.

I was four or five steps down when I heard the door open behind me. I didn't turn around until I heard her speak.

'Hey. I've just had a thought.'

I stopped and walked slowly back. The woman was fully out of her apartment and waiting at the top.

'I've just thought of something, not sure if it means anything.'

It did.

21

I waited for the woman to say something, but I could sense some kind of hesitation. I thought about what I was asking from her. A stranger just turning up out the blue and asking about some unknown woman – a supposed friend I didn't even have a picture of to hand.

'I'm Stacey,' I said, stepping forwards and offering my hand. She took it slowly, but didn't hold onto it for more than a brief moment. I tried to think of where the name Stacey had come from and failed. I didn't know a single person in my life with that name, but the lie had come so easily I shocked myself. 'I should have introduced myself first, sorry.'

'Kim,' she replied, seeming to regard me anew. 'It's probably nothing . . .'

'Any help you can give me, I'd really appreciate it.'

'Well, I'm not even sure if I'm remembering it right. It was a while ago.'

I waited, deciding to let the silence grow enough that Kim would feel obligated to fill it.

It didn't take long.

'There was a guy who seemed to be renting the apartment,' Kim said, folding her arms across her chest. 'It was for about six months last year. I only saw him a few times, but I remember going out to work one evening and he was just coming in. He didn't say anything to me – just put his head down when I walked past – but he didn't look right.'

'In what way?'

'Just . . . look, if you're living here, it's because you can't afford a nicer place, right? It's because you're probably just keeping your head above water most of the time. Only this guy . . . this guy looked to be doing okay. He was wearing a nice suit, smelled good, you know? Like he had a good job. Like he had money.'

I wasn't sure what this had to do with Ella, or whether it was anywhere close to important. Still, I was listening.

'Anyway, he puts his head down, even when I said "evening" to him. Didn't get so much as a grunt back from him. Which, to be fair, is usual for round this place. No one seems to talk to each other any more. He slid past me and disappeared up the stairs. I knew he wasn't the old guy from number nine, but I thought maybe he was a son or something like that. I poked my head up the stairwell, not because I was being nosy or anything, I was just curious, you know? Anyway, he let himself into number eight and I realised that he was my neighbour and had been for a while.'

'Sorry, Kim, I'm not sure how this helps me . . .'

'I'm getting there,' Kim said, dismissing my interruption with a wave of her hand. 'I remember shrugging to myself, thinking he was rude, and then letting myself out of the door downstairs. I was walking to my car out back, when another car pulls in on the other side. I didn't really give it a second glance, but then a young woman gets out.'

I was listening properly now. I stood up a little straighter.

'She was around mid-twenties and was blonde – gorgeous, right? But, like she knew it. Carried herself like she was too good for the place, nose in the air type. Anyway, she got out of her car and walked right to my apartment building and get this . . . she had a key. Let herself in. I'd never seen her before in my life and I get the feeling I might have noticed her before. Both of them.'

Too much of a coincidence, I thought. Even though the Ella that had been in my office the previous day had seemed broken down and shy, I could see her suddenly in my mind – a very different woman. Someone who knew what she had. Someone who carried herself differently.

And more importantly, she had been there, at this apartment building.

'Did you ever see them again?'

Kim shook her head. 'Never again. It was just that one time. Which is weird, right? You'd think I'd pass them in the hallway, but I didn't even hear them together in there, or alone. Never heard a TV or a shower. Nothing. It was just quiet. And then suddenly the apartment was listed for rental. You think it could have been your friend?'

I was still trying to process the information and didn't answer instantly. Her eyes narrowed a little, prompting me into a response. 'Possibly, but it doesn't sound like her, really. I think she was living alone. I guess she might have had a boyfriend or something, but she never told me. What did he look like?'

'Didn't really get a good look at him, sorry. I couldn't tell you. I only saw her for few seconds. Not sure I could pick her out of a line-up now. It was last year.'

'Right, right,' I said, wishing I could be sure. It was still possible it was all a coincidence – just another woman in her mid-twenties with blonde hair – but I didn't think so. It made no sense why Ella would give this address though, knowing I could come here.

But I would have found exactly what I did – an empty apartment and no one sure of its occupants.

'Anyway, that's all I got and I need to get some sleep,' Kim said, shrugging her shoulders and moving back to her apartment door. 'Back on night shift later. Like every day. This is the most I've been out of the place in the morning in a long time.'

'Thanks anyway,' I managed to say, before Kim closed the door behind her and left me staring at the number on her apartment. I turned slowly to apartment eight and thought about trying to break inside. Wondered what the point of that would be. Instead,

I walked back down the stairs, outside, and into my parked car. I pulled out my phone and searched for the apartment listing on Google and found it quickly on Zillow.

The photographs probably didn't do it justice, but I wasn't sure reality was much better. Cheap and available. And empty.

Maybe they were old pictures, but I doubted it.

It was a dead end now. If Ella had been here – and not alone, as she'd made out to me two days ago – then she was long gone now. Why she'd not made up an address if she didn't want to be found, I wasn't sure.

I checked the time and realised I was running out of morning. I thought about my patients that afternoon. Listening to their problems, their issues. The idea of it made me feel sick.

I didn't want to do this any more. I wanted to be normal again.

★

I didn't know what to do with myself, for the couple of hours I had until my afternoon appointment. I just knew I couldn't be alone.

That's how I ended up driving into the city.

I parked up in the lot closest to Jack's workplace and then second-guessed myself. I hadn't shown up at his office in a few years at least. In the past, at least once a month I'd drive over and meet him for lunch, but that hadn't happened for a long time. Not even mentioned by either of us.

I hadn't realised how much I'd missed that. Those brief moments of it just being the two of us, if only for an hour or so.

I got out of the car and walked towards his building – the familiar sign pointing the way towards the various landmarks of New Haven greeting me at the exit. Yale University only a short walk away. A place I'd only ever known from movies and television. I had always wanted to go see what it was like, but never had the excuse.

A few minutes later, I was in the lobby of the building where Jack worked. The company was housed within the financial centre, the buildings surrounding it looking more gothic than ever in the low spring daylight.

In summers past, we'd sometimes walk over to New Haven Green and sit in the sunshine. I'd bring a blanket from the car and we'd lie intertwined together – our bodies resting against each other. A brief oasis in the day. A moment in which we were simply Jack and Sara. Together. No JJ and Olivia. No siblings. No parents. Only the two of us.

When this was over, I was determined to find moments like those again.

I made my way up in the lift – *elevator, Sara* – to where Jack's firm took up multiple floors of the building. I wondered who would be working reception – I remembered a rotation of two young women, who I always enjoyed chatting with for brief periods. I couldn't recall their names. Probably something pretty and bright. Britney or Charlotte.

I didn't recognise the woman sitting at the desk. A new face, with the same high-wattage smile and tanned skin.

'Can I help you?'

'I'm here to see my husband,' I said, trying to return the smile and failing to meet the shine. 'Jack Edwards.'

'One second,' she replied, busying herself calling through. I motioned that I'd take a seat and wait, and she nodded.

I didn't have to wait long for Jack to appear. It seemed like he'd sprinted out of his office to see me. I shook my head at the sight of him out of breath. 'Jack, you didn't need to run . . .'

'What are you doing here?' he said, reaching me and placing a hand on my arm. He didn't so much as pull me to my feet, but gently made me follow his hand upwards. 'You never said you were coming.'

Somehow we were already walking away from the reception desk. 'I wanted to see you,' I replied, unable to think of the reason now. What had made me drive an hour into New Haven and to Jack. I checked over my shoulder, but the receptionist wasn't looking our way. 'I just needed to see you.'

I felt Jack's touch relax. 'Are you okay?'

'Yes, I'm fine,' I said, suddenly feeling like I was out of place. That I shouldn't be there, putting this on Jack. I could see the stress lines in his face. I knew that work was tough right now and me turning up at his office was only going to make things more difficult. 'I'm sorry, I shouldn't have just turned up here unannounced.'

'Don't be silly,' Jack replied, placing an arm around me, leading me away from the lobby area and into a quieter corridor that led to the elevator doors. 'You know I'm always here for you. Has something happened?'

'No, I . . . I just wanted to see you.'

'I'm really busy,' Jack said, looking over his shoulder as someone shouted his name in the background. 'But I could get out for a few minutes in a little while, if that works? We're real busy right now, but I can try and escape for a little while, at least?'

I shook my head. 'It's fine, honestly. I wasn't thinking straight, that's all. I know how busy you are right now and I shouldn't be here without calling you first. It's not fair. Besides, I've got appointments this afternoon. I should get back already.'

Jack frowned, then pulled me into him. 'Sara, you're making me worry about you.'

'It's okay, really,' I said, hoping he believed me, as I enjoyed the feel of him temporarily, before pulling away. 'I'll see you later on.'

I left before he could say anything more, feeling like I was losing my mind. Feeling like I was a burden.

Feeling like a failure.

22

Back in my office, I should have felt on safer ground.

All I had to do was ignore the fact that the woman sitting opposite me was definitely a cop. That was all.

Not just a cop. A detective.

I'd discovered exactly who Alex was a few minutes earlier.

'I thought it was time I was completely honest,' Alex said, once she'd finished.

I wish I'd been able to say the same thing. To her. To anyone. I wondered if she could see the beads of sweat on my forehead. Whether she could sense the fear that was twisting and turning inside me.

Whether she could see the same image that was rolling around my head, over and over.

I couldn't believe we had been sitting across from each other in a diner a day earlier, as if we were simply two friends catching up.

Was I being set up?

'I've been a cop for almost twenty years,' Alex said, her voice flat and monotone. A rehearsed quality to it. 'Became a detective ten years ago. I've never had any regrets about it. Not until recently.'

I had to focus. If I sat there not saying a word, it was only going to make it more obvious that I had something to hide. I cleared my throat. 'Your dad – he was a police officer as well, right?'

'I guess the apple doesn't fall far,' Alex replied, a humourless smile playing across her lips. 'He was second generation – his mom, she came to America back in the late fifties, when my dad was only a baby. He never knew his own father. My abuela, she never liked to talk about him. He more than made up for his own father being absent with me and my sisters though. He's been the perfect father.'

'Do you think you became a cop because you wanted to make him proud?'

'I guess it was something like that,' Alex said, leaning back in the chair, lacing her fingers together across her stomach. 'It's not like he ever tried to make me join up or anything. He encouraged us all to do whatever made us happy. That's what made *him* happy, if that makes sense?'

'It does,' I replied, feeling more comfortable. I realised that it wasn't just being in my own office, talking to patients, that made me breathe more easily. It was Alex. She had a calming way about her that made me wish I could tell her the truth. That we could be friends. 'He never put any pressure on you at all then?'

'No, never. We would talk, of course – especially when I told him I had decided to become a cop. He was proud, but made sure I knew what I was getting myself into. Truth is, he did the opposite of putting me off the job. I wanted it more. And I knew what it meant to him.'

'Still, it must have been difficult for you.'

'Sure, but I was determined.'

We were close now. I could feel it. The reason Alex was sitting in my office. 'Tell me what happened.'

Alex breathed in slowly. I could see how much of a struggle it was for her to tell me. To just say it out loud, probably for the first time.

'When I was a beat cop, we would be called out on domestic calls all the time. Like, most of the calls would be because some guy had too much to drink and started using his partner as a punching bag, right? So, anyway, there's this guy that I must have put in handcuffs almost every weekend. Then, the next day, his wife would be right there to pick his sober ass up. I talked to her so many times, about leaving him. Every time it got a little worse – the beatings would just go a little further. More bruises, more blood. And this woman – she was only a few years older than me. Such a small thing – so skinny, so short, she probably had to run around the shower to get wet. My last shift as a beat cop before making detective, we get a call to that house again. Me and my partner roll our eyes, and make our way there. When we arrive, she's nowhere to be found. He's in the kitchen, absolutely tearing the place apart. The floor is just covered in every appliance going, the refrigerator door is hanging on by a thread, the microwave has gone through the window. He's just gone absolutely crazy.'

I was listening intently, despite knowing where this story was going to end. I couldn't work out why it had taken this long, as I worked out the years since this event must have taken place, but I knew how trauma has a way of lingering.

'So, me and my partner, we call for backup, but once he sees us there he calms down quickly. Even sticks his hands out to be cuffed. Once he was lying on the floor, hands cuffed behind his back, I go looking for the wife.'

I held my breath.

'She was upstairs, locked in the bathroom, absolutely petrified that he was going to finally kill her. Took me at least five minutes to get her to open the door, because she didn't believe that he wasn't there right behind me to finish the job. He . . . he'd beaten her so bad, I didn't recognise her. There was so much blood, that I thought she'd bleed out in my arms. I couldn't believe she was alive, to be honest. She barely looked human.

'He'd gone out drinking, come back to find her trying to leave. She'd waited, after the last time we'd been out to them, for him to be away long enough for her to get her shit together and get out of Dodge. Only, he'd been thrown out of the bar early, after picking a fight with someone he really shouldn't have. Came home, his manhood bruised, and seeing her with a bag packed sent him over the edge. Not that he usually needed an excuse. Anyway, we got her to hospital and because we had her willing to go on record, he was charged and convicted of a felony. Assault with a weapon – he'd beaten her almost to death with a tyre iron. Eight years he got.'

I didn't know where the story was going now. I had been so sure she'd go up those stairs to find this woman dead, that I hadn't considered any other possibility.

I just knew the story didn't end there.

'I'd told her so many times that she just needed to help us get him away from her. That she could be free if she just cooperated, and I really think that last time was just too far. She'd already made the decision to leave and now, she could really see a way out. So, she got up on the stand, told the court how many beatings she'd taken, how she really thought he was going to kill her that night, how scared she'd been, that she'd really wanted to leave that night and how he'd stopped her. Eight years, that was worth. Anyway, this woman, she is finally free of him. She went to live with an aunt, up in a place called Middletown. Away from this guy's family, who blamed her of course. She was happy. I'd check in every now and again the first few years, but I guess that tailed off. I got busy and just didn't think I needed to. She recovered, she got better. I hadn't even thought about her for a few years. Then, a couple of months ago, I found out he'd been released from Danbury and immediately went to find her.'

Now I knew how the story ended.

'He killed her. Didn't leave it to chance this time. He found her and didn't beat her or nothing. Just put a bullet in her head, then one in his own. Barely made the papers. No one talked about it at all. Just another domestic that went too far.'

'And did you feel a responsibility for it?'

'No. It wasn't that. I just couldn't shake the feeling that nothing I did mattered. I'd got her out of that situation, eventually, with a little push. She'd listened to me, as I convinced her to testify against him, telling her it was going to be okay. That her life was going to be better afterwards, that once he was out of the picture, she was going to be fine. But that was a lie, because I couldn't control that. I couldn't keep her safe, because who could? He spent eight years waiting to get out, just so he could kill her and then himself.'

I let her breathe through the anger, her face reddening, her chest rising and falling rapidly. I glanced at the clock and realised we'd run over our time by ten minutes. She was my last appointment of the day, but I couldn't stop her now. I thought about JJ and Olivia, waiting for me back home. I was going to be late, unless I hurried Alex along, but I knew I couldn't do that.

'Alex, we can't control the world around us. As much as we'd like to, it's just not possible.'

'I know that,' Alex replied, dismissing me, but not with any bitterness. 'I just can't shake this feeling that nothing I do – nothing I'll ever do – will ever make a difference.'

I leaned forwards, wanting to take hold of her hand. Wanting to comfort her in some way. Only I knew she wouldn't want that. 'You have to recognise something. The job – the career, the *life* – you've chosen, is one of the most thankless. You're always going to be there to pick up the pieces after something has already happened. This woman, the time to save her was the moment before she met this man. After that point, this was always an outcome that could happen, unless something happened to him first. It's a horrible fact of life, but it shouldn't take over your state of mind. It's evil, what he did, but it had nothing to do with you or your actions.'

'Well, unless we'd put him out of the picture back when we'd picked him up, maybe.'

'But then, you're just as bad as what he became. What he already was.'

'I guess. It still doesn't mean I can shake this feeling that it doesn't matter. Nothing matters.'

'What you need to focus on are the things you do that have an impact on people. I'm sure you've helped many people over the years. Get justice, get answers. Heck, even just being there for them, when the worst has happened. I'm sure, beyond a doubt, that there are people out there now, who you don't even remember, who think about you and what you did for them.'

Alex seemed to think about it. Wiped away a tear from her cheek and looked back at me. 'I'd like to think that.'

'Alex, we've made great progress here today. Now you've told me why you're here, we can really work together to get you through this. Okay?'

'Thank you.'

I felt the guilt again then. That there was someone who would love to get justice for Adam – that man who I held in my arms as he died – and all who loved him. Who still missed him.

I felt a fraud.

'Talk to Gina at reception,' I said, hoping she couldn't hear the tears I was holding back in my voice. 'Any day you want to come back this week we can keep talking, okay?'

I managed to get her out of my office before I told her everything.

23

I was late for JJ and Olivia.

I swore quietly under my breath and quickly tapped my home address into the sat nav. GPS. The thing. Unable to trust myself to find my way home without help. It didn't matter that I'd done the journey for so many years. At that moment, everywhere looked foreign to me. I backed out of the space and heard my tyres almost squeal in protest as I put my foot down.

The traffic was murder on the way back to my home in Westport. I was already seeing Stephanie's face when I walked through the door – that mix of disappointment and regret. That the two of us were now bound by those kids forever and by her brother. That she had to tolerate the mess that was me. All of it hidden by the stupid smile of hers – that knowing smirk that told me how much better she was at everything.

I'd love to wipe that smile off her face.

I was making myself angry for no good reason. By the time I was turning onto my driveway, it was past four thirty and I almost crashed into the back of Jack's car.

He was never home this early. Not now. In the past, he would make any excuse to get home before dinner, so he could spend some time with JJ and Olivia, but that felt like a lifetime ago now.

The pressure on him was so immense, and I felt it in the pit of my stomach – what I had just added to that day.

I couldn't see Stephanie's car, so at least I didn't have to deal with her.

Still, I couldn't shake the feeling of nervousness as I got out the car and started walking towards the front door.

I hadn't even thought about how Jack would be dealing with all this. What he'd be thinking, how he would be worrying. He'd messaged me a couple of times since I'd shown up unannounced at his office and I'd just blown him off.

Nervousness gave way to guilt. But marital guilt I could deal with. Even if this wasn't on the same level as forgetting to wash a shirt, or not asking about an important meeting.

This was about forgetting that Jack would be worried about me.

I took a breath at the door and then opened it, placing my keys on the hook near the entrance. Went inside, barely registering the silence.

There was a bang from the kitchen – what sounded like a plate crashing onto the floor – and it startled me. I paused in the hallway and glanced upstairs, expecting to see at least Olivia come onto the landing as she heard me come home.

No one came.

I moved swiftly down the hallway and into the kitchen and saw Jack bending down, picking up the pieces of broken plate.

'Jack, are you okay?'

I heard him mutter something under his breath, but he didn't turn around. Just continued on, placing each piece he picked up on the counter above him.

'Where are the kids?'

'Stephanie has them.'

His voice was cold, unlike him. I moved towards him, as he stood up fully and leaned against the counter. He still hadn't turned to look at me and I hesitated as I reached him.

'What do you mean?'

Finally, he turned to me and his expression was one I hadn't seen in a long time. Dark, foreboding, shadowed.

'Where did you go today? Before coming to see me? I know you wouldn't have just turned up to my office for no reason.'

I took too long to answer. My mouth hung open, as I considered lying to him. Again. I couldn't do it. 'I was trying to find her.'

'And?'

I shook my head. 'Dead end, I think. The address she gave to the practice was empty. A neighbour told me there was someone there last year, but it could have been anyone.'

Jack fixed me with a stare, but his eyes changed a little. He was searching my face, as if it was something alien to him. 'Sara, I need you to tell me the truth.'

'I am telling you the truth,' I snapped back, almost on instinct. 'I don't know who she is, but I'm going to find out.'

'I sent the kids with Stephanie,' Jack said, turning his back on me. 'I think we need to have a long talk about what we do here. I left work early, because I need you to let me help you. So, we're going to sit down and work our way through this.'

He turned back to me, as a tear rolled down my cheek. Reached out and laid a hand on my shoulder, before bringing me towards his chest. I fell into it.

'We'll get through this. Together.'

I barely heard his words, as I felt safe for the first time in days.

2018

The wine that should have relaxed me was having the opposite effect. We were alone now. Late in the evening. The kids fast asleep in another room. My mum sitting downstairs. We had come up to my old bedroom, to finally be by ourselves. We had gone through two bottles between us already. That was on top of what we'd had at the wake.

And I knew then. I was going to tell him. The guilt that always lingered. I could spend my days not thinking about it, about what happened, but it was almost like a black cloud hanging over me. Sometimes I could ignore it, but it never went away.

Ten years.

I swallowed the last of my wine and looked at Jack. He stared back at me, daring me to get lost in his eyes. I looked away. 'I need to tell you something and I don't know how you're going to react. So, please, just let me get it all out before you say anything.'

Jack sat forward, placing a hand on my knee. I wanted to take it away, but I couldn't move.

'What's wrong?' Jack asked, a look of drunken concern across his face. 'Tell me.'

I couldn't back away now. I knew he might never look at me the same, but I had already opened the door up an inch and I couldn't close it again.

'Before we met, in 2005, I did something bad. Really bad. And I need to tell you about it.'

'Okay,' Jack said, his face scrunching up in confusion. 'Unless you're about to tell me you cheated on me, before we even met, I don't know why you look so scared.'

'Jack, please . . .'

'I'm sorry, go on.'

I breathed in deeply and then started talking. 'Remember when we talked about ex-partners? I told you about the guy I was with before we met and how it was a bad relationship?'

'Yeah, I didn't like the sound of him.'

'Right, but I never really told you the whole story.'

I could feel him tense up next to me. He took his hand away from my knee and swivelled to face me fully on the bed.

'I was young and I guess not that experienced. When I met him, I thought he was the one. I know that's not true now, of course, but I just fell head over heels for this guy. I mean, it was ridiculous. We barely knew each other and we thought we were in this endless love. It would never have lasted, of course, but I want you to know where my head was at. Anyway, there were times when I got a taste of what he was really like – he had a temper . . .'

'Right . . .'

'Wait, Jack, please. It was never directed at me. He never laid a finger on me. But it was always there, just under the surface. If someone looked at him wrong, he wouldn't just walk away. If there was an argument, he would be the one involved, front and centre. It was like he had all this violence inside him, just barely being kept from pouring out of him. We'd be in a pub, or just out on the street, and I could see him scanning the place all the time. Looking for a reason, almost, to take against someone. Like a coiled spring.'

I stopped for a second, wondering whether I should be totally honest. Knowing I had to be.

'The thing is – it excited me. It made me feel safe. I don't know why. I can't explain it now. But back then, all I could think about *was him and how he made me feel. I would follow him into anything. And eventually I did.'*

I was feeling a little nauseated, but wasn't sure if that was from the wine or not. Jack stared back at me, not saying a word. Not interrupting.

'One night, there was a young lad in a pub. About eighteen, nineteen. We were with a group of friends, and this lad was quite obviously looking over at us. Well, at me. He kept trying to catch my eye, grinning, raising his eyebrows every time he looked over. I don't know why he zeroed in on me, but I knew I didn't like it. Dan had his back to him, so had no idea this was happening and it wasn't like I had made it obvious I was with him. An hour or two went by and I got up to go to the bathroom. This guy, he was standing in the corridor that led to the toilets, right? Just leaning against the wall. He spotted me and I could tell by the way he was moving that he'd had too much to drink. When he leaned over me, I could smell stale lager and cigarettes. I can still smell them now.

'I tried to push past him, but he put his hand on my waist. Drew me to him, and his hand went lower. He said something in my ear. I didn't understand it, but I knew what he wanted. I jumped away from him, but one of the other girls we were out with came behind us and saw me shouting at him not to touch me.'

'Disgusting . . .'

'She made it into a scene. I just wanted to leave it, but before long, both groups were shouting at each other, and Dan was there. Heard it all. He flipped out.'

I could feel my chest, my heart, beating wildly. 'We waited for him to leave the pub. Dan wouldn't leave without seeing him. Maybe if he hadn't been alone, it would have been okay. Only, he walked past where we parked up and he was stumbling all over the place. I found out later that his mates had sent him home alone, no one even cared enough to make sure he got back safe. Before I knew what happened,

Dan was out of the car. He didn't even wait – he just attacked him. The lad went down and . . .'

I couldn't say the next part. Jack reached across to me, wiping a tear from my cheek.

'I didn't know,' I said, my voice strangled by emotion. 'I thought it was nothing, but then he was just lying there, not breathing. He'd hit the concrete floor and something had shattered inside his head, I guess, looking back now. I didn't know at that moment. I tried to find a pulse, tried to see if he was breathing, but I was panicking. I didn't know what to do. I was scared.'

Jack was next to me now, his arms around me, holding me close. 'It's okay, it's all okay now.'

'It's not though,' I said, my voice louder than it should have been. 'Because we should have told someone . . . should have tried to get help. Maybe they could have brought him back.'

Jack pulled away from me slightly. Looked down at me. 'What did you do?'

'We . . . I can't believe we did this . . .'

'What?'

'We buried him. We didn't tell anyone about it. Didn't call the police, didn't call for an ambulance. Nothing. Dan told me why we couldn't. How we'd be charged with murder, that because we waited for him it would be so much worse. Basically made me so frightened to do anything other than what he said. I wasn't thinking straight, so I just went along with it. And now, every day, I wish I hadn't. I should have stopped and thought about what we were doing, but he was so manic, so out of control, I was scared.'

'What happened next?'

'We took him to a place in the woods, where we knew he wouldn't be found easily. We dug a hole – so deep – all through the night. It took hours. Both of us. And then we left him.'

I couldn't talk any more. My throat burned with the effort. I collapsed, waiting for the inevitable.

I waited for Jack to stand up, to start shouting. To call the police, to tell them what I'd done.

Instead, he held me, as my body shook uncontrollably, tears cascading down my face until I was nothing but a puddle.

'It's okay,' he kept repeating, over and over, even though I knew it couldn't be. He waited for me to calm a little, before he held me in front of him.

'I'm not angry,' he said, sensing my fears somehow. 'I'm just so sad. For you, for the guy who Dan killed. I just wish I had been there . . .'

'How could you have . . .'

'I know, I know,' Jack said, waving away my question. 'It's just difficult for me to imagine a time when it wasn't us. When you weren't mine. I hear this and I think about you and what it must have been like. How scared you must have been, and I don't think of this like it was a "before-time". Like it existed before we were together. It was still the same woman who this happened to that I love now. And I just wish I could have been there to help you.'

I wanted to feel relief. I wanted to feel safe. Only I was awash with guilt at reliving that night.

'We're going to be fine,' Jack continued, bringing my head to his chest. 'It's done. It was a mistake, but it wasn't yours. He did it. Not you. Who knows what he would have done if you'd called the cops or something. You might not be sitting here right now. It wasn't your fault. I know being back here has probably brought all these memories back to you. It's going to be okay.'

I wanted to believe him. More than anything. There was still that ball in my stomach that knew it wasn't true. That I had to share the blame.

But, as he held me there, I knew that I loved Jack.

And he loved me.

24

When I told Jack what had happened that night with Dan, it was after we'd been together a long time and I was sure that he wouldn't leave me. Two children, a happy marriage . . . he couldn't walk away easily from that. That's how long it had taken for me to trust him. Not that I didn't trust him in so many other ways – it wasn't difficult to. He made me feel something different than I'd ever felt before.

'Remember when we first met?'

I smiled as the memory came back to me easily. Transported back in time almost fifteen years – to a time before we had pressure, children, exhaustion and worries.

I couldn't say a 'happier time' because you weren't allowed to do that if you were a parent, but the dirty little secret is that it was difficult not to think of it like that.

We were sitting at the table in the kitchen, opposite each other, but still close enough that I could see the lines in his face more pronounced than ever. The grey of his hair twinkling in the light above us, like the reflection of stars in a dark river. The light was fading outside, slowly, carefully almost. The house was still, silent. Only broken by the sound of Jack jabbing at the food on the plate in front of him.

I had offered to light a vanilla candle, to try and calm us both, but he'd scoffed at the idea.

'We should never have been in the same place at the same time, really, when you think about it.'

I glanced up at Jack, who finished his sentence and took another mouthful of spaghetti into his mouth. I looked for regret, but saw only wistfulness in his expression.

'We're from very different worlds,' I said, twirling food on my plate in the tines of my fork, but not attempting to eat. 'But, I guess sometimes things are meant to be.'

Jack hummed a response, but once he'd swallowed he looked back across the table at me.'What I mean is that fate is probably not real, but sometimes it's difficult to pretend it doesn't exist. I mean, I wasn't supposed to be there that night, was I? And neither were you.'

'I remember deciding at the very last minute that I was going to go,' Jack said, a wistful, nostalgic smile creeping across his expression. 'I was with Claire – do you remember her? – and we were just going to go into town instead, but we decided to drop in to that party first. We both didn't even know the person who was hosting the party. What was his name?'

'Oh, I can't remember now.'

'I remember you walking in and knowing straight away. I turned to my friend and said "I'm going to marry that girl".'

I felt the feeling wash over me, of happiness, of love. I'd heard the line so many times over the years – he'd even included it in his wedding vows – but it still didn't lose its lustre. 'Still made you work for it though, didn't I?'

'That you did,' Jack said, a brief closed-mouth smile appearing and then disappearing in an instant. 'That you did. I was prepared to do the work though. I didn't think a work placement of a year in London would have led to me finding my wife and the mother of my children, but there you go.'

'It could have been so different. I'm glad it wasn't.'

'Yet, if we hadn't met that night, then we wouldn't be where we are now. There was something about meeting then that changed everything.'

'True,' I replied, wondering what Jack was saying. What he was trying to get down to. 'I guess we should be thankful. Because of that night, we have JJ and Olivia. And we've been happy, right? I know things are tough now, but we're good?'

'Of course,' Jack said, but I didn't quite believe him. I knew what he was thinking – how the events of that week were having an effect on everything he said right now. 'I just want to talk about the night we met.'

'Okay,' I replied, when it became obvious that was the end of his sentence. I didn't know what he wanted to talk about. I didn't know where this was going.

'Do you think you should have told me then?'

'Told you what?' I said, knowing already what he was intimating. But, I wanted him to say it.

'What you did.'

'It wasn't like it was an STI or something,' I said, not thinking before speaking and hearing my tone come out a little harsher than I'd intended. I softened my voice. 'I didn't think I'd ever tell anyone about what happened. Never mind telling someone the first night I met them.'

'Of course,' Jack replied, reaching across the table and taking hold of my hand. 'I'm sorry, I didn't mean it that way.'

I knew he was lying now. He'd simply been talking from a position of hurt – tiredness, perhaps. It didn't mean it stung any less.

'I'm just trying to say,' Jack said, taking his hand back and returning to the meal in front of him. 'Maybe I could have done something sooner. While we were still over in England. Being so far away, and then this happening now, it makes it all so much more difficult to handle, right?'

'I guess.'

'So, if we'd confronted it while we were over there, maybe things would be different now.'

I knew he was talking about Dan.

I knew what he was suggesting.

'If it's him, then what's his game?' I said, placing my fork down quietly on my plate. I didn't have an appetite. I'd managed a few forkfuls before giving up on the idea. My stomach was still doing its tumbling routine. 'I don't know what he gets out of sending someone to see me? And then not even asking for anything. Or who this man and woman are who attacked me yesterday.'

'This *Ella* . . . she didn't even make it obvious that she was talking about you?'

'No, not in the slightest,' I replied, wishing I could speak to her again. Wishing I could make sure. 'She came in, told her story and then left as quickly as she'd arrived. Like she was scared to talk any more.'

'Then, maybe we're getting ahead of ourselves and there's nothing to it.'

I could see his mind whirring until it landed right.

'But then, that doesn't explain the two people showing up to your office.'

'Yeah,' I said, searching Jack's face for any sign that he blamed me for this. For the situation I'd placed our family in. I knew it was my fault, but I wasn't sure I could handle the idea of Jack hating me for it. 'She was talking about me. I just don't know why or what they're getting out of this.'

'They're trying to scare us.'

I let the idea roll around in my head for a few moments and decided it made sense. 'They're putting us on edge, so that when they do ask for what they want, we'll be too frightened to say no.'

'Exactly.'

'What do we do then? I don't want to wait around for that to happen. Is there something we can do to get ahead of them?'

Jack had been twirling spaghetti absentmindedly on his fork long enough for it to start disintegrating on the plate. He pushed it away. 'I have no idea what to do. That's my answer. This is all happening at the worst time, Sara.'

'I didn't exactly plan for it to happen at all.'

'I know that, but it doesn't help any. It has to be him. There is no other explanation.'

Dan.

I knew Jack was right. The only other person who could possibly have told Ella our story was him. 'I just don't think he would tell anyone – doesn't it affect him too? If people find out what he did, then it's him who gets it worst.'

'Then, who else knows?'

'Other than the two of us?'

I left the question hanging there, waiting to see anything from Jack. Any glimmer of a hesitation. Any note of fear.

There was nothing. He held my gaze until I finally backed down.

'I would never tell a soul, Sara,' he said, standing up and coming over to me. He placed his hands on mine and then bent down to his haunches until he was in my eyeline. 'You trusted me, right? I would never break that trust. Not for anything. It would destroy us, our family, I could never do anything like that.'

'I know . . .' I began, but the words caught in my throat. For a second, I had doubted him. I don't know why. He had never given me a single reason to do so. 'I'm just . . . I'm scared, Jack. I don't know what to do. I don't know how to get out of this. If she comes back . . .'

'*If* she comes back,' Jack said, interrupting me before I had chance to go on. His hands moved up my arms and drew me to him. 'It's going to be okay. We can get through this together. Just talk to me, okay? Tell me what you're going to do, before you go off on your own. I don't want you thinking I am going to let you go out and face this alone. We're in this together, okay?'

I nodded, because I couldn't do anything else. I couldn't speak. I couldn't make a sound, because it would all come out – all the fear, all the emotion I had been holding back for the past two days.

It would spill from me like an endless cascade of blood from a dying man.

'If they want money, we can get it,' Jack said, a finality to his tone. 'I know we still owe my parents, but we can get more.'

'Jack . . .'

'No, this is important. I just wish work was going a little better. We wouldn't have this problem.'

'Still issues with the last quarter?'

Jack waved a hand dismissively. 'Just some people getting a little worried. They shouldn't. I'll make it right eventually. We only have to wait. This time next year, everything will be great. We'll be more than comfortable.'

'Okay, Del Boy.'

Jack looked at me, a question mark for an expression. I shook my head, laughing quietly to myself. 'Don't worry, just another Britishism that you don't need to know.'

'We're going to get through this,' Jack said, then he held me tighter, until I couldn't take it any more and he sensed the need to let me go.

We didn't go far.

25

A decade in. Years of me hiding my story from him.

I had wanted to tell him sooner, but it had never felt like the right time to confess something like that. How do you tell someone you were part of the murder of a man? How do you tell the love of your life that you weren't the woman he thought you were?

How do you risk everything and hope it won't be the end?

There was no big plan. I hadn't marked a date on the calendar as being the time I would tell him everything.

It had just happened.

We had been together just over ten years at that point. JJ was six years old, about to turn seven. His mother had been delighted when we told her that I wasn't pregnant before getting hitched. I think she'd always suspected that would be the reason we would finally get married. She hadn't trusted me.

I'd known there was an element of suspicion from his family from the moment we'd met. Jack had always batted away my worries, my nervousness around them.

'They love you!'

Yeah, right. I was the English broad who had come back with him from his work placement in London. Just arrived on a plane and never gone home. Those first few years had been difficult, Jack working all the hours he could in order to continue his rise through the ranks.

The million-dollar house was a new development. Before that, we'd had an apartment that wasn't a world away from where Ella had said she lived. We'd moved on to Westport and its opulence and maybe that was all it was.

Jealousy. That I had something I shouldn't have.

I knew being back in England for my father's funeral had been the reason I'd told him then. I couldn't remember why I'd finally given in, though. Why I'd finally decided it was time. No warning. No long discussion that led to it.

I just recall the overwhelming feeling that I had to get it off my chest finally – as if it were a weight that needed to be unloaded. One that was becoming heavier every single day I kept quiet.

'I need to tell you something and I don't know how you're going to react. So, please, just let me get it all out before you say anything.'

I'd known that he would think I was going to confess to cheating on him. That was every married person's fear when a sentence began with those words. His complexion had whitened, the colour draining from his face. His forehead springing a sheen of sweat. I could feel him shaking a little as he sat down on the sofa next to me.

It was the worst night of my life.

It was the best night of my life.

To be seen, finally, by someone for what I was . . . for everything I had done, everything I had been party to. It was a burden that perhaps I didn't deserve to share with anyone else, but that didn't mean I wasn't glad to.

Wasn't relieved to.

I told him everything that happened that night. My story. He had asked in the past about ex-boyfriends, just as I had asked him about his past relationships. Those normal conversations you would have at the beginning of a relationship. Late at night, when you could stay awake past eleven, because you didn't need as much sleep for some reason.

He'd been in a few relationships – nothing serious. I was the first woman he'd seen a future with. I told him the same went right back at him.

I had mentioned Dan in passing, unable to give him anything but a cursory mention, for fear of giving anything away.

When I'd him the full truth of the two of us – how close we'd actually been and what we'd done together – he hadn't done any of the things I'd worried about. Instead, he'd held me tight and told me it was all going to be okay. That I had been put into an impossible position and done the only thing I could have.

He'd said all the right things and made me feel a fleeting moment of guiltlessness.

Jack didn't know that was how my thought process had gone, of course. We hadn't mentioned it more than a couple of times since then. We had continued to bring up our children. We'd had people over for parties, we'd made love.

We had been a happy little family.

Then, Ella came along and everything changed.

Only Jack could make me feel that lack of guilt momentarily again.

We lay in bed, me nestled into the crook of his arm, as he stared up at the ceiling. Only the sound of our breathing disturbed the silence – a small shaft of light permeating from the hallway outside our bedroom.

'I wish we could stay here forever,' I said, my hand tracing patterns on Jack's bare chest. 'This is my favourite place to be. Favourite time.'

I felt him murmur an agreement, before he shifted and drew himself up on the bed. I lay on the empty space beside him for a moment, before pulling myself upright.

'We can't just wait for the next thing to happen,' Jack said, swinging his legs from beneath the bedclothes and starting to get dressed. 'We need to do something.'

'That's what I was trying to do today,' I replied, covering myself up with the bedsheet as I watched him move methodically through his redressing. 'I don't know what else we can do.'

'I'm going to make a few calls.'

I tilted my head, as he lifted himself from the bed and walked into the ensuite. 'Who to?' I called out, but there was only silence in return.

I was confused for a moment, then I realised who he might mean. I got out of bed and moved towards the bathroom. I didn't knock, pushing my way through the closed door. Jack was leaning against the bathroom sink. Staring into the mirror above. I sat down on the toilet and waited.

'They'll be able to help us.'

I shook my head. 'No, Jack, please . . .'

'We don't have to tell them everything,' Jack said, turning to me finally. 'Just a basic outline. Something like, you were caught up in something that you don't want to revisit back in England and now someone is trying to blackmail you. Maybe. We're not sure. We just need to find this girl and work out what she wants.'

He was talking about his parents – over in their palatial home in Greenwich, with enough money that people went to see them for help and never the other way around. 'Jack, your mum already thinks I'm not worthy of you. Stephanie too. This is only going to make things worse.'

'That's not true . . .'

I gave him a look. 'You know it's true. Please, there has to be something else we can do.'

'If you have a better idea of how to find a ghost?'

I hesitated, trying to think of something, anything. Failed. 'She hasn't even asked for anything yet. She doesn't have any evidence, how could she? Maybe it's all just a coincidence. Can we wait first, before we do anything we can't take back?'

Jack stared back at me for a few seconds, before turning back to the sink. He washed his hands and dried them on the towel next to him. I could hear my heart beat in the silence, wary of the thud that seemed to fill the small space between us.

'I'll wait until the end of tomorrow. But that's it. I have to protect us, Sara. And they can help us. They can hire someone – a private detective or something – who can look into who these people are. They could get someone who might protect our family. Just please, accept it. Tomorrow, no later.'

I nodded eagerly, standing up and taking Jack in my arms. I felt suddenly exposed – realising I was still naked while Jack was fully clothed. I felt his hands on my back and closed my eyes.

Years ago, his hands might have wandered and we would have gone for a second round. Now, he let me go and moved past me, leaving me in the bathroom alone.

Age gets to us all.

*

Stephanie came back an hour later. Olivia with her eyes half closed, JJ shoulders slumped – probably annoyed he'd lost valuable gaming time, or YouTube time, or whatever else he could do that wasn't productive in the slightest.

I got Olivia into bed, as JJ complained about not having any time to do his homework. Wanting extra time before bed, the usual kid moans.

It was a joy to hear normality.

It took me half an hour to deal with the two of them – Olivia fast asleep and full of whatever healthy food Stephanie had managed to get them to eat, JJ sitting at his computer, pretending to do homework for the next twenty minutes he'd managed to haggle from me.

I went downstairs and found Stephanie in the kitchen.

'Where's Jack?' I asked, trying to keep my tone light, soft.

'Working, as usual. Poor man can't ever have a moment to himself.'

I know the feeling, I thought, but didn't say aloud. I'd long since discovered that it was pointless voicing those kind of ideas around Stephanie. 'Thanks for taking the kids for a few hours. It really helped us out.'

'Yeah, well, I'm glad to be able help out,' Stephanie said, running a finger over the kitchen counter and shaking her head at what she found. 'I mean it. I know we're not as close as we might have been if I'd been around more when they were younger, but I'm here for them now. Despite any limitations.'

I wasn't sure if she was joking. If she was trying to make me feel like the guilty party for not trying harder.

'I love spending time with those two,' Stephanie continued, picking up her bag and heading for the door. 'But, I wouldn't mind if things between the two of us were a bit easier too. Maybe we could meet up for coffee – away from the kids, from Jack. Just the two of us.'

'I'd like that,' I lied, struggling to think of anything I'd like worse. I was sure she was a nice person, but I couldn't stop the feeling that I was being patronised.

'Great,' Stephanie replied, a smile that could cut glass appearing in an instant. 'I can be there for you, Sara. I don't have many friends here any more. It would be nice if we both had someone we could lean on, right?'

I knew the feeling. I felt it more intentional on my part, though. Even so, I still felt like I was being played with. 'Sounds like a plan.'

'And you're sure about Jack? About what I asked in the restaurant the other day?'

I shook my head at the quick reversal in topic. 'He's fine.'

'Only, he seemed really stressed out earlier. Like something had happened.'

My fault. Again. But I wasn't about to admit that. 'Work, as usual.'

Stephanie narrowed her eyes and for the first time, I don't think she quite believed me. 'As long as that's all it is. I remember him being so laid back when we were younger. He looks like he has the weight of the world on his shoulders these days. I really wish he'd take some time off for himself. Anyway, we'll work something out later in the week, yeah? We can talk about this more then.'

'Okay,' I said, wanting her to leave now. Perhaps it was all in my head – maybe Stephanie was perfectly fine and I was the one who was the problem between us. Only I didn't think so. 'I'll see you tomorrow.'

'You will.'

And with that, she was gone. I went over to where I'd left my bag earlier and found my phone. Called up Facebook and switched accounts. Still no response from Dan.

I left the kitchen and went towards the office, seeing the light coming from beneath the door. I thought about knocking and telling Jack that there was absolutely no way we could ever say anything to his family about what was happening. My hand was raised when I heard an odd ping from the kitchen.

My phone. And I knew that there was only one app that made that noise.

Facebook Messenger.

26

I'd been expecting more. Better.

I thought he'd be more surprised. More worried. Instead, Dan had sent me a short reply.

I don't know what you're talking about. You have the wrong person.

I began typing out a reply, but everything sounded wrong. Accusatory, angry. I needed to take a breath. A little time.

Maybe half a glass of wine.

I got up and poured myself a generous helping from a half-empty bottle of white from the refrigerator and went back to the kitchen table. Straightened the fruit out in the bowl on top, which Jack must have moved back there after we'd eaten.

My phone screen had gone off in the meantime and I brought it back to life. Took a long swig from the glass and then began to type.

Glastonbury, 2004 – You wanted to watch Basement Jaxx on the Saturday night, and I wanted to watch Paul McCartney on the Pyramid stage. We argued and didn't see either one. It's me, Dan. Please. We need to talk.

I pressed send.

I finished the wine waiting for him to reply, then poured myself another glass when it didn't come.

There had to be more I could do. I thought about Ella. Who she could be, where she had come from.

I began trawling through the internet, calling up every single mention of Adam and his death. Looked at every photograph, seeing if there was even the possibility that she might be linked to his family in some way. A blonde girl in the background, young, but familiar. If Ella was around twenty-six or twenty-seven now, that would mean she'd be not even a teenager back then.

I didn't find anyone I could point to for sure. I switched back to Dan's Facebook friends list and scrolled through the names and photographs – went through each account and looked at everyone I could.

All that time, I had only the ticking of the clock on the wall behind me for company.

I didn't find Ella.

She seemed to have appeared from thin air, told her story, and then disappeared again. That couldn't be the case, surely?

She would be back. And I had to be ready for her this time.

It was eleven in the evening when I gave up waiting for Dan to reply. It would be four a.m. back in England, so I hadn't been expecting anything really, but I knew it would be a restless night. I switched back to my own account, then decided to take my phone upstairs with me just in case.

I'd never known Jack to go through my phone, but I'd never had anything to hide before.

He was still working in his office, so I left him there and went to bed alone. Again. Only this time I didn't go straight to sleep. I kept checking my phone – hoping that Dan would get back to me.

I stared at the ceiling for a long time. Going over that night again and again – seeing everything I'd done wrong. Everything

I could have done to save myself from living with the guilt I'd had for a decade and a half.

The sound from outside the room didn't register at first.

I was asleep. Not that I immediately knew that at first – I'd been lying awake for so long I wasn't aware I'd actually dropped off at some point. I came slowly to consciousness, unable to distinguish at first the difference between dreams and reality.

The second noise made it easier.

'Jack,' I said, my voice a whisper, lost in the darkness of the bedroom. I reached across and found an empty space beside me.

I heard something move downstairs and sat up in bed. I looked across at the clock on my nightstand and saw the time.

1:34 blinked back at me in red.

I shook my head, wondering why Jack was working this late. I swung my legs out of bed, now fully awake, and made my way over to the bathroom. Closed the door behind me and sat down. Washed my hands afterwards and opened the door back into the bedroom.

Jack was still not upstairs. I thought for a moment and then decided that he needed to come to bed. It wouldn't do him any good to be getting less sleep than he already was.

I moved downstairs and made my way up the hallway, shivering at the cold air that greeted me. I rubbed my hands over my bare arms, wishing I'd grabbed my gown before coming down.

I approached the office, seeing the light coming from underneath the door. Knocked softly and waited. When no answer came, I knocked a little louder and said his name.

'Jack.'

I moved my hand to the door handle and pushed it down, just as the air grew even colder around me.

There was a little resistance as the door caught on the floor before I opened it fully. I saw Jack in his chair, sitting back, his hands interlocked behind his head. His eyes were closed and for a second, I thought he wasn't breathing.

Then, I saw his chest rise, and heard the slow rhythmic sound of his breath.

I almost sighed with relief.

I hesitated for a moment, considered leaving him there to wake by himself, before realising how uncomfortable he must be. The computer in front of him was casting a glow on his pale skin. I took a step towards him, when I heard a noise behind me.

It was coming from the kitchen.

The first mistake was turning around. The second was not waking up Jack.

I moved back into the hallway, the light from the office disappearing quickly. I blinked, my eyes adjusting to the dark.

It was coming from the kitchen. I didn't even consider what it might be. I didn't think at all. I was already moving, as if my body was betraying me in real time. Doing things I never wanted it to.

I could feel a breeze stronger now, goosebumps crawling over my skin. The hairs on the back of my neck rising, sensing something my mind couldn't.

The back door was open.

Outside, I could hear a wind chime clinking in the darkness. It was coming from the Weavers' house next door.

I didn't think it was anything to worry about. I didn't think it was something I should be scared of – I just assumed Jack hadn't closed the door properly. I shook my head and crossed the kitchen floor, reaching the back door and closing it softly. It had obviously not caught the latch and had blown open in the wind was all that I was thinking.

A mistake, of course. I'd like to say that it was because I was still half asleep. Only it wasn't just that.

I was ignoring a voice inside my head, the whole time I was walking around the ground floor of my home.

My home. Where it was safe, where no harm could be done to me.

Where I could be sound in the knowledge that everything was going to be okay.

I still felt that way right up until I heard a scrape on the floor behind me and a shadow fell over me.

A sudden shift in the atmosphere around me. A thickening, a presence.

I was turning as the first hand landed on me. The second one struck my arm, as I raised it in defence, but I was already falling to the ground. The world became a blur of movement, of confusion. I could see two boots directly in my eyeline, standing next to me. I heard a shout, before hands gripped me in the armpits and I was being dragged across the kitchen floor.

Thrown down to the ground with a crash, and I curled into the foetal position, waiting for another blow to land. Only it didn't come.

Not then. Not straight away.

I heard a whispered voice, but couldn't decipher any words. I wanted to call out for Jack, but something had crawled up my body and closed off my throat. Nothing but a squeak came out.

There were two of them, was all I could think of in that moment. Two people in my kitchen, and I didn't know why.

My head hurt from hitting the floor, the same place I'd been hit the day before. It had all happened so fast, as if it wasn't really happening at all. For a moment, I thought maybe it was a dream.

But I could smell them.

The scent of a stranger. In my house. Standing over me.

'Stay down.'

I froze. My body shut down, as those two words came out from the darkness above me. A man's voice, filled with violence.

I couldn't move.

The clock ticking on the wall seemed to grow louder, as I waited for the next thing to happen. I knew it would be coming. I knew I would finally get to feel what Adam had felt on that night years earlier.

If I didn't do something, I was going to die there, in my own kitchen.

I waited for it.

27

There was nothing but black.

Inside me, outside me. I could think of nothing other than what was going to happen to me next. How they would do it. Would it be quick, would it be slow. Torturous. Merciful.

In the silence, my thoughts seemed like a cacophony of noise.

I tried to get to my feet, on instinct more than anything else, but something pushed against my back and I hit the ground again. The air sucked out of me, as my arm was tangled up beneath me, driving into my stomach.

'Stay down.'

It was the only two words I'd heard him say, but the second time it sounded more desperate.

My head was spinning as the floor began to blur, but still I tried to get up. It didn't matter to me that I couldn't see straight. That I could already feel blood dripping from a head wound.

I was thinking about JJ and Olivia.

I was thinking about them and the two people in my house. And what could happen if they heard a commotion and came out of their bedrooms. What could happen if they stood at the top of the stairs and those two saw them.

They were my children and they were in danger.

The scream came from somewhere I'd never known was inside me. At first, I wasn't even aware it was coming from me – I almost winced at the sound of it, before feeling the rattle in my chest and the edge of the chair my hand had fallen on.

I was getting to my feet, a roar of anger following me.

I couldn't even see them properly, but I didn't care. I was still screaming and grabbing hold of anything that wasn't nailed down beside me. I didn't look to see where I'd thrown the candle holder, the chair, the remote control – I was simply making as much chaos as I could.

Jack had to hear this. Call 911 and get help. Come to fight with me.

'What the . . .'

I heard the words through the echoes of my screams. Then, a grunt, as something finally connected. I could only see their shadowy outlines in front of me – one in the doorway, the other holding onto their head, braced against the kitchen counter.

'Grab hold of her,' I heard a woman's voice hiss.

I roared again, moving behind the kitchen table and picking up a chair, as if I were about to tame a lion.

'Get away from me,' I said, the words hurting my throat as I growled them out. 'Get out of my house.'

I jabbed the chair out in front of me, backing into the corner of the room. I wanted their full attention on me and I think I was succeeding in that.

The guy in the doorway took a step towards me, as the woman at the far end of the kitchen swore under her breath.

'I don't care who you are, just leave,' I said, moving around the table, as the man came closer. He wasn't a shadow any more – now I could see him a little clearer. Or what there was of him. At first, I thought there was something wrong with his face, but then I realised he was wearing a mask.

He was a little over six feet tall, broadshouldered and looking like it would take more than a chair to knock him to the ground.

It was the pair from my office the previous day. As if it could have been anyone else.

He had his hands out in front of him and I looked at the distance between us.

I had to wait a little longer.

'Put the chair down, lady.'

This wasn't a simple home invasion. This wasn't two drugged-up people, looking for a quick burglary. Maybe a TV they could sell on.

They were here for a reason.

I waited until I could almost hear his breathing, before I threw the chair to the side of him, purposely missing. His head followed it for a brief moment and in that split second, I picked up the horrible horse ornament that I hated so much and swung it towards the man's head.

I missed, but it connected with his shoulder and then fell from my hand. I felt the shockwave of impact travel up my arm like pins and needles.

There was a burst of silence, before he cried out – stumbling backwards and crashing onto the table.

I was already moving. I ran to the open doorway, my feet sliding on the hardwood floor. I made it to the bottom of the stairs, just as Jack emerged finally from the office.

'Sara . . .'

I was already moving up the stairs, taking them two at a time, making it up onto the landing above and positioning myself between JJ and Olivia's bedroom doors. I looked around for another weapon, but I heard Jack shout from downstairs instead.

'What the hell is going on?'

I didn't answer. I was too busy looking for something to protect my kids with.

Jack was on his own.

He would be okay with that, I thought, my mind still racing as fast as my heartbeat was. He'd understand. The kids came first.

I felt pain in my arm, my shoulder, but I was ignoring it.

I don't know how long I was standing there before I heard footsteps on the stairs.

'Don't come any closer, or I'll kill you.'

I wasn't sure if they believed me, but I did, and that was enough. If they came near my children, I was going feral. That was all that was in my mind. On a sideboard sitting on the landing, was a glass photocube. It weighed heavy in my hand, as I grabbed it and crouched, breathing hard, waiting for them to come. And it wasn't going to be pretty.

'Sara?'

It was Jack's voice, but for a brief moment I didn't believe it was actually him. Then his face appeared in the darkness as he reached the top of the stairs.

'Jack, get out of the way,' I hissed towards him, as if he were a nuisance. As if he was in the way of what I needed to do. 'They're coming.'

'Who is? What's going on?'

'The man and woman,' I said, annoyed at his questions. 'They're in the kitchen.'

'Not any more,' Jack replied, getting closer to me now. 'It's just a mess down there.'

I shook my head. 'They'll be back. They're coming for me. I've got to stop them.'

Jack finally came onto the landing proper and approached me as if I were a wild animal, holding his hand out in front of him. He slowed a little and then took what I was holding from my hand and wrapped his arms around me. I heard it thud on the ground, as I buried my head into his chest.

'What happened, Sara?'

'They came after me. I hit one of them, hard in the shoulder, otherwise he was going to grab me. Kill me, probably. They must still be down there.'

'There's no one down there now,' Jack said, keeping tight hold of me. 'The doors are locked. No one can get in.'

'Why are they doing this?'

'Shh, it's okay, it's all over now.'

I wanted to believe him, but I knew he didn't realise the truth of it. That this was far from over.

My body began to shake, as the adrenaline began to quell inside me. I pulled away from Jack and gripped his arm. 'Where were you? Why didn't you come sooner?'

'I was asleep, I'm sorry.' He tried to pull me towards him again, but I didn't let him. I couldn't stand there, I couldn't be calmed down by an embrace. I looked down and saw what was in his hand. I grabbed it from him before he had chance to grip it tighter.

'I need to make sure they're gone,' I said, making towards the top of the stairs before stopping and going into our bedroom. The gun in my hand felt comfortable. A weight I wanted to carry.

'What are you doing?' Jack said, as he followed me in. 'Let me take that back from you. It's not safe.'

I grabbed hold of my phone and tried to unlock it. My hands were shaking too hard. 'I need to call the police, Jack. I can't believe you haven't already . . .'

'Sara, you can't do that, remember?'

I barely heard him, managing to finally unlock my phone and then staring at the blurred screen in my hand. My finger hovered over the call button, before I took in what he'd said.

'It was them,' I said, voicing what I'd already known. 'Why would they come here?'

'I don't know,' Jack replied, shaking his head, coming towards me. 'But they've gone now.'

'We have to get out of here. We need to get the kids somewhere safe.'

'Are you sure it was two people in our house?'

My head shot up. I could sense the tone underlying his words. 'It's not my fault that you slept through it, Jack.'

'I'm just saying, it sounds like there must have been a hell of a racket, but I didn't hear a thing until you were running back through the house. I went into the kitchen and there was no one there.'

'Are you calling me a liar?'

Jack reeled from that. 'Of course not.'

'They came into our house. I'm not making it up.'

'Okay, okay,' Jack said, but I wasn't sure I believed him. I could hear the tone of his voice – his desire to just have the conversation be over.

'I need to check for myself.'

I heard Olivia's voice call out as I pushed past him but I wasn't concentrating. I glanced back, seeing Jack disappear into her room as I made my way downstairs. I paused in the hallway, listening for any sound that didn't belong. The house was still now – no whispers in the darkness. I switched on the light in the hallway and everything changed. No longer were there shadows crawling from every corner. No hidden places for someone to hide. I did the same for the kitchen, before stepping inside.

The back door was closed, no breeze flowing through the house. I could see two chairs upturned on the floor. I moved slowly, catching sight of the horse ornament broken in a few pieces on the other side of the table. I was staring at the back door, reaching out and trying the handle with my free hand. It didn't budge.

'See, we're safe now.'

I wasn't listening. I pushed past Jack and towards the front door. Unlocked it and went outside, my finger resting against the trigger of the gun in my hand.

It was cold. Still. I raced into the street, looking left and right, hoping to see a car pulling away. Not really knowing what I was going to do if I did see something, but not really caring.

The street was empty.

'Where are you? Come out and face me.'

My voice was a scream. My throat burned with the effort, as it reverberated around the darkened houses and yards. I could feel sweat running down the back of my neck.

'I'm here. Waiting for you. Show yourselves.'

Still nothing. Not a sound, not a crunch of gravel.

I saw a light go on to my right and spun towards it, the gun in my hand levelled in its direction. My finger resting on the trigger.

'Come out! I can see you!'

I was breathing hard, stepping towards the light slowly, ready to fire at the slightest provocation. In the distance, I saw headlights come on and heard a car engine turn over. I squinted in the darkness and swore I could see her behind the wheel.

Ella. Staring back at me. A grin on her face, ready to slam her foot down and wipe me out. Mouthing words soundlessly towards me.

'I'm coming for you.'

But I couldn't see any of those things. Only the lights.

'What the hell . . .'

I heard the voice and almost squeezed the trigger. My aim wouldn't have been great, but I still would have managed to at least scare the hell out of my neighbour.

I suddenly realised it was Burt Johnstone standing at his door, looking out towards me pointing a gun in his direction. Well, he had been. Now, he'd scurried back into the house.

I felt a hand on my shoulder and I almost screamed in surprise, before turning my hand around, just as Jack took it in his own and removed the gun from it in a single movement.

'Sara, what are you doing?'

I pointed towards the end of the street, where I'd seen the headlights, but they'd gone now. There was only darkness.

It didn't take long until the sirens started up in the distance.

28

They sat in their car, drinking what Colby hoped was decaf coffee. He was never sure if that was the case – how would you know?

'That was a trainwreck.'

Colby waited for Penny to disagree, but only got silence in return. He took another sip of coffee and turned the radio down.

'We should have taken her down there and then,' Colby said, feeling the anger, the embarrassment return. 'She deserved it for that little display. My shoulder is killing me.'

'Yeah, well my ears are still ringing.'

'I'm sorry about that,' Colby said, earning a frown from Penny. 'I don't like it when you get hurt.'

'I'm a big girl, Col . . .'

'Don't matter. Anyway, we got the cars, that's something.'

'I got one in the kitchen, before she came in.'

'You did? I didn't even see it.'

'Yeah,' Penny said, her tone changing a little. Playfulness creeping in. 'Well, I thought it was a good idea to move quick, you know? Given it was the middle of the night and we'd made too much noise getting inside.'

'Did you hide it properly?'

'I put it under the table. I don't think they'll find it. I made sure the table was upright before we left, just to make sure it wouldn't be found.'

'Well, I don't know how well those things work, but hopefully well enough for the boss in this situation.'

Colby didn't want to have to explain that they had made quite the scene at the house. That there would now be no doubt in Sara's mind that she was under threat. He wasn't sure how she was going to react to that.

'I'll call her in a few hours,' Colby said, finishing off his coffee, and watched as a homeless guy shuffled his way across the intersection. Glad of the fact he wasn't in his position. He had a bed for what was left of the night at least.

'The ones in the cars will work okay, I guess?'

Colby turned to Penny. 'Should do. Not that they'll be useful, I would say. Who talks all that much in the car? Just feels like she wanted to go back in time and hear what they had to say yesterday.'

'Why?'

Colby shrugged. 'Who knows. I'm not going to try and work out what her deal is about any of this. You think we should push for more answers from her?'

'I don't think we'd like what she has to say. The bottom line is this – we owe her a favour, so we're not about to walk away. And she's paying us as well.'

'You're not worried about where that money might be coming from?'

'If she'd asked us to do it for free, we'd have been ready to do it.'

'Maybe,' Colby said, not sure that would be the case. 'When we started doing what we do, didn't we have a list of rules?'

'Yeah, but what does that matter, really? It's not like we're going to be in trouble for not following them. We'd be in trouble for way more than that.'

'I guess.'

'And what is it that we do exactly? I don't think we could go and find a set of rules for it anywhere out there. It's not like it's a normal line of work.'

'You got that right.'

Colby sighed, wishing not for the first time that it was a normal line of work that they did. Knowing he could never see himself in a suit, in an office, working a nine-to-five job.

Some people weren't cut out for it.

'Still,' Penny said, finally relenting a little. 'It's not like I could care less about all of this. We're professionals – that's why we've been able to do this kind of thing without ending up in jail. Let's keep our wits about us through this.'

'We'll just continue doing as we're told and get this over and done with. That's the way forward. It's the only we get paid.'

'I guess so.'

'Some home, am I right?'

'Nicest one I've been in for a long time,' Penny replied, glancing across at Colby with a raised eyebrow. 'Makes you wonder how they've managed to get themselves in the sort of position they have.'

'It does,' Colby said, thinking it over. 'I mean, the house isn't so expensive that they could be into serious stuff. Not cheap enough that they're living hand to mouth. Just . . . comfortable, right? Pool out back, nice kitchen, good artwork. Tasteful.'

'Wouldn't mind a place like that myself. One day.'

'I doubt your taste would be the same as theirs,' Colby said with a smirk. 'It'd be posters of the Kardashians and that drag race thing you watch.'

'Well, you've got to put your own spin on it, right?'

There was a smattering of rain on the windshield as Colby watched the homeless guy pause on the other side of the street, then pull his hood over his head.

'Yeah, well we could have it worse, I guess,' Colby said, his voice barely above a whisper, as he pulled the car away from the curb and made his way down the increasingly wet streets ahead. 'But we'll have that one day. I promise. I want to give you the world.'

'I know you do.'

He wasn't sure what they'd be asked to do next and that worried him. Colby already had a headache – probably the pain from something clouting him in the shoulder moving upwards. The thought of where this job would take him after that night was making it worse.

Sara was a fighter. That was never a good sign. Most people when confronted by two strangers in their house in the dead of night would have pissed their pants and crawled into a ball. Penny had caught her good and true and still she had risen to her feet. The roar that had come from within her was unlike anything he'd heard from a woman before.

The fact that she had then faced both of them down was not something he had been expecting.

'If we have to go back in there,' Colby said, seeing the motel lights up ahead and thinking about finally lying in a cold bed. 'Then we have to be more careful this time. She's not going anywhere without a fight. You ready for that?'

Penny hummed a response. 'Whatever it takes.'

Colby nodded, as he pulled into the parking lot outside their motel room and turned the car engine off. He sat there for a few more seconds as Penny got out and ran towards the motel-room door. Opened it up and went inside without looking around for Colby.

'Whatever it takes,' Colby said to himself, his words sounding empty in the silent confine of his car.

He didn't know what that meant any more. He didn't know what he wanted any more. It wasn't as if this was a normal job for them – they were only doing this to repay a favour. And given they didn't have the full details, it seemed like they might be going against a fair few of the ground rules they'd laid out for themselves when they started out.

That wasn't going to stop him from seeing this out, though.

More than anything, his curiosity had been piqued now.

He needed to know what happened at the end of all this. What happened to Sara, to Jack. To that family.

Two kids, barely old enough to understand the fragility of life.

Colby was worried that they were about to learn the lesson.

29

Ella sat in the car outside Sara's house. Sara and Jack's house. Their home. Children sound asleep in bed. Sara probably the same by now. Dreaming a guiltless sleep. Jack sitting in the kitchen, a gun on the table next to him.

She knew all of those things.

Still, she had never felt further away from them all.

It was just after six a.m., which meant she didn't have too much time before she'd have to move her car. She didn't want one of the neighbours becoming suspicious, parting those white shutters that seemed to adorn the rooms at the front of the houses. Looking out onto their quiet street and wondering who was sitting in that strange car. Maybe calling over their husband or wife to check.

She didn't need any questions.

Especially after she'd first turned back into the street a few hours earlier and found the cops sitting outside the house.

That had made her heart quicken a little. She'd never thought about how someone was supposed to look while driving past a cop car so as not to look guilty. Staring straight ahead at first, before deciding that would look too obvious. Staring at them too much maybe a little suspicious.

She'd driven around for a while, waiting for lights to appear behind her. They never came.

So she'd come back and listened to the conversation that was happening in the kitchen. The cops talking to them, Jack doing most of the answering. Sara trying to stay calm.

It had been fun. Almost as fun as watching Sara standing in the middle of the street, staring towards her in the car. There had been a moment when she'd wanted to floor it. Plough into the killer and be done with it all. End the game there and then.

But she wasn't like that. She wasn't like Sara. She wouldn't take her life. It wouldn't be as easy as that.

There was the faint sound of snoring coming from the speaker of her phone, as the microphone picked up Jack asleep at the kitchen table. Finally. He couldn't have been comfortable in there. Ella pictured him, slumped over the tabletop, his arms protecting his head from the surface. The gun next to him, waiting to be picked up by a curious child. Maybe turned over in their hands, a finger slipping round the trigger.

They deserved better parents. They deserved more.

That was something that made her stay in that car, watching the house – the thought of those two children, oblivious to what their parents were doing. What they were hiding.

They shouldn't have to live in ignorance.

Ella knew they spent most of their time in the kitchen anyway. She had been watching the house for a long time. Over a year, in fact.

Longer than she wished to think about.

She had been waiting for this moment for too long.

There was a sense of finality to this whole thing. Like a film that had gone on too long. You'd be checking the clock, to see how much longer you had to endure it, but you couldn't leave until you knew how it ended.

The story wasn't over, but she no longer wanted to wait to see it out.

That was how she felt most of the time now. Eager, impatient.

That was how mistakes were made.

Ella waited. For what, she couldn't say. There was no reason for her to be there. The bug under Sara's kitchen table was wirelessly transmitting everything it was capturing and uploading it to a secure site online. Ella could listen just as well at home.

It was because of a mistake.

When she'd been at Better Lives and they'd asked for an address, she had panicked. She had given them the Maple apartment one and knew that could be traced, despite her not having been there for months.

It was still lying empty now. But that was a mistake she shouldn't have made. Sure enough, she'd followed Sara there the previous day. Waited down the street, to see what she'd do.

Ella knew she'd spoken to a neighbour, but hadn't been able to get close enough to hear what was said.

A mistake. Not deadly, not yet, but enough that Ella didn't want to leave anything to chance again. She had planned too carefully up to that point to let it fall apart due to something as stupid as giving not only a real address, but one in which Ella had actually stayed. It was a stupid thing to do.

No more of that.

The plan would be different now.

Things had to move quicker. More quickly than Ella had envisioned, but it would be fine.

It was all going to work out.

Ella shifted into park and pulled away from the curb. Turned her radio up and sang along to Taylor Swift as if she felt every word.

It was going to be a good day, Ella thought.

And she felt much better by the time she pulled into the parking lot outside Sara's office and shut off the engine.

Much better.

★

Alex got into work ten minutes early. A new personal best for the year, given that the previous few months hadn't been exactly a lesson in punctuality.

She'd slept better than she had done in a while. At least five hours all in one go. Another personal best.

She was greeted with a smile from a beat cop she knew well. Just getting off the night shift, it seemed. Tom Cooper – a guy in his early thirties, who always went out of his way to say hello.

Alex was feeling okay. Not good. Not great. Just okay. But that was a marked rise from the norm. She knew why, of course, and wanted to thank Sara Edwards for it.

'Hey, Detective Garcia,' Tom said, as she got closer. 'How are you doing?'

'I'm good, Tom,' Alex replied, only lying a little. 'And call me Alex. For the fiftieth time.'

'Sorry,' Tom said, blushing a little. For the first time, she hoped he would ask her out. Again. She might feel like saying yes this time.

'How was the night shift?'

'You know how it is,' Tom replied, leaning against her desk, as she got behind it. Took off her jacket and placed it on the back of the chair.

'You don't have to remind me. The memory is still lingering.'

'Not bad for middle of the week,' Tom said, suppressing a yawn, making his eyes widen a little. 'Had a strange one halfway through our shift. Had to bring a woman in from Westport. Local PD asked for backup.'

'Really?' Alex replied, her ears pricking up. She always did like a good cop story. Even now. 'Short-handed?'

'You know how it is now. They've got an excuse ready-made all the time. Anyway, we went over and took the call.'

'So, why is it interesting?'

'It's up in Westport, you know, the wealthy part of town? Where the houses are never in foreclosure . . .'

'At least for now.'

'Yeah, right,' Tom said, not impatient. A sly smile playing across his face. 'Get this – a neighbour made the call. Said there was a crazy woman, screaming in the street, and he thought she might have had a gun. We get there and the street is dead. Quiet. Knock on this guy's door and he opens it like we might be the devil himself, about to take him down. All squirrelly and nervous. He started babbling about the crazy woman across the street, how she'd been screaming in the street and he'd thought she was waving a gun around. Thought he was a nutjob. Anyway, we go over to the woman's house and she answers, looking like she'd been on a coke binge for the past day and a half.'

'Go on,' Alex said, wondering where the story was going. Tom seemed to be telling her something that he knew wasn't all that interesting, but trying to make it more so, in order to what? Impress her? She wouldn't be too bothered about that.

'She lets us in and is all wired. Breathing hard, shaking, the lot. We're instantly on guard, but her husband is there. He goes into control mode. Tells us they'd had a break-in, that they were going to call it in, but then we showed up, so he decided to wait. It was strange, you know? He shows us the back door, which has quite clearly been smashed in, the kitchen area looked a mess, and there was broken stuff everywhere. Like there'd been a fight or something. We take statements, of course, and then ask about what the neighbour had told us. The woman, she's about to speak, but the husband cuts her off straight away. Starts telling us that they've had problems with him for years and that he's a liar. They have a gun in the house, but he swears it's locked away and they had no chance to get it out, and wouldn't go waving it around the place. They have kids, who are sleeping through all of this.'

'So, what did you do?'

'Not much we could do. We spoke to the neighbour again, but he couldn't be certain there was any gun, and it was quite obvious there was no threat anyway. What's weird is that this is all happening on this really upscale place, right? The guy, he's some financial bigwig, and the wife is a therapist or something.'

Alex was getting bored by that point, but that made her ears prick up. 'Westport, you said?'

'Yeah, up by Clinton Ave.'

Alex knew the place. She could be mistaken, of course, but she knew if she'd said the name of the street where her own therapist lived, Tom would be surprised that she knew.

Before she'd gone to Better Lives she'd looked into Sara Edwards. She knew where she lived, who with, everything. Not for any other reason than curiosity, but now, this was a coincidence and a half.

She managed to extricate herself away from Tom, before he told her the end of his story, but with a promise she would catch up with him again. Then, she went and read the report on what had happened the previous night.

Alex was left in two minds about what to do next. Whether to bring it up with Sara, or find a new therapist.

30

The office looked different that morning – darker, somehow. More foreboding than ever before.

The drive had been done in a daze. I probably shouldn't have got behind the wheel, but I was determined that the previous night's events weren't going to stop me living.

When the cops had arrived the night before, I had wanted to just give up. Tell them everything and get away from the house. Get *myself* away from there so everyone could be safe. Instead I'd let Jack do all the talking, then gone upstairs and crawled into bed. JJ and Olivia were blissfully unaware of anything untoward whatsoever. I envied the bliss of complete ignorance. Was grateful for it too, of course.

The last thing I needed was the two of them becoming fearful of people breaking into their home.

Jack had at least waited until I was up and preparing breakfast before leaving for work. I could see guilt written all over his face over the slice of toast he was eating slowly. Joylessly.

'Did you get any sleep?' I'd asked him.

He'd shrugged and given me a grunt.

I'd slept for the last hour before my alarm went off. I'd considered going downstairs and sitting with Jack during the night, but had never quite made it.

I couldn't sit with him. Hear him tell me everything was going to be okay. I knew it wasn't going to be.

I'd tried to soothe him somewhat, but he didn't seem in the mood for that. I guessed it was because he didn't want this to be happening any more than I did.

Another difficult conversation shelved for another day.

I braced myself. Breathed in and out slowly and then got out of my car, looking up at the office as if it was a beast to be dealt with.

'Sara.'

I jumped out of my skin. My purse went flying, scattering its contents across the ground, as I tried to get back in my car.

'Sara, it's me.'

I wasn't listening properly, so it was only when Alex placed a hand on my arm and I turned with my fist raised that I realised it was her.

'Woah, woah,' Alex said, holding up her hands in mock surrender. 'It's just me. Nothing to worry about.'

'Sorry,' I managed to stutter out. 'I just didn't hear you coming.'

'It's fine, I didn't mean to scare you.' Alex tilted her head and looked me over. 'Everything okay?'

I wanted to tell her. Confess to it all. I swallowed it down. 'Yes, just a rough night, that's all.'

'That's why I'm here, actually,' Alex said, bending down and starting to pick up the things that had fallen from my handbag. Purse. 'Here, let me help.'

'Thanks,' I said, watching her carefully as I bent down to join her. 'What about last night?'

'I heard you had a break-in?'

She must have seen the confusion in my face, as she instantly went into defence mode.

'Sorry, a cop buddy of mine told me about a call-out he had in the early hours and I worked out it was you. I'm sorry. I just wanted to check you were okay.'

We both stood up and I tucked my purse under my arm. Shook my head. 'Yeah, I guess we had an issue. Nothing to worry about.'

'Are you sure about that?'

'Maybe not,' I replied, with a joyless chuckle. 'It hasn't been the best of weeks.'

'I knew something wasn't right,' Alex said, leaning against my car. 'Listen, if there's anything I can do to help, just say it. I owe you.'

She may not have been able to see me for what I was, but Alex knew I was holding back. And I decided I could use this opportunity that had fallen at my feet by Alex checking up on me.

Trust is so important. Especially when people are telling me about the deepest parts of their lives. They're placing their faith in me to not use that information outside of my office. For discretion, for secrecy.

I was about to use those things to my advantage.

'I don't know, Alex,' I replied, the feeling of a horde of butterflies fluttering inside me. 'It's . . . it's all a little delicate.'

'Shoot.'

'Well, it's about another patient of mine,' I began, wondering if I could sell this story. Wondering if Alex would see through me in an instant. 'I don't want to betray any confidences, but there's things that have happened. I don't know if it's all connected, but I can't be sure. This patient . . . she's *troubled*. And now she's not showing up for any sessions. I'm worried about what she might do. Now, ordinarily, we'd go above board on this and go through the proper channels, only this is a different case altogether in this instance.'

'How so?'

'Well, she's told me some very concerning things about her home life. About certain aspects that have made it tricky to get her to stick to appointment times, schedules, that kind of thing. As you know, it's important that she can trust me. I'm worried that by going through official channels, she'll back away from treatment and end up in a far worse place. I don't want to go into what was said in our last appointment, because that's confidential, but I'm hoping you can read between the lines here.'

There was a period of silence before Alex made a low humming sound.

'I'm not sure about this,' she said, and I could hear in her voice that she was uncomfortable. I was losing her swiftly.

'I would never usually do this, but I'm fearful that something is stopping her coming in for sessions. Or, *someone*. And now, in the past couple of days, I've been attacked at work and at home. I think this patient is the reason.'

I was gambling. I was taking what little I knew about Alex's history and making a judgement call.

Bad relationship. Domestic violence in her past, I would suggest. Out of control, stuck in a pattern of trying to leave and being unable to. Coupled with domestic violence issue at her job.

I was gambling that she would subconsciously place herself in Ella's shoes and want to help.

I've never felt more guilty.

'You should tell the cops on your case about this . . .'

'I tried to,' I said, cutting across her before she had chance to cement herself in the narrative of being unable to help. I needed to do that before it grew larger. 'They looked at me like I was an idiot. I should never have said anything. I just . . . I just don't know what else to do.'

I could feel the churning of guilt in my stomach like a ton weight. It wouldn't leave me any time soon, I knew.

'I can help,' Alex said finally. 'What details do you know about her?'

I didn't breathe a sigh of relief exactly, but that weight became a little heavier. I told her Ella's name and the little information we held. A fake address, an approximate age. A couple of observations about where she might be from.

Nothing that concrete, I thought, saying it out loud. I doubted Ella was her real name. I was guessing at her age.

'I'll look into it,' Alex said, after writing down everything I'd said. 'Listen, maybe you should take some time off? I can wait for our next session. The last one made a huge difference.'

'I'm glad to hear it, but I'm okay. I'll see you Tuesday, as scheduled.'

She eyed me for a second, then nodded to herself. Left me standing in the parking lot, watching her leave.

That ball of guilt inside me growing larger and larger by the second.

31

I entered the building and steeled myself for the day ahead. I wasn't sure how I was going to deal with listening to other people's problems all day. I couldn't imagine not slipping and screaming in their selfish faces:

'You think you have problems?!'

I made my way up to reception, feeling a little better as soon as I saw Gina – she greeted me with a smile that I returned. I felt I was forcing myself, but I was so glad to see a friendly face, I didn't care.

That was, until I realised someone was sitting in the waiting area opposite. I caught sight of a flash of blonde hair and stopped breathing. My smile fell and I took hold of the reception counter as I felt the strength in my legs disappear.

'She's back,' Gina was saying, but it was as if she was miles away. I couldn't hear her properly as the blood rushed through my body.

'I've told her you'll see her first, as you don't have anyone until ten thirty. Hope that's okay. It's just, I know you've been worried about her.'

I managed to glance in Gina's direction and give her a nod. Her eyes narrowed as she took me in. I cleared my throat and the sounds of the office slowly returned.

'Yes, that's fine,' I said, praying the words that fell from my mouth sounded normal. Right. 'Thanks, Gina. Send her through in a couple of minutes. Let me get settled.'

Gina continued to stare for a few seconds, then she reached out and placed her hand on mine. 'Are you okay? You look a little pale.'

'I'm fine,' I said, trying another smile that this time hurt my cheeks. 'Bad night, that's all. Olivia had a nightmare. Had us up half the night.'

Gina rolled her eyes so hard, I was worried they'd never come back in place. 'Oh, I know that one. Give them a bit of attention and that's it for the night. She'll be regretting it now, all tired in school. I think they know what they're doing to us most of the time. Keeping us honest, right? Making sure we still care.'

'Yeah, I guess,' I said, barely listening. I was glancing over my shoulder, towards the waiting room. Hoping and not hoping to catch a glimpse of Ella inside. Wondering what I'd do if she caught my eye. 'I'll be in my office. Five minutes, okay?'

'Of course.'

I almost jogged towards my office, ignoring the other people on the way. Ignoring Phyllis, ignoring Vicky, all the other workers in the office. I unlocked my door, pushed it open and then closed it behind me. I shook my bag from my shoulder and then leaned against my desk.

I needed a plan.

I couldn't think of a single question. Not one that wouldn't involve me threatening her physically in some way.

Maybe that's what I should do? Simply push her up against the wall as soon as she walked in. Get my hands around her throat and tell her to get out of my life, or she'd never be seen again. There had to be family that would miss her. There had to be something she wanted to live for, right?

Not just to torment me.

I couldn't do that. I had to control myself. Or I would lose everything.

I sat down in my chair, leaving the notepad on my desk, out of reach. It was just going to be me and her.

The clock ticked on the wall, counting down the seconds. I tried not to join in.

There was a soft knock on the door, just as I was about to pass out from holding my breath. I closed my eyes briefly, then spoke.

'Come in.'

Then, she was there. In the doorway, looking down at the floor. Blonde hair, thin-figured. The bones poking through her hands, as if they were trying to escape. Red nail polish today, immaculately manicured. She was wearing an azure-blue dress that just caught her knees. It clung to her body for dear life. Scooped neckline, displaying a simple silver locket on a chain.

'Is this okay?'

I gripped the side of my chair to keep from screaming out. I nodded slowly, scared to speak.

I wished I could call Alex now. Or just the cops. Tell them I had someone threatening my life.

Only I had zero evidence of anything happening because of this woman. Simply my own guilt, my own actions.

I needed answers, and if Ella was brazen enough to come back to my office, I wasn't about to ruin it by screaming obscenities in her face.

She came in slowly, her bag almost falling from her shoulder as she did so. Closed the door softly behind her and then hesitated at the sofa before sitting down. She took up the same pose as three days previously – wrapping her arms around herself in protection.

Only this time I didn't buy the act as quickly as I had done. This time, I knew what she was trying to do.

I waited for her to speak.

Thirty seconds can feel like a lifetime, but she wasn't going to get the satisfaction.

'I didn't know where else to go.'

She was going for the same act then, I thought. She was going to keep pretending. That was fine with me, for as long as I could stand it. She had to know I wasn't buying what she was selling.

Or just didn't care.

'So you came here,' I said, unable to take my eyes off her. I caught a hint of her perfume as it floated across the space between us. I recognised the scent, but couldn't name it. Her shoes looked designer at first glance, but I could see the strap on one side was frayed. I wanted to catch her gaze, make her look me in the eye as she lied to me. 'Why?'

'I need help.'

'I can't disagree with you there.'

The atmosphere in the room was thick with tension, but looking at Ella, you wouldn't think so. She seemed tense, yes, but like a coiled spring ready to unravel at any moment. She was barely flustered by my presence. It was almost as if I could have been anyone sitting there – rather than the person she'd been tormenting for the past few days.

'What do you have to say, then?' I asked, wanting to hear the lies first, before I made my move.

Whatever my move was. I hadn't planned that far ahead. I was just hoping to get through the first few minutes without flying across the room and gripping the girl by the throat.

I couldn't do that, as much as I wanted to. Unless I was prepared to go all the way, Ella could walk out of that room and end my life with a single phone call.

'I can't sleep, I can't eat,' Ella said, sliding a finger through her hair and tucking it behind her ear. She was wearing silver stud earrings that looked like they had a diamond set in the centre. Probably glass, I thought. Cubic zirconia.

Or a gift from someone gullible.

'I just don't know how to live with myself after what I've done.'

I shifted on my chair and dug my fingers into my thighs. 'Maybe talking about it isn't enough. Maybe you need some kind of medication to help you.'

'I don't take any pills,' Ella said, finally looking up and catching my eye. There wasn't a flicker on her expression – not a single sign that she was nervous about being in front of me, pretending her story wasn't my own.

'They won't help me anyway,' Ella continued, looking away after a few moments. 'Nothing will, I guess. I'm just stuck here, in this room, trying to find an answer to a problem that only has one right one, when you think about it properly.'

'And what's that answer?'

'Simple really,' Ella said, leaning back on the sofa and folding her arms. She looked back at me and met my stare. She wasn't blinking. 'I need to go to the police and tell them everything.'

32

I could feel my teeth grinding against each other.

'You want to go to the police and tell them what you did?'

Ella nodded slowly, seemed to wipe away an invisible tear from her freckled cheek. 'I think it's the only thing I can do.'

I didn't know what to say. There was no training for this kind of situation. Mainly because they didn't tend to give people who had been involved with a murder the ability to give therapy to normal citizens.

I cleared my throat and managed to extricate my teeth from grinding against each other. 'Ella, why don't we talk about why you're really here?'

There it was. The first confrontation. The first moment I'd had the courage to acknowledge that I knew something.

'I don't know what you mean . . .'

'You know *exactly* what I mean,' I said, feeling the words shoot out of my mouth, the taste of them foul in my mouth. I took a breath. I didn't want to lose control of the situation. I needed answers. I needed to know what she wanted from me. 'Why don't we start over. Talk properly to each other.'

Ella's hesitation looked real. Felt real. 'I'm really confused about what you're asking me.'

'You really want to carry on with this game? I'm not buying it any more. So, we can continue and waste both our time, or you can tell me what you want.'

'I don't want anything from you . . .'

'Is it money?' I said, becoming more exasperated by the second. 'Is that it? Do you want me to go to the police? Tell them everything, so I'm punished? Tell you where Dan is, maybe?'

'I don't know what you're talking about.'

For a moment, I thought I'd made a mistake. That Ella really was who she was saying and that I'd invented everything that had happened the past few days.

That she wasn't really there to get something from me.

That she was telling the truth.

My heart sank. It felt like it actually did – moving through my body to join the fluttering of butterflies in my stomach. I felt a sheen of sweat on my body suddenly spring from nowhere.

I could barely breathe. It was as if I had forgotten how to.

It was only seconds, but it felt so much longer than that. I felt the air change around me; warmer, thicker.

I had almost confessed to murder. To someone who was there for my help.

I had forgotten about the two people at my house. I had forgotten about what they'd done. At that moment, I was sitting in a room with a scared young woman, who was looking at me like I had lost my mind.

And it suddenly felt like I had.

Then, in the briefest of moments, I saw it.

The curling of her lips, bright red, turning upwards. Her eyes once imploring, concerned, now darkened.

She was smiling at me.

'Sara, you don't look well.'

I opened my mouth to say something. Glanced at the door and wondered what would happen if someone knocked or came in. Wondered how long it would take me to get past her and out of the room before she did anything.

'You should close your mouth,' Ella continued, her voice changing. Once soft, now harsher on the ear. It was sultry, almost.

Inviting. Alluring. Dangerous. 'It makes you look dumb. But then again, you did let me leave the other day without saying a word. Even though you knew *exactly* what I was telling you.'

I knew her. That's why I was finding it hard to speak. I was trying to place her. Where I'd seen her, *when* I'd seen her.

I was scrolling through the rolodex of my mind, flicking past names and faces of my past. Trying to make her fit.

'I don't want money,' Ella said, leaning back on the sofa, crossing one leg over the other. Her shoulders were back now, her body more open. 'If that's why you think I'm here. I just want to make sure you understand that.'

There was a beat of silence, but then I finally found my voice. 'Why?'

Ella rolled her eyes. 'That's the question you want to ask me right now? I thought you'd be better than this.'

I could feel the rushing of something through my ears, my brain. My vision was blurry, my heart beating faster than the ticking clock on the wall. My index fingernail broke on the arm of my chair, the sharp bite of pain following as I gripped harder.

There was nothing stopping me killing that woman in that room. Nothing at all. I was bigger, stronger. I had more to lose, I bet. She looked calm. I was filled with nothing but violence.

'Lay a finger on me and everyone you know will find out what you are.'

I was breathing hard, staring back at Ella as she smirked her way through her threat. The dirty little secret I was thinking?

I didn't care in that moment.

I didn't care if everyone knew what I'd done. If everyone found out about Adam Halton. If everyone knew I'd killed some poor, young patient in my office.

Anything to stop her smiling at me.

'Get out.'

It was all I could say. It wasn't a warning. It was me making it a little fairer – because in that moment, I was going to rip that woman apart.

'Sara – I know where your children go to school. Those people who were in your house last night – they know too. If I don't call them in thirty minutes, they're going into that school and taking them away. You'll never see them again. You'll never know what happened to them.'

'Don't you dare . . .'

'This isn't going to end here, in this room. Not with you trying to kill me. Not with you assaulting me. Not with you doing a thing. You're going to listen to me, then you're going to do as I say.'

My body was almost moving out the chair of its own accord. If I hadn't been gripping the arms, I think I would have flown across that room and mauled the woman.

JJ and Olivia were all that stopped me.

They didn't deserve this. None of it. Yet I believed what she said. I believed something would happen to them before I could reach them.

I knew the right thing to do, even though every fibre of my being screamed at me to do the opposite.

'I didn't think I'd be back here so soon,' Ella said, smoothing out a wrinkle on her dress. I watched her, trying to exude nothing but calm, but I caught something she didn't want me to see.

There was an almost imperceptible shake in her hands.

She was nervous.

It hit me then – she wasn't as sure of herself as she was making out. She was making a great show of it, of course. Given her performance in the two times I'd been in her company, I guessed she had done some acting in the past. Probably high school, maybe even college. Shown some talent, but never gone any further with it.

Yet that shake let her down.

I just had to work out how to use it to my advantage.

'It seems like you're not getting it quickly enough,' Ella continued, standing up now and gazing at the framed prints on the wall. 'This isn't something you can fight against, Sara. This is happening. It's all over. The lie that is your life is finally coming to an end.'

'You need help,' I said, swallowing down the bile of violence that threatened to spill out. 'I can give you that help. If you just sit down and tell me why you're doing this, we can work it all out.'

Ella giggled to herself, her shoulders working up and down. I couldn't see her face any more as she scanned the wall behind my desk. 'I guess that's what you tell yourself, right? That you're helping people, sitting in this awful room and listening to people go on and on about their problems. Their issues. Do you tell them it was all Mom and Dad's fault and they aren't to blame for the bad things they do? Or are you less of a hack than that?'

'Right to the parents. That's interesting.'

Ella snapped her head towards me. 'My mom and dad are the best. Not like you. They're not liars. They're not murderers. Don't try and suggest otherwise.'

I held my hands up in mock surrender. 'Right, I guess I was wrong.'

'Good, I'm glad to hear it,' Ella replied, turning back to my certificates on the wall. I'd hung them up because that was what everyone else did. I wasn't sure it was right – it seemed like everyone had seen counsellors' and therapists' offices on TV and decided that was the done thing.

I knew there was something about her parents, despite her protests. I also thought she'd been telling some truths the first time she was in my office.

If I'd had more time, I could have gained her trust. I could have helped her.

Instead, I wanted to hurt her.

'This is about you, Sara,' Ella said, taking one of the framed prints from the wall and studying it more closely. 'And about what you did to that poor man.'

'And what do you know about that?'

'More than I care to,' Ella replied, sitting down in the chair behind my desk and resting the frame on top. 'Do you still think about him?'

I was being careful. I didn't want to admit to anything in that room – I didn't know what she was thinking of doing. Whether she was recording this entire conversation, or if she was simply playing with me. 'Think about who?'

'You know exactly who I'm talking about. Don't try and play dumb now. It's not going to work. We need to be honest with each other. Don't you think?'

'I'm not sure I need to say anything to you, after you threatened my children.'

Ella smiled, her teeth perfectly straight. Perfectly white. 'No threats here. I just detailed what would happen if you touched a hair on my head. Got to have my protection, you know?'

'Why do you care what I think about?'

'I'm just curious, that's all. If I'd done what you had, I'm not sure I could live with myself. It would be all I ever thought about. I couldn't do what you did – leave your home country, come all the way over here. Then, become a therapist, listening to people's deepest, darkest thoughts. Tell them how to live their lives. How to become better people. All the time, knowing that you were worse than any of the people who came in.'

'Interesting. So you don't think I'm qualified to help people?'

'Something like that, I suppose.'

I leaned forwards in my chair, glancing over towards the door. I hoped for a knock I knew would never come.

'Is that because you don't think you can be helped?'

Ella stared back at me, as I waited for an answer. Small lines appeared on her forehead, as she frowned at my question, before she seemed to catch herself and shook her head. The giggle came again not long after. 'Maybe you're better than I thought.'

'Why are you here? What's your name at least? Maybe we can talk this over and work out what you need from me.'

'You know my name,' Ella said, stretching out on my desk chair. I half expected her to prop a foot up on my desk, but she didn't. 'And you know what I want.'

'I don't. I swear.'

Ella studied me for a few seconds, then shook her head sadly. 'I want you gone, Sara. I want you to pay for what you've done.'

33

I knew what I wanted to do.

I wanted to silence her. The longer she spoke, the longer her odds of making it out of my office alive became. It went over and over in my mind how I could get rid of this woman. How I could quickly quieten her. Then, how I would deal with the aftermath.

Could I call it self-defence? Could I stage a fight, show that I was only saving my own life?

Could I get away with murder again?

That seemed to be the only way to stop her.

Outside my office, I could hear soft footsteps, walking past my door. Keeping themselves to themselves, because they knew how important it was not to interrupt me. My phone was in my bag, close to Ella's feet under my desk.

I had no way out, other than to end it somehow. With Ella, in that room.

'I can't do what you want me to,' I said, trying to keep my voice level. Calm. 'Because I don't know what you're talking about.'

Ella shook her head. 'If you're worried, I'm not wearing a wire. I'm not recording this conversation.'

'And I'm supposed to believe you?'

'You can either believe me or not, it makes no difference to me.'

'Well, it's not like you've made any efforts to make me trust you.'

Ella sighed and ran a hand through her hair. Her nails were still perfect, manicured. Small details that I hadn't given any weight earlier. The antithesis of what I should have expected from an anxious patient in desperate need of help.

I had become complacent, I guess.

'Here,' Ella said finally, standing up and opening her bag. She emptied the contents onto the desk in front of her. I didn't move for a second, then Ella stood and pulled down her dress to show more of her chest. Patting down her stomach area, so I could see that there was nothing attached to her.

'My cell is here, but look,' Ella continued, holding up her phone and unlocking it. 'I'm switching it off, you can watch me.'

I did, but I had to be careful. I scanned the desktop, seeing Ella's scant bag contents – a couple of things that looked like make-up, keys, tissues. Nothing that screamed out that I should be worried, but I don't think I would have known what a recording device would have looked like anyway. They could be the size of a pin-head for all I knew.

'Believe me now?'

'Of course not.'

'Well, you don't have much choice here,' Ella said, rocking on the desk chair a little. 'You can either talk to me, or worse things start to happen.'

'Are you enjoying this?'

The question made Ella stop rocking and her forehead creased as she frowned back at me. 'Enjoying?'

'Yes, you seem like you're having fun, threatening me. Threatening my family. You and the man and woman, trying to intimidate us. Breaking into my house at night, attacking me. Now, you're here, saying someone will harm my children. I'm asking if this is fun for you? Do you like doing this sort of thing?'

'I never said any harm would come to your children . . .'

'Oh, not in so many words,' I said, quickly interrupting before Ella could get back on track. 'But I think I understood your point fine. You used my feelings as a mother to try and make me sit here and listen to you. Why would someone do that if they weren't having the time of their life? If they weren't loving the power that gave them over another person.'

I felt calmer. On steadier ground. I was able to keep eye contact with Ella without being worried about what would happen next, because I understood her.

She was scared.

Of what, I wasn't sure. Maybe she was forced to be there, in that room, opposite me. Someone making her say these things. Or she had learned somehow about what I'd done all those years ago, and thought I was an easy mark for blackmail.

I didn't much care.

'This isn't about enjoyment, Sara,' Ella said, clearing her throat, smoothing out her dress again. 'This is about justice.'

'Oh, I'm sure that's all you're concerned with. Nothing else at all. That's why you're here, trying to play games with me, rather than talking to the cops, right? Because you're just so willing to give me the opportunity to tell them myself. That's how kind-hearted you are, am I right?'

'We both know what you did . . .'

'Do we? I have no idea what you're talking about. And I'm very worried about your mental state right now, that you would come in here and confess to a murder. Then, threaten my family. I think the authorities would be very interested in hearing what I have to say. Don't you?'

Ella didn't respond, staring back at me, before looking down at her hands in her lap. I was beginning to feel back on track. More like me. Defending myself, my family.

I was winning.

'I mean, who are they going to believe?' I continued, beginning to see how I was getting through now. Seeing a way out of this. I could make her go away, just for today, so I could work out how to get myself out of this position. To work out what Ella actually knew and how much it could harm me. 'A young woman, who voluntarily came to see a therapist with a laundry list of complaints about her mental health? Or someone who has respect, standing in the community, with not so much as a speeding ticket on her record? You tell me. How do you really think this is going to go?'

I settled back in my chair, studying her as I saw the cogs in her mind begin to whir. Working out what to do next.

'That's good, Sara,' Ella said finally, nodding to herself. 'That's really good. I can imagine that would work on someone if they were just playing a game.'

The calm feeling that had washed over me after I'd finished talking began to dissipate. I didn't like the way she was talking.

'See, the problem is,' Ella continued, leaning forwards and smirking. 'The problem is, that I know more than you realise.'

'You know nothing,' I spat back at her, losing control for a second. Only a second, but it was enough.

'Adam Halton. That was his name. The man you killed. And you did it with a man called Dan, isn't that right? Back in England. I even know the name of the town where he was killed. It wouldn't take much to link you two to the bar where you first encountered Adam. Witnesses could place you there, even after all this time. Not only that, you'd have to place all your trust in Dan to make sure he wouldn't crumble at the first line of questioning.'

I wasn't sure I was breathing. I was so still, I felt dead.

'I know more than you realise and that's probably why you think you can get away with this. Making out that you would be believed? That's not going to fly when I start telling them what I know. And it'll be so much worse if I do, because it won't just be about Adam. I'll tell them there's more. That you've been doing this for years. That they should investigate you for unsolved murders across two continents.'

'Stop . . .'

'And we both know that won't lead to anything – I'm assuming, of course, that you just made the one mistake, but who knows? Anyway, it won't matter any. You'll be destroyed publicly by the end of the day. You'll never see your children again – they'll only know you as a monster. Jack too. It'll be over.'

'You don't know anything—'

'If you do it my way, you can make it look like it was all a mistake. Blame Dan for it all. Say you weren't there when it happened, but you've known about it. The guilt has finally got to you and you need the Halton family to know the truth. You'll be looked on kindly – as you say, you have no record. You might have to go back to England, but at least you'll see your kids a few times a year. They might even let you back into the States, if you don't have your green card cancelled.'

I stood up, looking around me for something. Anything that I could use to shut this woman up.

'I can see you're not going to give up too easily,' Ella said, standing up from the chair and walking around the desk. She paused, then swept the few things back into her bag before continuing. I tensed up as she stopped a few feet away and faced me.

'I think you should leave, before I do something I'll regret.'

Ella smiled at me, showing me those pearly whites again. 'Let me make this perfectly clear to you. You're going to leave here now and go to the nearest precinct. You're going to tell them exactly who you are and what you did. You're going to call Jack and tell him what you're doing and then say your goodbyes. That's how things are going to go.'

I could see she was trying to keep the upper hand. Yet, I could see her confidence waning. She couldn't keep eye contact with me, taking a step backwards towards the door.

'I'm not going to do that,' I said, taking a step towards her now. 'And I think you know I'm not. So, what now? What are you going to do?'

I noticed the hint of hesitation, as she finally settled her gaze back on me.

'I don't think you understand the position you're in here . . .'

'I don't think *you* understand,' I said, talking over her. 'You come here, to my place of work and expect me—'

'JJ and Olivia are going to be very upset to hear what their mother really is.'

It was almost as if I lost a moment of time. Not saw red, not a blackout, or anything like that. It was simple really.

I heard her say my children's names and I lost all control.

The space between us was covered quickly and my hands were on her throat in an instant. She grabbed hold of my arms, but I locked in.

I heard something crash to the floor, but I was barely aware of what it was. I was entirely focused on squeezing the life out of her. She was trying to pull my hands away, but they weren't budging in the slightest. She slapped, punched at them, but they didn't move.

I tried to sweep her legs out from underneath her, my hands slipping as I did so. She sucked in a breath, but my hands locked back in.

Ella pushed me back, sending me onto the chair, but she fell on top of me as I kept hold of her throat.

It was as if I only had one thought. That I was going to silence her. Stop her talking. I could feel something pounding against my chest and realised it was Ella driving her fist into it.

The chair teetered and then crashed to the ground. We both fell and she was finally released from my grasp. She now had her back to the window and her escape blocked by me. I saw her wipe a hand across her mouth, her dress ripped at the shoulder. Black marks running down her cheeks.

I saw all these things as a blur, as I looked down quickly and picked up the globe from my desk and threw it towards her.

She ducked at the last moment and the crash as it hit the window blocked out any other noise. Ella turned as the glass shattered, and I ran towards her, grabbing her by the shoulders.

I forced her towards the open window, feeling a scrape against my hands as we reached the sill. I could feel the wind from outside blowing against me as I pushed harder, and my ears began to ring as the sound became deafening.

Then I realised what the sound was.

It was coming from me. Screaming, as I tried to throw this woman out of the window.

34

I could see the white in Ella's eyes, staring back at me, as she grabbed hold of my arms and refused to let go. She flinched as I screamed into her face, tears of fear springing to her eyes.

I wasn't formulating words, but I was shouting something at her. I wasn't sure. I wasn't thinking straight. I had one goal and that was to make sure she didn't leave my office alive.

There was no way I could let her go.

The black marks of mascara cascaded down her cheeks like an oil spill.

'Please, please.'

Her words may as well have been in a foreign language for all they meant to me. Now she wasn't trying to prise my hands off her – she was desperately holding onto me, as gravity threatened to take over and pull her out of the window.

I could feel her bones underneath my hands. The thinness of her body, the fragility of it. I wasn't breathing, the guttural sound of my screams scratching at the back of my throat.

'I'll kill you. I'll kill you.'

I heard the words I was chanting over and over, as if I was watching myself from another part of the room. From above. Observing a mad woman trying to kill.

She was almost gone. I could see the fear in her eyes, as she began to lose her balance. I could see the ground below us – the unforgiving concrete, ten floors down.

Ella would be dead on impact. And I would be happy.

'Don't, please . . .'

I pushed harder, half of Ella's body now out of the opening. I could see blood seeping through my fingers, broken glass around us. I couldn't feel any pain, adrenaline taking over and blocking out everything normal in my world.

Then, I heard the door slam open behind me, then the thud of footsteps rushing behind me. Hands pulling on my shoulders, someone shouting. I lost my grip on Ella and she almost fell out of the window. Instead, she teetered to the side, then fell to the floor inside the office. I felt an arm around my body and tried to shrug it away.

'Get off me,' I said, unaware who it was. My focus was solely on Ella, who was slowly getting to her feet.

'Sara, what are you doing?'

I knew the voice, felt comforted by it for a fleeting moment. Then I saw Ella rise up and my attention snapped back to her. I felt hands pulling me away, but I managed to shake them off.

'Let me go . . .'

I moved towards Ella again, but she was too quick. She escaped my lunge and moved swiftly across the room.

Ella was crying hard now. 'Get her away from me.'

'Come back here,' I said, moving towards her again, but hands gripped my shoulders, harder this time.

'She's crazy,' Ella screamed and was then moving out of my office.

'Sara, stop this.'

I tried to go after her, but the grip on me was too strong. I struggled against it, but my energy was sapped from the effort I'd given trying to force Ella out of the window and I couldn't move. Suddenly I was falling, the sofa providing a soft landing.

'What the hell is going on?'

I looked up and saw Gina standing over me, but it wasn't her asking the question. Simon was standing in the doorway – an incredulous look on his face. I looked between Gina and then Simon, unable to formulate a sentence.

'Call 911,' Gina said, sitting next to me on the sofa and putting an arm around me. 'A patient has attacked Sara.'

I tried to get to my feet, but Gina wouldn't allow me to. I was breathing hard, my chest tight with every intake of air.

'Right, of course,' Simon said, about to leave before I stopped him.

'Don't,' I shouted, the word coming out almost like a plea for my life. 'Please. Just . . . just let her go.'

'Sara . . .'

'No, it's okay. I'm fine.'

Simon looked at me for a second, then turned on his heels and left. I looked down at my hands and realised that there was a long slash across the back of my left hand. Blood was seeping from the wound, but I didn't feel any pain. I looked across at the broken window and the glass covering the sill. Outside, ten floors down, would be where the majority had fallen.

'What happened?' Gina asked, her voice low, comforting. Her arm around me, bringing me close to her body. 'Are you okay?'

'I'm . . . I'm fine,' I replied, my voice shaking almost as much as my body was. 'I don't know what happened.'

'Let me take a look at your hand.'

I almost took it away from her gaze, but I relented and allowed her to examine it. She took her cardigan off and wrapped it around my hand, applied pressure. It made me cry out in pain, but it was better than looking at the wound.

I didn't look up as Simon reappeared in the doorway. 'Cops are on their way. Building security are looking for the patient now.'

'We need medical attention as well,' Gina said, her hand gripped around mine. 'She's got an injury to her hand that'll need looking at. Grab the first aid kit.'

'Right, okay, right.'

I looked up at Simon and realised for the first time how flustered he was looking in his immaculate suit. His silver hair was still plastered to his head, but I thought I could see a strand out of place finally.

I caught a glance shared between Simon and Gina that seemed to last a lifetime, and I knew that it was over.

That was it.

My time at Better Lives was done. Maybe not quickly, but it would never be the same.

I felt relieved at the idea and didn't know why.

'I'll go and work that out,' Simon said finally, and then he was gone. I felt the enemy of a tear escape my eye and roll down my cheek. Gina reached across and wiped my face.

'It's okay, it's over now,' Gina said, releasing her grip slightly and sitting a little more forwards on the sofa. 'You're going to be fine.'

I let out a quiet, short laugh at the idea. 'I don't know what happened.'

'Did she attack you?'

I wanted to shake my head, but I couldn't. I didn't want to lie to her. 'It all happened so fast. I just remember fighting with her. That's when this must have happened to my hand.'

I wanted to take away Gina's cardigan and inspect the injury to my hand, but she kept hold of it.

'Well, the police will be here soon. And we'll get it looked at, make sure there's nothing to worry about. It'll all be fine, don't you worry. And they'll find her. Make sure she can't do anything like that again.'

I shook my head now. 'I need to go.'

'Shh, you just rest yourself now,' Gina replied, not showing any surprise at my protestations, if she had any. 'Just try and calm down. I just wish I'd got here sooner.'

I thought about what Gina must have seen when she came into the office, drawn by the smash of my office window. The sight of me trying to force Ella out of the window.

There was no way that she wasn't aware that I'd been in the process of ending someone's life. Yet there she was, holding an item of her own clothing over a small wound on my hand.

Maybe she was more of a friend than I thought.

'Listen to me, Gina,' I said, pulling away from her properly and removing her hand from mine in one move. 'I can't be here when the cops show up. They'll ask all sorts of questions and I don't want any of that. Ella is just a troubled girl and she doesn't need any of this. It'll only make her worse. And I don't know what I'd even say – I don't remember what happened . . .'

'Sara, you can't just leave.'

I knew she was right, but at that moment, I couldn't face the idea of having to explain what had gone on in that office. I couldn't think of a lie that would make any kind of sense.

'I need some water,' I said, settling on something that was true. My throat was burning. 'Can you get me some, please?'

'Don't you have any here?'

'No, sorry,' I said, wanting her away from me suddenly. Wanting to be away from everyone. 'Do you mind? I think the shock is starting to kick in, that's all.'

'Yeah, course,' Gina replied, eyeing me carefully and then finally standing up slowly and moving towards the doorway. 'Should I get someone to sit with you? Should I get Simon back?'

I shook my head. 'I'm okay, honestly.' I gave her a small smile, which seemed to placate her enough to leave.

I didn't hang around. I lifted Gina's cardigan away from my hand and saw that the wound on the back of my hand was barely anything to worry about. A deep scratch, if anything. The bleeding had stopped, so I left the clothing on the sofa. Grabbed my bag from the floor, made sure my phone and car keys were inside and then bolted for the door.

I couldn't go out the front way through reception, but thankfully the stairs leading up from the floor below were located in the opposite direction. I put my head down and headed for them without looking around.

'Sara?'

I heard Gina's voice from behind me, but I didn't flinch. I flung open the door and started running down the steps.

There was no stopping now. No turning back.

I had to finish what I'd started.

I made it to the floor below and moved through the offices, ignoring the confused glances of people standing up from their desks, and made my way to the reception area.

'Can I help you?'

The young man at reception was standing, but I didn't even shoot him so much as a glance. I pushed my way out and towards the elevators. Pushed the button and waited a few seconds.

'Come on, come on,' I whispered to myself, pushing the button again and again, as if I could make it come quicker.

Finally, the elevator pinged and the doors opened.

Inside, a man was breathing hard, standing almost in a fighting pose. His beard was what I noticed first – thick, bushy. As grey as any English sky in winter. His skin was the colour of mahogany, lined and weathered. Bloodshot eyes and a smell of sweat and fear emanating from him. He made as if to push past me, before taking another glance at me.

'Sara?'

And that's when I realised who the man was.

I pushed my way into the lift and pressed the ground-level button, before Dan had a chance to say anything more.

35

Ella was in her car within seconds of leaving the building. Driving out of the parking lot a moment later and a mile away before she guessed the cops had even been dialled.

It couldn't have gone much worse.

Much better, either. There was never going to be a good outcome once Ella had been confronted.

By the time she was on the highway, back towards Hartford, she was laughing to herself. To have come so close to being thrown out of that window, to have been that close to death . . . there was something of relief and despair hitting her all at once.

She thought she'd had Sara all worked out, that she would have folded in an instant. That had proven to be an utter mistake.

She wasn't even sure why she'd gone there that morning. There was nothing to be gained really – she was already aware that Sara knew she was under threat from what Ella knew. By putting herself in the same room as her, she'd risked everything.

Still, it had been fun at first, watching her squirm. She just hadn't factored in the fact that Sara would fight to keep the life she had built for herself.

Well, that wasn't going to happen. Not now. She'd passed too many people on her way out of the office to not realise how much attention Sara had drawn.

There was no way back for Sara now.

It was still a mistake.

Ella was aware of her slowing crashing heartbeat, and occasional lapses of giggling to herself brought on by the adrenaline coursing through her body.

There really had been a moment when her life had hung in the balance. The rush she'd got from that wasn't going to leave her any time soon.

Sara deserved everything that was coming to her.

That was what was keeping her going. Knowing that no matter what she did, it still wasn't in any way comparable to what that murderer had done.

What now? That was the problem. Ella had deviated from her plan to such an extent, that she was almost making it up as she went along.

No, that wasn't right. She knew the end point. That was the important part. She could unleash Penny and Colby – make sure they repay the debt they owed her.

And she had so much information about Sara that there was no chance she could be blindsided again.

Still, the fact that she had been so close to losing everything put a chill through her body. She had thought that if she had ever found herself in a physical confrontation, that she would have easily bested Sara. That hadn't been the case.

Which meant next time she would have to be better prepared. Have a better defence.

Sometimes, though, the best defence is a good offence.

Ella smiled to herself as she saw the formulation of a new plan come to mind. She took out her cell and dialled the last number she'd called. Waited for him to answer.

A new plan. One which would eradicate everything that had come before it.

One which would work.

One which would see Sara's downfall in all its glory.

★

Alex followed the car, not really knowing or understanding why. Maybe it had been the desperation in Sara's face when she'd told her about the woman who had been possibly responsible for the break-in at her home. That at least made her aware of the seriousness of the situation.

That was why she hadn't gone that far. She was waiting for something to happen. Gut instinct, they called it.

She called it experience.

The guy rushing past the car and into the parking lot had stirred her suspicions. Then, only a few minutes later, this.

The woman matched the description Sara had given her. Maybe that was enough for a further investigation into where she was going. Along with the look on her face when she'd pulled out of the parking lot and almost clipped her own car, parked up on the main street outside the parking lot.

She had been laughing, even as make-up streaked across her face. Maniacally, breathing hard.

Maybe it was just that Alex felt like she owed Sara for something.

The motive for why she decided to follow the woman, on nothing more than a hunch, could have been any or all of those things. It didn't change anything, though.

It just meant Alex became part of something that was out of her control. Without even knowing why.

And the world turns on decisions made for no good reason.

36

I bundled Dan into the passenger seat, running around the car and getting behind the wheel. Stuck it in drive and peeled out of the car park, the wheels underneath us screeching in protest.

I looked over at him, wondering if I had conjured him into existence. If he wasn't really there.

'How are you here?' I said, my tone a few touches too harsh. I saw him flinch momentarily at the sound of it. I took a breath.

'Sara . . .'

'I don't understand how you can be here.'

I could almost feel the cogs of my mind start turning. Locking in place. I thought about having him next to me, so close. What he was capable of. How unsafe I was right at that moment. Then, he asked a question I didn't want him to.

'Who was that?'

I could barely believe Dan was sitting next to me – and might not have were it not for the smell of him. Wafts of nostalgia assailed me as I turned right out of the exit ramp and searched ahead.

'That's the woman who somehow knows about Adam,' I said, looking for his reaction. He didn't give me any. Didn't say anything for a few moments, holding onto the dash as I turned a corner a little too quickly, and almost rear-ended a car going slowly ahead. I braked hard, then manoeuvred around the car and found clear road again.

'I don't see her . . .'

'She can't have got far,' I said, barely believing myself. 'She only has a couple of minutes on us.'

'It's a maze here, we're not going to find her,' Dan replied, using that voice I remembered so well. That *stop being so silly and illogical and listen to me who knows everything* voice. It made me grip the wheel harder and put my foot down further on the accelerator.

'She's here somewhere.'

But I knew he was right. She could be a mile ahead of me already. More if she'd hit the highway. I wasn't going to just fall across her, parked up to the side of the road, almost waiting for me to find her.

It wasn't going to be that easy.

I wanted to scream. I wanted to pound the steering wheel in frustration. I wanted to find Ella, grab her by the throat and never let go.

I couldn't do any of those things.

I gradually slowed the car, checking the rear-view mirror, expecting to see red and blue lights flashing at me. Expecting to be pulled over by local cops and asked for my licence and registration, before getting an overpriced ticket for some of my driving choices.

I checked the clock, seeing it wasn't even midday yet. It felt much later, as if the day had already slipped into night.

'Sara, what happened back there?'

I glanced across at Dan, who was staring back at me from the passenger seat. I could see a glimpse of the man I'd once known – his blue eyes, now looking a little greyer somehow. The smell of him. That was all that was familiar though. The rest of him was so different.

'How the hell are you even here?' I said, ignoring his question for now. 'Did you get on the next flight out from London after I sent the first message? Or did you already know?'

Dan hesitated, formulating an answer that I was sure I wasn't going to like. When he spoke, I knew he wasn't telling me the whole truth.

'I got here as soon as I could,' Dan said, fidgeting in his seat. 'You sounded desperate.'

'Well, you've got that right. You have no idea what my last few days have been like.'

'Maybe you should tell me. And then we can work out what we do.'

I shook my head, making a quick decision. 'First, we've got to get off this road and somewhere I can think straight.'

*

An hour later, Dan was sitting in my kitchen, looking a little more alive. I'd made him shower, which hadn't taken much persuasion to be fair. He seemed glad of the offer, as if he knew how bad he'd allowed himself to get.

He was now dressed in an old T-shirt and sweatpants of Jack's I didn't think he'd ever miss. *Metallica* scrawled across the front, which was a band I don't think Jack had listened to in about twenty years.

I bandaged up my hand, after stemming the bleeding. The cut didn't look as bad once it was cleaned up. The sting of pain became a dull ache. I didn't think it was as bad as I'd first feared, but I would need to get it checked out at some point. Not any time soon though.

I made coffee for us both, but couldn't drink my own. I watched as Dan almost inhaled his, his wet hair plastered to his head, less scraggly than it had been an hour earlier. It was thinner than when I'd last seen it, even if it still retained most of the colour I remembered.

His beard was what continued to catch my eye. He'd been clean-shaven the last time I'd seen him this close. It was as if he'd grown a mask, so I couldn't see the old him.

Still, despite the time and distance that had kept us apart for so long, it was Dan sitting at my kitchen table.

'You look great.'

I smiled at the compliment, despite myself. I tried to remember the last time I'd received one. It had been a while. Not Jack's strong point, that. He was loving in so many ways, but he sometimes forgot that the easiest way was a few simple words.

I wasn't sure how to respond, though. I could hardly say the same. 'You're a skinny thing now,' I settled on, which didn't really make me feel comfortable. 'I remember you being a much bigger . . . presence? Is that the right word?'

'Well, I don't really keep track of my weight.'

I felt the smile fall from my face, as I took him in. 'How are you here so quickly?'

It was a simple question, but I could see how much Dan was struggling to give an answer. There was no way he could have got here so quickly, without already knowing where I was.

Just no way.

Dan shook his head. 'Do you really want to hear this?'

'Yes.'

'You always knew how to make me feel awkward,' Dan said, a ghost of a smile playing across his lips, before his eyes turned downwards. 'I didn't know what else to do when you left. I tried to live my life, but it didn't quite work out. And I wanted so much to make sure you were okay.'

'How long have you been here?'

'A week or so.'

I rocked back in the chair. 'Are you kidding me?'

'I knew you'd need me.'

'Again, how? This girl only showed up a few days ago.'

'I've wanted to reach out so many times,' Dan said, setting his cup back down on the table and refusing to maintain eye contact in the slightest. 'I just didn't know how to do that, without messing up the life you've made for yourself.'

'How do you know about my life?'

'You're not the only one with fake Facebook accounts,' Dan replied, a boyish smirk on his face. It made him look two decades younger for almost a full second, before he returned to the forty-odd-year-old dishevelled man sitting across from me.

'Google is also good for that kind of thing,' he continued, the smirk disappearing. 'I just needed to be sure that you were okay. Then, I guess, I got stuck for what to say. It's not like things ended on a good note. Or that you'd even want to be reminded of me.'

'I don't understand how you got here. In the States, I mean? I know why I came here . . . you can't just be here to keep an eye on me.'

And then it hit me. Why he was really on the same soil, the same land as me.

He was making sure I was going to keep my promise. That I would never tell anyone what happened that night. I tried to think of a reason why he would ever doubt me and came up with a thousand answers. Everyone was human, after all, I guess. You can never fully trust a person.

'Well, why now? You've never been here before?'

'I'm not going to lie and tell you that I had a premonition or something,' Dan said, scratching at his beard, dry skin falling onto the table top in white flakes. 'Someone sent me a message. Told me that things were coming to an end, in so many words. It wasn't like I had anything else going on. I needed to come to make sure you were safe.'

I knew he was lying. I also knew how he would react if I accused him of doing so. I remembered that temper – never turned on me, thankfully – and it was the last thing I needed at that moment.

'I wasn't sure where you lived, but I knew where you worked. Your picture is on the website.'

'Right,' I replied, wishing I'd never agreed to be featured for that damn thing. 'Still, you've been here for days and you've not tried to make contact until now. I don't understand.'

'Does it matter?' Dan said, his tone bitter, sharp. As if he were tired of the questions he must have surely known would be coming. 'I'm here now and we have a problem, right?'

I tensed up at the harshness of his tone. 'What if I don't believe you?'

'What?'

'Maybe you're working with them,' I said, enjoying the flinch he gave as I leaned towards him. 'You're here with that girl. And those two people. All part of the same team. Maybe that's what happening, Dan? Because I don't know how you could be here otherwise.'

'I told you – someone got in contact with me . . .'

'Why didn't you reply to my message, then? Why pretend that you didn't know what I was talking about?'

'I didn't know it was you.'

I remembered I had used my dummy Facebook account to contact him and had to concede that point. Still, something didn't sit right with me.

I couldn't quite tell what he was feeling. Ashamed, perhaps. Of what he had become, or of the reason he was there in the first place, I wasn't sure. Either way, it wasn't the way to move any of this forward and I desperately needed that to happen.

'Anyway, it doesn't matter, because I'm here now. I want to help you. Help us. We're in trouble here.'

'You could say that,' I replied, biting down on my bottom lip, trying to stay in control. I had calmed significantly since trying to throw Ella out of my office window, but I didn't think it would last. I shot a look at the front door, wondering how long we had until the police showed up at my home. 'This woman . . . she knows about what happened and wants me to confess.'

'How does she know?'

'I have no idea,' I said, treading carefully. I didn't want to spook him too much. 'I was kind of hoping you might be able to help with that.'

Dan finished his coffee and stared back at me. 'I haven't told a single person about that night. How could I?'

'Well, that's what I thought, but are you absolutely sure? Not a single slip in all these years?'

'No.'

His answer was firm, but I still wasn't sure I believed him.

I decided against pushing the point at that moment. 'Well, neither have I, so how could she know?'

'I don't know what you expect from me, but I can't answer you on that.'

'I'm just saying, how else would someone find out about this? It's not like I'm going around broadcasting it. I don't want anyone to ever know about this.'

Dan sighed heavily, filled with sadness. 'Maybe it is time that people found out. I don't know about you, but life hasn't really been going well for me.'

I tried not to look around me. At the designer kitchen we were sitting in. The interior design that could have come from a catalogue. Little touches that screamed that we weren't short of money. 'I know what you mean.'

He looked up at me and rolled his eyes. 'I guess living somewhere like this probably helps. Having a family too. A job that no doubt pays well and is rewarding. Can't say I have any of those things to fall back on when the guilt gets too much.'

I opened my mouth to answer, but I heard something outside. A car pulling up on the driveway. I got up from my seat and moved towards the kitchen entrance, the hallway leading to the front door, and heard a car door slam shut.

'No,' I managed to squeak out, then turned back to Dan, who instantly saw the fear on my face and got to his feet. 'You need to go out back. Now.'

He didn't question me. He crossed to the back door and I turned my back to him, running for the front door, just as a key started turning in the lock.

I managed to grab hold of the door, just as it was opening inwards, taking a deep breath.

I plastered on a smile and held the door open.

'Sara,' Stephanie said, key in hand, a shocked look on her face. 'What are you doing here?'

37

I didn't move. I could see she was stuck in place. Eyes darting over my shoulder and past me into the house.

'I could ask the same of you,' I said, ignoring the nervous feeling inside that was threatening to overwhelm me. This was my house. 'It's a bit early to be picking up JJ and Olivia, isn't it?'

'I was . . . I was just driving by,' Stephanie replied, caught in an obvious lie but deciding to roll with it. 'I saw your car and thought something might be wrong.'

'Nothing's wrong. Honestly.'

Stephanie's eyes narrowed, unable to hide her disbelief. 'Are you sure? I was worried that something might have happened to you, that's all.'

'Of course not,' I said, wishing that my dislike of this woman didn't colour everything I said and did around her. It would have made it easier to get rid of her quickly. 'Everything's fine. I'm just surprised you were driving past here. It's not exactly close to your home or the restaurant.'

'It . . . it was just on my way from seeing someone on business. What are you doing home anyway? I thought you were working all day?'

'I came back for lunch early. Left some paperwork back here that I needed to pick up for an afternoon session.'

I didn't think she bought my lie any easier than I did hers. Yet we were at an impasse now. I wasn't about to step aside and let her in, in case Dan was discovered. She wasn't about to leave in a hurry.

I wasn't sure which one of us was going to blink first.

'So, are you going to invite me in?'

'What for?' I said, trying to remember a time we'd ever been alone – when the children weren't only a few feet away, or Jack was in another room. 'I'm going back out myself soon, so you'd only be sitting here by yourself until JJ and Olivia get back home. I'm sure you have better things to do . . .'

'Well, don't you have some time at all?' Stephanie replied, averting her eyes, shifting around a little. Nervous, perhaps. 'We could have that coffee now? Just the two of us. I'm worried about the both of you. The past few days . . .'

It was as if she knew I was trying to hide something. I shook my head at the idea – hoping that the invitation was genuine. 'I'm really sorry . . .'

'Of course,' Stephanie said, cutting across my apology. 'I guess I thought you might need someone to talk to, that's all. Right now. I know you've been struggling with something and maybe you need someone to help you out.'

That got my attention. 'Why would you think that?'

'I was talking to Jack . . .'

That was enough for me. 'I really have to go,' I said, and began closing the door, before she stuck her foot in the way as it almost closed. I felt my heart rate increase again. Had she noticed something behind me? Was there the whiff of another man in the air, perhaps? Or was she just not easily lied to?

I was beginning not to care.

'Really,' I said, opening the door only halfway this time, 'I don't have time—'

'Your hand?' Stephanie replied, concern in her voice. 'What happened?'

I had almost forgotten about it. I looked down at it, as if it wasn't attached to me. 'Oh, nothing. Just a small cut. Got a little clumsy making a sandwich, that's all.'

'That's a large piece of gauze for something like a cut. Must have been bad. Are you sure it's okay?'

'It's fine, honestly,' I said, hoping she would begin to sense my impatience with her now. 'Just a silly little thing. Nothing to worry about.'

She eyed me for a few seconds, as I waited for her to make her mind up. Believe me or not. I was losing whatever tolerance I'd had for her.

'Well, I hope it's not too bad,' she said finally, taking a step back. 'I'll see you later with JJ and Olivia then.'

'You will,' I replied, then closed the door fully. I hung onto it for a few seconds, letting my breathing return to normal. My heart rate calm a little. I waited for the sound of her car starting up but didn't hear anything.

I moved towards the lounge and almost skulked into a shadow, not wanting her to see me. I needn't have bothered. She wasn't looking my way.

She was talking to Pam across the road. I knew they got on well – as Pam Caulfield did with most people. One of those gossipy types that people seemed to enjoy the company of – until she was talking about them, of course.

I didn't think Pam had seen me turn back up at the house, but I thought about Dan and the way I'd pulled onto the drive and bundled him into the house quickly. It was possible. I'd only scanned my surroundings.

I swore under my breath at my own stupidity. I should have made sure no one saw him come inside. Now, she could be telling Stephanie that I'd brought a man back here and I just knew she'd have nothing but joy in telling Jack all about it.

Which meant I had to tell him first.

It didn't matter in the great scheme of things. I still had bigger problems to deal with.

The first of them was making sure JJ and Olivia were safe. I didn't believe Ella when she'd threatened them earlier that day, but I wasn't going to leave that to chance. Which meant I would have to pick them up early from school and make sure they didn't come to any harm.

Which meant calling Jack anyway, because I was going to need his help.

I sighed, still watching Stephanie and Pam talking outside. They seemed to be finishing up, so I held my breath as Stephanie turned and looked back towards the house. She wouldn't be able to see me, but that didn't mean I didn't suddenly have the urge to duck out of her sight. I stayed in place instead. She paused as she reached her car, but then got inside. I heard her engine turn over and then she was pulling away out of the street. She was gone in a few seconds.

I let out a breath and then made my way back into the kitchen.

'She's gone,' I called out, seeing the back door closed and no sign of Dan. I made my way to the door and then paused. Waiting for him to come back in.

A few seconds passed by and he didn't appear. I raised my voice, so he could hear me. 'Dan, it's okay to come back in.'

Still no sign of him.

Any other time, I wouldn't think anything of it. I would just suspect he hadn't heard me. That he was at the bottom of the back garden, yard, hiding in some bushes. Trying to stay quiet and out of sight. Too far away to hear me.

I didn't feel like that.

My pulse quickened, as the hairs on the back of my neck stood on end. I could almost see what was happening behind that solid wood door. I could see two people, waiting for me to turn the handle and step out. I could see Dan lying on the floor, a pool of blood around his body. A lifeless face staring back at me.

I could already feel the guilt. Of coming back here. Of getting him killed.

Yet nothing was stopping me reaching out. Taking hold of that door handle and twisting it down. Nothing was stopping me pulling the door towards me, a rush of cool air blowing towards me and passing me by.

I stepped out into my backyard and braced myself for the inevitable.

Only there was no blood. No people. No Dan.

Nothing at all, other than the covered pool, the grass bristling in the wind, the smell of spring in the air. Wet leaves and cold sunshine.

My eyes were squinting in the light, two small lines of sight. I was a ball of tension, each muscle screaming to be relaxed.

I was forty-two years old and my body hurt with stress and anxiety. A constant companion for the past few days. And now, after finally starting to feel that I wasn't alone any more, there I was. Standing by myself, waiting for the hammer to fall.

Nothing happened. No one made a sound out of the shadows. No one barrelled towards me, ready to take me away from my home, or worse, kill me where I stood.

I wasn't sure if it was relief I was feeling.

It wasn't.

It was loneliness. For a few moments, when Dan had been with me, I'd felt like I wasn't going through all of this on my own. Now, he was gone. He wasn't hiding at the bottom of the garden, he wasn't hiding in the bushes. He hadn't been able to hear me, because he wasn't here any more.

He was gone.

I was on my own.

If I wasn't so filled with fire, I would have cried. Instead, I balled my hands into fists and knew what I was going to do next.

I was going to protect my family.

Whatever it took.

Whatever the cost.

38

Alex followed Ella out of Stamford, onto the freeway, always a few cars behind hers. It had been a long time since she'd followed anyone – it wasn't something that she had to do all that often. She couldn't even think of an actual date.

Her memory hadn't been the best in the past few months. Cases bleeding into each other.

She was on the road for at least enough time to wonder why she was even following this woman. Alex didn't usually go by intuition. And it wasn't as if she owed anything to Sara.

That was a lie, she told herself. Of course, she knew it wasn't the case.

Before she'd started seeing Sara, she'd barely been able to make it through each day. The nights were even worse.

She owed her something. On top of the money it cost to see her for an hour, she thought with a wry smile.

Peace, serenity, sleep . . . they do come at a price.

She had tried calling Sara's office number, a few minutes into the drive, but she hadn't answered. Instead, it had been the receptionist, and from what little she could ascertain, it sounded as if there had been some kind of physical confrontation between Sara and this patient. One that had ended with a broken window, police being called, and Sara going missing.

Alex didn't even realise it had been more than an hour of sticking behind Ella's car. A 2019 BMW convertible, bright white and glistening in the spring sun. The top was up, of course, but Alex occasionally caught a glimpse of the orange headrests inside.

And the blonde-haired woman behind the wheel.

It was a fifty-thousand-dollar car, if Alex knew a damn thing about anything. She was sure of it. Which was the real reason she was still following her.

Because it didn't make any kind of sense, given what she'd found out about Ella Morley.

Of course, that wasn't her real name. Almost, but not quite.

She'd called Tom back at the station – knowing she would have to go on a date with the guy now. A favour for a favour. Not that it was much of a hardship. She didn't think spending an hour or two in his company would be a bad thing.

It was what would come after that was the problem.

But that was for future Alex to deal with. For now, she was concentrating on the road ahead.

They hit some traffic around North Haven. Always the way on the 15. A given, at any time of the day. You never knew when it was going to hit, but it was usually when you needed it the least. This time, it actually helped. As they slowed to a crawl, it gave Alex a chance to sidle up beside the BMW and have a proper look inside.

Ella was smiling. Bright, white teeth on show. Alex could hear music escaping from the confines of Ella's car – some new song she would never recognise if she heard it again.

The rhythmic bass was annoying. Ella singing along was worse.

Given what had happened back at Better Lives, Alex had expected her to be anxious, nervous, adrenaline-filled. Scared even. Anything other than this.

Ella looked as if she'd just won the lottery and was on her way to pick up the cheque.

Another reason Alex continued to follow her. All the way on the 15, until they turned off onto the I-91 and she realised where they were heading.

It was a long journey from Stamford, but Alex stuck with her all the way. Watched as she turned into the parking lot outside of a building. Alex pulled over on the street and risked the ticket.

She had to work out what to do next.

Call Sara, or go speak to Ella herself.

She chose the latter option.

Alex got out of her car and waited to cross the street. If there hadn't been more than a single car coming, she would have made it across. She would have been striding towards the office building lobby and having a chat with the receptionist. Maybe showing her badge and getting access.

Maybe she would have found Ella and had a quiet word. Maybe she could have found out what the hell she was doing and why she was going after Sara.

Only there were a few more cars, which meant she didn't hear the approach of footsteps. She didn't feel the breath of a man behind her.

She didn't see them coming.

What Alex did feel was the unmistakeable jab of the barrel of a gun in her side.

She could smell him – cheap cologne fighting a losing battle with terrible motel showers. She heard his voice in her ear.

'Don't make a single move. Do exactly what I tell you.'

39

JJ and Olivia's school was only a few minutes' drive, but it may as well have been on the other side of the country. It felt as if it took an age to get there, as I ran through so many different scenarios in my head. I thought about Ella turning up there, pretending to be a family member, getting inside and taking them away. I thought about those two people, breaking into the school, threatening Mrs Amsick on reception and taking my children out of their classroom.

I'd always thought they were safe in school, that nothing could ever happen to them there. Of course, that wasn't true. I'd seen the news often enough to know that a school wasn't a safe place for a child any longer.

I wasn't thinking straight. I was already thinking two steps ahead – about what I was going to do when I turned up at the school and was already too late.

I slammed on the brakes in the car park outside, leaving it across two spaces, and ran towards the entrance to the low-level building. I pressed on the buzzer and when no one answered within a few seconds, leaned on it again. And again.

A tinny voice came through the intercom. 'Yes?'

'Hi, hello . . . er . . .'

Now I was there, I realised I hadn't thought of an actual plan that wouldn't make me sound like an absolute crazy person.

It didn't take long to think of one.

'It's JJ and Olivia Edwards's mum . . . mom,' I said, talking quickly, before I had chance to question the idea that had flashed in my head. 'I'm here to pick them up.'

There was a moment of silence – Mrs Amsick checking her notes, I imagined, before she came back on the intercom.

'Hi Sara,' she said, which was the first bit of relief. 'I don't have anything here about you picking them up early today?'

'Oh, that can't be right,' I replied, thrilling myself at how surprised I really sounded. Almost as if I weren't making this all up as I went along. 'I sent a note in with them both earlier this week. I've got to take them up to New Haven for an appointment, this was the only time I could get for them, and I can't cancel it again. I'm so sorry that you haven't been told.'

'Hang on,' Mrs Amsick said, before the sound of the buzzer went and I was able to pull on the door. I moved inside and flashed a smile at her behind her desk.

'Honestly, they'll have put it to the bottom of their bags and not handed it in to their teacher.' I tried to act calm, but I was sure Mrs Amsick could hear my heart beating from a few feet away. Or see the sweat prickling my forehead.

'Give me a sec,' she said finally, getting her ample body up from her seat and walking through the doors that led towards the classrooms. She left me alone and I let out a long breath.

As long as she came back with JJ and Olivia, everything was going to be okay. I could feel it. I didn't have a plan as such – that would come later. For now, I just needed to make sure they were safe.

That was all that mattered really. Everything else could wait.

A minute went by. Then another. I started to think bad thoughts, that I couldn't easily push away. Logic was trying to push its way in – of course no one had already been and got them, Mrs Amsick would have said so. It was impossible to listen to that, though. All I could think about was that she was going to walk back in with a confused look on her face and tell me they had already gone.

Another minute, and then I heard a sound that made me smile. It was Olivia's laugh. I closed my eyes and lodged it away in my mind.

I saw JJ first, a scowl on his face that made me roll my eyes. He could be as annoyed as he liked – I didn't care. They were both okay.

'Here we are,' Mrs Amsick said, pushing the door into the reception area and letting the two children file past her. 'They both had no memory of any note, but I'm sure it's just been misplaced.'

'I could have sworn I gave it to them both,' I replied, shaking my head. 'It's been a long week, I'm so sorry. Is it still okay?'

Mrs Amsick gave me a warm smile and I could have hugged her there and then. 'Don't worry about a thing. I bet they're both happy to miss an afternoon of school, right children? Will you be back at all today?'

I shook my head. 'They'll be in tomorrow as usual,' I said, as Olivia wrapped her arms around my legs and her bag almost knocked me over. 'Come on you two, let's get you out of here.'

We signed out and Olivia skipped alongside me as we left the school. JJ was scraping his shoes along the ground behind us as I checked outside. I stopped them in their tracks, scanning the surroundings for anything that didn't look right, before leading them towards the car.

'Here we are,' I said, unlocking the car and opening up the back door. Olivia jumped inside, but I had to wait for JJ as he shuffled towards me slowly. 'Hurry up, we haven't got time for this.'

'What's going on, Mom?' JJ said, coming to a stop as he reached the car finally. 'Where are we going?'

I hesitated, seeing the look on his face. He was confused, but also annoyed by the interruption to his school day. I could read him easily, like you can with eleven-year-old boys. 'Just get in the car and I'll explain,' I replied, buying myself a few more seconds' thinking time. 'Nothing to worry about.'

He gave me a look that said he didn't quite believe me, but got inside anyway. I closed the door behind him and then jogged around the car, looking around me quickly one last time. Still clear.

I got behind the wheel and pulled away.

'We've only just had a check-up,' JJ said from the back seat, leaning forwards, his face appearing at my shoulder. 'So, why did you lie to Mrs Amsick?'

'Just sit back and be quiet for a little while, okay?' I replied, trying to concentrate on keeping the car on the road, even as my hands shook as I gripped the wheel and tried to work out exactly where I could take them. I glanced up at the rear-view mirror and tried a smile towards him. 'It's all going to be fine. I had to take you out of school for today, that's all. I'll explain it all soon, trust me.'

JJ sat back in his seat with a thump, as Olivia sat quietly behind me. She seemed much happier with the shock of me arriving, but I could already see JJ was an issue. I should have guessed at that, but I didn't have time to worry about it.

They were safe with me for now, that was the main thing.

I drove on, past the turning towards home, and down towards the coast. By now, low February sun was bright in the sky and I wished I'd brought sunglasses with me. I quickly decided on a destination and felt better for it.

It took us less than fifteen minutes to cover the five-mile journey down towards Sherwood Island, and the beach that lay beyond. I pulled over in the parking lot and took a deep breath.

'Are we going to the beach?' Olivia said from behind me, her voice equal parts surprised and excited. 'Mom, can we walk on the sand? Can we go in the sea?'

'Give me a minute, darling,' I replied, finding my cell and stepping out of the car. I left the windows open, walking a few steps away. 'Let me just make a call.'

I could see the light in her eyes and my heart warmed at the sight of it. Then, the weight of reality came crashing down and I almost winced at the way it hurt me.

My cell, my mobile phone, both terms interchangeable for me now, was in my hand and I scanned around the car park. Nothing looked out of the ordinary, but it wasn't as if I would know what to look for anyway. By the time we'd made it to the approach road to the island, we were the only car travelling south, but that didn't stop me keeping an eye on the entrance to the parking lot.

I opened my phone and found my recent call list. Pressed call and waited.

'Hello?'

'Jack, it's me.'

'I know,' Jack said, already a note of irritation in his voice. 'I'm at work, Sara, I can't really talk . . .'

'I need you here, now.'

There was a moment of silence, then a sigh from Jack. 'What's going on? Has someone done something?'

'Just listen to me, Jack,' I said, knowing he would back down. Knowing he would relent and listen to me, as soon as he realised how serious things were. 'I have JJ and Olivia with me, but they're not safe here. I need you to come and take them to your parents', or Stephanie's house. Away from home, away from me. Just for a while, until I can work all of this out.'

'This is about . . . Jesus.'

'We're at the beach on Sherwood Island.'

'It's going to take me at least at least an hour to get there,' Jack said, a note of nervousness in his voice. 'Can you wait that long? Shouldn't you call the police or something?'

'Just get here, Jack,' I replied, quickly, getting a little irritated myself now. 'We need you.'

'Of course, sweetheart. Sorry, I'm just worried, that's all. Has something happened? I can call Stephanie and ask her to meet you if that's better? Before I get there, I mean? So you're not on your own.'

'It's okay,' I said, tiredness washing over me. I was surprised Stephanie hadn't already called him. I continued looking around the parking lot, making sure there was nothing new. Nothing out of place. 'Please, just get here, okay? Quickly. It's important.'

'Of course, I'm on my way now. Love you.'

Then he was gone. I stood in the parking lot for a few seconds more, before I heard Olivia shouting me over. I turned to look at her and tried a smile.

'Let's go for a walk, kids,' I said, trying to sound normal.

Feeling anything but that.

40

Dan was running. Feet pounding against the pavement, breathing so hard it was burning the back of his throat. Not looking at where he was going properly, just head down, barrelling forwards. Probably not the best thing to do in a strange town, in a strange state.

A bloody strange country as well.

All of it. All of it was wrong. Being there, thousands of miles from where he'd once called home. Escaping the UK for what? Because he was scared? Of being found out, maybe. Of being discovered. Of slipping up and telling the wrong person what had happened back in 2005.

All of those things, yes.

More than that, though. It was all wrong because he should have been dead. That was the truth of it. His body should have given up on him a long time ago. His mind had tried to, but his flesh and bone refused to keep up.

Right now, it was screaming at him to stop. It wanted to give up, to lie down and recover from the distance he'd just put between him and Sara back at the house.

He hadn't wanted to leave. There was so much still there between them. He wanted to still be sitting across a table from her. To still be talking to her. To still be breathing the same air as her.

It was as if all those years had slipped away, time becoming nothing, despite them both looking so different now.

He wanted to help her.

Only that wasn't going to happen.

He'd known as soon as he'd stepped out onto the back porch and looked at her back garden. Turned and seen the size of her home. Seen the life she had built for herself, while he had wasted his.

Wasted away.

He had spent almost twenty years on standby. As if he had been waiting for the call from her. The call for help, the call for his presence.

The call that said he was wanted. Needed.

Now it had come and he was running.

Because it turned out that after all these years, he'd been wrong about himself. He'd thought after that night in 2005, and what happened to Adam Halton, that he wanted to die. That he was too cowardly to do it himself, so he was waiting, hoping that someone would finish him off instead. That the decision would be taken out of his hands and someone would do the deed for him.

Only, as he looked at what Sara had become, what she had managed to do after that night back in England, he realised that he had been wrong all this time.

He wanted to live.

And that wasn't going to happen if he stayed around Sara any longer than he had to. Someone was coming. They'd told him themselves.

He came to a stop, his hands on his knees, as he breathed hard and fast. His lungs burned with effort. He looked back over his shoulder, to where he'd run from. No one was following him. No one was sitting idly in a car, watching him. No one was around at all.

He had no idea where he was now. That suited him okay. It wasn't as if any of it mattered any more.

His phone was still in his pocket – fully charged, like it made any difference. It was useless away from the house. He brought it to life anyway and the reason he had run flickered back at him from the screen.

A single message.

He caught his breath and then continued running.

41

We were walking on the beach when Jack arrived a little over an hour later. Both kids had seemed to accept the idea that I'd pulled them out of school for a surprise trip to the beach and were now busy making nuisances of themselves in the sand. I didn't dare think of what I was doing to them by having them out of school and here instead, but I could see them both and that was the main thing.

I didn't think I'd breathe easily until I was sure they were safe.

Or think clearly.

I saw Jack in the distance at first, shielding his eyes from the low sun. I raised my hand in greeting and then looked over at JJ and Olivia. They were on the edge of the water now, probably daring each other to dip a foot in the freezing Atlantic sea. Both had their pant legs rolled up, barefoot in the sand, as I carried two pairs of socks and shoes.

Any other day, it would have been bliss. The middle of the day, Jack joining us . . . it should have been a moment to savour.

Instead, I was rolling on the balls of my feet, itching to get away.

Jack was shaking his head as he approached me. He'd called me again from the road, but I'd ended the call after simply telling him to hurry up. That we were safe, but he needed to get there fast.

'What's going on?' Jack said, as he reached me. He stopped a few feet away, before catching himself and closing the gap between us and enveloping me in an embrace. 'Are you okay? What's happened?'

When I was in his arms, I felt colder. As if I were betraying him in some way by making him come all that way and not explaining first. 'I'm sorry . . .'

'It's okay,' he said, holding me closer. I could feel his warm breath on the top of my head and I closed my eyes.

'I didn't know what else to do.'

'It's fine, I'm here now,' Jack said, pulling me away from him and searching my face for a clue as to what had happened. His eyes scanned down my body and finally alighted on my hand.

'What's this?'

I almost pulled it away from him, as if I were embarrassed by it. 'It's nothing.'

'Let me take a look,' Jack said, pulling it back towards him. He took hold of my hand and stroked the bandage covering the cut I'd given myself on the broken window in my office.

'Tell me.'

I took a breath and told him everything that had happened that morning. From Ella arriving without warning, to her switching in my office. The whole story.

Everything.

Except Dan.

I didn't tell him about Dan turning up at my office. About taking him back home and then hiding him away when Stephanie arrived. About him disappearing and me panicking that whoever was after me had turned up and taken him away.

I left all of that out, because I didn't want to see that look in Jack's eyes. That hurt, reflected back at me.

There was no way I could deal with that right at that moment.

When I was finished, we both looked towards where JJ and Olivia still played at the water's edge. Gazed at our children and were silent together. He had been holding onto me to begin with, but now he was a step or two away. I wanted to reach out to him, to feel his hands on mine.

I didn't move. I couldn't. I felt like I was betraying him with every decision, every step I took.

'What the hell are we going to do?'

It was a good question and not one I had a simple answer for. 'She threatened the kids, Jack . . .'

'Don't worry, I heard that bit,' Jack said, a bite in his tone. 'Which is why I'm struggling to think straight right now. But we have to do something, right? We can't let this go on.'

'I want you to take JJ and Olivia. To your parents', to Stephanie's, anywhere that's away from me.'

'Sara . . .'

'Don't, Jack,' I said, before he could say anything more. I turned to him and took hold of his arm. 'If anything was to happen to them, or to you, then I would be to blame. And I can't have anything more on my conscience. I wouldn't be able to live with myself. It's all escalating. She knows she has to make a move now and I don't think it's about the police. I don't think that's her endgame here. She wants me for something, and I don't know what that is, but she's dangerous. Those two people who broke into our house, they're dangerous. I need you three to be far away from me whenever she comes back.'

'I'm not just going to leave you to deal with this. I can't do that.'

'You have to,' I said, imploring him now. I thought about this being the last time I spoke to him, the last time we were together as a family, and my heart felt as if it were tearing in two. 'It's the only way. I'll be okay. I just need to deal with this on my own.'

'We're a team. I can't let you go through anything alone. I know I've been distracted by work lately, but this is serious. It's too dangerous.'

'Which is why I have to deal with it by myself,' I said, stepping away from Jack and turning my gaze back towards the sea. I wished I could stay there all day. I wished we could run towards the water, kicking and laughing with JJ and Olivia. I turned back to Jack. 'Remember when we used to come here when they were younger? We'd spend a day on the beach, not worrying about a thing.'

'Of course . . .'

'I was always only ninety per cent here,' I said, unable to look Jack in the eye, keeping my focus on his chest. His shoulder. Anything but his eyes. 'There was always a part of me that had this feeling that I didn't deserve any happiness. A gnawing feeling in my stomach, that wouldn't go away.'

'Sara, you don't need to feel like this.'

'Maybe. Maybe I do. Because, remember, it's not like I should forget what I left back home. What I know. What I did. It doesn't matter how many people I help now, Jack, because when it really mattered, I didn't help, did I? When it came down to it, *really* came down to it, I made damn sure I put myself first.'

'Then, perhaps you should go to the police,' Jack said, carefully, choosing his words as if he were worried any single one of them might be like stepping on a mine. 'Because none of it was your fault. They'll tell you that. They'll want the actual perpetrator, not the person who was forced into helping him. He's the one who should feel guilty, right?'

I let out a humourless chuckle. 'I'm just as guilty. That's how they'll see it.'

'Listen, they'd have to get you back to the UK first and that won't be simple. We'll get you a lawyer – a good one – and it will be fine. You just tell your story, exactly what happened, and then we can fight whatever comes next.'

'What if the story isn't exactly what I told you?'

I could feel Jack's eyes on me now. Piercing my skin. I could feel the weight of his look like a burden on my shoulders.

'What are you talking about?'

I wanted to tell him the truth. The whole truth. Nothing but the bloody truth, so help me one of the three thousand Gods that existed. Only I couldn't. I had never told a soul. I had given Jack part of the story, of course. The 'sanitised' version.

There was no way I could ever say out loud what really happened that night to anyone.

There would be no way back from that. There would be no way Jack would want to be around me. There was no way he would let me be a mother to his children any more.

He would see me for what I was.

A monster.

I couldn't take that. I couldn't live with that look on his face. That judgement from the one person in the world who was supposed to love me no matter what.

Because it was never like that in the real world.

Love was conditional.

'It doesn't matter,' I said finally, grinding the sand beneath my toes. Enjoying the feeling of it. Of normality, before I let the darkness take hold and become everything. 'That was just me talking before thinking. The bottom line is this, Jack. My actions have led to you all being in danger. I'm not going to continue on that path. This is my problem, I'll fix it.'

'But we're a team . . .'

'We are,' I said, stopping him from finishing the thought. 'But this is just the way it has to be. I'll deal with it.'

'How? How are you going to deal with it, Sara? This isn't something that can just be settled with a conversation. We're talking about your life. *Our* life.'

'And that's why I'll deal with it. They just want me to destroy everything. I want to save it. There's no greater motivation a person needs than to save her family. That's what I'm going to do.'

'I think this is crazy, Sara,' Jack said, taking hold of me, his hands on my upper arms. I could feel the strength there, the desperation to make me see sense. 'What if they're dangerous? What if they try and hurt you if they don't get what they want?'

That was the problem. He was trying to make me see sense, but I'd already seen it. There was no way I was going to put any part of my family in danger because of me. 'This is my fight, Jack. You have to accept it. We can't both go running off, because we have two children . . .'

'Who need their mom.'

'I'm coming back,' I said, finally looking into his eyes. They were wet with emotion. With fear. 'Just keep them safe. Don't take them back to the house. I'll be in touch soon.'

'Where are you going to go?'

I pulled him close to me, kissed him and then wrapped my arms around his body. I closed my eyes, inhaled the familiar scent, the way his body felt against mine. I almost lost myself in his embrace, before letting him go.

'I'll tell you when it's over.'

And those were my last words to Jack before leaving. I walked away, across the beach towards JJ and Olivia, my mind trying to make me go back. Every thought telling me I was making a mistake.

I saw my two children laughing and playing and living. I almost stopped walking, my legs turning to jelly at the prospect of saying goodbye. At the thought of it being the last time I would ever see them.

I felt a pain in my heart I didn't think was possible.

I kept walking, seeing JJ and Olivia turn to me as I got closer. I smiled towards them, seeing a flicker of apprehension flash in their eyes. As if they knew what was about to happen.

'JJ, Olivia,' I said, calling them over. I watched as they padded over to me, their feet yellow with sand. A breeze swept across the beach, but it was still balmy enough that I wasn't worried about them being too cold. A nice, spring day, that I was about to walk away from.

'Listen,' I continued, as they finally reached me. 'Dad is here, and he'll be taking you over to Nana and Grandpa's house. There's a problem at home that I've got to take care of. Hopefully you'll be back later, but if not, you'll both be good and stay at your grand-parents' house, right? Like an adventure?'

Olivia nodded, but JJ didn't look convinced in the slightest. I wrapped them both in a hug before he had chance to say anything.

'I'll see you later, okay?' I said, my words almost lost in my children's embrace. 'Love you both.'

And then I walked away before I could change my mind.

42

As I drove onto our street, I slowed down, looking at each vehicle in turn. I was almost at a crawl as I reached the driveway, before turning onto it and facing the house.

My house.

It looked darker, even as the sunlight glistened off the sidings. More strange, unfamiliar than it had ever been before.

I switched the engine off and sat in the driveway for a few seconds. Waiting for someone to emerge, for people to maybe peer through the blinds covering the living room. For a noise to emanate from somewhere within. The unmistakeable sound of a threat.

I could barely hear anything from inside the car, so that wasn't exactly going to work.

In my rear-view mirror, I could see someone pop out from the house opposite. I angled it and saw Pam Caulfield appear on her front porch, shielding her eyes from the sun. I sighed softly and got out of the car.

I thought about going straight in, but knowing Pam like I did, I knew if anyone would have information, it would be her.

She almost shrank back into the house, as I jogged over the road to her.

'Hey, Pam, how's it going?'

She usually greeted me with a smile. A bit of local gossip and sometimes a terrible joke. Now, she looked at me like I was a stranger. Someone to be wary of.

'Sara, how are you?'

'I'm okay,' I said, stopping halfway up her driveway, as she came down her final few steps. 'I was just wondering if you'd seen anything over at my house while we weren't there? During the day, or something like that? Maybe in the past couple of hours?'

She eyed me with a look that I couldn't work out. It wasn't one I'd seen before from Pam.

'I can't help you . . .'

'Pam, please, do you know something?'

'I don't know what you're talking about,' she said, taking a step backwards. 'Maybe you should call Jack? You shouldn't be on your own.'

'What do you mean? I'm fine. I just wanted to know if you'd seen anything, that's all.'

'I haven't seen a thing,' Pam said, her voice cold now, but also a hint of nervousness in it. 'I don't know what you want from me.'

I couldn't help myself. I could feel that red ball of anger in my chest and Pam Caulfield was becoming an annoyance. 'You're telling me that you, Pam Caulfield, haven't seen a thing that might look out of place on this street? I think you have and you're not telling me.'

'I need to go back inside . . .'

I stepped forwards and pulled her around as she turned away from me. 'No, I'm not buying it. You know everything that goes on around here, so why are you pretending that you don't know anything? You know what happened last night. Well, it's important that you tell me everything you saw.'

'I didn't see anything,' Pam said, trying to pull away from me, as I kept hold of her arm. 'Please, let go of me, I just want to go back in my home.'

'No, you're going to tell me what I need to hear,' I replied, my voice echoing around the empty street. She winced as my voice turned into a shout. A screamed plea for help escaping from within me. Her eyes were watering, as she tried to escape my grasp.

For a moment, I thought I was going to hit her. Maybe more than once. Until she told me what she knew. Because I was sure she knew something that would help me. I had no idea what it was, but she *had* to know something.

'Please, Sara, let me go . . .'

I was breathing hard, as Pam cowered away from me, her pleading eyes staring back at me.

'I'm . . . I'm sorry,' I said, letting go of her suddenly. She stumbled back and almost lost her footing. I reached out to catch her before she fell, but she jumped back with a squeal of surprise. 'Pam, I didn't mean to scare you.'

'I . . . I'm going inside now,' she replied, moving slowly backwards towards her open front door. She took the steps leading up with her back to the door, slowly, carefully. 'Please, call Jack, tell him you need him to come home.'

I took a step away, looking down at my hand. Blood had seeped through the bandage covering the cut on my hand. I stared at it for a few seconds, as if it wasn't attached to me. I turned around quickly, jogging back across the road towards my house. I could feel Pam's eyes on me as I kept going.

I knew she'd seen me last night. That she had probably spoken to the idiot next door.

I couldn't think about it at that moment. We could move when this was all over.

The house looked empty, but I knew it was a mistake to think of anywhere as safe. I pulled out my keys and placed them in the lock, swinging the door open and ducking away from the entrance. Nothing, no one, jumped out into the empty space. I peered around and into the hallway inside, my heartbeat slowing as everything looked normal.

I walked inside, my senses on fire as I listened for any sound. I closed the door softly behind me as I stepped forwards. I could hear the ticking of the clock in the kitchen, silence otherwise.

I moved around the house, checking every room, the process taking much longer than I needed it to. I finally came to the office and walked inside, crossing the room quickly and finding the safe at the back.

For a moment, I thought Jack might have changed the combination – JJ's birthday – but the door swung open and I reached inside.

When Jack had told me that he'd bought the gun, I'd told him that it was a bad idea. That having a gun in a house with a small child was asking for trouble. He'd looked at me like I was soft – that we needed it for protection and that we never knew when we might need it, and anyway, isn't it better that we have it and don't need it, rather than need it and not have it?

I didn't buy into any of his arguments, but I relented before he mentioned the second amendment. I did manage to convince him that it had to be locked away at all times. He had agreed and I hadn't seen it again until last night. Never mind that the point at which you might so desperately need it, would probably be about five minutes before you managed to get it out of a safe.

The gun felt heavy in my hand, a black piece of metal that seemed to scream violence at me. I turned it over in my grip, careful not to point the barrel anywhere near myself.

I barely remembered holding it the night before. Now, it felt more real. I was making a decision to have it in my hand right then.

One thing Jack had taught me right at the beginning was how to check two things – that it was loaded and that the safety was off or on.

I checked both of those things now and then placed the gun in my purse. I ran a hand through the safe, to see if there was anything else I needed. Our passports were inside and I paused as I picked mine up. Turned it over in my hand, opened it and saw the photograph inside, years old now. I didn't want to compare it to how I looked now.

I put that in my purse too.

There was money in my account if I needed to go anywhere. There was probably a better way of leaving the country without being found, but I didn't have time to think about that right then.

I closed the safe and stood up. Jack's laptop was sitting on the desk, and as I turned, I saw the lid was open, but the screen was black. I hesitated, then placed a finger on the touchpad and the screen came to life.

A photograph of the four of us stared back at me. Taken maybe five years earlier – Olivia couldn't have been more than four or five. I wasn't sure when the picture had been taken, but I recognised the background.

I slumped down in the chair, staring at my family – all of us smiling, as if we were the happiest damn family in the world. And we had been.

Until I'd ruined it all.

Well, until my past had ruined it.

The picture was a screensaver, the time and date staring back at me too. I pressed the space bar on the keypad and the password box popped up on screen.

I had never looked through Jack's things in all the time we'd been together. Never seen any reason to go snooping through his phone, or on his computers, or through his pockets. I'd never even considered it. Never needed to. I was too busy worrying about my own guilty conscience to consider his.

Which is why it felt so wrong to type in his password and gain access to his laptop now. I was just glad he used the same one for everything – online accounts, email, everything, the same password.

I'd mentioned to him once that it probably wasn't a good idea, but he'd just shrugged his shoulders at me.

I don't even know why I was sitting at his computer, waiting for the desktop to show up on screen. At that point, I was simply desperate, that was all.

I needed anything that would make me feel normal. And at that point, I just wanted to know when that picture was from.

I navigated around his desktop, saw a folder titled PHOTOS and clicked on it. The folder opened and I was suddenly looking at our entire life together.

Hundreds, no, thousands of photographs. All stored there, going back more than a decade.

I didn't know Jack kept them all like this. We had various external hard drives, USB sticks, all filled with the same photographs I imagined. Taken on cell phones, digital cameras, the lot over the years. But Jack had stored them all together it seemed, in one place.

There were pictures of us, back when we'd first started dating. Only a couple of those. Then, more numerous as we moved in together. Me pregnant, my growing stomach. JJ after he was born.

Moving into this house. JJ's first day at pre-school. Days out at the beach, at Jack's parents', Stephanie's parties. I scrolled down, the pictures becoming a blur of colour. Olivia joining eventually. Her first days, first years. The four of us.

I stopped scrolling by so fast, as I came to the picture that served as Jack's screensaver, in amongst a set of photographs that were immediately obvious. It was from 2019, from a trip we took to Mystic, further down the coast. I could see in the next picture a shot taken from outside the pizza place there – made famous by a 1980s movie. I smiled at the memory of Jack trying to explain the film to me, as I'd never seen it.

More photographs – not many in 2020 and 2021, for obvious reasons. Mostly from when the pool had been installed, employees wearing masks as they worked. Then JJ and Olivia shirking, having schoolwork from home, and splashing around in the sun.

Then they came to abrupt end in the middle of 2022, with a party at Stephanie's restaurant, a few familiar faces in the crowd.

I looked through them, feeling so far away from that feeling of security as it was possible to be.

Then I saw another familiar face.

And I screamed.

43

Colby went inside the motel to clear out the place, as Penny paced alongside the vehicle, checking her cell phone every few seconds, waiting for the call to come in from the 'boss'.

He didn't like this. Not one bit. This hadn't been in his plans. This was supposed to be an easy job – intimidate a rich woman and make sure she listened to the girl. Now, he had some other woman tied up in the trunk and he wasn't sure if he wanted to be in this line of work any more.

'Idiot,' he said under his breath. This was as bad as the time he'd got involved with some rich guy over in Greenwich. Thankfully, he'd managed to get out of that situation before that guy had most of his crew killed or arrested. And then his mansion burned to the ground.

This . . . this was different. Now, he wasn't working on behalf of someone with actual power. Or alongside an army of people. It was just him and Penny, having to deal with the fallout from whatever this girl had got them into.

Killing a cop wasn't top of his to-do list that week. That month. That damn century.

He wasn't going to do it.

'We good?' Penny said, as Colby came jogging from the motel room, throwing a bag in the back seat of the car. 'Got everything?'

'Yeah, all good,' Colby replied, pulling out a pack of cigarettes that looked bashed up. He took one out and realised his hands were shaking.

'We could just . . .'

Penny didn't have to finish the sentence. Colby knew what she was going to say. They could just walk away now. Drop the woman in the trunk off somewhere and be out of the state within a couple of hours. They could keep driving until that place was a speck of dust in the rear-view mirror.

But, Colby knew Penny and Penny knew Colby.

The one thing that made them do the things they'd done in the past was on offer.

Money.

Colby wouldn't kill the cop. No doubt about that. And he hoped Penny wouldn't either.

Only, if that girl told him to jump off a cliff, he'd ask her if she wanted him to go forwards or backwards, if it meant there would be more money in this thing. Enough so that Penny didn't have to work in this field again. Maybe throw in a half-pike while he was at it.

He was in trouble.

They both were.

'What's the plan then?' Colby said, pausing at the driver's-side door, looking over the car at her. 'Has she told us what she wants us to do?'

Penny shook her head. 'We have to get out of here, that's the first step. Then, we wait for her call.'

'You think she knows what to do about this thing?' Colby nodded towards the trunk, as if he were talking about trash they had to get rid of, rather than a person. A *cop*, of all 'things'. It sent a rush of fear through his bloodstream.

'I don't know,' Penny said, running both hands through her hair. She looked tired, which made Colby feel a failure. 'I think she was surprised when she showed up.'

'She seems to have been on top of things since this all started.'

'As long as she's paying, I don't mind what she tells us to do.'

Colby wished this wasn't their line of work for the umpteenth time that day.

He wished he could take her away from that place. That they could live in peace, wih normal jobs. Normal lives.

They were just too good at what they did, though. And it was too lucrative. A normal job wouldn't do.

'I guess we have to get out of here,' Colby said, opening the door and getting in the car. Penny took a final look back at the motel they'd called home for the past week and then got inside herself.

Colby wondered how far he could drive before he was far enough away from the problems he'd caused for himself.

He wasn't sure he had enough gas for that.

Instead, he drove on. Waiting for the call to come. It took longer than he would have liked, but eventually, it did.

★

This was the problem with inserting herself into situations that didn't have anything to do with her. There was always a chance that she'd end up duct-taped and shoved into the trunk of a strange car.

Alex thought about the last cop she'd heard about being tied up by some criminal. It hadn't ended well for him. She wished she could remember the poor guy's name, but it wouldn't come to her. Just a story that had been shared around the station.

She could hear their voices outside. They didn't seem to know what was going to happen next, which was a good thing, she decided. Yes, it could lead to them making a mistake that wouldn't end well for her. More likely, they were panicking already.

She had seen that panic on their faces when they found her badge.

That should have been an end to the ordeal, but of course, her luck didn't extend that far.

Alex hadn't even had enough time to reach for her weapon when they'd grabbed her off the street. Two of them, with the element of surprise, the odds hadn't been in her favour, but it still rankled with her.

She had been careless.

Running after that woman had been a mistake. Not taking her time, speaking to Sara first, working out what this was all about . . . all of it had been a massive mistake.

And now, she was paying for it.

The only good thing was that they hadn't pulled her out of the trunk as soon as they'd come to a stop.

Killed her there and then.

It was still daytime, she thought. Maybe they were just waiting until it was dark to deal with her.

That would give her enough time to work out a plan, at least.

Not that she could think of a single one right at that moment. Her gun was gone. No one knew she was there. She had no idea who this pair were and she was currently lying in the foetal position, unable to move her hands or legs. She could barely breathe, with the tape over her mouth.

It wasn't an ideal situation to plan from.

That wasn't going to stop her. Because she wanted something more than anything else at that moment.

She wanted to be alive.

And she wasn't going to give up on that.

44

I swore at the printer as it took its sweet time to finally comply and print the damn photograph. As it finally took the paper from the tray and slowly made its way through, I enlarged the photograph on Jack's laptop again, and made sure I wasn't seeing things.

No, nothing had changed.

My phone buzzed on Jack's desk and I picked it up. A text from him.

At mom and dad's house. Kids are fine. Call me. X

I didn't call. I was just glad they were safe, because now I realised just how much trouble I was in. How far this went. The print finished and I snatched the paper from the tray. The quality wasn't great, but you could still see it well enough to recognise what it showed.

Her.

I shook my head as I grabbed my purse and rushed out of the office, down the hallway and towards the front door. I almost flung it open, but looked through the glass first. There was no one outside. The street was as empty as it had been when I'd arrived. I still opened the door cautiously, waited a few seconds, then left the house. I walked quickly to my car, opened the driver's-side door and got in. Locked it after me instantly, then took a breath.

I had something to go on, that was the important thing. That was better than nothing. It didn't matter what it meant, I could deal with that another time. I made sure my purse was in easy reach on the passenger seat and then reversed out of my driveway and onto the street. I took a look over the road at Pam Caulfield's house and saw her blinds snap back into place.

Something else I would have to deal with at some point in the future, but not important at that moment.

I knew where I was going, which meant I didn't need to rely on the GPS, thankfully. I wasn't sure I could deal with driving down any unfamiliar streets or highways. I wanted to just switch off and try to make sense of the thoughts running through my head.

It was a thirty-minute journey; I covered it in less than twenty. I had the radio blaring the entire way – some eighties radio station that I'd found one day accidentally. Heart and Journey blasting out the car speakers, as I tried not to think about my life falling apart around me.

I parked around the back, grabbed my purse from the passenger seat and the printed photograph that it was resting on top of, and got out of the car. Any calm that had seeped in was now dissipating quickly as I approached Stephanie's restaurant.

We had been here for dinner a few times, not often enough for Stephanie's liking, though, I bet.

I knew she didn't like me, but she didn't need to do this.

The sign outside said open, but it didn't seem like anyone had told people living close by. There wasn't anyone inside as I walked in, a young woman leaning against the desk didn't even look up at me as I approached.

'Welcome to La Bella's,' she said, finally putting her cell phone down long enough to realise I was standing there. 'Oh, hey, aren't you . . .'

'Is Stephanie here?'

'Yeah, I think so.'

I raised my eyebrows, wondering if there was anything that could make this nineteen-year-old girl move quickly. 'I'll go through,' I said finally, annoyed that I'd waited this long. 'It's fine, she knows I'm coming.'

I walked past her before she had chance to complain and passed a horde of empty tables. It was late afternoon, so I wasn't expecting it to be busy exactly, but it was still deathly quiet in there. If it got any later, though, I could imagine that Stephanie would be worrying away.

Her office was past the bar area, through a door marked Staff Only and next to the kitchen. I went through and paused at the kitchen, seeing only unfamiliar faces peering back at me, before going back to doing whatever they had been before.

I knocked on the office door and went in before I heard an answer.

Stephanie was sitting behind her desk, phone in one hand, her other resting on the mouse connected to her computer. She barely moved as I walked in, staring at the screen on her left.

'Yeah?'

'Stephanie,' I said, finally getting her to tear away her attention from the screen. She looked more confused than I'd ever seen her before. Screwed up her face, as if she was trying to work out how it was possible for me to be there.

'Sara,' she replied, placing down her phone and pushing her chair back. 'What are you doing here? Is everything okay? Kids, Jack?'

'They're fine,' I said, knowing that she would know full well by now. That Jack or his parents would have called Stephanie the moment they'd arrived there with the kids. I didn't know why she was lying. 'You know they are. Why don't we, for once, have an honest conversation?'

'I don't know what you mean . . .'

'I know you hate me,' I said, saying out loud something I'd screamed inside my head for so long. Kept to myself, never telling a soul. Not even Jack. 'I don't know why. I've always been nice to you – you helped us so much. You're the reason I have . . . had, probably, now, I guess, a career after having JJ and Olivia. They love Aunt Stephanie, Jack adores his sister, so I've just kept quiet. But I know you hate me. I can see it in every conversation we have. Every shared word, shared glance. You detest me. The disgust, it comes off you in waves.'

'Sara, you're wrong.'

'Let me finish,' I cut in, determined to finish my thought. Determined to finally get my say. 'You don't have to pretend any more. You have your reasons, I'm sure. I don't care what they are. It never mattered to me. Sure, I'd prefer if someone didn't hate me for no reason, but I can't change how you feel.'

I could see her squirming in her seat, desperate to talk over me. Deny, argue. I held up my hand as she opened her mouth to speak, as I took a breath.

'I could live with it all,' I continued, feeling more confident the longer I spoke. 'You were good with JJ and Olivia, Jack loves you, and we don't exactly have to like each other, or get on, for us to live our lives. Everything was fine. Nothing had to change. We saw each other for a few minutes, here and there, when we crossed over after I finished work, and that was it. A few family functions here and there. Nothing major, right?'

I stared at her across the desk, I looked down and saw the picture I was holding. The blurred quality, shaking in my hands. 'So, why would you do this?'

I tossed the print out across the desk, watching as it skidded across the surface and came to a stop as she stuck her hand in the way of it. She lifted it slowly, turning it one way, then another, giving it a glance and then setting it back down in front of her.

'Sara, I don't know what you're talking about.'

I had known she was going to say that. My jaw was pulsing with tension, as my teeth ground against each other. I wanted to bite down on my tongue, but I started speaking before I had chance.

'You know *exactly* what I'm talking about. You know what's been going on this week. You know what's being done to me. I just want to know why.'

'Please, help me here, because I'm clueless as to what you're talking about.'

'See that,' I said, pointing across the desk towards the picture. 'That's what I'm talking about.'

'I'm seeing you, Jack, and the two children, here, at the restaurant.'

'Yes, that's right.'

'And that's supposed to explain why you've burst into my office in the middle of the day, ranting about me hating you without any kind of proof of that fact, and accusing me of knowing something I couldn't possibly know?'

'Stop playing games . . .'

'Let's stop everything,' Stephanie said, standing up from behind the desk and walking around towards me. She stopped a few feet away. 'Why don't you go home. I'll call Jack and he'll come back and then you two can talk about things. He knows you've been under a lot of pressure lately and maybe that's having an effect on your . . . your mental health, maybe?'

I stared back at her. 'There's nothing wrong with me.'

'I talked to your neighbour earlier,' she continued, as if she hadn't been interrupted. 'She told me that you were out in the street in the middle of the night. Shouting about two people breaking in? That . . . that you had a gun.'

'Yes, that happened. Jack was there. He'll tell you. And you know all about it anyway.' I pointed back at the photograph, where she'd left it on her desk. 'And that proves it.'

She couldn't have looked more patronising if she'd tried. Head cocked to one side, eyes soft and looking down on me. 'I spoke to Jack about it. He told me he didn't see anyone breaking in. Just woke up to you screaming the house down. Add that to you making him leave work the other day, telling him you'd been attacked. And then what happened at work this morning . . .'

'How do you know about that?'

'They called Jack, of course,' Stephanie said, resting against her desk, only a foot away from me now. 'They're worried about you. You . . . you attacked a patient, they're saying?'

'Yes, but she's not a patient, Stephanie. You know her.'

That stopped her in her tracks for a moment, but she was about to go on, before I stopped her. I stood up, reached across her desk, and snatched up the photograph. 'See this here,' I said, pointing at the space behind Jack, me and the kids. 'That's her.'

She looked at it for a second, before her eyes settled back on me. 'I can't see anything.'

'It's her, it's Ella,' I said, jabbing a finger at the photograph, before thrusting it towards Stephanie. 'Take it, see her. She works here.'

'I don't have anyone working here called Ella.'

'You're a liar,' I said, spitting the accusation at her. 'Why did you tell her to come to me? Why did you get her to say those things?'

'I don't know what you're talking about,' Stephanie replied, but she did take a closer look at the picture now. 'This woman does work here, but she's not called Ella. You must be confused, Sara. I don't know what's got into you, but I should never have left earlier. You're not yourself.'

'You're damn right, I'm not. You have no idea what I've been going through these past few days and you're the one to blame.'

Stephanie moved closer to me. That look of hers making me feel sick.

'Listen, why don't you sit down and I'll get you something to drink. A water, or a fruit juice? Coffee maybe? And then I'll call Jack and he can take you home . . .'

'Tell me who she is,' I said, jabbing at the photograph again. 'Is she here now?'

Stephanie shook her head. 'She's just one of the servers,' she said, not a hint of a lie in her tone. 'She's a sweet girl, who wouldn't do anything to hurt you. Come on, just sit down . . .'

'No!' I was losing my patience. Everything inside me was screaming that Stephanie was genuine, but I knew better. I knew what she was like. She was playing some kind of game and I wasn't going to let her win. 'Tell me her name.'

'Amy,' Stephanie said, her voice still soft. Still trying to calm me and failing miserably. 'I swear to you, she's got nothing to do with anything you've been going through.'

'Amy,' I repeated, testing the name on my tongue. It burned. 'I need to see her. She's threatened JJ and Olivia, Stephanie. She wants to destroy my family. Why would you do this?'

'I haven't done anything—'

I looked at the photograph. Ella standing behind the four of us, holding a plate of something, but looking directly at the camera. She wasn't in focus, but I knew it was her.

There was no denying it, despite Stephanie's protestations. I knew what was happening. 'You wanted me out of the picture, but it's not going to work.'

I pushed past her as I turned on my heels and headed for the door. Stephanie tried to place a hand on my shoulder, but I brushed it off. I flung the door open and walked into the kitchen. The staff there looked up, bemused expressions as I called her out.

'Amy? Where are you?'

I couldn't see her in there, as I walked all around the prep stations, down to the back and pulled open the large refrigerator door. I turned and stormed back towards the restaurant area. Stephanie was waiting in the doorway and held up her hands to try and slow me down.

'Get out of my way.'

She didn't step aside and I almost pulled out the gun there and then. Shoved the barrel under her chin and watched her cry and moan and beg for her life.

Instead, I placed two hands on her chest and shoved her as hard as I could, then kept moving.

'Amy?'

The woman who had been on the door as I'd arrived was standing in between tables, almost shielding the space behind her.

I could see her. Cowering by the entrance.

'You . . .'

I rushed forwards, pushing the woman out of the way, as Ella backed away, bumping up against the door.

I'd found her. Ella. Standing there, pretending not to recognise me.

I stopped in my tracks, trying to decide what I was going to do next. Then I remembered the threats she'd made. What she'd done to my life that week.

I was going to finish the job I'd started earlier that day.

I was going to kill her.

45

I could almost hear my heart beating in my chest, as I thought about how to take the next step. Whether I should shoot her there, in front of witnesses. Whether I should take her somewhere to finish the job.

There was no doubt in my mind that I was going to end her life. That I was going to keep my family safe.

From both of us.

'Sara!'

I heard Stephanie's shout from behind me, but I was too busy concentrating on Ella, standing in front of me. She was dressed differently – in a smart white shirt, black skirt, hair tied back. She looked younger than she had earlier that day.

There was a moment when I wasn't sure that I had the right person. That she looked so childlike, innocent, that I'd made a mistake. She wasn't even looking me in the eye – trying to make herself as small as possible.

'Did she put you up to this?' I said, jabbing a finger over my shoulder towards Stephanie. I could hear her footsteps behind me. 'Did she make you come to me?'

'I . . . I don't know what you're talking about.'

That wasn't what I wanted to hear. I reached forward and grabbed hold of Ella's arm and she shrieked out in pain.

'You know exactly what I'm talking about,' I said, gripping her bicep hard, as I tried to find the opening to my purse, hanging across my body. 'And I'm not going to let you get out of it this time. You're coming with me.'

I felt a hand on my shoulder and I tried to pull away from it. The grip was too strong. I turned and saw Stephanie, a look on her face that I had never seen before.

Fear.

'Please, Sara, let her go.'

'You don't understand,' I said, finding the opening to my bag and placing my hand inside. 'She's trying to ruin us all.'

'She's just a young girl,' Stephanie pleaded with me. 'Please, just let her go and we can talk about this.'

I looked back at Ella, tears rolling down her cheeks, her shoulders shaking, and doubt hit me. She looked so different. So unlike the woman who had sat in my office earlier and threatened my family.

I shook my head. I wasn't wrong. My free hand came out of the bag and I pointed the gun at Stephanie.

'She's lying,' I said, seeing my hand shaking in front of me. I heard a scream and the clatter of chairs behind Stephanie. I locked eyes with my sister-in-law, as hers widened at the sight of me. And what I was pointing in her direction.

'Sara . . .'

'Don't,' I said, moving the gun around and pointing it at Ella. 'Tell her, Ella. Tell her what you're trying to do to me.'

'I . . . I don't know what you're talking about.'

'Please,' I said, and I could hear the whine in my voice. The pleading. I just wanted someone to believe me. To tell the truth. 'Tell them I'm not crazy.'

'Call 911. Don't worry, Amy, it's going to be okay.'

I heard someone shout that out. I took one last look behind me, saw Stephanie pleading, crying, shouting, but all I could hear was a ringing in my ears.

'I'm sorry,' I said, dropping the gun to my side, before putting a hand to my head. Rubbing against it, as if that could bring some comfort. 'I've made a mistake.'

I pushed past Ella, sending her stumbling over, but I was already moving. Out of the restaurant, around the back, to my car.

I couldn't do it there.

I'd almost screwed everything up. If I had done what I'd wanted – taken hold of Ella and marched her out of the building. If I'd done that, everything would have been over. The police would have been looking for me, called by Stephanie, who would make sure I'd never see JJ and Olivia again.

I had gone too far. It was all over.

Why did I take the gun?

I had to breathe. I could feel my body panting, trying to suck in air. My chest felt tight, my vision swirling, the world spinning around me.

I made it to my car, but only barely.

I flung open the car door and collapsed into the seat. Gripped hold of the wheel and leaned my forehead against my hands.

Tried to control my breathing.

It took too long.

I had to think straight. I had to get away from there. I had to work out what I was going to do.

It was impossible to do any of those things while I couldn't catch my breath.

Minutes went by that felt like hours. I risked lifting my head up, expecting to see police surrounding my car. The lot was empty.

I started the car, backed out of the parking lot, and onto the street. Circled around the restaurant, before parking up the road, out of sight.

It wouldn't be long, I told myself. They'd send her home. They had to. She'd just been attacked by a mad woman. They didn't know the truth. Only I did.

My phone rang from within my purse. It was nestled up against the gun, which I'd thrown inside at some point.

Had all that really happened?

Yes, was the answer. All of it.

I lifted my phone out and saw Jack's name on the screen. I thought about not answering, but I needed to hear his voice.

'Jack,' I answered, feeling the sob in the back of my throat. 'Are you okay?'

'Sara, where are you? Stephanie called me. What are you doing?'

I could hear the panic in his voice. The fear. It was there so often now that I would have been more surprised not to hear it.

'I'm okay,' I said, swallowing back the emotion that was threatening to overwhelm me. 'She's involved somehow, Jack. The woman who came to my office, she works for her.'

'What? I don't understand.'

I told him about Ella. Finding the photograph. Finding her at the restaurant.

'She denied it, Jack,' I said, hitting the wheel in frustration. 'But how can she? She was there, this morning, in my office, threatening our children. And Stephanie employs her. Why else would she be there? Why else would she be doing this?'

'I . . . I don't know. You need to come here. Where are you? I can come get you. We should be together right now.'

I shook my head, knowing he couldn't see me, but I couldn't get the words out. 'Jack, you need to be honest with me, okay?'

'Always, but please, just tell me where you are. I'll come find you. We'll take you home . . .'

'Jack, listen to me,' I said, more force in my voice than I was expecting. 'I need you to tell me the truth.'

There was only one answer now. Stephanie knew what I'd done, all those years ago. And Jack must have told her.

He must have betrayed me.

I took a breath. I wished he was in front of me, so I could tell if he was lying or not. That was one thing that I loved about the man. I could always tell when he was lying. Not that he ever did. He was honest to a fault. It was why I never tried on new clothes in front of him – I'd know in an instant if they looked wrong on me.

I never asked him anything I didn't want an honest answer to.

'Did you tell her what I did?'

'Sara—'

'Just tell me,' I said, my voice reverberating around the car. Spittle flew from my mouth and landed on the dash. 'Tell me if you told Stephanie what I did.'

'I would never tell anyone. You know that. I wouldn't tell a soul. She doesn't know anything.'

I listened to his words, took them in, tried to spot any hesitation, any uncertainty. There was nothing.

I thought he was telling me the truth. I believed him.

'Please, just tell me where you are.'

'It's okay,' I said, my voice soft now. I could feel the tension leaving my body. Not shutting down, no. It was different. 'I'm going to be fine.'

I wanted to tell him why it was going to be fine. Why I was suddenly more relaxed.

I'd worked it all out, that was all. I knew exactly who was to blame. Who had told Ella and why she was doing this.

Dan.

'Jack, tell the kids Mom won't be home for a little while. Tell them I love them and I'll see them soon. And I love you. More than you'll ever know.'

I ended the call, before the tears that had begun rolling down my cheeks turned to a waterfall.

Dan.

I should have told Jack. I should have told him that he'd been at our house that day. That he'd obviously been in the country for days. Not wallowing in his guilt back in England like I'd thought.

He'd been working out how to get revenge.

I'd managed to make a life. I had a family. And he wanted to ruin me for being able to do that, while I imagined he rotted away back in England.

I didn't know how he'd managed to link up with Ella. Probably while stalking me, knowing that Stephanie was my sister-in-law. Found her restaurant. I remembered how charming he'd been with me, all those years ago. How he'd sweet-talked me into a relationship within hours.

There was no way he had lost those skills.

She was a young woman. Working a minimum-wage job in a restaurant. Probably struggling to get by. It made sense that she would be easily bought with promises of something tangible.

Dan wouldn't want money. He'd want me to pay for his guilt.

I'd invited the man into my life. Into my home. And as soon as Stephanie had arrived, he'd disappeared. I knew why now – because he was scared of being recognised.

It all fell into place.

I hadn't seen Ella walk by. I wanted to go back to the restaurant, calmer now. Walk in and tell Stephanie that I just wanted to talk to the girl. Relaxed, smooth.

That wouldn't work.

I was sure she would walk out of that place alone. She was too brave for her own good. Once away from all of those people, she would revert back to who she really was.

I wouldn't have to wait long.

46

Ella walked out of the restaurant in the distance. Dabbing at her eyes, as if she'd been crying. I imagined she'd been taken into the office by Stephanie, who had been oh so concerned and sorrowful. Had told Ella how I was a mixed-up person, placated her with platitudes. Maybe given her a few holiday days, just so she didn't make a song and dance about it.

Not that she would. There was no way she'd go to the cops about any of what happened. She had her own plan to carry out. She was going to meet with Dan and finally make me pay.

This would all be about the perception for Stephanie. I had no doubts that she'd be instantly on the phone to her parents, telling them how I'd gone crazy. That Jack needed to let me go. That it was best for the children that they wouldn't be around me.

I used all of it as fuel.

There was no way I was going to let any of this happen. Jack loved me. He wouldn't let his family break apart. He knew the real me and accepted it, warts and all.

They couldn't break us. None of them could.

I got out of the car, leaving my purse on the passenger seat. I looked up and down the street, people walking by everywhere. I fell in with the crowd, keeping an eye on the blonde woman on the other side of the street.

Ella stopped at the crosswalk, a couple of hundred metres away from the restaurant. I stood behind the five or six people waiting to cross, keeping my head down low. When the lights changed, and the people started walking, I followed them.

I met her in the middle.

She didn't see me.

I took hold of Ella and jabbed the gun into her ribs. 'Make a move without my say-so and I'll kill you.'

She opened her mouth to shout out, but I pressed harder. No one could see what I was doing. If you happened to glance our way, it would just look like we were walking arm in arm.

'I swear, say one word, or shout out, or make any sudden movement, I'll kill you here and now. You know I can do that.'

I took hold of her arm and led her back the way I'd come.

The sunshine had disappeared. Dark clouds forming above us. A soft breeze rippled through the street and I could feel the cold air hit Ella's arms, goosebumps breaking out.

'This way,' I said, pulling her alongside me. I reached my car and thought quickly.

'You drive,' I said, opening the driver's-side door and bundling her inside. 'Get in.'

'Where are you taking me?'

She was still acting. Still playing the part, pretending like she had been back at the restaurant. I ignored her question and made my way around the car, getting in the passenger side.

I tossed her my keys and motioned with the gun for her to drive.

I watched as she slid the key home, her hands not shaking any more. The first indication that the mask was slipping.

'Just keep driving and follow my instructions,' I said, pulling my seatbelt across my body, while still holding the gun on Ella. Amy. Whatever her name was. 'Don't try and run us off the road, or the last thing I'll do is pull this trigger, you understand?'

She nodded, glancing towards me, her eyes still wet with tears. She had black streaks down her cheeks. Waterproof mascara obviously not something she'd invested in.

'Just pull out and drive towards the highway.'

I had to think about where to take her. Where we wouldn't be interrupted. I needed to talk to her and make sure I had it right.

I felt better than I had all week, but I was nowhere near home and dry yet.

One thing I hadn't expected was for Ella to actually be at the restaurant. It seemed wrong that she had still picked up her shift, when she was doing what she was.

'Just keep driving, back towards the coast,' I said, Ella not saying a word as she threw on her turn signal and kept going. Her hands were resting on the wheel as I wiped my brow and then lowered the gun a little. 'Does Stephanie know about this? About what you've been doing? Did she have anything to do with it?'

'I don't know what you're talking about.'

'You can drop the act now,' I said, turning in my seat a little. 'It's just you and me. I can still see the scratch on your neck from earlier this morning.'

'And I can see the cut on your hand,' Ella said, glancing my way for a second. 'You have to admit, you came out of that little scuffle we had worse, didn't you?'

'Why are you doing this?'

'Where are you taking me?'

I wanted to scream. Grab the wheel and force us off the road, just so I could see her face smash into the dashboard. 'Answer my question.'

She shrugged her shoulders. 'Why does anyone do anything?'

'Money or something else?'

'Money is as good a reason as any,' Ella said, her voice calm, level. It was as if she'd had a gun pointed at her many times before and it had no effect on her in the slightest. It was unnerving.

'So, Dan is paying you to do this?'

Another shrug of the shoulders.

'You're going to have to start talking to me,' I said, growing even more impatient. 'Who are the two people who attacked me at work? Who broke into my house? Are they with you or Dan? Or both of you?'

'Don't you think you deserve all this, Sara? Is there no guilt in your mind at all? Don't you just want to make all this stop?'

'I want it to stop.'

'Well, you can do that. Look, I'll drive you to the local station now and you can make a full confession. It might be okay. You might not get extradited. Yeah, you won't be able to live in your house for a while, I'm guessing, but at least you'll be unburdened.'

I laughed, trying to make sense of what she was saying. 'You're saying that will be it? That's all you want me to do? You must be crazy.'

'Not as crazy as you.'

'Careful,' I said, the laughter disappearing in an instant. 'After you threatened my children, this might just go off at any second. Then, I'd just find Dan and get him to give me the answers instead. I'm not crazy. I'm the one who decides what happens next.'

'Yeah, holding a gun on a simple waitress . . . totally not crazy.'

'Why are you doing this?' I asked the question again. One she didn't seem to want to answer. 'What has Dan promised you?'

I saw her shoot me a sideways glance, before she focused on the road again.

Every time I mentioned Dan's name, I noticed she tensed up. I didn't think she realised he'd been to see me.

'Sara, where do you want to go? What are you going to do? This isn't going to work.'

I checked the time. The sun was getting lower in the sky now, masked as it was by darkening clouds. Only a few hours ago, I'd been standing on the beach with my family, spring sun in our eyes. Now, I was heading towards a storm.

'You know where I live,' I said finally. It wasn't a question. I knew she did. That was how the two people had been able to break in. 'Take us there.'

'And then what?'

'You'll see.'

I already knew the answer. I didn't need to tell her that, though. Home would be good. It would be marred forever, of course. I'd probably want to move. That's if I got away with what I was going to do, obviously. And that wasn't at all likely.

I knew Jack, though. He wouldn't just accept that I needed him to stay at his parents'. He'd come looking for me.

Which meant my house would be the first place he would look.

'On second thoughts,' I said, noticing her grip harden on the wheel. 'Take us to Bluff Point.'

'I don't know where that is . . .'

'Just head towards Westport and I'll direct you.'

A plan was forming in my mind now. One that didn't exactly make me feel confident, but a plan all the same.

I was tired. My muscles were aching, my bones the same. I just wanted to lie down and sleep for a week.

And maybe I'd have the chance to soon enough.

My phone pinged in my purse. Probably another message from Jack. I ignored it, keeping my focus on Ella. Or Amy. Or whatever her name was.

'What's your name?'

'Why do you care?'

'I want to know,' I said, struggling to keep an eye on both her and the road ahead. I wanted to make sure she was heading in the right direction. 'Tell me the truth.'

'It's Amy,' she replied, without a hint of hesitation. 'Although, I've grown to like the name Ella. I might save that if I have children.'

I shook my head. 'You're deluded.'

'Why, are you going to kill me before I get chance?'

'I might if you don't wipe that grin off your face,' I said, wondering if I actually could do it. Squeeze the trigger and watch her fall to the ground lifeless. Would I shoot her in the chest? The head? Could I actually do that?

To save myself. To save my family.

Yes.

Yes I would.

I should have been feeling hungry. I hadn't eaten since a couple of slices of toast that morning and it was almost evening now. Yet I felt hollow inside. As if I was becoming a shell of what I had once been.

'Keep going,' I said, as we reached an intersection. 'Not much further now.'

I had to make a decision. I knew where we were going, but not what I was going to do at the end of that road.

Or how I was going to deal with Dan afterwards.

47

It was almost dark by the time we pulled up at Bluff Point. We came to a stop in the parking lot outside the yacht club, empty save for one or two other cars.

My phone was still beeping and buzzing away in my purse. I didn't know how many people were trying to get in touch with me. How many police were looking for my car right then. I certainly hadn't seen anyone following me on my journey, but it wasn't like I would have known what to look out for, in any event. I had been solely looking for red and blue flashing lights and there hadn't been any of them.

'Stay here,' I said, opening up the passenger-side door and closing it behind me. I wanted to put my hands on my knees. Take a deep breath and try to quell my rapid heartbeat and swirling insides.

I couldn't do that.

I had to be strong.

Inside my purse, my phone buzzed again, and I pulled it out now. I walked around the car, putting my body in the way of any escape from Ella. Amy.

It would take some time to not think of her as Ella.

I didn't think I would need to.

My cell phone was lit up, a call coming through.

Jack.

I wanted to pick up. To hear his voice. I couldn't do that. If I spoke to him now, he would only talk me out of what I was going to do.

No, I had to stay strong. I didn't think it would take that much time to end this.

I placed the phone back in my purse and glanced towards the sea. An open expanse of blue that seemed to stretch out forever. It was a beautiful place, there, south of Westport. There was a beach a little down the coast, but it was here, at Bluff Point that I remembered being happiest.

I reached over and opened the driver's-side door. Held the gun at my side and motioned for Ella to get out.

'Walk this way,' I said, closing the door with my foot and walking behind her. She glanced over her shoulder, but I nodded for her to keep going.

This place, this beautiful place. It was where Jack had asked me to marry him. For a brief moment in time, I'd forgotten everything else. I'd forgotten about Adam Halton. I'd forgotten about Dan. I'd forgotten about my past and could only see my future, laid out before me.

A future of a loving marriage, children, a fulfilling career. A comfortable home, a healthy pension fund. Kids going off to college, without worrying about student loans. Having careers of their own, families of their own. A future of old age, of love and of happiness.

And this woman was trying to ruin that future.

I didn't care that she was being led to do it by someone else. I didn't care that while she had been the face of it, Dan had been pulling the strings all along.

We reached the wall at the edge of the parking lot and Ella turned towards me.

'Keep going,' I said, the sun setting behind us. I wished I could sit a moment, enjoying the view. Enjoying normality. 'Climb up on the rocks and walk towards the sea.'

'Sara, you need to tell me what you're planning to do.'

There was only a hint of nervousness in her tone now, but I could hear it there. It should have been more. She should have been cowering.

'Walk to the edge there,' I said, keeping calm. Keeping composed. 'Just a little further.'

The terrain was more difficult to traverse now. The sandy beach was over to our left, while we climbed over the rocks that jutted out towards the sea. Huge boulder-like things. One wrong step and you could turn your ankle. Worse, break it if enough went wrong.

Not many people would think of clambering over them in the dying light. Which meant we were alone.

I scanned around us, not seeing a single other person. I wondered what someone would see, if they looked in our direction. Two women clambering over the rocks, trying to keep themselves upright. Would they stop and stare? Would they be intrigued enough to come for a closer look?

I didn't think so.

Ella – it was still difficult to think of her as Amy – stopped after almost falling twice. She turned to me. 'I'm not going any further.'

'You'll do what I tell you to.'

She shook her head. 'You're not going to do anything. You're just trying to scare me.'

'Do you really want to test that theory?'

'Yeah, I don't mind at all,' Ella said, folding her arms across her chest. An act of defiance, it seemed, but in actuality, she was probably trying to keep herself warm. 'You're not going to shoot me here. You're not going to push me into the sea. You're not going to do a damn thing. So, tell me, what are you *really* going to do?'

I hesitated, knowing that she was right.

As much as I wanted to – as much as I *needed* to – I wasn't going to do any of those things. I'd been trying to gee myself up, trying to give myself the confidence to do just that, but when it came to actually pulling the trigger and shooting this woman, I knew I couldn't do it.

It wasn't me.

Not any more. I wasn't that person.

'Sara, why don't you just be truthful to yourself?' Ella said, looking back at me – that same patronising look that Stephanie had given me earlier. 'You're out of options here. Unless . . .'

'What?' I replied, knowing that this was it. This was the moment when she would tell me what they really wanted. 'You and Dan, what do you want?'

Ella laughed, forced, loud, but every echo hurt my ears.

'You don't get it,' she said, still chuckling to herself. 'Dan isn't the one in control here. I am. He's not important. Never was.'

'Stop lying to me. I know he's the one who came to you and made you do these things. I know he's the one who told you what I did. What has he promised you? Money? Is that it? I can't give you the amount you'd want. I don't have it. I know you might think we're rich, but it's all fake money. It doesn't really exist. We make our mortgage payments, we save for our kid's college, and that's it. There's nothing to give you both. So, if this is the only way to get rid of you, I'll take it.'

'I'm not after your money,' Ella said, taking a step towards me. 'You know what you have to do for all this to be over.'

'And what's that?'

'You have to confess. You have to go to the cops and tell them what you did.'

'I didn't do anything.'

'You know that's not true, Sara,' Ella said, taking another step towards me. I held my ground, but tightened my grip on the gun hanging at my side.

I wanted to raise it. I wanted to point it in her direction and make her stop.

'It's time to give up and tell people what you really are,' Ella continued, her words being carried towards me on the wind that had picked up around us. 'It's time to tell the truth. Tell them what you did.'

'No. That's not happening.'

'It's over,' Ella said, her voice rising in volume now. More confident, as she looked down and jumped across to another rock. 'Don't you get it? You think you're going to walk away from all this and go back to your happy life, without a care in the world? It's too late. It's all over. You might have got away with it for over fifteen years, but you're done. The nice house, the family, the career — you don't deserve any of it. You're never going back to that life. We're not going to let you.'

'Dan will go down too,' I replied, feeling hopeless. Feeling desperate. I didn't want to hear her voice any more. I wished I could raise the gun in my hand and squeeze that trigger. Watch her fall on the rocks and stop talking. 'He killed Adam, not me. I never wanted any of this. Tell him. Call him now and tell him that if I go down, so will he.'

'I've never spoken to Dan in my life,' Ella said, stopping a few feet away from me. She glanced around us, before staring back at me. 'I don't care what he does. I didn't even know his name until you told me. I'm not interested in him. I'm interested in what *you* do.'

'No. It's you and him. All of this. You're trying to get something from me. You're trying to make me crazy.'

'You're already crazy,' Ella said, mocking me. Shaking her head, as if it were the most ridiculous thing she'd ever heard. 'That has nothing to do with me. You've been pretending, Sara. You've been lying to everyone. Trying to pretend you're something you're not. You're not normal. You're a killer. You don't deserve anything you have.'

'I know,' I said, my voice quiet. My bones felt tired. I wanted to collapse to the ground. I wanted to roll into a ball and for all this to be over. 'But I'm not going to let you take anything away from me. You're not going to win.'

'I already have.'

I heard a noise behind me and spun around. I lost my footing, slipping on the damp rocks and falling to the ground. My elbow caught most of the blow, my outstretched hand the next to take the fall. My arm exploded in a sharp burst of pain that made me cry out.

The gun was skittering away, into the dark recesses between the rocks. My purse flying from around my shoulder.

None of it mattered.

The pain was a blur, a peripheral figure on the edge of my consciousness. I knew I shouldn't concentrate on it, otherwise it would be all I would feel. And I couldn't do that. I had to get up. I had to do something.

Or I was going to lose him.

The noise I'd heard, the footsteps on the rocks behind me. I could see his face and I wished I could be happy to see him. As if he were there to help me.

'Please . . .' I said, as I tried to get to my feet. I couldn't catch my balance. 'You shouldn't be here.'

He came closer, standing over me. I waited for him to offer his hand, to help me to my feet, but he didn't do that.

I should have known. He wasn't on my side.

Instead, he looked past me, towards where I'd last seen Ella standing.

'I got here as soon as I could,' Jack said, his breaths coming in short bursts as he navigated the rocks. 'Did she hurt you?'

'No,' Ella replied, carefully making her way back. 'How did you find us?'

'The bug in the car. I followed you all the way here.'

'Jack . . .?' I managed to say, as I slowly got to my feet. 'What?'

He pushed past me, causing me to fall back to the ground. I landed on my back, looking up at them, as they came together.

And fell into an embrace.

48

Colby flicked on his turn signal and turned the car around. 'Bluff Point. Nice spot.'

'Where is it?'

'South of Westport,' Colby said, ignoring the cry from the trunk, as he slammed on the brakes so he didn't careen into the back of a slow car ahead. 'Right on the coast.'

'You think this is it?'

'I'm not sure what else she could want,' Colby replied, draining the last of the coffee they'd picked up twenty minutes earlier. 'I'm telling you now – this is worth more than five K.'

'I know, but we owed her a favour. After what her father did for us, we couldn't just walk away. A few grand to intimidate a woman seemed like easy money.'

Colby knew that was true. 'You called it from the beginning. The husband wanted her gone enough to make sure we stuck around. I'm just worried about how far he's willing to go.'

'Why he didn't just walk away is beyond me.'

'Because all men are idiots. Except me. I hope you know that at least.'

Penny smirked at him, before placing a hand on his arm. 'I know.'

He'd answered the call from Amy with one hand, as they'd cruised down the main street of New Haven. Down Whitney Ave, past Yale. A place that may as well have been a foreign land to Colby. Penny even more. They were forty minutes away, but he would try and shave at least ten minutes off that time.

'Did she say what's going on? What are we supposed to do with the cop?'

'I don't know,' Colby replied, wishing he'd never got involved with this woman. Or the guy she was having an affair with. It had been a shitshow from the beginning. 'Let's just get it done and we can walk away from this finally.'

'Really? I've been enjoying it. Seeing how other people live, that kind of thing.'

'Don't you have a bad feeling?'

Penny shook her head and Colby wondered if that should worry him.

'Just follow my lead,' Colby said, taking the turning that would lead them onto the I95. Ignored the views out of the left-hand side of his car and onto the dark coastline beyond. 'Unless we play this right, we'll end up in jail by the end of the night.'

'The cop?'

'We're not killing the cop,' Colby said, glancing over his shoulder, as another thump came from back there. 'That's one thing we're not having on our conscience.'

He looked across at Penny, hoping she heard the words. 'You listening to me? No matter what she says, what either of them say, we don't kill the cop. They can deal with her. If we do something as stupid as that, we'll never be able to step foot on the east coast again. Shit, with the technology they have these days, we'll have to leave the damn country. And I'm not prepared to do that. We just have to deal with the wife and get out of there with at least some kind of payment, you hear me?'

'Yes, darling.'

He wished they were anywhere else. Maybe back in his home town. His real home. Hours across country. Maybe he would have been able to make a decent living somewhere. They could have a family. Raise children. Maybe farm a little – that had always been the dream.

Instead, he was stuck in a car with a cop tied up in the trunk.

Colby was a religious man. And he was beginning to think that he was already being judged for his past actions while still walking around on Earth, rather than after he'd reached the gates.

*

Alex could hear them pretty well from inside the trunk. A few words were lost if they turned their heads, or mumbled a little.

But she got the main points.

The phone call from 'the woman' who Alex knew was Amy Morrison. Called herself Ella to Sara, but she knew her real name. That they had to go somewhere called Bluff Point, which seemed familiar to her.

She'd heard it recently.

Then she remembered. And her heart sank a little.

It was Sara who had told her about it. It was when she'd been talking about her 'happy place'.

Which meant that Sara had either taken Amy there, or been taken there by the husband.

This was the endgame now, she could feel it.

And she still had the problem of the duct tape around her wrists. She'd managed to get the binding around her legs off, but the wrists were proving to be more difficult. If she'd been sitting in a chair, it would have taken her seconds to get it off. As it was, she didn't have the space to do anything about it right there.

Which meant she wouldn't have much time to get away when they opened up the trunk. She would have to be running before they saw so much as a blur.

Alex braced herself as she felt the car turning, smacking into the side of the trunk as they came to an abrupt halt, hurtling towards the back as the car settled.

She could feel the tension in her muscles. The cramp beginning to set in.

There was no way she could allow that to happen. She had to be ready.

Alex didn't know how long she was going to have to wait, but she would be prepared when it finally came.

★

Dan wasn't going to make it in time.

That was by design, he guessed. When Jack had called him, Dan had asked too many questions. None of it made any sense. Why he was there in the first place. Why they had contacted him.

Why they had got him involved.

He was scared. Of being seen, of being known. Of being in the spotlight. It was too close to being found out.

A murderer. That's all he would ever be known as.

He should have been back home, in England, pretending none of this was happening. Letting Sara take the fall for them both.

He couldn't let that happen.

She would never forgive him.

He was the only person who knew what happened that night. The truth. And if he let her confess – or worse, if they were determined to make her pay – then he knew what would happen next.

Either they would come for him . . .

Or she would.

BEFORE

When Sara had finished telling Jack about the night a poor young man named Adam had died, her husband held onto her. Not because he wanted to be close to his wife. Not because he wanted to comfort her.

But because he couldn't let her see his eyes.

She fell asleep not long afterwards. He slipped out of the room, leaving her alone on the bed. He walked to the room down the hall, where JJ and Olivia were sleeping. Dead to the world, as Sara would say.

He was married to a murderer.

The realisation began to hit home. Of what he had brought into his life. Of what he'd been sharing his bed with, for all those years.

Of what had given birth to his children.

He couldn't pretend he didn't know there was something about Sara he'd never quite understood. Had never tried to.

He didn't know it was this.

The problem was – he didn't know what he was going to do about it. Not then. Not in the hours after she'd told him.

What he did know was that he had to find out as much as he could.

Sara's mom was sitting in darkness, staring at a blank screen in the corner of the room. TV remote still in her hand. She looked lost.

'Hey,' Jack said, coming into the room and sitting down on the other end of the sofa. 'Can I get you anything?'

She shook her head in response. Slowly. As if she were coming out of a dream.

Jack's mind was already whirring. Thinking ahead. There was no way he could stay with Sara. Yet he also knew he would be ruined in the event of a divorce. It would be messy. Unnecessary.

He realised in that moment that there was something he hadn't allowed himself to admit. He hadn't loved her in a long time. Perhaps he never had. He had been swept up in the romanticism of it all – meeting her in a foreign land, the sex was good in the beginning, bringing her back to the US and introducing her to his parents, knowing they wouldn't immediately approve.

Then, they'd had two children and fallen into a life together. It was comfortable, it was easy.

It was boring.

Now, years later, he had a way out. A way to keep all his family's money. Keep his good name. His good standing. His two children. Where he wouldn't be known as just another divorcee. Another statistic.

He had options. He could go to the cops. Tell them everything he knew. Blow the whistle and watch her fall apart.

He thought of what his parents would say. How they would view him.

He didn't want that.

He could divorce her, knowing she wouldn't be able to argue against it. He could get custody of the children. He loved them more than life itself. The thought of being forever linked to her, though . . . that wouldn't do.

Jack got up from the sofa and left the room. Moved through the hallway, feeling the need for fresh air – the atmosphere in the house was filled with death.

He opened the front door and went outside. Stood on the path and looked out into the darkness.

There was someone out there.

In the silence. As if waiting for him.

'Who's out there?'

Jack watched as a figure peeled away from behind a car, stopping underneath a streetlight. He was around the same height as Jack – skinnier, a little older perhaps. His cheekbones strained against the grey skin on his face. Hair cropped short, military style.

Somehow, he knew who it was. In a way, he'd felt his presence ever since they'd landed in the country. A piece of Sara's history, hanging around like a bad smell.

'What do you want?' Jack said, taking a couple of steps forward. He stopped a few yards away from the man. 'Why are you out here?'

The man shuffled forwards a little, before stopping at the end of the pathway. 'I need to see her,' he said, his voice barely above a whisper.

'You're him, right?'

'I don't know . . .'

'You're Dan.'

There was a pause, then Dan slowly nodded his head. 'Please, I just need to speak to her.'

'I know what you did,' Jack said, beginning to formulate a plan of sorts. 'And you're not getting anywhere near her.'

49

Nothing made sense.

I was getting upright, finally, but I was so confused, I couldn't be sure I was really conscious. I wanted to pinch the skin on my arm and wake myself up. To come out of the nightmare.

There was no way this could be true.

I got to my feet, standing only a few feet away from my husband, who was currently holding onto a woman who had been trying to destroy our lives.

'You're okay,' he said, pulling away from Ella and holding her face with his hands. His beautiful, soft hands that had held me every day for the past fifteen years. His eyes hidden from me, staring into hers. 'Where's the gun?'

'She dropped it,' Ella replied, smiling up at him, before pulling him close to her again. 'It's gone down into the rocks.'

'Jack?'

He finally turned to me and I saw the expression on his face. It was one I'd never seen before. Not directed at me, never.

It was disgust. It was sneering. It was soul-destroying.

'Why didn't you just go to the cops?'

I shook my head. 'I don't understand . . .'

'None of this would have had to happen,' Jack said, peeling himself away from Ella and coming towards me. He jabbed a finger in my direction. 'If you'd just done what you were supposed to, it wouldn't have come to this.'

'Jack, please? Tell me what you're doing?'

I still couldn't believe it. Not Jack. He wouldn't do this to me. He loved me.

'I had to do something,' Jack said, taking another step towards me. 'I couldn't let a killer raise our children any longer. Don't you get it? You're evil. I knew you wouldn't just leave us alone, so I had to do something. You forced me into this.'

'That's right, Sara,' Ella said, appearing at his shoulder. 'It's not his fault.'

'Shut your mouth.' My voice echoed around us, before the wind whipped up and stole my words. 'This can't be happening.'

'Sara, you can still make this right. You can still walk away from this, if you just go and tell them what you did.'

'JJ . . . Olivia . . .'

'They'll be better off without you,' Jack said, his voice rising in pitch, as if he couldn't believe that I didn't see his point. 'Don't you see that? If you just go to the cops, tell them what you did, it'll all be over. Don't make me do something you'll regret.'

I staggered back, almost losing my footing again. I scanned the ground, as Jack turned back to Ella.

'Why don't you go back to the car and I'll deal with this?'

'I'm not leaving you alone with her,' Ella said, taking hold of Jack's arm. 'There's no telling what she's capable of. I don't want anything to happen to you.'

'It's fine, don't worry,' Jack replied, kissing the top of Ella's head. 'I can handle her, I promise. I just need to talk to her, so she understands what her best option is here.'

Ella smiled at him, looked at me and rolled her eyes. Then she skipped along the rocks, going past me in a blur, leaving me and Jack alone.

'Why?' It was the only thing I could think to say. The only thing I could possibly say.

'I really didn't want you to find out this way,' Jack said, talking as if he had been found skipping on a diet. Forgetting a party invitation. Not taking the garbage out. 'But you have to see things from my point of view. I couldn't sleep easy knowing there was a killer living under my roof. I could barely look at you, much less allow you to be around our children for much longer.'

'How long have you been seeing her? When did it start?'

'Why do you care?'

I stared back at the man I loved, wondering when I'd lost him. When he'd changed into something I didn't recognise. 'Because it matters. To me.'

Jack shook his head. 'The only thing that matters to you is walking away from this unharmed. Because I swear to you, there's no way back now. It's over.'

'You told me you understood. That you knew I wasn't a bad person.'

'I was scared of you, Sara,' Jack said, not a hint of a lie in his voice. Although I wasn't sure I'd know the difference now. 'Of what you might do. Sure, you haven't slipped in a long time, but at any point, you could do it again. You wanted me to believe that it was all him, but you were there. You didn't stop him. And Dan told me you were right there with him – you told him what to do. I couldn't take the chance with the kids' lives.'

'It wasn't like that . . .'

'I'd say anything to keep us all safe. Me, JJ and Olivia. I didn't know what you might do. I asked Stephanie to come back, so you weren't alone with them any more. It wasn't until Amy came along that I saw a way out.'

'You could have just told me that you didn't want to be together. You didn't have to lie, you didn't have to cheat. You didn't have to do any of this.'

'And have you still in my children's lives? Why do you think Stephanie is always around? It's so I know they're safe.'

'I would never hurt them,' I said, spitting the words at him. I couldn't believe he would even think I would. 'I'd die for them, you know that.'

'Until they were in your way, just like Adam Halton was. Until they become a problem for you.'

'It wasn't like that . . .'

'You killed him, Sara,' Jack said, his fingers reaching up and finding the bridge of his nose. His telltale sign of stress. 'That's the truth. You don't deserve what we have. You don't deserve to be a mother.'

'You can't take them away from me,' I said, my hands balling into fists. 'They're my children. I'm not going anywhere.'

'You're out of options,' Jack replied, chuckling, as if this was just a game to him. Maybe it was. Only it was a humourless sound. He was tired of the conversation. Of the argument. 'It's done. I tried to do this the right way. I wanted them to make you understand that the best way out was to just leave us and confess what you'd done. Pay for your crime. You'd leave us alone and I could tell the children the truth. But instead you brought Amy here for what? To do what to her?'

I opened my mouth to reply, but I couldn't find the words. I knew what I had planned to do, but it only made everything he had said right.

Maybe he was.

'It's inside you,' he continued, his words chosen carefully. 'This evil. It's a sickness. And it's been there all along. You can't change who you are. Adam Halton was a problem for you and you dealt with it. Then, you sleep soundly. You trick me, you have my children. You have a career. You sleep next to me, you treat your patients, and all along you have this thing deep within you that you can't hide any more. It's never going away.'

Maybe he was right. Maybe for all of our safety, I should have been locked away.

'I can see it in your face,' Jack said, his tone softer, more concil-iatory. 'Look, you still have a chance to do the right thing here. I'll take you there now. You can tell them what you did to him. You'll take your punishment.'

'What about JJ and Olivia? You think I should just walk away from them?'

'They'll be okay,' Jack said, smiling at me. 'They'll have me. And Amy. We'll make sure they're brought up well. You've had your chance. I know you think you love them but after what you did, you can't possibly think that you're fit to be a mother? Who knows when you might snap again? When you're backed into a corner . . . I mean look at where we are. Look at what you were going to do. You can't be around my children any more. I don't want you around me, never mind them.'

'You're a monster,' I managed to croak out. My heart was rac-ing, my mind going a million miles a second. Nothing made sense. I couldn't believe it was Jack saying these things to me. I couldn't believe he would do this.

'There's only one monster here,' Jack said, picking his way across the rocks and getting closer to me. 'And that's you. Can't you see that?'

I stepped back, trying to work a way out of the situation. To not claw at his eyes, place my hands around his neck and squeeze until he went still. To not bash his head onto the rocks until my hands were covered in his blood.

Those images raced through my mind, so hard, so fast. All I could see was red.

'Last chance,' Jack said, from somewhere in the blur that had become the world. 'You either leave and confess, or . . .'

He didn't finish his sentence. Left the threat hanging there. I didn't want to think about what he was talking about. What he was suggesting. Only I needed to hear it.

'What will you do to me if I don't?'

He smiled again, a horrible, sick-inducing smirk. 'Then, it'll be so much worse. You've done some crazy things this week. It won't be difficult to get you put under a psych hold. In fact, I think it'd be incredibly easy. Then you'll end up in the nuthouse for the rest of your life, because you'll never be able to get out. Think about that – every day, you'll be locked away with no chance of escape. I'll tell them stories, Sara. I'll tell them about how you talked about killing yourself. That I was scared about the way you looked at me, at the children. That we weren't safe around you. The neighbours will back me up. Stephanie, your work . . . everyone thinks you've gone crazy already. I can make sure that you never have another life.'

He came closer to me and I could smell his aftershave. The scent that had always made me feel comforted. Now, I felt my stomach flip, a nauseated feeling that made me want to gag.

'Think about it,' he said, his voice barely above a whisper now. 'This way, you can move on. Eventually, of course. Just not with us. This life is over. You're going to walk away and never see us again. Never come back. You might have to spend some years behind bars, but at least when you get out, you'll be able to have another life.'

'No. You're not going to do this to me.'

'I already have,' Jack said, taking hold of me, his hand rough on my upper arm. The grip tight. 'Choose.'

I couldn't. There was no way. 'There has to be another way. Please. Don't take my children from me.'

'They'll be better off without a killer for a mom.'

He didn't know what he was doing. He didn't know what he was asking.

He didn't know *me*.

A scream came from somewhere deep inside. A roar. And then he was backpedalling away from me, stumbling over. I didn't wait until he fell.

I was already running.

50

I could feel the burn in my lungs. The ache in my legs, as they slammed against the rocks, but I wasn't looking back. I was going forwards.

There was only one way out of this.

I managed to get across the rocks, jumping down and into the parking lot. I could see Jack's car, parked up near the edge. Mine was further away and I made my way towards it.

I heard a shout from nearby, but I ignored it. I was only concentrating on my car, getting inside, driving to Jack's parents' and getting JJ and Olivia.

That was all that was important right now.

I could see headlights in the distance, as the sky turned black and I felt the soft tears of rain falling on my skin.

Almost there.

The car turned into the parking lot, the roar of its engine breaking the silence of the night. I could almost feel it turning my way, racing towards me. It didn't matter. I was almost in touching distance of safety. Of shelter.

I almost slammed into the side of the car, coming to a stop from my flat-out sprint towards it at the last moment. I pulled on the door handle, expecting it to give instantly.

It didn't move.

I felt across my shoulder and cried out when I realised what was missing. I looked back quickly, but I couldn't even see the rocks now. And I knew what was waiting for me back there.

I heard another shout, my name being screamed across the parking lot. I spun quickly, trying to find something, anything that I could use to break the window. Not that it would help me. I didn't have a key to start the damn car.

The car that had been hurtling towards me came to a stop a few feet away, and I heard the door open. I was frozen in place, as out of the darkness I saw a figure emerge.

'Grab her, now,' Ella said, shouting in the direction of whoever had got out of the car. 'Don't let her go anywhere.'

I screamed and the world became a cacophony of noise.

I didn't even know it was me at first. My ears rang and my throat burned with effort, but it wasn't until I felt the man's grasp on my wrist that I realised I had to move.

There was no pause. I pulled away, felt the man's hand fall from mine and ran. Hard. I couldn't see all that far in front of me, but I took off as if I was in pursuit of hidden figures ahead of me. I heard shouts behind me – warnings, threats, anger – but I tried to concentrate on only my legs pumping ten to the dozen beneath me. Desperately trying to keep my balance, as the ground grew soft and muddy around my feet. Trying to grab and pull me down, pull me under.

I'd hit the fields that surrounded the parking lot. The houses were pinpricks of light in the distance.

I ran as fast as I ever had in my life.

My lungs screamed, the muscles in my legs wailed in protest, but I kept going. I couldn't look over my shoulder, so convinced was I that they would be just behind me. The man who had jumped out of the car, reaching out, waiting for me to stumble or fall so he could get me in his hands again.

I could feel my shuddering breaths and tried to ignore them.

I reached the end of the field, then onto the road, seeing the large houses that lined the approach to Bluff Point. I told myself that I could make it there. That I could bang on someone's door and that they would come out and help.

I told myself I was almost safe.

I didn't need telling twice.

I rounded a corner, heading towards a small cut-through – an alleyway that would lead to the open street and the closest house. I put my head down and sprinted the remaining yards that separated me from them. A last effort.

When I made it to the alleyway, I almost collapsed with exhaustion. I finally allowed myself to look behind me.

There was no one there.

I moved the last few feet, then leaned against the wall breathing hard in and out.

One last effort and I would be okay. That's all it would take.

I heard something smash nearby and my heart stopped for a beat or three.

I moved away quickly from the wall, getting a few steps away, and then I was flying through the air. It felt as if it were in slow motion – one moment standing upright, catching my breath. The next, unable to exhale, in mid-air, hurtling towards the ground.

I landed with my elbow tucked underneath my body. It drove right into my ribs, knocking the wind out of me. That wasn't the problem. I wanted to throw my hands out to break my fall, but the fall had already come.

My head smacked against the concrete and I felt the shock of the impact travel through my entire body. A shockwave that pulsed through every vein, and sent my body into spasm.

It went dark. For a moment. Maybe two, I wasn't sure. I could feel a weight on me, but I couldn't move to shift it from me. I didn't see stars, not even in the black sky above me, but then, I didn't really see anything at all.

I was almost outside of myself. My mind. Floating away, as the rain began to fall harder and I struggled against my own failing body.

I came to, properly, more aware of my surroundings, bit by bit. Second by second. I heard breathing in my ears, and then a hand shift against my body.

'Stop struggling,' someone said. I didn't know who. It could have been me. My own thoughts. Only it didn't sound like any voice I'd heard before.

I felt hands grip me around the wrists. Spinning me around on the ground, as my body began to respond. As air entered my lungs finally and I started moving. Slowly. Trying to struggle, but failing.

'Stay down,' a voice said, his voice sounding slurred in my dead ears as I felt hands grip me around the wrists.

I wanted to get up. Get away. But I couldn't move. My arms moved up my back and pain exploded in my shoulders. I cried out, but it was lost as soon as it reached my throat.

I could feel myself being dragged along. Two bright lights suddenly flashed in my eyes, blurred vision, bright orbs dancing in my sight.

'She almost got away.'

'Yeah, but she didn't, Penny, so all's good.'

I felt an arm slip around my body, then another across my mouth. I could taste stale cigarettes on my lips. I tried to shake free, but my head was pounding and it only made it worse. I couldn't feel the ground beneath me.

Then, I was thrown to the ground again, as we reached the edge of the parking lot. I heard breathing around me. Heavy, wet.

I thought it was a dog. Or some kind of animal. Instead, I realised I'd heard that breathing before. The two people who had broken into my house. The voices from the office car park. Distinctive. Memorable.

'What do you want us to do?' I heard a woman's voice say.

I turned my head slowly, seeing Ella illuminated in the head-lights. 'Let me think.'

'Amy, let me speak to them.'

Jack's voice. For a split second, I forgot about what had happened. I looked up, seeing him holding his hand against his head. Rubbing at it absentmindedly.

'Please . . . please let me go.'

My voice didn't sound like my own. It was rasping, each syllable agony. I was getting my breath back, but my head was still swimming. I felt rough hands on me again, keeping me from getting up. I could focus now, as my vision began to come back.

'We can't just leave her here?'

'Jack . . .'

'Can't you shut her up?'

I felt the hand over my mouth and I tried to move my head away from it. His hold was strong. Too strong. I was locked in place.

'She's not going to the cops,' Ella said, and I could see her, close to Jack. 'We need to get rid of her.'

'I know, Amy. We can turn her in – get her on a psych ward. Like we talked about. It's the only other option.'

'No it isn't,' Ella said, her hand reaching up and touching the face of the man I loved. I felt my stomach flip.

'We'll never be truly free of her,' Ella continued, looking up at Jack. Imploring him with her eyes. 'The children will never really be safe. Unless we're completely sure she's gone.'

I began to struggle again, as I saw something change in her expression. I saw Ella turn towards the man holding onto me.

'How much?'

'For what?'

Ella stepped forwards, letting go of Jack. 'You know what I'm talking about. My father helped the two of you out once upon a time. Now, he's gone and you've repaid your favour to him for me. Now, this is separate. I'm asking you how much it will cost to do what I know you've done before. The two of them. To disappear for ever.'

Two of them, I thought. Who was the other person?

Dan, of course. They must have got him back at the house.

'There's no price. We're done here . . .'

Jack came up beside Ella. Placed his arm around her. 'We can pay. Just give us a price.'

'No, it's not happening . . .'

'Colby,' the woman said. 'Let's talk.'

51

Colby let Jack take over restraining Sara. For a moment, he hoped she would escape there and then.

He tore his attention away from them and looked at Penny as if she'd gone mad.

'We can't.'

He looked back towards where the husband was currently struggling with Sara. Watched him pin her to the ground and seem to regain control.

They didn't have time to think properly.

'Listen, Colby,' Penny said, turning him away from the scene unfolding ahead of them. 'It's not like we haven't done this before.'

'It's a bit different, don't you think?'

'Killing someone is killing someone.'

'She's a mom,' Colby said, trying to see the logic. Failing. 'And there's a cop. We absolutely cannot do this.'

'They're desperate,' Penny replied, getting closer to Colby. 'Can't you see that? They'll pay whatever we want. We can take a break from this – I know you want to. When we started, we never wanted to do this kind of thing, right? Well, maybe this is our chance to get out of it.'

'They won't have enough for that. How long would it take them to raise the sort of cash we'd need to go off the radar for any sort of time? They don't have the cash now.'

'Well, they'll have enough to keep the wolves from the door at least. And then, eventually, enough to allow us to be a little bit more picky about the jobs we take on.'

'I'm not killing a cop,' Colby said, as firmly as he could. 'And neither are you. She doesn't know who either of us is, she doesn't know anything. We're not doing that.'

'But . . .'

'No, Penny, we can't do it. There's no amount they'll be able to give us that will make it worth the trouble. This is their mess. They have to clean it up.'

Penny pouted, as if he'd just told her they couldn't buy an expensive piece of jewellery, rather than kill a cop. Colby rubbed at his forehead, massaging life into himself.

'You're stressed,' Penny said, coming to his side and slipping her arm around his waist. 'I know why. So, I'll do it. It's not a problem.'

'She has kids . . .'

'I know,' Penny said, a hint of sadness in her tone. 'But, we don't know her. We matter more, right?'

'Not the cop,' Colby replied, hoping he wouldn't have to say it again. 'It's too much heat on us. Let them deal with it.'

Penny nodded and he let her go.

*

'Sixty K,' the woman said, once she'd returned. 'For her.'

I began shouting, screaming, but they were lost in the rough skin of a hand across my mouth. The man had returned and taken over from Jack.

I saw Jack look at Ella, weighing things up. He turned back to the woman, refusing to look at me.

'I never wanted this,' Jack said, glancing back at Ella. 'I just wanted her to confess and be out of it. I don't want to . . . you know, end it.'

'Fine, then we can just be on our way in that case,' the woman said, matter-of-factly. 'But I'll tell you now – whatever you had planned was never going to happen. You had kids with the woman and she loves them more than you. More than herself. She'll never let them go. So, you either run off with your new girlfriend, or you take care of your wife here and now. It's up to you.'

I watched my husband – the man I trusted more than anyone else in the world – seemingly make his mind up over whether I should live or die.

And I couldn't believe he wouldn't come to the right decision. He was a good man, despite the situation we seemed to be in. He wouldn't let this go on. He wouldn't let the mother of his children be hurt.

He couldn't.

Jack turned back to Ella. 'If we let her get hurt, we're just as bad as she is.'

There it was. Humanity, poking its way through.

'Jack,' Ella said, placing a hand on my husband's arm, causing me to struggle and fail to break free from the man holding onto me. 'You know what she is. We talked about this. She's a monster. You talked me into doing this whole charade. I had to sit in a room with her and pretend to be what she is. We knew that there was a chance she wouldn't confess. Look, she's been around the kids for too long – who knows what she's filled their heads with. We can fix this. We can fix them. But we need to stop her before it's too late. We don't know how many other people she has hurt over the years. We're doing everyone a favour by making sure she can't hurt anyone else.'

'But this . . . this is murder. If we do this, we're just as bad.'

I waited for Ella to lose her patience with him, but instead she only seemed to become more sympathetic.

'I know, I know,' she said, pulling him close to her. He held onto her like she was a piece of driftwood in the ocean he'd found while drowning. 'It's okay. I wish she'd done the right thing, but she's not going to. And we don't have enough to go the cops ourselves.

We just don't. So, she'll take everything from us. The house, the kids, the money. All of it. She'll try to destroy us. We won't have a life together. And it won't be murder. Think of it like we're putting down a rabid dog. She's sick. We have to do the decent thing. And you or I won't be doing it ourselves.'

I was listening, but I couldn't take it in properly. I wanted to rip them apart. I wanted to get at them, get my hands around her throat. His throat. Squeeze until they went blue.

'Okay, I understand. This is the only way. But I can't watch.'

My heart broke in two, as Jack looked back at the woman standing over me. He still refused to look at me.

'We'll give you forty thousand.'

I strained my eyes, finding Jack. He was standing six feet away, his polo shirt ripped at the neck. Something black was on his hands. Blood.

'Fifty,' the woman said, folding her arms across her chest. 'And we make the cop disappear.'

He looked down at me finally, shook his head sadly, as if I were a dog he was having put down. Then, back at the woman.

'Deal.'

52

I was already struggling, but that increased tenfold as I saw Jack and Ella walk away. Not even looking back at me. Not staying to watch.

Not giving me a second thought.

I was left with the man and woman. The stench of sweat dripping in the atmosphere around the man. Dirt and grime.

'You can't do this, Penny, please,' I heard the man say. 'You'll not be able to live with yourself.'

'Fifty K will make it much easier.'

'I'm not going to help you. You know that, right? I can't be here when you do it.'

'That's fine.'

'Please, just listen to me,' the man said, his grip on me slackening. 'Fifty grand isn't enough. Not for what you've got to do here. It's two people. Two lives. Two women. One a cop. Doesn't that mean anything to you?'

'You think I should've charged more?'

'No, I'm saying you can't do this.'

They went back and forth, talking about taking my life as if it were nothing but an inconvenience.

I stopped struggling, as it became clear I wasn't going anywhere. I moved my hands slowly around me, trying to find something on the ground. I heard a banging coming from the direction of the car.

The two continued to talk. I could tell they were a couple – that they'd done work like this together for a long time, but both wanted out. That the work they did probably included murder.

I thought about the end.

There was something on the ground next to me. Shards of something. I felt along the asphalt and tried to find something bigger than a centimetre or two.

It was clear Penny was going to win the argument. I learned the man's name. Colby. What a stupid name. I didn't want to die at their hands. I didn't deserve this.

'I'm not going to watch you do this,' Colby said, his grip disappearing in an instant. 'If you're really going to do this, you're on your own.'

My ribs screamed in protest at every slight movement. I concentrated on breathing through it.

'Fine, I can deal with it on my own.'

I looked up and found Penny's eyes. They were black in the darkness.

'Please, I have . . . my children.'

'Not my problem, lady.'

I could see a flash of something. It turned dull as it pointed towards me. Her hand was steady.

'Listen, I can give you more than fifty thousand. A lot more. You just have to let me go.'

That got her attention. 'How much more?'

'I don't know,' I said, trying to come up with a figure that would save my life. 'Seventy-five. Would that be enough? Anything, please. Just don't do this.'

Colby cocked his head, listening, absorbing. 'A hundred.'

I nodded my head, far too eagerly. Not caring in the slightest how it looked. 'A hundred, yeah, whatever you need. I'll get it for you.'

'How?' Penny said, a disbelieving tone cutting through the single word.

I hesitated, not thinking straight. 'I . . . I just will, don't worry.'

'You don't have it,' Penny said, shaking her head. 'Your husband – he's the one with the money. He can get it, but I bet you can't put your hands on anything. It'll be worse for you now, with him shacking up with her. He'll control everything.'

'No . . . no, I have my own money, I promise. I can give you a hundred thousand. I guarantee it. Please.'

Penny was thinking, I could see it. The cogs turning in her mind. Considering the offer. I knew what she was going to do. The idea of double her previous fee would be enough to convince her to change her mind. That's how these type of people worked. It didn't matter that I had no idea how I was going to get that kind of cash. I could figure it out.

Jack was insured, after all. I could collect on that without a problem. Once I'd dealt with him as easily as he seemed to have dealt with my fate. I wouldn't farm it out either. I'd do it myself.

'No.'

I was already planning my next move, so when Penny spoke, I didn't quite realise what she was saying.

'Way I see it,' she continued, speaking slowly, as if her thoughts were forming as she spoke. 'I have fifty guaranteed here. You might be offering more, but I don't see it as being as solid as what they're promising. They can get it to me – I don't know what you're capable of actually paying, so it's a risk, right?'

I didn't know if she was actually asking me, expecting an honest answer. Getting an opinion on whether I could pay enough to save my own life.

'I can get it,' I said, hoping she could hear the honesty in my voice. The desire. The plea. 'I swear.'

She thought for a few seconds, then my heart fell as she shook her head.

'No, I think I'll stick with the fifty,' she said finally, as if she was on a gameshow. 'That seems to be the right call.'

'Please . . .'

This was it.

If I didn't do something now, I wouldn't even hear when it happened. It would just be over.

She was almost on top of me, her feet within touching distance. And that's what I concentrated on.

I grabbed hold of what I'd found on the ground, feeling the sharp edge of a broken headlight, and thrust it towards her leg.

Found flesh, as I used all my strength to drive it home.

There was a beat of silence, that I used to get to my feet, almost losing my balance as I stood up so fast. My head whirled with light-headedness, but I was already moving while behind me Penny squealed like a wounded animal.

I took off across the parking lot, in the direction of the sea. I could hear it in the distance, waves lapping against the shoreline, as the rain grew heavier around me. I couldn't see much in front of me, but I knew if I just kept putting one foot in front of the other, I would be okay.

I would be safe.

I would walk away from this.

I reached the wall and clambered over it, onto the rocks. I wanted to get close to the spot where I'd lost my purse, try and find my keys, my phone, anything that would help me. I couldn't search for long, but I started whispering a silent prayer that they would be right in my line of sight.

There was a shout from behind me, but I ignored it, continuing to skip across the rocks, landing on each soundly, so I didn't lose my footing.

'Stop running . . .'

I didn't stop.

There was a gap in the rocks and I jumped from one to another, before spotting something on the surface a few rocks ahead.

My purse, my handbag, its contents spilled out.

I pushed on, new hope given. I reached it in seconds, sliding to my knees and picking up my bag. I thrust my hand inside and my fingers instantly touched upon my car keys. I grabbed hold of them and gripped them tight in my hand.

I struggled to my feet, my free hand flying to my side as a stab of pain hit me in my ribs. I took a deep breath and looked left and right. I needed to find somewhere to hide. Until they gave up looking for me.

There wasn't anything obvious.

I could hear steps coming towards me, so I turned and headed to my left, towards the beach I could barely see in the darkness.

There was only the sound of my feet smacking against the rocks. I couldn't even hear my own heavy breathing, as I kept going.

The silence was broken.

It was as if a snake had jumped up and bit me on the leg. I was running with one leg for a second, before trying to put weight on the other.

I slammed onto the rocks, the pain wiped out in an instant as my leg screamed with fire.

My hand instantly went to the back of my leg, just below the knee. I could feel heat there, as I pulled up my trouser leg and felt the wound. I pulled my hand away, as my vision went white with agony.

I'd been shot.

The thought was like a neon sign in my mind, flashing over and over. Someone had fired a gun at me and hit me direct in the leg.

I tried to stand, but I couldn't get to my feet. And I could hear him coming now.

'I didn't want to do this. I want you to know that.'

I was crying, screaming, but it was as if he couldn't hear me. I started dragging myself across the rocks, almost at the edge now. I could hear the waves, the sea, the smell of salt on the air.

'Sorry,' Colby said, finally reaching me. 'You put up a good fight, I'll give you that. But you hurt my wife. I can't have that.'

I could only watch as he levelled the gun.

I thought about JJ and Olivia. About the beach. About the sea. I tried to keep their faces in my mind, as I turned my face away from the man standing above me.

I didn't even get a final word.

It was just over, in an instant. He squeezed the trigger and my body was hit with a thud. An explosion of heat.

Two more times.

And then, I was gone.

BEFORE

'You're going to tell me everything.'

Jack waited for Dan to speak. To tell him what he was already suspecting.

'We waited for him to come out,' Dan said, his voice quiet. Devoid of emotion. 'She told me he deserved what was coming to him. So that's what we did. We waited and waited. Then, he was there, in front of us. We both got out of the car – I took the lead. I went up to him and got in his face. I could see how scared he was, but I could hear Sara next to me. She was screaming at him.'

'Who hit him first?'

'Me,' Dan said, ashamed, scared of the truth. 'I caught him square in the jaw. Then it all became a bit of a blur. I couldn't stop myself. I knew Sara was with me – I could hear her hitting him too. I got so close to him that I realised how young he was. I know he was nineteen, but he could have easily passed for younger. It didn't stop us.'

'You beat him to death.'

'We both did.'

'Why didn't you go to the cops? Why didn't you try to save him?'

'It was too late,' Dan said, unable to meet Jack's eyes now. 'By the time we found ourselves, he was already gone. Then it became more about making sure we weren't going to get into trouble. I know how selfish that sounds, but it really was too late by that point. I remember just staring at him – this stupid gold chain he had around his neck, with the initial A hanging from it. He was so young. But *he shouldn't have touched Sara. I always told her I would keep her safe, and that's what I thought I was doing.'*

'She told me a different story,' Jack said, moving closer to Dan now. Still a little wary of the smaller man. Knowing what he knew, it didn't make any sense – how could someone as diminished as the guy in front of him be a threat to anyone?

'I'm telling you everything . . .'

'She told me it was you alone,' Jack said, interrupting him before he could say another word. Another lie. 'You killed him. She was there, she didn't stop you, but she didn't help you. You did it.'

Dan didn't speak. Shifted from one foot to the other.

'Is that what happened?'

Dan still wouldn't answer. Jack took another step towards him. 'I want the truth. I want to know exactly who I'm married to and you're going to tell me.'

Dan told him the truth. As much as he knew. As much as he suspected.

'Give me your phone,' Jack said, once he was done. Once he had finally admitted what he'd suspected.

'Please . . .'

'No. It ain't happening. And if you don't want me to go to the cops and tell them what you did, you'll do exactly as I say. Where did you bury the body?'

Dan shook his head. A tear escaped, rolled down his cheek. The last part was always the hardest.

'Dan, if you don't tell me . . .'

'Okay, there are woods near a place called Wambrook. We dug a hole, buried him there. No one will ever find him.'

'You're sure about that?'

'Positive.'

'I'm going to call on you at some point. I know enough to make your life very difficult, you know that. At any moment, I could tell someone what you did and you'd be locked up within seconds. That

means you work for me now. You're going to do whatever I say. I own you.'

Jack returned inside a few minutes later, not knowing exactly how it was all going to play out, but knowing it was going to end up with Sara gone from his life.

He didn't know it would take so long to do that.

Years.

53

Dan saw Sara's husband and the woman getting into the car together.

Jack and Ella.

They kissed and held onto each other once inside the vehicle. Smiled and giggled, as if it was all a game.

He was too late.

He saw a man in the distance and froze. He was holding a gun.

Dan didn't move. Not even when he saw Sara go down. Not even when he heard the shots. Not even when he knew that they had killed her.

He would be next.

That made him move.

It took him longer without his own car, but he made it to the house only a couple of hours after them.

It's not difficult to break into a house. The actual act itself, that is. Gaining entry, even as technology moves forward, is never the issue.

It's all about what comes next. The risks, the dangers. What happens once you're inside. How you deal with the possible things that can go wrong. A dog, an alarm, a camera.

A person. With a baseball bat, with a hammer.

Or a gun.

Although, in this case, he knew that was kept locked away. Safely out of the hands of the children in the house. He'd always thought there was little point in a gun being in a safe, when he was already inside the house by the time they'd need it. By the time it had been taken from its safe space, it would have already been too late.

Breaking in was the easy part. Loud or silent. It's all about dealing with the fear that courses through your veins once you're inside. Dealing with controlling that, slowing your breathing, not allowing it to take control.

Dan had done this kind of thing before. It had been a necessary evil in order to survive, over the years since he'd killed a man. Since he'd struggled to hold down a job for any length of time. A way to make a bit of money here and there. Some jewellery that he could pawn. A bit of food. Shoplifting was more difficult, he'd found. Breaking into houses was easier. The fear was still there – but he could control it.

He could weigh up the risks and possible outcomes within a few seconds. Hundreds of previous jobs had given him all the experience he would ever need. The different doors, windows, shutters, you name it, he could break them.

He could pop a window open without you even turning over in your sleep. You wouldn't hear a sound. A soft click, a few turns, and he'd suddenly be standing in your kitchen, or your dining room.

Or your bedroom.

Sure, sometimes it would be a little messier, but those were the jobs he saved for the empty homes. The ones without security dogs and multiple cameras pointing at him.

The break-ins were all different. Whether it was a nice house, with cars on the driveway that simply needed to be 'resituated' to the highest bidder. Those were the easy ones, where all you needed was the keys. And Dan knew most people left them out in the open, near the front door. Despite being told numerous times that it wasn't the best place to keep them. Easily accessed, on display. Your new Audi or Mercedes disappeared in the middle of the night, with nothing left to show for it.

Technology was moving on, but it hadn't made much difference to his life. The increase in cameras had driven him to cover his face, but that was no big deal. A balaclava suited him fine. He'd always worn gloves, so that was again no issue.

The blurred and distorted images of home CCTV was no issue to him either. Something for an exasperated homeowner to post on a local Facebook group, or one of those neighbourhood watch apps, hoping someone would recognise a blob of black.

This wasn't that type of break-in, though. This wasn't like anything he'd done in the past.

Dan wasn't looking for money. For stuff to sell. Food to eat – although that would be nice. It had been a while since he'd had a proper meal.

This time, he was looking for revenge.

He'd been too late to save her.

He'd come back to Sara's house, because that's where her husband and the woman he'd been having affair with would be.

It wasn't going to be an issue getting inside. It was what he was going to do once he was in there that was bothering him.

He was in the back yard, having scaled the short wall that separated it from the side alleyway, when he realised he was probably making a mistake.

Sara had been killed by these people.

Which only meant one thing – this had been the outcome from the beginning in their minds. Sara out of the picture, the cheating husband able to move on with the new woman.

He didn't have a weapon with him. Something to defend himself with.

He kept moving all the same.

The back door wasn't an issue. He still had the key that he'd taken when he'd been at the house earlier that day. He didn't know why he'd taken it then, but was now glad he had.

It really is easy to break into a house.

Especially when you have a key.

The blonde woman was waiting for him inside. He almost bolted back out, but he was so surprised to find her there that he was frozen in place.

'Keep your voice down,' she said, lifting a finger to her lips. 'Everyone is asleep.'

Dan couldn't move.

She was sitting at the counter in the kitchen, drinking a small glass of something. His mouth watered at the sight of the liquid. He could feel his hands shaking.

She finished her drink in one last gulp.

'Amy,' she said, raising a hand his way as a greeting. Her voice barely above a whisper. 'And I'm guessing you're the infamous Dan?'

He nodded his head slowly as the barstool spun as she got up from it.

'I knew you would come,' she said, shaking her head sadly. 'I knew you'd been here earlier today. I've listened to the whole conversation you had with Sara.'

Dan could hear his heart beating as he realised what she was holding in her other hand. It almost stopped when she pointed it at him.

'So, I know you were planning to double-cross us,' Amy said, stopping a few feet away from him. 'Now, she's gone. And there's nothing here for you.'

'What did you do with her?' Dan asked, finally finding his voice. 'Did you leave her there to die? Have you buried her?'

'Why didn't you just run? We don't need you any more. And you're not getting anything that was promised to you. No money. No salvation. You don't deserve it.'

Dan hesitated. 'Was it you or him?'

Amy cocked her head in confusion. 'What do you mean?'

'That messaged me,' Dan said, willing his body to move. Feeling bereft when it wouldn't. 'That paid for me to come over here.'

'Oh,' Amy replied, a smile playing across her lips. 'Both of us. Jack didn't think you'd come. You were an insurance policy that we didn't need in the end. That's why I've been waiting for you. I knew you'd be close by. And after what happened tonight, I knew I wouldn't have to wait long.'

'What did you think I'd do? Why bring me here in the first place?'

'I wanted to see what you would say when you came face to face with Sara. I thought it might have been enough to make her go to the cops, but we know now that she was never going to do that. Unfortunately for her.'

'So why involve me at all? If this was between you and her, why complicate matters by bringing me here?'

Amy shook her head sadly. 'Because it took a little longer to convince him that she needed to be gone for good than I wanted.'

Dan finally made his feet move. He took a few steps towards Amy, but then saw her grip the gun tighter in her hand and that stopped him in his tracks. He shook his head. 'Where is she?'

'I don't think you understand what gone means. It's over. She's finally been made to pay for her crime. Well . . . your crime. Both of you, guilty as each other.'

'It was an accident. That's all it was. It should never have happened. I only came here to make sure you both knew that. I know I spoke to Jack before, but I wasn't thinking straight. It wasn't Sara's fault at all. She didn't know what I was going to do. She didn't know I was going to hurt the guy. It wasn't supposed to go that way. She was just scared, frightened. This is all my fault. Not hers. So we need to find her and fix all of this.'

'Save it,' Amy said, getting closer to him. The small gun in her hand disappeared from his view. A tiny little thing that fit nicely in the palm of the much younger, much smaller woman standing in front of him, and gave her all the power in the world. 'I'm not interested in hearing your life story. She's dead.'

Dan looked in her eyes and saw no lie.

And then he knew why she'd really been waiting for him.

'You're just as bad as us if you do this,' he said, his voice shaking with fear. He could feel his bladder wanting to let go. He wanted to run, he wanted to fight, but all the energy within him had left.

'Maybe,' Amy replied, lifting the small .22 gun up and levelling it at his head. 'But at least this can't be called an accident.'

Dan made as if to move, but the pop came first. He felt a thud in the side of his head. His thoughts being cut off.

Then, it was only darkness.

He didn't hear another sound.

He didn't see another image.

He didn't feel a thing.

He didn't even get the chance to wonder if he'd deserved it.

54

'What have you done?'

Amy turned to see Jack, standing in the doorway. The gun was still in her hand, still extending out.

Jack raised his hands, slowly. He was wearing only boxers. Amy could see the hair on his chest standing on end. His eyes flitting one way then the other. 'Why?'

She placed the gun down quickly on the kitchen counter. 'No, I didn't mean to point it at you, I'm sorry.'

Jack's hands slowly lowered. He walked to her side before picking up the gun quickly. She ran to him and threw her arms around him, but he shrugged her off.

He walked over to where Dan's body lay on the floor. Looked down at him. Got down on his haunches and felt his neck for a pulse that would never be there.

'Amy, what did you do?'

She couldn't see his face, but she could hear the tone of his voice and it sent a shiver through her body. She started talking. Slowly, for a few words, before it became like rapid fire. 'He . . . he broke into the house. I had to do something. He was going to kill me. He knew what we'd done to Sara and was going to tell everyone. He wanted me to die for it. Said I deserved it. He wasn't going to stop there. He was going to ruin us both, Jack. I had no choice. He came at me, so I didn't think. I was thinking about the kids . . .'

'They didn't wake up, thank God,' Jack said. He puffed out his cheeks, as Ella began to talk again. Placed a finger to his lips and shushing her. 'Thankfully it wasn't too loud. You need to figure out what to do with him.'

'Don't worry, we can sort this out.'

'I can't deal with this, Amy,' Jack replied, breathing more heavily now, swiping a hand through his hair. 'We'll move him for now. To the office.'

'What are we going to do?'

'Hide him there, until you call your two friends and tell them you need their help to move a body.'

'We can't do that,' Amy said, too quickly. She took a breath. 'I mean . . . I don't even know where they are right now. They'll have gone to ground after what happened tonight.'

'Well, what else are we going to do? Tell them we have their money. They'll soon come here.'

Amy knew what they should do. They were going to have to move him. Dump him somewhere where he'd be found after months, or years, had passed. Down at Bluff Point, as a symbol that it was all over for Sara and Dan. Poetic. By the time his body was found, there would be no way anyone would link him to her or Jack.

Only, she couldn't say that to him right then. He wasn't acting the way she thought he would.

'I don't know, Jack,' Amy said, her voice quiet. Pleading. 'I was protecting us. Can't you help me deal with this?'

'Call them.'

'Jack, why don't we deal with it ourselves? This was to keep us safe. It's all over now and no one can stop us being together. Don't you see that?'

He chuckled humourlessly at that. 'Amy, there's no way I'm doing a damn thing. I'll help you move him into the office, but that's it. I can't get involved in something like this. It's why I wanted Sara gone in the first place. This is your mess. You can clean it up. And then we can talk later.'

Her heart broke a little at that. She hadn't seen this side to the man she loved. How cold he was. How little he cared about the situation they were in.

She hadn't expected this.

An hour later, she sat in the kitchen, staring at the wall, wondering if she had got everything wrong.

Only, she knew it was going to be okay in the end. They would be together soon enough, with nothing holding them back. She just had to get through the next twenty-four hours.

That was all.

*

Amy stepped out on her front porch and waved the kids good-bye. They bounded down the path and didn't look back until they were stepping onto the school bus. JJ with one foot inside, waiting for Olivia to catch up to him.

She felt the rush of love that can course through a parent every now and again. That indescribable sensation that can surprise you by its sudden onslaught. Rock you back on your heels with its intensity.

She would die for those two children. She would do anything to keep them safe.

Yet there she was, waving them off onto a bus that she wasn't driving. With other people she couldn't control. Sending them off for hours at a time, where she couldn't protect them.

The thoughts came and went quickly, before life slipped back into focus.

On the other side of the street, Pam Caulfield was standing outside her door, arms folded across her chest and the *Westport Newspaper* dangling from one hand. She gave Amy a quick look before turning and going back inside. No cheery hello, no catch-up about local events. No gossip shared.

Amy knew it was going to take time. She was going to be an outsider to them for a while. Someone to be viewed with suspicion. Maybe she would have to watch them share barbecues and parties without an invite. Conversations that would suddenly fall silent if she was noticed at the periphery.

It was going to take time.

It mattered little to her in the main. She would get on with her life without the need to be liked, without the desire to be a part of the community. She knew it would hurt Jack that she wouldn't integrate herself with the other families in their street quickly. He would want to move on from Sara quickly. The new normal accepted as fast as he wanted it to be.

She would have to make the effort, she guessed. It wouldn't come as naturally to her as it seemed to for him, all that type of thing. Making friends and ingratiating yourself into a group.

He was worth it. *This* was worth it.

She went back inside, closing the door behind her slowly, carefully. As if she was worried about making too much noise. Looked down at the hardwood floor, the early-morning light streaming through from the back of the house giving it a sheen that couldn't be replicated in photographs. Closed her eyes and sighed softly.

Then she clasped her hands together and allowed herself to be drawn through the house. She floated through, as if she wasn't in control of her actions. As though someone else was controlling her body, making her move, making her blink, making her breathe.

She passed the living room, perfectly still, perfectly clean. The dining room opposite, the same. Into the kitchen, the source of the light that ran throughout the house. Stole a glance out back to her perfectly manicured garden. The blue of the pool water looked so inviting.

Amy turned away before she could be tempted, down to the locked door at the back.

She pulled the key from the pocket of her jeans and twisted it open. The door opened and the darkness within escaped into the hallway.

The office was small, but large enough for a desk and a couple of bookcases. A small window that looked out towards the pool and barbecue area. The blind had been pulled down, probably at some point the night before. Possibly Jack, if he had come inside to do a bit of work in the evening, when she wasn't around. The kids never came in there, so she didn't think it was them.

Maybe it had been her. She couldn't remember.

She didn't *want* to remember. It was much easier this way – to pretend she was being guided in all her actions. That she didn't have full control of her body, her mind. That there was some unseen force making her move.

He was still dead.

Nothing had changed since a few hours earlier. No matter the amount of wishing she had done.

She had to do something. He couldn't stay here. It wouldn't be long until someone would notice.

Amy took a step closer, expecting the body to move. Grasp hold of her wrist and not let go.

That wasn't going to happen.

As she felt the tears she'd been holding onto since he had taken his last breath begin to roll down her cheeks, she got to work.

He wasn't going to ruin her perfect life.

Not any more.

She had made sure of that.

*

Amy couldn't believe it had only been a few hours since they'd been out on the rocks at Bluff Point.

They had already made plans of what would happen next.

Jack would play the crying husband, as he begged for information on Sara's whereabouts. She got chills as she thought about watching him on local news. On social media. Of course, there would be so many people ready to say he must have been involved, but he had a strong alibi for the entire period.

Stephanie, his family, all ready to get behind him. He was with his children. The police wouldn't suspect him for very long. Especially after they found her car out at Bluff Point.

Couple that with the fact her workplace colleagues would talk about her attacking a patient. Her neighbours would talk about her screaming in the middle of the street.

Given everything that Sara had done in those days before she went missing, it wouldn't be difficult for Jack to make it look like she had simply lost her mind.

They both knew, of course, that Sara's body would never be found. Penny and Colby would make sure of that.

They had already sent her a picture of Sara's body, lying on the rocks. Sent from a number she didn't recognise.

It was a sad ending for Sara. It didn't have to be that way, but people make their own choices.

JJ and Olivia would accept her eventually, even if they had to pretend for now that she and Jack weren't together.

She would just be helping out at first. Stephanie would be surprised, she guessed, when she left the restaurant and took the offer from Jack.

Suspicious was probably a better word. But she would come round as well.

They all would.

And the time apart would only make Amy and Jack stronger.

It was all going to be okay. She just had to put a call in to the two people who had helped her before and everything was going to work out. Jack would understand eventually – he would know that she only killed Dan to keep them safe.

This wasn't like what happened with Sara.

He would understand.

She stood over the body, pulled out her cell phone, and found the number.

It was answered within a few seconds.

'Penny, it's me,' Amy said, surprised at how calm she sounded. How calm she felt. 'I have another problem I need help with.'

*

Penny ended the call and then looked across to the other side of the table. Different diner, but same menu. They all seemed to be the same these days. The only choice being what food might kill you slower.

'That was her,' she said, pushing away her plate, which was still filled with pancakes, bacon and syrup. It had been a good idea when she'd ordered it, but she'd suddenly lost her appetite. 'She has another problem.'

'She say what it was?'

'No,' Penny replied, shaking her head. She motioned to the waitress to refill her coffee cup. 'But I think it's a big problem. Said she needed help to take care of a package. Too big for her to deal with herself.'

'A body?'

'That'd be my guess.'

'Well then. I guess we should probably help her out. She say how much? On top of the fifty, of course.'

Penny shook her head and then sat back, as the waitress filled her cup and she stirred some sugar into it.

They had known that she would make a mistake.

That she would need their help again.

And now here she was. Already. Only a few hours later.

Maybe Colby had been right all along. Not that Penny would ever admit that. It wouldn't do for him to realise now that he was usually right.

55

A my waited for Penny and Colby to arrive. She wished she could have dealt with Dan's body herself, but there was no way she was going to be able to move it alone. And they were good workers.

The bigger issue was Jack.

He hadn't listened when she'd told him that they could dump the body somewhere that night. That they couldn't keep a dead man in the office.

It was as if he had checked out mentally from it all.

When he'd left for work that morning, he hadn't kissed her goodbye. He hadn't even said a word to the children as they left. He was sleep-deprived, that was all. He was working too hard.

And he'd ordered his wife be killed only a few hours earlier.

It was going to be a difficult time, she knew. Telling JJ and Olivia that their mother had gone missing was going to be the most difficult part, she guessed.

Amy could tell that the knowledge of having to do that was going to take a big toll on Jack.

She didn't know why that would continue in private with her, though. He should be happy right now. He should have taken time off work and been there with her. They should have been dealing with the fallout together.

So many times, she had tried to talk to him about what would come after Sara was gone. In the more than a year since they'd first met. Sitting in that apartment she had over in Norwalk. It wasn't just about sex. They would cuddle on the sofa, watching movies, binging TV programmes, talking until he would be forced to leave. About their plans for the future, about Jack's work and where it might take him. About his family and how they would react when they finally met Amy.

Back then, he hadn't been able to keep his hands off her. His stamina was something she struggled to keep up with.

In the past few weeks, things had changed. She knew it was because of the stress of what they had decided to do.

It was all going to be okay though. She could feel it.

Dan was the last piece of the puzzle that needed to be dealt with, thrown away in the garbage. Then they could live their lives together, happy and content. Nothing would ever get in their way again.

Amy heard a car pull up outside and she moved to the front door, looking through the glass and seeing two figures approach.

A knock on the door.

Penny and Colby had arrived. Now she knew everything was going to be okay. Life could begin.

She turned back to the door as a louder knock came. She brushed herself down and reached for the handle. Opened it.

Amy saw the life she had planned begin to blur in her mind. She saw everything begin to fall apart, little by little.

She saw. Her.

And she knew it was over.

All over.

'Hello, Amy,' Sara said, walking into her home. Smiling. 'Happy to see me?'

★

I remember coming round in the back of a car. People shouting over me, someone holding onto my hand.

I had felt the movement of something underneath me – the car whizzing down a road. High speed. Two voices in the front, arguing with each other.

I had looked across and seen Alex holding onto my hand. Talking to me, even though I couldn't understand the words she was saying.

I said only a few words to her before I fell into darkness again.

'Where am I? Where am I going?'

It wasn't long until I'd worked out the answer to those questions.

Now, I was standing in my home. The place I had once felt so safe. Amy standing in front of me, open-mouthed. Her mind disbelieving what her eyes were telling her.

She finally found her voice. 'How?'

I closed the door behind me, breathing the same air as her. 'You shouldn't trust people, Amy. Not those two people you hired, not Jack, not anyone.'

'It's not possible . . .'

'Yet, here I am.'

I was enjoying this moment. Perhaps more than I should have been. After all, after what almost happened to me the night before, I should have lost my mind entirely.

Penny and Colby helped a little.

The image was only a few hours old, but it came to me over and over. Colby, standing over me, firing his gun into the rocks beside me. My body going into shock. A flash of light. Remembering being pulled across Bluff Point.

Then, what he and Penny said to each other.

'I couldn't do it. She's a mother. And I'm not being responsible for taking her away from her children. I just can't let that happen.'

'Colby . . .'

'Penny, you know what happened to me. You want one or both of those kids to end up the same way?'

Now, the only thoughts I had were of my children. And making sure I could get them back.

I kept walking, as Amy backpedalled into the kitchen, until she bumped into the kitchen counter.

'Sit down,' I said, not asking. 'I want to hear you tell me.'

I watched as Amy looked around her, probably for something to hit me with. Maybe something worse than that. I moved quickly, taking her by the shoulders and shoving her towards the seat.

'I have people outside waiting for me,' I said, motioning towards the back door with my head. 'Oh, and there's this.'

I took out the .38 I'd been holding in my pocket. Colby had given it to me a few seconds earlier. I let it hang limply in my hand. 'I don't want to use it though, Amy. I just want to talk. No . . . sorry, I want to *listen*.'

'We thought . . . we thought you were gone.'

'I barely have a scratch. A graze from a bullet that flashed past my leg. Looks worse than it feels.'

'But . . .'

'Enough, Amy,' I said, enjoying the wince as my words landed on her ears. 'I'm not Lazarus. I haven't risen from the dead. You just chose the wrong people. They made a different call to the one you wanted them to make. That's all. So now we're going to chat, you and I.'

'Okay,' Amy replied, her eyes darting to her left for a split second. Only a slight movement, but I caught it. 'What do you want to know?'

'How long?'

'How long what?'

I sighed. 'How long were you seeing my husband?'

'Oh,' Amy said, her eyes drifting to the floor. I could see her mind whirring. 'You want the truth?'

'Tell me.'

'Almost two years.'

I tried not to show a reaction, but it hurt too much. I couldn't fathom that amount of time passing without me knowing something was going on. 'A long time then. Tell me everything.'

I waited, as I saw Amy work out what she was going to say. Probably so used to lying that she was trying to figure out the one she was going to tell. Then I saw her shoulders relax a little, as if she was making a decision. To tell the truth for once, I realised.

'Stephanie introduced us,' Amy said finally, her voice quiet, but filled with a certain kind of strength. Of knowing. 'I don't think she intended for us to hit it off in that way, but I've always wondered. I guess we'll find out. Jack came into the restaurant, to pick up something or other, and Stephanie made a point of bringing me over to say hello. I knew instantly that there was a connection there. A glint in his eye, the way he smiled. He came by a couple of times after that, for one reason or another, but always made sure that we spoke. Then he came by when Stephanie wasn't there and we ended up talking for a long time. Just the two of us.'

I could feel my breathing becoming shallower. My heart rate increase, as anger and betrayal coursed through me. I hadn't had enough time to get used to the idea of what Jack had done. Hearing it from Amy's mouth was only making things worse.

'I knew he was married, so I had no intention of doing anything,' Amy continued, a wistful look on her face. 'But we both knew that something was going to happen. He took his time, though. Got to know me. Then he found me on Instagram and we started talking even more.'

I waited, knowing there was more to come, even though I didn't want to listen any more.

'It wasn't just sex. That wasn't all it was, even in the beginning. We had a real connection. We love each other.'

'A forty-two-year-old man and . . . what are you, twenty-five, twenty-six?'

She didn't respond, but I knew I was close.

'It just happened,' Amy said, a shrug of her shoulders giving me all the information I needed. 'We fell in love.'

'How did it come to this? Why did you come to my office that day?'

Amy sighed, as if she was bored of the questions now. Then, she eyed the gun in my hand and realised she had no choice.

'He wanted to leave you, but he told me it was difficult. That there was a lot of money at stake, that he couldn't face the idea of co-parenting, or the looks he would get for leaving his wife for someone younger. All that blah, blah, blah. He wanted out, but couldn't see a way. Then, he got drunk one night and he told me your story. Told me that was the real reason he'd looked for me. Why he needed me. Why he needed to get him and his children away from you.'

I didn't want her saying it out loud. 'So you came up with this plan?'

'It was both of us.'

'You know, Amy, I need you to be clear on this. You're saying Jack was as much a part of this plan as you?'

Amy nodded in response, confirming it. 'If not more so,' she said, compounding the point.

I felt the betrayal complete. Reached into my pocket and placed my hand on what was inside and found the switch. 'Just so you know, Amy, it wouldn't have worked in the slightest. I would never have gone to the police. I would have never told anyone what happened.'

'You would never tell people you murdered someone?'

'Well, would you?'

Amy looked away, her answer clear as day.

'I only told Jack because I trusted him, but that was a mistake. He was the only person I would have ever told. There was no way I was going to do what you thought I would. You would have had to kill me to take my children away from me.'

'What are you going to do now?'

'I could ask you the same question,' I said, knowing it had been burning through her tired mind for the past few hours. I was only interested in JJ and Olivia and making sure they were back under my care. That didn't mean that there wasn't going to be an unholy mess to clean up, though. Jack. Amy. Everyone at Better Lives. Jack's work, the neighbours. Jack's family. Everyone was going to have questions. 'You've made a mistake, haven't you? I know how that can be. I know exactly how easy it is.'

I took my hand out of my pocket.

'He broke into the house . . .'

'Only we know that's not true,' I said, interrupting before she could spin a tale. 'He had a key. I gave it to him. And you don't have a mark on you, I'm willing to bet, so he didn't attack you. You killed Dan in cold blood, isn't that right?'

'He deserved it.'

'Tell me what happened,' I said, making sure she could see my finger curled around the trigger. 'And remember, I'll know if you're lying. Give me an excuse. Any excuse.'

'I knew he'd be back,' Amy said, looking me square in the eyes, her voice clear and calm. Confidence oozing from her. She wasn't scared of me. She wanted to tell me. She wanted to hurt me.

'I waited for him. I knew he'd be coming back here, looking for you. I didn't realise he had a key. I sat in this kitchen and shot him within a minute of him coming inside. He didn't have a chance to do a thing.'

'And now he's where?'

'Jack's office.'

'Thank you,' I said, placing the gun back in my pocket and taking the voice recorder from the other. 'I think I have everything I need.'

'What's that?'

'I want you to call Jack now,' I said, coming to the end of my patience at being in her presence. 'Tell him you need him to go to Bluff Point.'

'What are you going to do?'

'Unless you do this, I'll send this recording to my friend in the police. She'll do the rest.'

I could see the panic start to creep into her face now. 'I'll leave. Now. You'll never see me again.'

'I know that,' I said, enjoying the moment. 'But first, you're going to call him.'

She reached for her cell phone and I tensed up waiting for her to make any movement. She swiped it open and called Jack.

When it was done, I took her cell from her. Shook my head. Took my own cell phone out and called the last number on the recent call list.

'Alex, it's me. I got it. There's a body here and she's confessed.'

'Wait . . .'

*

Alex ended the call and then breathed in slowly.

She looked down at her cell and found the number she needed. Within a few seconds, she had spoken to the station and knew that within minutes, half the local PD would be converging on the house.

When she thought about how close she had come to not surviving the night, a rush of relief ran through her body.

She closed her eyes and she was back in that car. Waiting. Then, Penny had opened the trunk and she had sprung out, immediately backpedalling to give herself room. She'd lifted her arms to the sky and thrust them down to her sides, breaking the duct tape in an instant.

Alex had been about to run, but the sight of Penny's gun had stopped her in her tracks.

At that moment, she'd thought it was all over.

Instead, Penny had spoken to her. Told her the truth. The whole story.

She'd even given her back her possessions as an act of trust. Alex had contemplated taking her gun out, ordering Penny to the ground, and calling it in there and then. Making sure they were both sent down for what they'd done.

Something had stopped her.

Colby walking back with Sara.

She had never seen her therapist look more defeated.

And Alex had seen a chance to make a difference. Maybe one she hadn't been able to make before. She had thought quickly – telling Colby and Penny that in exchange for them not killing her and Sara, she could make sure they went free.

And they'd accepted that.

That didn't mean that Alex wasn't going to make sure they paid for their part in all of this too.

In some ways, Alex had felt sorry for them. It was clear that they hadn't intended on getting involved in anything like this.

Sara had known what would come next, it seemed. That someone would go looking for her at the house. That Amy and Jack would do something bad.

There was guilt running through Alex's veins now. She could have prevented a death.

Which meant that she wouldn't let Colby and Penny get too far when this was all over.

Alex wondered if she should be there with Sara when she finally ended all of this. Back at Bluff Point.

Wondered if she could trust that she was just going to talk to him.

Whether that would ever be enough.

Alex wanted to tell her colleagues. To give them everything she knew and let the dust land where it may. Only she was well aware that sometimes these things are best not left to someone in authority.

She had done that once and regretted it.

She wasn't going to let that happen again.

56

I only had a couple of hours. This part, I was less comfortable with. I wasn't sure how it was going to play out. How things might change in an instant. I needed to be quick, but clear.

I was waiting for Jack at Bluff Point. And I didn't think it would take long. Amy had played her part perfectly. I'd left her in the house, just as a dozen cop cars turned into the street. She wouldn't have got far.

I'd made sure of that.

Now, as I saw Jack's Mercedes turn into the parking lot, I got ready for the last part. He came to a stop in an empty space, over to the front of the lot. I watched him get out, look around, a crease lining his forehead as he didn't see Amy.

I got out and started walking.

He saw me coming. I wasn't sure if he was going to start running, but Colby and Penny getting out of their car nearby seemed to stop any thoughts he may have had of doing so. Still, he didn't look all that surprised to see me. Not like Amy had.

'You look older,' I said, as I came within a few feet of him. 'Sleepless night?'

'How?'

'Strange, that's what Amy said too.'

I expected him to ask about her. What might have been done, where she was. Instead, his next question told me everything I should have known about him.

'What do you want?'

I stared at him, hoping to see some small part of the man I'd once trusted, loved, more than any other. I don't think I would have seen it given infinite time to search. 'We're going to talk.'

'You're not getting the kids and you're not getting a single penny from me.'

'We were possessions to you, isn't that right?'

He smiled, but I could see something slipping through the arrogant surface. Nervousness. 'Was I proud of my family? Of what I had brought together? Of course. I'm not going to deny that.'

'But that changed.'

'Yeah, it did. Right around the time you told me what you really were.'

I shook my head. 'I told you that when I'd been young, I'd got into a situation that, granted, was worse than just a bad time with drugs, or drinking too much. But it shouldn't have destroyed us. I didn't kill Adam Halton.'

'You covered for him. For Dan. That makes you just as bad.'

'Imagine what I would do for you in that case,' I said, getting drawn in. Enjoying it. 'I loved you more than I could have ever loved him. That was silly young love. Not real. Me and you . . . that was something deep. To the roots. I would have done anything for you. For us.'

Jack hesitated, on less steady ground now. 'It doesn't matter,' he said finally, turning away from me. 'None of it does. You killed a man.'

'You know that's not true, Jack. I might have been there when an accident happened. I might have allowed myself to be talked into covering it up, when I should have done the right thing. And trust me, that decision haunts me and will haunt me forever, but that's not who I am. If you knew me at all, you'd know that's not me. If you loved me . . .'

'I did.'

'If you loved me, truly, you would know I would never hurt anyone. I couldn't. So, all this talk about being worried about the kids – *our* kids – is just a smokescreen. Why don't you tell me the truth? Why don't you tell me why you really did all this?'

Jack shrugged his shoulders, glancing towards where Colby and Penny were standing, just out of earshot.

'Let me tell you,' I said, starting to lose my patience. 'I think you had your head turned by a younger woman. Happens every day, to weak men as they get a little older. You've been with the same person for over fifteen years. You're working hard, life gets a little boring for you, and then there's this fresh girl, almost two decades younger than you, who comes along and puts you on a pedestal. She tells you what you want to hear, listens to your stories, your lies. You're distracted by the shiny new thing and you start thinking, "I deserve this. If it wasn't for my boring old wife, I could be happy." Time passes and you start thinking about how you can have this life you've dreamed about. She makes you feel young, she's exciting, she dotes on you, hangs on every word. To her, you're a god. You can do no wrong. This isn't like your life with me. You're finally in complete control. But, you've got this problem, haven't you?'

Jack turned back to me. 'And what's that?'

'Me. You didn't get a pre-nup, so you know that everything you've told Amy isn't going to be possible. You'll lose the house, half of everything you've worked for. Also, you're hanging on by a thread at work, because they know you're not as good at your job as you like to believe. You don't know how long you'll be able to keep hold of it. You're facing losing everything.'

'I'm not losing . . .'

'Jack, I know what's been going on. I saw the emails. You've lost them millions of dollars in bad investments. They're going to fire you soon. Then it really would be all over.'

'You . . . you don't understand.'

'You're scared of losing everything. So you tell her about what happened to me when I was younger. You tell Amy all of these awful things, lies, about me. Of course, she wants to help you get rid of your problem. You'll keep the house, the kids, and your family will be none the wiser. They won't cut you off, because they never liked me. Because if we know one thing about your parents, it's that they wouldn't have anything to do with you if they knew you'd cheated on your wife, right?'

'You seem to have it all worked out,' Jack replied, still attempting to keep a semblance of confidence, but I could see the veneer was starting to crack. 'It doesn't make any difference, though. We're still over. It's just more messy now.'

'Oh, I agree. Because I know, whatever you might have told Amy, that you always planned for me to die at the end of this. I think you either thought I'd kill myself or would have those two over there do the job for you. You're too much of a coward to try it yourself.'

'I'm not like you.'

'You would have made a pretty penny from my death. Enough for you to carry on with the life you've always enjoyed. With a new, younger woman. You would have played the part of a grief-stricken husband well, I'm sure.'

'It doesn't matter now,' Jack said, sighing heavily. 'You've just made it a little more difficult. That's all. But I'll win in the end. I always do.'

'Maybe not. Especially because right about now, Amy will be having handcuffs placed around her wrists. They'll have found Dan's body in your office. They'll be taking photographs, evidence. Everything.'

I stepped forwards and I saw Jack flinch. I felt the grin stretch my face and enjoyed it. 'Not only that – not just a murder charge, that I'm sure Amy will take the fall for – but they'll take away things from the house. Your things. *Your* computer.'

This time, the realisation did hit.

'That's right, Jack,' I said, getting closer to him now. 'All of those times you've spent in your office, doing whatever it was that kept you afloat at work, that's about to be discovered. What you were trying to do, to claw back all that money you lost. It'll all be found now.'

'You . . .'

'Bitch? Right? That's what you were going to call me? Just tell me – how much did Stephanie know?'

He shook his head. 'Why does it matter?'

'I just want to know.'

'She didn't know a thing,' Jack said, a humourless chuckle escaping his lips. 'She just happened to introduce me to Amy. And had no idea about what was going on. She did like you, not that you'll believe me.'

I wasn't sure if that was true. But, if Jack was this messed up, maybe his sister was as well. Probably the parents, the therapist part of my brain said. I'd never thought too much about them, but seeing how Jack really was made me realise *what* he was.

Privileged. Entitled.

It gave me nothing but pleasure now to tell him it was the end.

'Everyone is going to know what you've done. Who you are. There's no hiding it any more. Your parents are going to know they failed. Stephanie will discover the truth of what her brother is. You'll be an outcast. It's over.'

Whatever I expected his reaction to be, it didn't include what he actually did. He lunged for me, his hands wrapping around my throat, crashing us both down to the ground. I could see the fire in his eyes, as he stared down at me and squeezed.

'I'll kill you . . .'

Sweat and saliva dripped over me, as I dug my nails into his hands and battered at his arms. He didn't let go, and for a few seconds I couldn't breathe.

I was going to die.

I wanted to laugh. I didn't feel scared, or sad.

I was just glad I had pushed him this far.

Then there was a sudden release and I sucked in oxygen hard and fast. Penny had her arm around me and pulled me up so I was sitting. I looked across to where Colby had hold of Jack, pinning him down.

'Lady, are you okay?' Colby said, as bystanders began to gather. 'We've called the cops. It's okay, we'll tell them everything.'

I looked across at Jack and saw the defeat in his eyes.

*

JJ and Olivia got off the school bus and fell into step alongside each other. The clouds above them began to slowly disperse, allowing the sun to provide a little more warmth to the late afternoon.

It didn't help either of their moods. All day, Olivia had had this sick feeling in the bottom of her stomach. It had started the day before, when Mom had taken them to the beach. When Dad had arrived and Mom had disappeared.

'Who is she?' Olivia said, hoping her older brother would have the answer to the question that had been bugging her all day. 'I know she works with Aunt Stephanie, but why is she in our house?'

'Who cares?'

That was typical from JJ. If he didn't know the answer to a question, he pretended like it didn't matter. Olivia tried another. 'Where's Mom? Do you think she'll be back by now?'

'Why don't you stop whining?' JJ said, his voice low and angry. It made Olivia take a step to the side, so she wasn't too close to him. 'I'm sure everything is okay.'

Olivia knew it wasn't. Mom didn't look good yesterday and when Dad had picked them up the night before, he wouldn't answer any questions about where she was.

She thought it was weird the way he'd been acting that morning. Like it was normal that Mom wasn't around. That it had been him who had made sure they got up for school, dressed and ready. When they'd asked for breakfast, he'd acted like it was a surprise that they needed to eat.

Then, there was that woman in the house. Trying to stay hidden – but they had both known she was there. Then, Dad had left them with her, telling them she was the "babysitter", as if they ever had anyone other than Aunt Stephanie watch them.

Olivia didn't like the new babysitter already. She was too scared to say anything, but she was worried that Mom wasn't around and Dad didn't seem to think he should tell them where she was.

As they approached the house, they saw a police car sitting nearby. The door opened and they both stopped in their tracks.

Olivia spotted her first. JJ quickly after.

Then they were running towards their mom.

They crashed into her, as she wrapped her arms around them. Heard a wince of pain, but felt a strong hold on them.

'It's okay,' Mom said, holding them tight, holding them close. 'I'm here. I'm back. But listen, we've got to move, okay? We've got to get out of here.'

'Where are we going?' JJ said, pulling away from her.

'Is it the beach again?' Olivia said, her little voice high-pitched and full of excitement. 'Can we go?'

'Something like that,' Mom replied, pulling them close again, before leading them away. 'Come on, let's pick up some things and then see where we're going.'

★

Holding my children was a gift. In the moments after I'd crashed onto the rocks and Colby had stood over me, it was one I'd thought I would never get to experience again. I had wondered if there would ever to be a way to see them again. To touch them, to hear them.

To be their mom.

Our home was a crime scene for days. We were unable to pick anything up, even go near the place in those first few days. Alex helped me out, made sure we had somewhere to stay locally, that we were looked after.

The whole time, she kept me up to date on what charges Jack and Amy would be facing.

Both would be charged with murder and attempted murder. Alex was going to testify that she'd heard them both say that I should be killed.

Colby and Penny were long gone. In exchange for our lives, Alex and I had decided that we wouldn't tell anyone we knew their names. They hadn't really done anything other than intimidate me, in the end. When it came down to it, they hadn't been able to actually go through with killing me.

For Jack, it wasn't just the murder and attempted murder charges, of course. Once his computer had been forensically analysed, he was in deep trouble. The firm he'd worked for was now distancing itself from him, but it was obvious he had been involved in some nefarious practices for a long time. I think if I'd been out of the way, he and Amy would currently be in a country with no extradition agreement with the US. With my children.

If Alex knew why I hadn't gone to the cops as soon as Amy had come into my office as Ella, she made no effort to tell me so.

I knew it was going to come up at some point.

I knew that Jack and Amy's credibility was shot. And that it wouldn't be easy for them to prove a thing. Only two people had known where Adam's body was and one of them was dead.

Poor Dan.

I hadn't had chance to grieve for him. It was unlikely I ever would.

It was his fault all of this started in the first place.

I moved back into our home, once the police had finished investigating the scene, but I didn't think I would be able to stay there long. Jack had made every part of it feel alien to me now.

I knew about keeping secrets in a marriage. It turned out I wasn't the only one.

The only good thing that came from it was JJ and Olivia.

I was worried about JJ. He had been quiet before the events of that week and had become even more sullen now. He missed Jack, of course, but there was more to it than just that.

One day, he might tell me.

Olivia was holding my hand as we entered the restaurant. I was used to the looks in public now, but it still took a little effort to ignore them. To not react.

The waitress showed us to our booth in the window. Menus offered. I smiled and waited for JJ and Olivia to order the same thing they always did.

Instead, Stephanie came out from the back and made her way over to us. She wrapped her arms around the two children, as they bolted for her. Disturbing other diners with their yelps and screams of delight. I couldn't help but smile.

They hadn't seen her for weeks.

'Okay, JJ, Olivia, you can let go of her now,' I said, with a laugh. 'She isn't going anywhere.'

I stood up and faced Jack's sister. Held her gaze.

'Kids, sit down, drinks are coming over,' Stephanie said, as she stepped back and let me follow her out of earshot.

I went along with her. Waited as she continued to breathe slowly and stare at me.

I wasn't going to speak first.

'You could speak for him,' Stephanie said, finally. Not an impassioned plea, but as close as she was probably ever going to get to it. 'He is the father of your children, after all.'

I shook my head. 'He wanted me dead.'

'I know,' Stephanie replied, not a hint of emotion, of contrition in her tone. 'And he told me why.'

My heart slowed a little, as she leaned forwards. 'I know exactly what you are,' Stephanie continued, her voice low, so only I could hear it. 'And my brother is going to pay for what he did to you. And you're going to get away with it. But I'm not going anywhere. I told you I'd do anything for those kids – and that includes making sure you don't do anything to put them in harm's way again.'

I wanted to protest. To tell her it was her own brother who had done that. Only the words wouldn't come out.

'I know what you are,' Stephanie said again, pulling away from me. Giving me that same, sickly smile of hers. 'I'm always going to be around. You can't escape that.'

She left me standing there, open-mouthed, before I heard Olivia's voice pulling me back.

It didn't matter to me.

I was back with them. And it didn't matter what I'd done, or what I'd been. I was their mom and that was it.

I dreamed of moving away. Somewhere new, somewhere exciting. They might miss friends, but they could make new ones.

Kids were resilient.

I would go back to work – not at Better Lives, given what had happened – but everything was going to be okay.

We could create a new family.

A new reality.

A second chance for them.

Yet another for me.

Only, Jack's family would find me.

Stephanie was always going to be close by. Watching me.

As I made my way back to the booth, I realised I was never going to escape my past.

I was never going to be free.

From them.

From what I did.

From myself.

2005

We had pulled the lifeless body of Adam Halton across the ground, and then struggled to get him into the back of the car. Dan got some old blankets from the boot and placed them over him in the back seat and then turned to me.

'We'll need to wait until morning,' he said, his hands shaking as he lit another cigarette. 'We've got nothing we can use right now.'

I shook my head. 'It's now or never. What do we need?'

'A shovel, for one.'

'We can get one from my parents' shed, not a problem.'

'Bags, as well. Big black bags.'

'Same place,' I said, nodding my head up and down. 'It's all fine. We can do this.'

'Are you sure? Because we have to be in this together. Until the end.'

'Of course,' I said, taking hold of him. 'I love you.'

I did. I would have done anything for him. In that moment, I didn't know that this would be what destroyed us as a couple, of course. In that moment, I was only thinking about how to get out of the situation we'd been placed in.

We drove to my parents' house after picking up keys from our place. Let ourselves into the back garden. I unlocked the back door as quietly as possible, finding Dad's keys on the hook where he kept them in the kitchen. Crept back out, without a sound, and then crossed the garden to the shed.

I had prepared a million excuses in case I was caught, but they didn't wake up at all. They never knew we were there.

In the shed, I got everything we needed, then put the keys back inside the house and left.

We drove along a country road, towards woods that backed onto a farm place near Wambrook. Somewhere that I knew was completely isolated. Where he wouldn't be found for a long time, if ever.

In silence. Neither of us daring to speak. Barely able to breathe.

We planned to dig a hole, taking hours to make sure it was deep enough. We'd pick a spot that was well hidden. It would be a long time in the future before someone came across it, when you wouldn't even be able to tell the ground had been disturbed. We thought of everything.

We were miles away from the car park where Dan had attacked him. We should have been safe.

In the silence of the car, as we tried to concentrate on what we had to do, the noise from the back seat was a cacophony.

Dan nearly took the car off the road when the gasp came from behind us.

'No . . .' Dan said, as he regained control of the car, and I turned around and saw the young man's body stirring beneath the blankets. I shook off my seatbelt, not thinking straight.

Only thinking about keeping us safe.

'What's going on?'

I stared into the guy's eyes, as he mouthed something soundlessly.

I really hadn't known what I was doing when I'd taken his pulse earlier in the night. I didn't know he was still alive.

I didn't know. I promise that.

I had a moment to think. About what would happen next. About what Dan might do. He might panic, decide that it was better if we let him go. That he wouldn't tell anyone, we could make him promise.

Dan was an idiot.

'It's nothing,' I said, reaching forwards and placing a hand on Dan's shoulder. 'Just air being expelled. I've seen it on those crime dramas. I'll sit back here though, in case of anything else happening.'

'Okay, okay, good,' Dan said, sounding unconvinced. Sounding like he knew exactly what I was doing.

I never asked him if he really did know what happened next. I was only aware of how he acted towards me after that night. The fact he didn't fight for us. Didn't argue when I said I was leaving. The way he couldn't look me in the eye ever again.

He was scared of me. Of what I was capable of, I guessed.

I shifted myself next to Adam's body, as his mouth opened and closed. As he tried to come to. I held him down.

It takes a long time. Longer than you think.

I held the blanket over his face for so long, that I couldn't feel my fingers afterwards. Until he wasn't moving any more. Until he wasn't breathing.

Longer than you think. To kill someone. To take their life.

To make sure they can never tell a soul what you've done.

So, so long.

ACKNOWLEDGEMENTS

As ever, this book wouldn't exist without the help, support, and assistance of so many people. My absolute and unending appreciation to the following . . .

Jo Dickinson, who continues to be the reason I get to tell stories. A more supportive and hardworking editor would be impossible to find. Thank you, thank you, thank you. For everything. Working with you for almost a decade has been the greatest time of my life. Here's to many more years together.

The whole Hodder team, who have welcomed me into the family and are always enthusiastic and diligent – Alainna Hadjigeorgiou, for being an ace publicist, Alice Morley and Sarah Clay for all their work. I couldn't appreciate it any more than I do. Thank you.

My agent Kate Burke, who has come in and elevated the book to new heights. You have the best notes and I'm so excited to be starting this new journey with you. Sian Ellis-Martin for her assistance and thoroughness.

All the readers who got in touch online or in person, championing my novels to other readers, telling me how much they have enjoyed reading the books – thank you so much. You're the reason I get to tell more stories.

My FLCWers, Val, Mark, Chris, Doug, and Stuart.

My boxing shenanigans crew – Tony, Rob P, Rob S, and Mik. One day we'll be ringside for a big fight altogether!

Andy Theo, for plastering my walls.

Mike Hale, for being yet another brother. Marie Ennis, for being my biggest fan, and ergo, my favourite cousin (don't tell the others).

Daniel, Natalie, Alex, Alice, Josh, Santino, and Vincenzo, for making me proud every day.

My family, for always being there for me.

And finally, as always, my reason for being. Emma, Abigail, and Megan. I love you all more than anything.